To everyone who inspired me, encouraged me, and guided me.

Without you, this could never have happened.

Dim vales- and shadowy floods-
And cloudy-looking woods,
Whose forms we can't discover
For the tears that drip all over!
Huge moons there wax and
wane-
Again- again- again-
Every moment of the night-
Forever changing places-
And they put out the star-light
With the breath from their pale
faces.
About twelve by the moon-dial,
One more filmy than the rest
(A kind which, upon trial,
They have found to be the best)
Comes down- still down- and
down,
With its centre on the crown
Of a mountain's eminence,
 While its wide circumference
In easy drapery falls
Over hamlets, over halls,
Wherever they may be-
O'er the strange woods- o'er the
sea-

Over spirits on the wing-
Over every drowsy thing-
And buries them up quite
In a labyrinth of light-
 And then, how deep!- O, deep!
Is the passion of their sleep.
In the morning they arise,
And their moony covering
 Is soaring in the skies,
With the tempests as they toss,
Like- almost anything-
Or a yellow Albatross.
 They use that moon no more
 For the same end as before-
 Videlicet, a tent-
Which I think extravagant:
 Its atomies, however,
 Into a shower dissever,
Of which those butterflies
Of Earth, who seek the skies,
 And so come down again,
(Never-contented things!)
Have brought a specimen
Upon their quivering wings.

"Fairyland"
by Edgar Allen Poe

Strange Woods

Prologue

The forest was quiet and peaceful. It was a beautiful summer's day; the sun was shining with all its strength. The only movement was that of the tall maple trees swaying in the morning breeze. The animals, squirrels, deer, nymphs, and rabbits, had disappeared into the dark depths of the forests early on, as if they already knew what was about to happen in their quiet sanctuary.

It was not until almost noon that something began to stir in the calm forest. A large clearing, deep into the forest's center began to come to life. The wind picked up, circling around the clearing like a tornado, bending the trees almost to their knees. This lasted for mere seconds before the winds died down and the trees were able to stand straight again. As soon as the giants were back to normal, four humans appeared in the center of the clearing, a ripple of air coming off them like a shock wave off a nuclear bomb.

As soon as the forest settled from the surprise materialization of these four humans, it went back into relative silence, except for the conversation of the four women now in the clearing. Three of the four women immediately fell to the soft grassy floor of the clearing, their bodies still in shock from the sudden dematerialization and rematerialization of their Travel.

"I don't think I will ever get used to that," one said, the shortest of the group, as she stood up and brushed the dirt off of her dress.

"At least I warned you this time," the fourth woman snapped, the only one who never had a problem with Traveling. It was her ability, after all.

"Though that doesn't help much with the splitting headache we all get afterwards," the tallest said. She had a powerful tone and demeanor, the leader of the group.

"I'm not so sure about this, you guys," said the shortest of the four. There was a hint of foreboding in her voice.

"Peri, this is the only good idea we could come up with. We're doing it, " the leader said.

"You're only saying that because it was your idea, Kendra! Don't you understand? We could *die* doing this! As in, cease to be living!"

"I think we know what dying means, Peri," the Traveler said. Her hair blazed like fire in the sunlight.

"Was I talking to you, Aideen?"

"Don't be so snippy. I'm only trying to lighten the mood."

"Cut it out, the three of you. We can't do this if we can't get along!"

This came from the fourth of the group. Even if she wasn't the leader, she was obviously someone the rest looked up to, because all at once, the clearing became eerily still once more.

"Yeah. What she said. And besides Peri, are you four or forty? Don't be such a baby! This will certainly be an adventure."

"Aideen, really? Must you always have the last word?"

"Sorry, Damia. Goodness, everyone really is on edge today."

At this, all three of the other women glared at Aideen. She only shrugged, and walked past them all.

"It'll be all right, Peri, you'll see."

"I'm sorry, Kendra, but I'm still not convinced this is a good idea. We could be in serious danger here!"

"Peri, that's why we split up the crystal," said Aideen, in a tone that was just short of patient. She didn't even look back at Peri as she said this. She continued to focus on the clearing around them, pushing all thoughts of doubt from her mind. She could focus on nothing but what lie ahead. If she focused on the past, what happened in Imladun with Atish, then she knew she could not stay strong.

"But splitting up the crystal isn't going to save us. The only thing it will do is stop Kenneth from getting to Earth," Peri cried.

"Well then at least we'll have saved Earth," Kendra said harshly. "If we can't keep Beindor and Hecate out of his grasp, we can be sure as hell that he will *never* capture Earth."

"All right, that sounds good in theory. But how do we know that once we're barely in the ground, Kenneth won't get the pieces of the crystal, and get to Earth anyway? I'm telling you, *we need a better plan.*"

"Peri, there isn't any other way. This is our last hope," Kendra whispered. This was the first time in Kendra's life that she let herself look defeated. Her face showed all the adventures from her years as one of the four protectors of Beindor. Somewhere in the past few years the laugh lines around her mouth had become the only remembrance for her that her life had at one point been even remotely happy. She continued solemnly, "Kenneth is too powerful for us; we cannot defeat him any other way. This is the only thing we can do to make sure his power will not surpass our own."

At this, Peri crumbled. She crouched down on the ground, with her head on her knees, "I'm just so scared. I don't want to die. I don't want my son to grow up without either of his parents."

Aideen, who had been pretending to ignore what the others were saying, looked up when Peri said this, looking distraught. What Peri had said seemed so final; Aideen began to question their plan too. She knew for a fact she didn't want to die. None of them wanted to die. Aideen knew they had to go through with the plan, but that didn't make it easier for her. Every fiber in her being told her they should look for another way, a safer way.

Yet she also wanted it to be over. She was tired of the constant battles with Kenneth, the never ending massacres he created. She knew that if this was the only way to make sure Kenneth didn't survive their attack, then they should try it. Saving the lives of millions across Hecate and Earth was worth the risk of losing their own.

Damia rushed over to Peri as soon as she began to fall, and enveloped her in a hug. Aideen made a move to follow her. They held her in a hug as Kendra watched from a small distance.

"I have an idea. A way to guarantee that we don't die. Or at least, our spirits wont," Damia said mostly to comfort Peri, but also for the others to hear.

Kendra looked up from her own brooding, surprised. Aideen looked up sharply from Peri, her expression changing from a soft, worried look, to a simmering glare. "And you choose to mention this *now*? Kenneth can't be more than moments away!"

Damia was not moved in the slightest by Aideen's glare.

"It's the perfect time," she said. Aideen's glare didn't smolder out . Instead, it got hotter. Just when Aideen might have erupted, Kendra stepped in.

"What's your idea, Damia? Hurry, please. Aideen is right, we haven't got much time..."

"All we have to do is say a spell," Damia explained, repeating the words of the Elvin Queen Bryndis who had given the spell to her after Damia had told her what the four cousins were planning to do.

"And when we die, we can guarantee that our souls will be reborn in four women who will be capable of killing Kenneth. They will grow up to look just like us; will have our powers, and even our temperaments," she added the last part as she looked over at Aideen. "The only difference is that we can *guarantee* they have the power to kill Kenneth."

"How do we do that?" Peri asked, moving away from Damia, to look up at her.

"We can make sure they find their soulmates."

"Why would they need their soulmates?" Peri asked.

"Because when they give into their powers, it will be their soulmates who keep them connected to the physical world."

This statement was met by silence. Staying connected to the physical world was exactly the problem they were having with their plan. It was the only drawback. There was a possibility that the four women, once tapped into their full powers, would not be able to stop their powers from taking full control. When that happens, their bodies would no longer be able to handle the power and would die simply from exhaustion.

The silence that had crept over the clearing was broken by Aideen's disbelieving snort.

"That's certainly easy for you to say, Damia. You're the one who found their soulmate."

"You have too, Aideen," Damia said, angered by Aideen's comment about Rohak, who also happened to be a very good friend of hers. "Or have you forgotten about Atish?"

Kendra took two steps toward Damia, but Aideen got there first. Her eyes flashed red, and she moved forward until she was so close to Damia, her chin nearly touched the other woman's nose. "Never say that. *Do you understand?*"

Damia blanched.

Usually her volatile younger cousin's temper didn't frighten her, but this was one of those rare moments when Aideen's temper showed in all its glory. Damia really shouldn't have mentioned Atish. She knew it was a touchy subject with Aideen.

"Aideen. Stop that right now, before you do something you might regret," there was more than a little fear in Peri's voice. She had been joking, of course, but they all had seen what Aideen could do when angered.

"Fine. And I didn't say I'd forgotten him. Do your little spell Damia, but do it fast. We're running out of time."

Peri muttered something under her breath that none of the three quite caught, except Aideen.

"I am *not* being bitchy, Peri. I'm just being realistic."

They all took hands, and gathered together in a small circle. Then, Damia closed her eyes, and recited Queen Bryndis' spell. They all repeated it, and then they broke the circle, and opened their eyes.

"Did it work?" Peri asked nervously.

"I don't know. Do you feel any different?" Damia asked.

"Not even a little bit." Aideen responded.

"Well it's not supposed to work until we die, right? So then it's probably a good thing that we don't feel any different." Kendra, ever the practical one, added.

"So we're saved then, right?" Peri asked, letting a little hope sneak into her voice. "If we die today, it won't be the end? Kenneth might still be defeated?"

"Oh, I don't think that will happen, *dear niece.*"

All four women jumped at the sudden voice that surrounded them, coming from the trees. The forest was so thick; none of the Keepers could tell where exactly the voice had come from.

"Come out here, Kenneth! Don't cower behind a bunch of twigs! Come out and fight!" Aideen called. She was in a fighting stance, with her fists in front of her body. Kendra shot her a harsh look. Her goading Kenneth would not help matters. But before Kendra could admonish her cousin for her reckless behavior, Aideen's fists burst into flames.

The fire didn't bother the woman in the slightest. Aideen had willed it to come, and so it had. A cold, harsh laugh followed Aideen's actions. It was a sound none of the women ever wished to hear again, it rattled the very bones in their bodies.

"You think your little parlor tricks will scare me? You had better have something much, much bigger up your sleeves, if you want to defeat me."

With that, he stepped out from the trees. Kenneth was not much older than the Keepers, just forty-six to their forty-three. He would have been truly handsome, if not for his coal black eyes, which showed no distinction between pupil and iris. They were the most frightening thing the women had ever noticed about him, even as a boy before Beindor. He was tall, with white blonde hair cut short, and close to his head. His skin was pale, but it wasn't sickly. It reminded the women of royalty, who dared not let their skin tan. He too wore clothing that would fit a fifteenth century nobleman. His clothes suited him, despite his ancestry in Austin, Texas. Like the Keepers, he had not been born in Beindor.

"You're delusional, Kenneth. If you think your power is stronger than ours-"

Kenneth cut Aideen off, "No, Aideen. I don't think. *I know.*"

Aideen looked angry enough to kill, "You forget who you're dealing with."

At this statement, Kenneth looked almost as angry as Aideen. His black eyes widened with rage and the muscles in his arms rippled under the fabric of his shirt.

"No, I know *exactly* who I'm dealing with. I'm dealing with four little girls who happened upon a world too powerful for them, you murdering bitch," He paused for a moment, gathering himself before he prematurely killed one of them. Then he continued, "But don't worry, I've come to take it off your hands."

On this last statement, his voice turned sweet, but murder flashed in his eyes.

"Now you're the one with delusions, Kenneth." Kendra said. "We will never let you have Beindor."

Kenneth growled.

"Don't call me that!" he nearly screamed. "My name is Tárquin now. Kenneth Rhed died when the glorious Keepers murdered his mother! Glorious," At this, he spit on the ground. "Tell me, did you ever stop to think that the woman you killed was your *family*? Your step-grandmother? Did you even care?"

"Did she care when she murdered our grandfather?" Aideen yelled back. "She got what she deserved!"

Kenneth closed his eyes, obviously trying to hold back the anger he was feeling. His entire body shook, but when he opened his eyes again, he wasn't ready to explode anymore. In a calm voice he said, "In any case, it no longer matters. That wrong done so many years ago will be righted tonight. But, in the meantime, you will call me Tárquin."

Damia snorted.

"Tárquin?" She asked in disbelief. "As in *Tarquinius Superbus*? You do realize that he was so miserable at his job that they overthrew him and replaced him with the Roman Republic, right? I don't think that's quite the image you want to send to the people of Beindor."

"Um, Damia?" Aideen asked quietly. "Are you trying to help him, or just stalling?"

Damia shrugged, "I'm just saying it was a poor choice." She looked back at Tárquin, and missed Aideen rolling her eyes.

"Enough!" Kenneth screeched.

He raised his hand, and pointed at the women. Out of his finger shot a stream of fire. Kendra quickly jumped in front of her family, and raised a tall glassy wall between the women and the fire. It moved slowly, rippling like the water in a shallow pool, for it was in fact a wall of water. Aideen shot a stream of fire of her own at Kenneth, by pushing one of her fists in his direction. He didn't seem concerned at all, and when the fire was less than a foot from his face, he raised his hand, and the fire simply vanished.

For a moment, the four women didn't know what to do. Then, Kendra's voice rang out in their minds: *Move towards him. We need to surround him!* Kenneth moved toward the women, and laughed. "You still think your powers are greater than mine, don't you?"

Aideen snorted, and moved slightly, shifting her balance. "I should think that was obvious," and then, without warning, she shot both of her fists toward Kenneth, releasing a huge column of fire towards him. At the same time, Peri shot out both of her arms, and a gust of wind picked up the fire, swirling it into a point before it made contact with Kenneth's chest. Before he could deflect the attack, Damia raised her hand out if front of her, and the earth moved, cracking under him. He lost his balance, and falling to his knees the wind and fire hit him square in the face. He flew backward and hit a tree. For a second they thought he was unconscious. Then he stood up, as easily as if he was rising from a bed, and smiled. There was not a scratch on him.

"My mother was able to teach me a few things before she died. You can thank her for that." Before he could move, they surrounded him.

He only laughed.

"You think that's going to help you? Nothing can help you now."

But the women just ignored him.

They stretched out their hands toward each other, and closed their eyes. Their hands were suddenly connected with a strand of brilliant white light, so bright that it hurt to look at it for more than a second. The light moved constantly, twisting and writhing between the women's outstretched hands, entwining in their fingers, dripping little bits of light here and there.

For a fleeting second, Kenneth thought he was in serious trouble. And then, the four women did something he never expected. He could feel them give up their control over their powers. He could feel them slowly being taken over by their respective elements. This was a dangerous game they were playing, and Kenneth knew what they were after.

After the women had given up their control, they could no longer think, they could hardly even feel, except for the pain. Damia felt herself being given over totally to the Earth, she felt her power running through her veins, wrapping around her arms, legs, body, and neck, like vines. Kendra felt her bones turning to Water. She felt her whole body melting away, as her element consumed her. Aideen was burning. Smoke was filling her lungs, and Fire was scorching away her skin, until there was nothing left. Peri could feel the wind inside her; blowing and blowing, taking away every sense of herself she had, until there was only Air.

And suddenly, light, concentrated power, shot out of every pore on the four women's bodies. Green for Damia, blue for Kendra, red for Aideen, and yellow for Peri. They shot out toward Kenneth, and enveloped him entirely. He let out a blood curdling scream. He too, could feel vines wrapping around him, he could feel the fire burning away his humanity, the little of it that was left, he could feel his bones slowly turning to water, and he could feel the winds ripping him apart. And then suddenly, he laughed. For in an instant, he had realized something fatal.

"You'll never stop me, Keepers. I am too powerful for you," and with that, Kenneth began to disintegrate.

It started in his fingertips, and moved its way up his arms, and down his legs, until finally it came to his head. The vines began to unravel from his limbs, the water began to evaporate, the smoke begun to clear and the wind ceased to roar. With a final laugh, Kenneth was no more. The women never noticed this. They never heard his mysterious last words. They were too caught up in the battle that was raging inside each of them. But as soon as the last little bit of Kenneth floated away, the lights all faded into nothing, and the women collapsed.

When they awoke, they were the only ones in the clearing.

At first, none of them could believe it. They scanned the area repeatedly, searching for any sign of the man that had been there only seconds before. The man that had caused so much pain and suffering to more than just the four of them. He had caused millions pain, burning cities and killing innocents with just a single word.

When they saw that he was nowhere in their sights, they all felt a wave of relief wash over them. Peri was the first to speak, her voice shaky and her words uncertain, "It worked... we killed Kenneth."

Aideen looked doubtful.

"Is it possible he got away?" she asked Kendra.

She shook her head, but turned to Damia anyway. "Well, is he here?"

Damia closed her eyes, and searched through the trees for any sign of human life. After a few moments, she opened her eyes again. "We're the only humans in the entire forest. Wait-"

And without bothering to finish her sentence, she took off in the direction of the trees. She stopped short of the thick growth, and glared into the dark shadows underneath the trees, with her arms crossed. She looked like she was about to scold a child.

Kendra began to call her cousin's name, but heard someone else do so first.

At that moment, a man sprang out from the trees, and made straight for Damia. Only when he had run headlong into her, and gathered her in his arms did he stop. The others could clearly see that it was Rohak, their closest friend, and Damia's husband. Before Rohak could kiss his wife properly, she had pushed him away, and was looking at him scornfully. "What are you doing here? I thought you were still in Vavia!"

This time, it was Rohak's turn to look at his wife in disbelief. "Did you really think I was going to let you fight Kenneth on your own? We've been in this together since the beginning, and you're mad if you think a little thing like not having any magikal powers was going to stop me!"

Damia smiled up at her husband, and gave him a little peck on the lips. "Sorry to be the bearer of bad news, but the battle's over. Kenneth is-"

But she couldn't finish her sentence.

She gasped, and fell limp, eyes wide open. Rohak barely caught her before she hit the ground. He held her close, and shook her. "Damia? Damia! No!" Hardly aware of the tears running down his face, he wheeled to face the other three girls, who where running toward the pair.

"What's wrong? What's happened to her?"

Kendra approached them, eyes wild with fear. She barely made it to Rohak before the same look came to her face, and she too fell limp, in a jumble of limbs and skirts, to the ground. Peri rushed over, and pulled Kendra's form into her lap, eyes streaming.

"What's happening!? Aideen! What's the matter?!"

Aideen just gazed down at her cousin, and then to the north and slightly toward the setting sun. After a moment, she began to sag, but seemed to keep herself up out of sheer will. Finally, however, her body won out over her mind, and as she fell to her knees, she whispered in a pain filled voice, "We failed."

And then, to no one in particular, or rather to someone who was not in the clearing with her, she whispered, "I'm sorry," and fell to her face in the moss. Peri covered her mouth in terror, and looked up at Rohak, who was still cradling Damia's limp body. Tears welled up in her eyes as she realized that they had failed, just as Aideen had said. They had not been able to keep their powers in check, and their worst fears were coming to life. They were killed by the very thing they depended on the most, their elements.

Rohak realized that there was no hope for Peri, but he still felt the need to reach her. To comfort her like he had not been able to for his dear wife. He pushed all thoughts of his motherless daughter from his mind, and looked at the last Keeper. He started to move to Peri, but before he could even take a step, she collapsed against Kendra's body.

Upon seeing Peri fall, Rohak fell to his knees. He was not dead, like the four women, but was in an entirely different kind of pain. A kind of animal wail left his mouth, and he wept. His four closest friends, his wife, they had given everything to save their people. They had made the biggest sacrifice, and yet he could not feel proud. He felt sick. Sick that they had left him and were not coming back. All he wanted was for them to come back, to wake up. He could care less if Kenneth Rhed survived. He wanted his family back together.

Suddenly, he felt the weight of his wife's body leave his arms and he spun around wildly, searching for her, for who might have taken her.

Rohak looked around, and realized he was kneeling, alone, in an empty clearing.

Chapter One

Ugh...what is that?

Damia Starke blinked open her eyes and looked around her slightly unorganized room. She sighed, adding cleaning her room to the never ending 'To Do' list that she kept in her head. Then she remembered why she had woken up, a loud buzzing sound coming from her right. She looked over to her dresser and found the source of the noise.

She grumbled as she saw the large flashing light on her alarm clock. She flipped the bedcovers off her body and slid off the bed. She reached out to her clock and shut off the alarm. The time read five forty-five: the time Damia got up every single morning before school.

It was February of her senior year of high school. All her transcripts had been sent out to her potential colleges, and she was finished applying for the government funding that would help her through the next four years. All she had to do was wait, to see which colleges accepted her and which ones would reject her.

She thought of one school in particular which she prayed with all her heart would not reject her. She had sent the application to them in secret. Her mother would never have approved of it, but if she can show that she was accepted, then there was nothing her mother could do to stop her. She would go.

Damia picked her way across the messy room and out the door. She walked into the bathroom and locked the door. She paused for only a second to look at herself in the mirror. She didn't even try to fix her wild hair. The curly mess was a halo of tangles that formed around her head. She rubbed the sleep out of her eyes and blinked in the sudden light of the morning.

She turned on the water in the shower, waiting for it to get hot. She looked around the small room, which she shared with her mother and older brother, Matt. They lived in an apartment, so all the walls of their home were the same standard beige color, but it was really the trinkets that made it special.

In the bathroom there was a small candle set on the tank of the toilet which was only lit in emergencies, a large square mirror on the wall that made the room look twice its size, and the light blue shower curtain that matched the toilet seat cover. Damia remembered the time Matt had pulled the shower curtain down while trying to climb onto the side of the tub, not three months after they had moved in. The rod had come apart from the wall and hit Matt smack in the nose, breaking it in two places. Blood covered the freshly painted room.

Their mother had to drive him to the hospital, and Damia stayed home to man the fort. By the time her mother and brother got home, five hours later, a nine year old Damia had cleaned the entire bathroom. There were no more blood stains on the floor and the shower curtain was back in working condition. There was only one spot of blood that Damia could not reach, which was half way up the wall. It was still there today, a reminder of what had happened nine years earlier.

Damia laughed to herself at the memory as she stepped under the warm cascade of water. She began shampooing her now soaking wet hair and let her mind drift off. As she was rinsing out the shampoo, she thought about the days ahead. It was Friday, February twenty-forth, which meant the day earlier was her cousin Kendra's eighteenth birthday.

Damia thought about giving her cousin a call, to give her belated birthday wishes. She had also thought about calling yesterday, but knew she wouldn't be able to do it. Despite being only five months apart, the two had not spoken in eleven years.

Eleven years, Damia thought. *What on earth could we have fought about?*

The truth was that she didn't know. She tried remembering back to when she was seven, but there was only one memory from that year she could remember, and it was not one she wanted to think about. Just a split second thought of her father's fatal car crash sent a shiver down Damia's spine and she turned up the water as high as it could go.

Moving away from that topic, she thought to herself, *I wonder what Kendra is like... I wonder what they all are like.*

Damia thought about her other two cousins, the two who were born in the months between her and Kendra. It was with the three of them she was not speaking, not solely Kendra. They had been a very close group of friends growing up. As many families tend to do, cousins born together are raised together. This family was no different, except for the fact that the four girls had suddenly stopped talking the summer of 1998.

I bet it was over something silly. What could make four seven year olds hate each other? It's not like we would be fighting over a guy.

Damia, now done in the shower, turned off the water and dried herself off with her towel. With the towel wrapped around her body, she walked back into her bedroom. She flipped on the lights and searched through her drawers for an outfit for the day. By the time she was done, she was wearing a pair of all purpose jeans with layered tank tops and shirts over. The top most shirt she wore had a scoop neck and was the color of a forest just before dusk.

She added some necklaces, including one with a wooden elephant pendant on it. She styled her long curly hair with some gel and pulled the front back into a small pony tail, leaving the rest of it down. She put on a light touch of eyeliner and mascara and smiled to herself in the mirror. She could tell it was going to be a good day.

Damia glimpsed at the bracelets on her right wrist in the mirror. She paused, almost forgetting that they were there. They had become such second nature to her that she didn't even feel their weight. There were two bracelets; both had not been taken off in at least eleven years.

The first was a simple gold chain. It had been given to her by her father on the day of her kindergarten graduation. She hadn't been able to get the clasp, so he had done it for her. She hadn't taken it off since. She couldn't bare the thought of taking it off. It was the last memory of her father she had. He had died in a horrible car crash two years later. A drunk driver had drove right through a red light, swerved and hit her father's car dead on. James Starke died instantly, while the drunk driver had walked away with less than a scratch.

After that crash, Damia had vowed to live a nonviolent life. She never swore, never drank, and never did anything that might cause other people harm. She couldn't bare it if she caused another little girl pain like she had felt when her father was taken from her.

The second bracelet was a homemade friendship one. There were four colors, green, blue, yellow and red. She had made it when she was seven years old; the summer after her father's passing. She had spent the summer at her Aunt Karina's home, with her three cousins Kendra, Peri and Aideen. The four girls had made the bracelets together one sunny afternoon, and Damia had not taken hers off since.

She wondered if the others still kept theirs. She could not remember the end of that summer and the fight that broke the girls apart. She wished she could, unlike the night her mother told her and Matt about the car crash. That night was forever sketched into Damia's mind.

~*~

"Hello?" Peri yelled, peaking into the dark room.

She was nervous. Not really sure she wanted to see what was behind that door. She opened the heavy door anyway, pushing against it. It swung open with a sudden effortlessness and Peri peered into the black before her.

There was a couple visible in the dark.

It was obvious to Peri why the two lovers had hidden away in this obscure room, but she couldn't stop herself from interrupting. In a quaky voice she whispered a name that made the couple freeze. They had been caught and weren't sure what to do.

"Joey?" Peri repeated, a little more confident it was her boyfriend she was seeing with another girl.

Joey looked up at Peri with pure horror in his eyes. "Peri? How could you-? I thought you were-"

Peri turned away and Joey's sentence trailed into silence. She could feel the tears begin to run down her face. She wiped them away, not wanting him to see her cry. She felt someone move close to her and felt a pair of arms wrap themselves around her, bringing her close to their chest. She turned up to face the man, expecting it to be Joey.

But the man holding Peri close didn't have Joey's brown hair and hazel eyes. This man was blonde and had green eyes. He kissed Peri's head and said, "Don't worry. Soon this will all be a bad dream."

Then he started singing a song. The odd thing about it though, was that it was a woman's voice coming from his lips, singing a not very comforting song. Peri looked up at the mysterious man, confused. Then she felt another pair of arms around her.

It was her cousin Kendra, and next to her was another strange man. The two of them were singing backup. Peri knew Kendra was a singer, but her voice was not as high pitched as the one coming from her mouth. And she could only guess that the man standing next to her wasn't a similar soprano.

It was then she recognized the song as one that frequently played on the radio. She quickly put two and two together, and the answer was her alarm clock. It was six AM and the alarm was going off, waking Peri Andes from her horrible nightmare.

She sat upright in bed. The song was still playing, and it was about to get stuck in her head. She quickly turned off the alarm and got out of bed. Trying not to think about her disturbing dream, she went into the bathroom she shared with her older sister, Zoe. She locked the door and turned on the light. Not ready for the sudden brightness, Peri was blinded for just a half second before regaining focus.

She didn't really care for the bright pink and yellow theme the bathroom had going on, but it was what she and Zoe had picked out years ago when they had first moved into the house. Peri didn't bother trying to change it since Zoe was dorming at her local college and Peri herself planned to go away to college in less than a year. The room would probably stay the ugly baby pink and yellow until the house was sold again.

With the hot water messaging her back, Peri let her mind wander back to the dream she was having before she woke up. The image was vivid in her mind, but she wished it would fade away like all her other dreams. This one had seemed so real, she had even forgotten she was dreaming for a second.

Ever since Peri could remember, she had been able to tell when she was dreaming as she slept. Every single time she dreamt, she knew from the beginning that it was a dream. Never has she woken up and realized she was dreaming, until this morning. She had felt as if she was really in that dark room; watching her boyfriend kiss another girl. She could still remember how it felt to have Blondie's arms wrapped around her, to have him kiss her head.

She shook away that memory and realized that something strange, something besides Joey kissing another girl had happened.

She had dreamt of her cousin Kendra. Kendra was comforting her in the dream, something she would never do in real life. Why would she dream of Kendra like that? She had barely thought of her since seeing her hidden among the faces in a chorus concert in the beginning of the year. It wasn't as if they were close friends.

Then Peri remembered that the day before was Kendra's birthday and she could have slapped herself in the forehead. That was why she had dreamt of Kendra! She was subconsciously thinking about the inevitable birthday party that went along with a birthday, and the torture it would be to go.

The last thing she wanted to do was spend even one evening with Kendra and the others. After the summer the three of them had spent at Peri's house, every family gathering was awkward. They had fallen apart in the most ghastly way, and were too mad to forgive each other. Now, eleven years later, they had still not forgiven each other, and the initial argument was long forgotten. How they could ever reconcile after all these years spent brooding was beyond Peri.

After getting ready for her six hundred and sixty-second day of high school, Peri was glad she only had to do this fifty-eight more times. Then it was off to do the exact same thing in college. However much she didn't want to repeat another four years of mindless schoolwork and drama, she was excited about leaving Seattle.

None of the colleges she applied to were remotely close to her, the farthest being NYU and the closest being the University of Southern California. She couldn't wait to leave high school behind and start her real life. Only fifty-eight more days until she could start fresh, away from the influence of her friends and family. Only fifty-eight more days until she was the one in control of what happened next.

She walked down the stairs and into the kitchen of the large home she shared with her mother and father. The two of them were sitting at the breakfast table, eating their breakfasts. They both had a section of the Seattle Times spread across the table in front of them, and were reading intently. Peri walked up to her mother and kissed her forehead, asking, "Are we doing anything this weekend?"

Karina looked up at her daughter, and said, "Yesterday was your cousin Kendra's birthday. Or did you forget?"

Shrugging, Peri lied, "It must have slipped my mind."

Karina frowned, looking over at her husband, who glanced up at her from the article he was reading. Karina then said to Peri, "Her birthday party is tomorrow night. We will be leaving the house a little before four. Will you be here?"

Peri frowned, taking an apple from a fruit bowl in the middle of the table, "If I *have* to."

She took a bite of the apple and turned to her father, already knowing the answer to her question, "Are you coming, Daddy?"

Maxwell Andes looked up from his paper at his youngest daughter, "I'm sorry, sweetie. I can't. I have to stay late at the office tomorrow. Boss's rules."

Peri would have laughed if her mouth wasn't full. Her father never made it to family parties, not even to his side of the family's parties. The boss always managed to be able to keep him at work on the days of birthday parties, graduations and holidays. And since Max was the founder and CEO of Andes Mountain Gear, Peri knew exactly how the boss managed to keep Max late on those days.

Instead of laughing, Peri gave her father a glare, and he returned it. She then turned back to her mother and said, again with a mouth full of apple, "But why do I have to go if Daddy doesn't? It's just as much his family as it is mine."

Karina sighed, knowing this was going to happen. "I know you don't want to see your cousins," she said. "But they are just as much your family as they are mine. And if I have to go, then you have to go. Okay?"

Peri bit into her apple, thinking. She frowned at her mother and said, "Fine. But it doesn't mean I'm happy about it."

She turned on her heal and walked out the door. She got into her car and drove to school thinking, *Only fifty-eight more days...*

Chapter Two

Two seconds... one second... the flaps slowly fell as the five and nine turned to zero and zero. No alarms rang, no music played. Those functions had been broken on this flip clock since Kendra's older brother, the clock's first owner, slammed it into a wall. Kendra never needed an alarm anyway. Her eyelids fluttered open just as the leaves of the clock face came to a rest.

She looked over at the old clock and smiled. Right on the dot. Again.

She moved out of bed and could feel the butterflies in her stomach. Yesterday had been her birthday, but tonight her two best friends had a surprise for her. She had gone to bed dreaming about what she hoped the surprise would be, trying desperately to ignore the fact that the next day was going to be the longest day of the year, and not in a good way.

She felt the butterflies again as she thought of Ryan, one of her best friends. Her heartbeat always went a little fast when he was around, and no matter what he did it made Kendra's face flush. She constantly looked like she had a fever when hanging out with him, but he never noticed. She had had a crush on him since they met in the seventh grade, but never had the courage to ask him out. She desperately hoped that was a part of her surprise.

As Kendra began to get ready for the day, her overworked mind went back to the dreadful thought of Saturday. Normally Saturdays and the weekend meant joyous times for Kendra and her friends. It was the only time during the week they didn't have to worry about school, not to mention the people or the homework that came with it. However, this Saturday sent Kendra's stomach churning in the most unpleasant way.

While she loved her family whole heartedly, birthdays always involved one awkward moment where Kendra would be forced to visit with Damia, Peri and Aideen. Normally it was their mothers who pushed the four cousins together, trying to rekindle the bond that had long ago separated. Paula, Kendra's mother, always seemed to be the most eager of the aunts to get the four girls together, with the other three following close behind her.

Kendra played with the idea of none of them showing up, as if by some miracle. She knew that Peri was the least likely to show. She had inherited her father's gift of disappearing without a trace when the word 'family' is mentioned. Aideen was in the middle, sometimes wanting to spend time with the family, other times just wanting to bolt back home. She wasn't the most comfortable with gatherings of large amounts of people, even if they were relatives. Damia, Kendra knew, would most definitely be there. She never missed a chance to visit with the family. It was like she actually enjoyed seeing everybody jumping at each other's throats.

After putting on a pair of dark blue jeans and a long, grey, formfitting sweater, Kendra ran her fingers through her shoulder length brown hair. It was still wet from last night's shower, but it was clean and tangle free. She put on a pair of black boots and walked out the door. She walked down the hall of her one story house and found her brother, Art, sitting in front of the large TV screen. He was in his dark red, terry cotton bathrobe eating a bowl of cereal. Art's eyes were glued to the random cartoon that happened to be on at the moment.

Kendra smiled to herself and walked into the kitchen, where the box of cereal Art had used was sitting open on the counter. Kendra was impressed. Most of the time it was the milk that he left out, leaving surprise chunks in Kendra's breakfast. She took a bowl from the cupboard and poured her own bowl of cereal. After adding the milk and grabbing a spoon, she walked out into the living room and sat down next to Art. He hadn't moved a muscle.

~*~

As she walked down the stairs, Damia could hear her mother and brother arguing in low whispers. They were whispering harshly, angrily and as if they were trying to make sure their voices didn't travel up to the second floor and into to Damia's ears. She waited a second at the bottom of the stairs to listen to what they were saying.

"You don't understand," Matt was saying. "If it's what she wants to do, then you shouldn't be stopping her."

"It's a terrible idea. Julliard?"

"It's a great school," Matt interrupted, but his mother didn't pause to listen.

"What is she going to do? She can't sing, so she wouldn't make it on Broadway," Melissa said. She couldn't believe she was even thinking of her daughter on Broadway. It was absurd. "What is she going to do? Be a *Rockette?* I'm sorry, Matt, but even if she does that, what is going to happen in ten years? When she's too old to work at 30! What is she going to do then? This is just impossible."

Damia couldn't believe what she was hearing. She knew that this was going to happen, but she had expected it to come after she told her mother about applying to Julliard. How could they have known? Unless...

Damia quickly walked around the corner and up to her mother and brother, both of whom were seated at the dining room table. They looked up, startled, and stopped talking. Damia put her palm out to her mother, who had an envelope in her hand.

Melissa looked down at the envelope, and then at her daughter. "Please, Damia..." she started, but trailed off when she saw the look in Damia's eyes. She reluctantly handed over the envelope.

Damia stared at it.

The Julliard letterhead was printed on the upper left hand corner of the envelope. Her name was printed on a label in the center. She noticed the envelope felt thick and she could feel her heart well up with emotion. Tears formed in the corners of her eyes as she tore open the envelope and took out the papers inside.

After reading and rereading the letter, Damia looked up at her mother and brother. A tear fell down her cheek as she said, "I got in!"

Melissa was not surprised, but not in the least bit happy. Confused, she asked, "I thought you needed to have an audition..."

Damia tried to hide her smile as she said, "Remember when I went with Noelle to visit her grandparents in San Francisco?"

Melissa frowned, "Yes."

"That's when. We planned that trip around my audition."

Melissa felt her body temperature rise, finding out that her daughter had lied to her. She had brought her up to be respectable, and the first chance she got at showing that responsibility, she betrayed it. *What would James think?*

She took a breath before saying through gritted teeth, "I have to get to work, but when I come home we are going to have a nice long chat. Am I clear?"

Damia knew this was inevitable. She nodded, not caring. She did it! She had made it into her dream school!

Melissa, with a frown on her lips and creases in her forehead, stood up from the table and went upstairs to get ready to leave. As soon as she was out of sight, Matt stood up and hugged his little sister, "Congratulations. I'm proud of you, Damia."

Damia beamed, "Thanks, Matt. That means a lot."

Matt smiled before bringing his breakfast dishes over to the sink. As he turned the water on, he watched Damia hug the letter in her hands to her chest and hop up and down on the ball of her feet. She whispered to herself, "I did it! I made it in."

Chapter Three

Peri pulled into the student parking lot of Placoid High, and into her parking spot. She turned off the car and sat still for a second. She watched other early arrivals pull in and walk up to the school. She then spotted the black pickup truck owned by her boyfriend, Joey. He pulled into a parking spot close by and Peri heard him turn off the engine.

Peri took a deep breath, trying to push the horrible images of Joey and the mystery girl from her mind. By the time Joey was there, opening her door, they were all but forgotten. She put on a smile and took the hand Joey offered her. After grabbing her purse and books from the passenger seat, Peri turned to Joey and said sweetly, "Good morning."

He smiled before kissing her, "Good morning to you too."

Peri smirked before taking Joey's hand and walking into the side entrance of the school. The couple walked through the halls of the school, where only a handful of teachers and even less students could be seen wandering around. They walked up to their lockers on the second floor and put away their books. They then went outside and sat down at a picnic bench in the courtyard.

Sitting next to Joey, Peri felt foolish to be worried that her dream would come true. Joey wasn't that kind of guy, that kind of boyfriend. He hadn't been anything but amazing, and there was no reason why Peri should think differently. She let out a sigh and Joey pulled her closer to him.

"What's wrong?"

Peri looked up at him, knowing he had said something, but she hadn't heard what, "I'm sorry?"

"You seem so far off." He then smiled, "Not thinking about another guy, are you?"

Peri smiled and shook her head, "No, of course not."

Joey then turned serious, "Then what's wrong?"

Peri debated telling him, now realizing the foolishness of the dream. After figuring why not, she said, "I had a bad dream last night."

"Was it about me?" Joey joked.

When Peri nodded, Joey asked, serious again, "Did I hurt you?"

Peri almost said yes, but knew it was a silly thing to do. There was no need to worry Joey about it. She shook her head again, and felt the familiar ach in the back of her throat. It always seemed to happen at the worst moment, like when she was trying to be strong.

Joey must have realized what Peri was thinking because he pulled her into a hug. He kissed her forehead, as the stranger had done in her dream, and said, "I would never hurt you, you know that. I love you more than anything else on Earth."

Peri smiled and looked up at her boyfriend. She couldn't believe she was acting so ridiculous. They had been dating since freshmen year without any more problems than what to get each other for their birthdays. There was no way Joey would cheat on her. No way. She nodded and gently kissed him, "I love you too, Joey. Thanks for listening."

Joey smiled, "That *is* what I'm here for."

Peri was about to kiss him again, her dream completely forgotten, when three girls sat down at their table. Annie, Peri's best friend since the eighth grade, coughed lightly into her hand, breaking Peri and Joey apart. She smiled apologetically and Peri smiled back, not excited to see them.

Annie looked at Peri, "We're going to Marie's after school. Are you coming?" She glanced at Joey and added, "Or are you busy?"

Jackie and Kelly, who were sitting on either side of Annie, giggled. Annie smiled innocently, wishing the other two would shut up. She couldn't believe Peri was still with this loser, Joey Montgomery. It had been four years, how could she not see what a mismatch it was? Every time Annie saw them together, she wanted to vomit. While he had a body of a star athlete, he was clumsy as hell. He had tried out for the football team, but had tripped over his own shoes while running out onto the field. Peri was star quarterback girlfriend material, not towel boy girlfriend material.

Peri knew what Annie and the others thought of Joey, they didn't try to hide their opinions, even around him. They were her best friends, and the only thing they disagreed on was Joey. It was what was tearing them apart, and Peri wished that they would drop it. It had been four years without any evidence damning Joey, but they still insisted that she broke up with him.

She sighed, saying, "Of course I'm not too busy to hang out with you guys!"

Annie smirked, before glancing at Joey, and said, "Good. I have *so* much to talk to you about."

Annie, Jackie and Kelly stood up and the warning bell rang. Joey and Peri got up as well. Annie lip curled as she realized that Joey would be walking with them to their first class, Physics. She pushed ahead of him and Kelly and Jackie quickly followed. She was not about to walk around school with that freak.

Behind them, Peri squeezed Joey's hand, "Don't worry about them."

She looked up at him and smiled, "I'll love you no matter what."

~*~

Aideen Norcross Morris is never late for school. Ever.

Okay, Aideen thought, *maybe that's a little bit of an exaggeration.*

Aideen Norcross Morris is hardly ever late for school.

Hmm... Aideen frowned. *That's not entirely true either.*

Aideen Norcross Morris is almost always late for school.

There. Aideen would have laughed, if she wasn't using all her energy to run. She had just been stepping out of her house when the bus drove down her street and right past her house. The bus driver hadn't even glanced over. If he had, he would have seen a frantic Aideen waving her arms and running down the driveway.

But he didn't, and now Aideen was running through her neighbor's backyard. She jumped over a child's plastic chair and wove through a maze of miniature jeeps and sandboxes and hula-hoops. She could feel the all too familiar pain in her side from running flat out for more than half a minute, but she could not be late for another day of school. She already had four detentions because of tardies, any more and she'd get a suspension. A suspension was not something Aideen was looking forward to.

True, she could get a much needed day off, but she absolutely didn't want a suspension on her record. College was the main goal right now. It was her escape route from Seattle and the life that seemed to be on an endless loop, day after day doing the same exact thing, nothing exciting ever happening. Although she knew that a suspension wouldn't bar her from getting into any college, she didn't want any imperfections... Nothing was going to stop her from leaving Seattle.

She unlocked the fence door and ran down her neighbor's driveway. She turned and ran to the corner of the street, where she could see the bus was about to turn. She came to a stop just as the bus reached the corner. The door opened and the bus driver looked down at Aideen in surprise. She just pushed past him, too winded to explain how she got there. She walked down the row of sniggering classmates, who had seen everything, and sat down in a seat next to a girl named Meg.

Meg smiled, "I didn't think you were going to make it."

Aideen put a hand on her side, where the splitting pain was just starting to reduce, "I don't think I am."

Chapter Four

Kendra walked into Placoid High School daydreaming. Again her mind was wandering off, thinking about after school, when she would be spending the evening with her two best friends. Actually, her friend Lisa wasn't in the daydream. It was just Kendra and Ryan...

"Thinking about me?"

Kendra snapped out of her trance and saw a tall boy with sandy brown hair standing in front of her. It was Ryan. And he was grinning.

Kendra blushed, "You think too highly of yourself, Ryan."

"Ahh..." Ryan said, falling instep with Kendra. "That means yes."

Kendra rolled her eyes and Ryan laughed. She just hoped her acting was believable. She would die of embarrassment if he found out he had been right. Either he would confess his love for her, or their relationship would be officially ruined. Kendra hoped for the former, but knew the latter was much more likely.

Changing the subject, Kendra smiled, "So, what do you and Lisa have planned for me tonight?"

Ryan shook his head, "Ah, ah, ah! You know I can't tell you that! It's a surprise!"

Kendra groaned, "You know how much I hate surprises. I'm going to be worrying about it all day. I won't get any work done. And I'll give myself a stomach ache."

Ryan chuckled, "Then should I return the birthday cake I got you?"

"Birthday cake?" Kendra asked excitedly. "Is it strawberry?"

Again Ryan shook his head, "You know I can't tell you that."

"It is, isn't it!" Kendra smiled. "You wouldn't get me anything else. I'm on to you, Ryan McPherson!"

"Okay, so the cake is strawberry, but you won't be getting anything else out of me!" Ryan said.

"Ryan! Are you giving away the surprise?" Lisa asked, walking up to her two best friends. She smiled inwardly at them. They were standing so close that they looked joined at the hip. It was obvious to her that they liked each other, had liked each other forever. It was obvious to the entire school except them. She had just barely been able to convince Ryan to take a chance tonight and tell Kendra how he feels.

He had said that Kendra wouldn't feel the same way. Lisa knew the exact opposite was true. While Kendra had never told Lisa about her crush, it was written all over her face. Whenever they hung out with Ryan, Kendra tended to stutter a lot more than normal. She also was a lot clumsier, tripping over nothing, dropping books everywhere. It was like she became a complete idiot whenever he was around. Not to mention the flushed cheeks which gave her away every time.

Lisa saw Kendra was blushing now and could not understand how they hadn't started dating years ago. Hopefully that would all change tonight. With a little encouragement from Lisa, they would be the cutest couple at Placoid. She could see them at the ten year reunion married with three kids. They were perfect for each other.

Ryan looked down at Lisa and smiled, sending her a look that showed how nervous he was. She smiled encouragingly back and he said, "Of course not! Nothing is going to ruin tonight."

"Good," Lisa said. "Tonight is going to be perfect."

~*~

"God! Can you believe her? A thousand words! On the Civil War! What the hell are we supposed to write about? That's a freaking book!"

Aideen smiled at Meg, "You know a thousand words is just about five pages long? That's hardly a book."

"Still!" Meg yelled, ignoring the looks she was getting from people passing her in the hall. "What are we going to write five pages about?"

Aideen shrugged, "We did it on the War of 1812, I think we can do it on the Civil War."

Meg shook her head, "I wish I could drop this class. I don't even need AP History! I'm going to be a *lawyer*!"

Aideen was about to point out the contradiction in her statement, but decided to let it pass. The two girls walked into the art room and took out their current works. Meg was drawing a picture of her baby sister at three weeks old. Aideen was working on a picture of a sunrise. It was half sketched, half painted at the moment. There were a lot of yellows and red and oranges, but Aideen had also included some blues and purples and blacks. That's what she liked about the sunrise, it included so many different colors, you could never know what to expect.

Aideen took some paints from a nearby cupboard and set up at a table in the corner of the classroom. Meg set up her own little work station on the table next to Aideen. She continued to rant about their newly assigned paper until she realized Aideen was no longer answering. She had gone off into her own little world, filled with acrylic paints and sunsets, a world without papers due and college applications needing to be sent out.

Chapter Five

Walking into the studio, Damia felt her troubles melt away; just as they always did when she stepped through the doors. She forgot about her mother, waiting at home to "discuss" Julliard with her. She forgot about the family party where she would have to confront her three cousins. She walked into one of the practice rooms, where a class of five and six year olds were about to start, clutching a piece of paper in her hand. She quickly walked over to the teacher, and held out the piece of paper to her.

Miss Diana was a middle aged woman who had been running her dance studio for over twenty years, after graduating from the Julliard School herself. Damia had taken lessons from her since she was three years old, but it wasn't until the year Damia turned eight that she doubled her efforts. After that, Miss Diana became Damia's idol; the woman who gave her private lessons all year round and her first job at the age of sixteen. Miss Diana was the one who first told Damia she was Julliard material. Miss Diana had even gone with Damia to the live audition. Damia knew she owed everything to Miss Diana.

Miss Diana stopped what she was doing - putting a cassette into the tape player - and her eyes widened. Damia bit her lip, holding in the emotions that were about to explode. She waited without a word as Miss Diana took the piece of paper, unfolded it and read it. Miss Diana read it once more before reaching out and wrapping her arms around Damia.

"Oh, Damia! This is wonderful! Congratulations!"

"Thank you so much, Miss Diana," Damia said, with tears in her eyes. "For everything. I couldn't have done this without you."

"Stop it, Damia," Miss Diana said with a small laugh. "You're going to make me cry."

Damia smiled and pulled Miss Diana into another hug. "You're the greatest woman I know. This is all because of you."

Miss Diana smiled and said, "Come on, Damia, we don't want to keep these children waiting."

Damia nodded, taking her acceptance letter back. She took off her jacket and sweatpants, under which she wore a leotard and tights. She slipped on her ballet shoes and followed Miss Diana over to the waiting students. Together they taught the class.

~*~

"Peri, honestly I don't see what you see in that Joey character," Annie said.

The four girls were sitting at a table inside Marie's Creamery, a local ice cream shop. They had just sat down when Annie blurted that out. She didn't mean to say it, but she was glad she did. She didn't like hiding her feelings about her best friend's boyfriend from her.

Peri sighed, knowing this was going to happen sooner or later. She took a sip of her root beer float and looked up at Annie. "Well I guess it's a good thing I'm the one dating him and not you."

Jackie and Kelly exchanged glances, and continued to eat their ice cream. They did not want to get in the middle of another Annie/Peri fight. They watched helplessly as the two girls quarreled, secretly wondering how their relationship lasted as long as it did.

Annie's eyes widened and she snapped, "I'm only trying to do you a favor. Montgomery is the *worst* kind of guy you could be dating."

"Why?" Peri asked. "Because he isn't on the football team like all your boyfriends? Tell me, Annie. How many meaningful, long-lasting relationships have you had with them? None, right? Have you ever had a boyfriend for longer than two weeks?"

"Meaningful? Long-lasting?" Annie could not believe what she was hearing. "Since when is that what you wanted? Last time I checked, we were in high school. Relationships are meant to be two weeks long."

"Well, then I guess our relationship is long overdue for a break-up," Peri snapped.

Annie smiled brightly, "Yes! You finally get it! You and Joey so need to be over."

"I wasn't talking about me and Joey, Annie," Peri said, standing up. "I was talking about me and *you*."

Peri grabbed her purse and stormed out of Marie's. Luckily she had brought her own car, so she was able to make a quick getaway without worrying about rides. She fought back the tears as she pulled away, but she knew they were inevitable. She had known her friendship with Annie was on thin ice, but she never expected to end it like that.

Back inside Marie's, Annie and the others were in shock. Annie couldn't believe that Peri had just walked out on her. She was trying to help her, and that was the thanks she got? Brushing the fight off, Annie said, "Fine. She doesn't want to listen. She'll see. Someday, I'll be right and she'll be sorry."

Chapter Six

"Get away from me! Leave me alone!" Little David Morris was screaming at the top of his lungs, running in circles around his living room like a cornered animal. "Help! Help! She's gonna kill me!"

Aideen walked into the room with a towel in her hand. She watched her five year old brother scream for help. She tried her hardest not to yell at the boy. It wasn't his fault that she got stuck babysitting him. It was her parents' fault. They were the ones who decided at the last minute to go out with a bunch of their friends. Aideen did have plans, to finish her sunset painting, but her parents didn't understand. They told her that she could paint and watch David at the same time. Really? How can she concentrate on her painting while worrying about what David could be sticking his fingers into, or even eating?

She wanted to yell at her parents. She wanted to get away from them. Aideen couldn't believe how typical of a teenager she sounded, but it was the truth. They didn't understand her and they weren't about to listen. They were teenagers once, why couldn't they remember that? They were too wrapped up in their own little world to bother to stop and think about Aideen and what she wanted.

They didn't even realize that she was going to be leaving in less than six months. Or if they did, they didn't seem to care. She expected a little bit more of a commotion about her graduating from high school and going to college, especially from her dad. She was going to be the first Morris to go to college. It only took four generations, but it was going to happen. He didn't even seem to realize that she was almost twenty.

Okay, so she had over two years before she reached twenty, but still. She was long past childhood, and they barely noticed that she had hit puberty. That's why she planned to move as far away from Seattle as possible. Maybe travel the world. Aideen had always longed for adventure. Perhaps she could visit Cairo before going to college. She wanted to do something big with her life; she just didn't know what yet.

Realizing that David was still running around the room, yelling for help, she put her hand on her hip and said, "I'm not going to kill you. I'm going to give you a bath."

David let out a loud screech that made Aideen cover her ears. She walked over to him and plucked him up off the floor where he had thrown himself. He started wriggling and trying to escape from her grasp.

"Stop it, David! Before the neighbors hear you and call the police. Then we'll both be put in jail, forever and ever! Do you want to go to jail? They don't have sandboxes in jail!"

David stopped wriggling and sat up in Aideen's arms. His eyes widened, and he began to wail, "I don't wan'ta go ta jail!"

"Then let's take that bath of yours."

David shook his head and started wriggling again.

Aideen didn't let go of him. Instead, she said, "Fine. You can go to bed now then. I was going to make some ice cream sundaes for us after your bath, but if you don't take your bath you can just go to bed now."

David stopped wriggling and again sat up in Aideen's arms. He threw his arms around Aideen's neck and said in warp speed, "IsorryAideen!Itakemybathnow!" Then he added, as if it were a afterthought, "Can I get sprinkles on my sundae?"

Aideen laughed at her little brother, "You can have as many sprinkles on your sundae as you want." She set him down and added, "Now go take your bath!"

David made a mad dash for the bathroom.

~*~

"Can I open my eyes yet?"

Kendra felt dizzy. He was so close to her; she couldn't think straight. She could smell his cologne, the one that she had bought him for his birthday back in December. Her heart did a flip, thinking of Ryan putting on cologne she had bought him. She could feel him breathing, his chest rising up and touching her back. It sent her head spinning, but it wasn't the only thing that made her feel woozy. His arms were wrapped around her; his hands covered her eyes. He was touching her face. Grant it, it wasn't in a romantic way, but he was touching her nevertheless.

Lisa could see how Kendra was reacting even with half her face covered by Ryan's hands. She wanted to laugh at how pathetically hopeless she was. She could see Ryan was just as ecstatic as Kendra was, his face also becoming flush as Kendra leaned up against him.

"No, we're not there yet," Lisa said with a laugh. "Stop asking!"

"I hate surprises."

"Yeah, we know," Ryan said. "You haven't stopped saying so for two weeks."

Lisa laughed and added, "You're going to love it. Stop worrying."

Kendra bit her lip, but stayed quiet. She let Ryan lead her through his house. She had visited his place enough times that she knew exactly where they were, and where they were headed. She listened as Lisa slid open the back door that led out to the back porch and smiled. Despite the cool temperatures in February, the three friends hung out in Ryan's backyard all year round.

Then Ryan stopped and Kendra asked, "Now?"

"Just a second," Kendra heard Ryan say. She could feel his voice vibrate in his chest and she smiled.

"Ow!"

"Sorry!" Ryan said. He had led Kendra right into a table. She could feel her knee pulsing in pain, but not even that could dampen her mood. She was still with Ryan, after all.

"Nice one," Lisa said.

"I'm sorry," Ryan said. "I'm just so excited! Sorry, Kendra."

"It's okay," Kendra said. "Can I look yet?"

"Yes!" Lisa said and Ryan removed his hands.

Kendra opened her eyes and looked around. She gave a gasp of surprise and turned to her friends, "You shouldn't have done this!"

They both smiled and Ryan said, "We wanted to."

The porch was covered with birthday decorations. There were streamers and balloons and even the tablecloth had little party hats printed on it. Sitting on the table was a small pile of presents and a birthday cake. She walked over to the birthday cake and read, "Happy 18th Birthday Kendra."

She smiled and turned to Ryan and Lisa. Ryan said, "Strawberry, your favorite."

Kendra reached out and grabbed Ryan in a hug. She then wrapped an arm around Lisa and pulled her into it. "Thank you guys. This means so much to me."

Ryan flushed again, and prayed Kendra didn't notice. He could feel the butterflies in his stomach as he thought of what he was going to do later. Somehow Lisa had convinced him to tell Kendra how he felt. He didn't even realize that Lisa knew, or that Kendra would feel the same. That's why he was so nervous. He didn't want to ruin their friendship by saying something as silly as, 'I love you.' He hoped it wouldn't.

He smiled, "I don't know about you two, but I am famished. Who wants birthday cake?"

"I do!" Kendra piped up, following after Ryan.

Chapter Seven

Wrapping her arms around Joey, Peri closed her eyes, "Thanks for coming here."

Joey squeezed Peri in a hug, "Of course. I just can't believe she would be so mean to you."

After Peri had stormed out of Marie's, she called up Joey. He met her at her house and she invited him inside. Once up in her room, she broke down crying. Joey immediately enveloped her in a bear hug and together they sat down on the floor against the side of her bed. Combing his fingers through her hair, he asked, "What's wrong? What happened?"

"I told Annie that we were finished. I broke up with her."

"Why?" Joey asked.

"Because," Peri said through her tears, "she told me that she wanted me to break up with you."

Joey wasn't surprised at that. Annie had hated him since the first time they met, and she didn't try to hide it. He just felt bad that he was the reason why Peri stopped being friends with her. "So you're never going to talk to her again?"

"I don't know," Peri sighed. "I mean, I want to be friends with her. We were so close! But sometimes she can be so *air headed*. She can't look past herself and I don't want to be friends with someone like that."

Joey nodded his head, "That makes sense."

Peri smiled, "Thanks for listening to me. Now can we *please* change the subject?"

Joey laughed and then said, "Oh, I forgot. I have tickets for the Billy Joel concert tomorrow. Do you want to go?"

"Forgot?" Peri said, looking up at Joey. "How could you forget that you have those tickets? I tried getting some! They are over three hundred dollars!"

Joey smiled, "Okay, maybe I didn't forget… but anyways, are you free?"

Peri's smile turned to a frown as she remembered that she wasn't free. She groaned and said, "I can't. My cousin Kendra's birthday was yesterday and her party is tomorrow night."

"Wait. Kendra as in Kendra Dodson?" Joey asked.

Peri sighed, "Yes, *her*."

Joey sat up, "I didn't know you were cousins! Why didn't you ever mention it?"

"Because," Peri said, still bummed about the concert, "we stopped talking in like second grade."

"Whoa," Joey said. "Did you have a fight?"

Peri thought back and shrugged. "I don't remember. We were all hanging out at my house for the summer. I remember one day everything was fine, and the next, none of us were talking."

"None of? There is more than just you and Kendra?" Joey asked. "How many more cousins do you have in this school?"

Peri shook her head, "None. Damia and Aideen go to schools across town."

Joey frowned, "So you're going to blow me off for a birthday party for a girl you don't even talk to?"

"I don't even want to go. But my mom's making me." Peri snorted, "I don't even think *she* wants to go, and it's her family."

"Well you can always sneak out and we can go to the concert," Joey smirked. "I won't tell if you don't."

Peri shook her head, "My mother would *murder* me."

She then glanced at the clocked, "Speaking of which, if she comes home and sees you up here, she's going to kill us both."

They stood up and walked over to the bedroom door. Joey opened it, but before he left, he turned around and kissed Peri. She smiled up at him and said, "Thanks again for coming over to listen to all my problems."

Joey smiled, "Any time. I love you, Peri."

"I love you too," Peri said, kissing him again. "I'll call you later."

Joey nodded before walking down the hall and down the stairs. Peri listened to him leave the house and drive off. She closed her door and fell face first onto her bed. A few minutes later she heard the garage door open and her mother's car drive in. Peri groaned and looked at the clock. It read seven o'clock. Peri wished it was Sunday and that the party was over. She wished she never had to go to another birthday party ever again.

~*~

Damia dragged her feet slowly up the stairs to her apartment. She knew what was waiting on the other side of that door, and she wasn't excited about it. Slowly she unlocked the door and stepped inside. She looked around, and was surprised her mother wasn't waiting on the couch, ready to pounce. She closed and locked the door without Melissa making an appearance.

It wasn't until she was halfway across the living room before she saw her mother standing at the top of the stairs. She stopped and looked up, waiting for her mother to say something. Melissa walked down the stairs slowly. She had reached the bottom before saying, "You missed dinner again."

Damia immediately looked at the clock hanging on the wall. It read seven thirty three. She looked back at her mom and said, "I'm sorry. The only clock at the studio is on the receptionist desk. I didn't realize it was this late until I got in the car to come home. I'll be here tomorrow, I promise."

"So you were at the studio?" Melissa asked, her anger slipping for only a second.

Damia nodded, "I help Miss Diana for three classes, and then I have my own lesson. That's how it is every Friday. I guess my lesson ran a little long. I wanted to make sure I got this one step."

"Damia," Melissa said, cutting her off. "I think you should spend less time at the studio."

Damia's mouth dropped, "What? Why? I missed one dinner. It's not like I was out getting drunk or high. I was at my job."

"It seems to me that your priorities are a little mixed up. Staying away from dance for a while might help you set them straight."

"This is about Julliard, isn't it?" Damia asked.

Melissa let out a controlled sigh, and instead of yelling, said, "Partly. You know my opinion on going to college for dance, and you blatantly ignored me."

"I didn't ignore you. I considered your opinion and chose to go with my own! Why is that such a big deal? I do stuff without your opinion all the time."

"But this is the rest of your life!" Melissa said, desperately trying to make her daughter see reason.

Damia interjected, "And it's my choice whether or not to go to Julliard, not yours! Stop trying to control my life! Just because it's not what you think is right, doesn't mean it's not right! I won't know until I try."

Melissa sighed, "I just wish you could look beyond Julliard. What is your life going to become afterwards? Do you really want to make minimum wage as a backup dancer?"

Damia realized it was a hopeless argument. Neither of them was going to convince the other to come to reason. She shook her head, "Of course I don't want to be a backup dancer. I want to come back and run the studio with Miss Diana, maybe even take over after a while. She told me today that I could be a choreographer just like her when I graduated. It would be well over minimum wage and I would be guaranteed a job. But that doesn't matter to you. You just want me to be a business major like you, and get a boring office job like you. You don't care about what would make me *happy*."

Damia walked around her mother and headed up the stairs. She stopped before she reached the top and added, "You aren't happy, so why should I be?"

~*~

"I can't believe I'm about to say this, Kendra."

Kendra took a breath. This was it. It was all going to end there. On her birthday. He had found out she liked him, and couldn't handle it. He was going to end their friendship and never talk to her again.

Ryan and Kendra were sitting together on the steps to the back porch. Lisa was inside, pretending to wash dishes, but in fact she and Mrs. Montgomery were watching through the kitchen window as Kendra and Ryan talked. Lisa had explained what was about to happen and Mrs. Montgomery rushed over to watch, with Lisa following right behind.

The sun was far below the horizon, having set around three hours earlier. Kendra had opened the presents Ryan and Lisa had bought her and they each had had at least three pieces of the strawberry birthday cake. Ryan knew he couldn't put it off any longer. He sat down next to Kendra on the steps, and on cue, Lisa ran inside to do the dishes.

Ryan sighed, "I have been trying to come up with something to say all day, but every time I think about you I become speechless."

Kendra looked up at Ryan, not expecting him to say something like that. She was quiet, waiting for him to explain what he just said. She didn't want to jump to conclusions and then embarrass herself even more in front of Ryan. He looked down at his hands, and took a breath. Then he looked up at Kendra and said, "I like you. A lot. I can't get you out of my head, and I don't want to. Kendra, I want to be with you."

Kendra's eyes widened. Was he kidding? Was this some kind of joke he and Lisa were trying to pull. She was about to ask, when he moved closer and took her hand in his. "Well?" he asked. "Will you go out with me?"

Kendra could tell that Ryan was not kidding. There was a fear in his voice that he could not fake if he had tried. She felt her heart fill with emotion and her throat start to dry up. She nodded and said quickly, "Of course I will, Ryan."

She then threw her arms around him and pulled him into a hug. After a moment he pulled away a little and kissed her. It was a light kiss, but it was a kiss nevertheless, and Kendra was floating on Cloud Nine. She put her head on his shoulder and closed her eyes, knowing that life was perfect.

Chapter Eight

"Daddy! Daddy!"

Jedrek Faal looked up from his meal just in time to see his little girl jump into his lap. She was wearing a simple brown dress, which looked like it hadn't been taken off in days, and her hair was pulled back into a long braid. He picked her up and threw her into the air. She let out a little screech, but giggled when he caught her and started tickling her. She squirmed out of his tickling hands and said, "Daddy! I don't wanna go to bed!"

"Oh?" Jedrek said. "Is it bedtime already?"

He let out a big yawn and let his head droop backwards. Sara, his five-year-old daughter laughed and pushed on his chest, "Wake up! It's not your bedtime! It's *mine!*"

Jedrek picked up his head and looked down at Sara, "Oooh... I see."

He stood, and scooped her up under his arm. She laughed again and said, "Put me down!"

He ignored her until they reached the second room of the two room mud-built house. He dropped her on one of the two beds in the room and she continued to giggle. She stood up and said, with her hands on her hips, "I don't wanna go to bed!"

"Will you go to bed if Daddy tells you a story?"

Sara's eyes widened and she nodded quickly. She then jumped down onto all fours and crawled under the covers of the bed she shared with her sister. Her sister's twin brother slept on a mat on the floor and her parents slept in the other bed in the room. Her father sat down on the edge of his bed and looked at Sara, "What story do you want to hear?"

"The Keepers!" Sara said excitedly.

Jedrek frowned, "But I told you a story about them last night. And the night before. How about one about the Great War between the Dragons and the Dwarves? Your brother loved that one when he was your age."

Sara shook her head and repeated, "The Keepers!"

Jedrek sighed, "Okay, what story about the Keepers?"

"All of them!" Sara said.

Jedrek laughed, "All of them? That would take years! The Protectors of Beindor had very busy lives."

"Then the first one! And tomorrow night we can do the second, and then the third, and then the fourth and the fifth and the sixth until we've done them all!" Sarah said eagerly.

Jedrek laughed again at his energetic little girl. "Alright. The first Keepers story? Hmmm.... Well many, many years ago, before you and I were born, four women discovered a portal between Hecate and Earth."

Sara giggled, as she always did when someone mentioned the fictional world of Earth. Even she, at five years old, knew that there was no such thing as Earth.

Jedrek continued, "These four women brought with them from Earth a group of people who settled this very city, Canhareth. It was the first human city in Beindor, this country, and on all of Hecate. Eventually humans expanded and built Vavia and Nérand, plus many other cities and towns in Beindor. They eventually even discovered the countries of Ohtalie and Úrdor, too. These people, your ancestors, lived in peace for a while, until a monster attacked Canhareth.

"This beast, a cyclops, began tearing apart the city. It tore off roofs of houses and stepped on the tiny people in the streets. The people thought they were all goners until the four women who created the portal between worlds came and saved the day. They had been away exploring the other parts of Beindor, but when they came back, they had changed. They had magikal powers, like being able to fly and heal with a single touch.

"They were able to defeat the cyclops, killing it without even getting a scratch themselves. The people of Canhareth, of Beindor, were amazed. They dubbed these four women The Keepers of Beindor. They were Keeper Aideen, Keeper Kendra, Keeper Damia and Keeper Peri, and they continued to keep order in Beindor until they mysteriously vanished themselves."

"Jedrek, honey," a woman standing in the doorway said, interrupting.

Jedrek looked back at her, "Yeah?"

His wife motioned to their daughter, "She's asleep."

He looked down at Sara, and realized that Fay was right. He chuckled to himself before patting Sara on the head, "Goodnight, my sweetheart."

Sara mumbled something incoherent before turning on her side, away from her parents. Jedrek laughed softly again before walking out of the bedroom with his wife. He stood in the doorway and watched as Fay took the wooden plate and cup off of the table and dropped them into a large tub filled with murky water. He watched as she began to scrub them clean.

After a minute or two, he approached her and kissed her cheek. She stopped scrubbing when his kisses reached her lips. She pulled away after a second and smiled, "What's gotten into you?"

Jedrek smirked, "What? Something wrong?"

Fay shook her head, bringing his face back to hers. She smirked back, "Nothing's wrong. I just haven't seen you this happy in a long time."

Jedrek shrugged, "I guess I'm just in a good mood."

He then closed the gap between them and kissed his wife again. The dishes made a popping sound as they fell into the water, completely forgotten.

Chapter Nine

Standing in front of the mirror in her room, Peri sighed. She was not looking forward to this party at all. She loved parties; she loved hanging out with her friends and having a good time. She loved taking pictures and having a couple drinks. It was her friends that made the parties fun, but she was friends with no one at this one. She barely talked to anyone in her family, and she refused to speak to the only relatives she had ever gotten close to.

She knew nothing good would come from this party.

She walked out of her room and down the stairs; an idea, one last ditch effort to stay home, forming in her head. She walked slowly down the stairs and up to her mother, who was taping a birthday card onto a box wrapped in birthday gift paper. Without looking up from the present, Karina said, "No. "

"Mom-" Peri started, but was interrupted.

"Whatever it is: no. You're not getting out of this, so don't even try."

"But I have a project due Monday that is worth-"

"Do it tomorrow," Karina said, grabbing her purse. She walked past Peri and towards the garage door.

Peri followed close behind, "Please, Mom. You don't under-stand. I hate these things. I don't want to see them."

"You're still fighting with your cousins?" Karina asked in dis-belief. "That was forever ago, and *that's* why you hate seeing your family? You should make up with them. Parties would be a lot easier on you if you did."

Peri groaned, "It's not as simple as saying, 'I'm sorry. Wanna be friends?'"

"I didn't say making up would be easy," Karina said as the two got into the car. "I'm saying afterwards would be easier."

Peri frowned and said, "It would be easier if we didn't have to go."

~*~

There were people *everywhere.* Aideen didn't even know she was related to so many people. She quickly counted thirty people and stopped, not wanting to know how many people were crammed into Kendra' backyard. The sight was already making her head pound. Maybe it would rain and they would all have to scramble inside. During the commotion she could just slip out the side gate. They wouldn't realize she was gone until she was at home in bed.

Aideen chuckled at the idea and looked up to the sky. She stopped laughing; it was bright blue with not a sign of cloud cover. There was no chance that the party would be rained out and Aideen had to come up with another way to make her escape. Unfortunately, nothing was coming to mind as her mother and father ushered her closer and closer to the large mass of people.

As Aideen was pushed closer to the masses of people mingling on the back deck and yard of Kendra's house, she spotted one of the few people she had wanted to steer clear of for the rest of her life. It seemed that at that same moment, her mother spotted Damia as well and said, "Oh, Aideen look! It's your cousin Damia! You two haven't chatted in a while, why don't you go over and say hi?"

Aideen's stomach dropped into her toes. She looked over at her mother and wanted to scream *Are you insane?* but knew that would hardly have been polite. Instead she just stared, until her mother realized that she was not about to move. Kelly Morris sighed and pushed her daughter in the direction of her niece.

Damia saw them coming just before they reached her and Aideen could see her eyes grow large for a moment. *I'm not going to kill you*, Aideen thought, glaring at Damia, who did look like she was facing her executioner.

Damia smiled at Aideen hesitantly, not sure what she should do.

"Hi, Aideen," Damia said quietly. "How are you?"

"Fine," Aideen said quickly, her throat tightening up. She refused to look at Damia, but instead focused on the lawn behind her. She watched as her cousins Matt and Art picked up a Frisbee and started throwing back and forth to each other. She had the sudden urge to go join them; they looked like they were having so much more fun than she was at the moment.

She glanced back over at Damia who was staring at her, waiting for her to say something. Aideen stared back, without the small smile that was playing at Damia's lips. She wasn't going to be the one to talk first; she was going to wait for Damia. She had taken up that honor by saying the first hello. Aideen didn't want to take that honor away from her, that wouldn't be nice.

So they just stood there.

After a moment of silence, the noise of the party began closing in on them. They felt the pressure to talk push at them from all around, and yet neither of them could find the right words. What do you say to a person you refused to speak to for eleven years? That was the question they were both struggling with, and neither could come up with an answer.

It was at this point that they realized there would be no conversation between them, at least not a comfortable one. That moment had passed almost as soon as they reached each other. Now they had to come up with an excuse to leave this awkward meeting in the past. Struggling with an exit line, Aideen opened her mouth. But nothing brilliant came out like she had hoped.

Damia then flushed slightly before saying, "I'd better..."

She walked away, trailing her sentence along behind her. Aideen let out a breath as soon as she was gone, so happy that moment was over with. She just hoped she wasn't going to have to do that two more times before she was allowed to leave. Putting that reunion behind her, Aideen walked towards Matt and Art. They were two cousins that Aideen had always gotten along with. They never pushed her to make up with their sisters. Aideen doubted that they even realized they were fighting.

Chapter Ten

In her hands was a plate overfilling with food. There was a veggie burger, trail mix, and a brownie. Damia scoped out the tables and saw the liveliest one. She could tell from across the yard that her grandmother was knee deep in a story from the good old days and her audience was captivated. Despite the fact that her mother was one of those audience members, Damia knew that was the table she was going to find the most enjoyable company. She hurried over, hoping to catch the last of the story. As soon as she sat down there was a burst of laughter from the table. Damia smiled at her family and asked, "What? What did I miss?"

"Oh, nothing, darling," Melissa said to her daughter, ignoring the fight they had the night before while in front of family. "Your grandmother was just telling a story from back in the day. When she was dating your grandfather."

Damia's eyes lit up and she turned to her grandmother, "Please tell me, Grandma. I'd love to hear about Grandpa James."

Frances Ferrando smiled at her second oldest granddaughter, "Maybe another day, sweetie. I'm liking the look of that brownie you have there. I might go and get me a few of those."

Melissa stood up, "Let me, Mom. You can tell Damia about Dad."

Damia smiled up at her mother, hoping this meant that she wasn't mad at her anymore. Melissa just smiled and walked away. Damia eagerly turned to her grandmother, who looked like she was off in a daydream. She said, "Your grandfather was the most remarkable man I have ever met. He swept me off my feet the moment we met, and somehow he still manages to make me fall in love with him everyday, even from the grave."

Frances sat for a moment in silence, thinking about her late husband. Damia wished she had met her grandfather, but he had died just a few months before she was born. He had caught malaria during the Korean War and survived. That was in the early 1950s. Then suddenly in 1989 he went into relapse and died shortly afterwards. He had been sixty years old.

The fact that both her mother and grandmother had fallen in love with a James had always fascinated Damia. She often daydreamed of her James waiting for her somewhere out there. She wasn't the first person to come to that conclusion, either. More than once, someone at some party or another would come up to her and ask her if she had found her own James yet.

If Damia ever did find a James of her own, she worried that his destiny might be as tragic as her father and grandfather's. Both of them had died prematurely. When her father had died, she vowed never to fall in love with a James. That way his fate would not be that of her father and her grandfather. So far no James had come into her life, and she figured it was a slim chance that one would. Two had been a fun coincidence, three would be plain creepy.

Frances Ferrando continued her story, with Damia listening eagerly. Melissa came back with a plate of brownies for the table, and everyone ate them contently. Damia knew she was lucky to have a family like this. There was no place she would rather be than sitting in her aunt's backyard, listening to stories from her grandparents' youth.

~*~

She couldn't deny that the party was a success, but Kendra could not wait for it to be over. Besides the fact that her newfound love interest would be there to help clean up and go through her new presents, Kendra just wanted to sit down. Though family gatherings had always sparked Kendra's interest; hosting one was never her idea of fun. There always seemed to be some controversial moment, and Kendra had enjoyed watching from the sidelines, not having to be the one to play referee.

So far she had gotten lucky. No such moment had occurred, and everyone's heads were still attached to their bodies. Once everyone had arrived things started to settle down. Kendra made her rounds to each of the tables, talking for a few minutes with all of her relatives. The conversations were all pretty standard. What was she going to do after high school? Did she have a boyfriend? (Which she answered with a glowing 'Yes.') Was she excited to be turning 18?

Soon her answers became the robot answers that matched the robotic questions. She wanted to have conversations with these people; she just didn't like having to make them all short and sweet, then on to the next table. Her cousin David's birthday was next, and she knew that she would be able to relax at that party. However, that wasn't this party, and Kendra trudged on, counting down the hours until she would see Ryan again.

~*~

She was being antisocial. She knew it. Her mother knew it. Everyone knew it. But she didn't care. She was happy. Music was pumping into her ears via two small earbuds. Reclining on a pool chair with her eyes closed, Peri could easily have fallen asleep. There was only one problem to that ideal situation.

She was continuously being hit by a Frisbee.

She was at her favorite part of a new album she had just bought when she felt the plastic toy hit her in the legs. Her legs, already having been hit twice, were now throbbing with pain. Peri bolted up and glared at her cousins standing in the large open backyard. They were looking over at her like mice trapped by a hungry cat. She screamed, "What the hell was that for?"

Matt, the oldest of the cousins, pointed behind her, "I threw the Frisbee too high for Art. My bad... could you throw it back?"

Peri looked over her shoulder, and sure enough, on the other side of her chair was the brightly colored Frisbee. She stormed over to it and picked it up. She looked back at Matt. Her cousins Art, Aideen and David were waiting for the toy as well. She then smirked, an evil idea quickly forming in her mind.

Without a word to her waiting cousins, Peri turned to the fence, the one that looked over to the front of the house and driveway, and threw the yellow Frisbee over with as much strength as she could muster. Ignoring the protests from her cousins, Peri turned to her chair and picked it up, moving it to a more secluded spot. A spot away from the lawn and those playing on it.

Chapter Eleven

Aideen was not surprised Peri had chucked their Frisbee down the driveway. She expected nothing less from a girl who sits out with her iPod at a birthday party. As Peri got situated in a new area to listen to her music, Aideen lost a game of Noses, and became the person who had to retrieve the Frisbee.

She ran past a group of tables where people were seated and eating some food. She noticed Damia was sitting with their grandmother, who was telling one of her infamous stories about Grandpa James. She shuddered at the thought of the moment that she and Damia had stood awkwardly with each other. Luckily, Kendra had steered clear of the Frisbee field and Peri was too engrossed in her music to want to talk to her. She didn't need any more uncomfortable moments this evening.

As Aideen searched the front yard for the bright yellow Frisbee, she noticed a guy a couple houses down, walking his dog. He was wearing only a long-sleeved shirt, and sweatpants, despite the cool February weather. His dog, a golden retriever, was running around him in circles and Aideen could tell she was happy to be outside with him.

The dog owner noticed Aideen watching him, and he smiled at her. She smiled back, tucking a strand of her wild reddish-brown hair behind her ear. She then frowned and looked away, realizing she was beginning to flirt with him. Flirting was not something Aideen wanted to be doing. She wanted nothing to do with men and their tricks.

Her last boyfriend promised her the world, and she believed every word he said. Instead of the world, she found out he had not only been dating her, but two other girls as well. Needless to say she dumped him right away, but she never got over the betrayal. She had tried dating again after him, but she quickly realized that they were all the same: manipulative and looking out for only themselves, with no regards to the feelings of those they stepped on. So, she stopped dating. She figured she would start looking again in a couple years, when the guys her age were more mature and ready to have a more serious relationship.

In the meantime, she removed herself from the dating scene. She refused to go out with anybody, even those who seemed to have a genuine interest in her. She refused to let herself fall for every guy she met, and if she did, she would mentally destroy them until she no longer felt anything for them except disgust.

She ignored the dog and owner, and resumed her search for the Frisbee Peri had tossed over the fence. Even though she was ignoring them, she was watching the man and dog out of the corner of her eye. She watched as the golden retriever spotted something across the street and froze. Aideen looked over at the spot where the dog was looking, and saw why she began running at full speed. The Frisbee lay in the grass on the lawn across from Kendra's. Aideen ran after the golden retriever, yelling at her owner to stop her.

But it was too late.

By the time Aideen was half way in the street the golden retriever had picked up the Frisbee in her mouth and began prancing around like a show dog. Aideen yelled at the dog, "That's *my* Frisbee!"

The dog looked over her shoulder at Aideen and, with the Frisbee still in her mouth, smiled. Aideen took a step forward, ready to rip the Frisbee from the dog's mouth, and the dog pranced a few steps backwards, away from Aideen. Aideen stopped and the dog stopped as well. *This could only happen to me,* Aideen thought sourly.

She moved forward and again the dog moved out of her reach. Chuckling came from behind Aideen, and she remembered that this dog had an owner. She spun around and yelled again, "That's my Frisbee! Tell your dog to hand it over!"

The golden retriever's owner was not intimidated by Aideen's yelling. Instead, he found it very amusing. He said with a laugh, "How do I know it's really yours? It's in Mrs. Herburger's yard, not yours."

Then he paused. "You don't live here, do you? This is Kendra Dodson's house."

"Yeah," Aideen said. "I'm her cousin. And this is her birthday party. And *that's* the Frisbee we were playing with until Peri throw it over the fence."

"Peri?" he asked. "Peri Andes?"

"Yeah..." Aideen said, arching an eyebrow. "You know her?"

The guy ignored her question, stunned by the revelation he was having. "I didn't know Peri Andes and Kendra Dodson were cousins! I don't think I've ever seen Peri talk to her in school."

"You go to Placoid?" Aideen asked.

The guy looked away from the house behind him and turned back to face Aideen. He smiled, "Yeah. And I assume you don't. I would have noticed you before this."

Aideen grimaced at his attempt to flirt with her, "Nice. Can you tell your dog to give me my Frisbee back now?"

He smirked, "Chelsea. Come here, girl."

The golden retriever's ear perked up and she trotted merrily past Aideen and to her owner. He took the Frisbee from her mouth and she sat down, waiting patiently for him to throw it. He glanced up at Aideen before a smile spread across his face. The dog stood up and started to dance in place, waiting for her chance to snatch the Frisbee out of the air.

Aideen realized what he was about to do seconds before he was able to throw it. She ran over and grabbed the Frisbee from his hands, "What the hell? This isn't yours! You can't give it to your dog!"

The guy shrugged, "Whatever."

He then started walking away, "Come on, Chelsea."

The golden retriever followed behind, glancing back at Aideen and the bright yellow Frisbee in her hands. Aideen stormed back into Kendra's backyard, only to be met with a loud, "Aideen! There you are!"

Chapter Twelve

Paula Dodson sat anxiously at a table in her backyard. There was a problem in need of fixing. She knew she had to be the one to fix it. It was obvious that they weren't going to fix it on their own. She watched as her daughter Kendra ate her dinner across the table from her. She smiled kindly over at her daughter, and then looked over her left shoulder.

Behind her sat Damia, with her back to them. Paula could tell she was laughing, talking to her Uncle Adam. She looked around and saw that Peri was sitting on a pool chair under a group of trees, trying to hide from the rest of the party. She tried finding Aideen, but she wasn't anywhere to be seen. She figured she must be getting some food, because that's where Matt, Art and David were headed. She had seen Aideen playing Frisbee with the boys earlier.

Paula knew that this silly feud the four girls were in was ridiculous. It had been eleven years and they still could not come to terms with each other. They had mastered the art of avoiding each other, and it was time that they were forced to face their issues. Paula knew it was her job to help, seeing as she was the host of her daughter's party, and all four girls would not say no to her.

She stood up and motioned Kendra to stand as well. Kendra put down her fork and stood, "What's up?"

Paula didn't answer. Instead, she walked around the table and tapped Damia on the shoulder. She smiled and said to her niece, "Come on, we need to do something."

Damia glanced at Kendra, who was standing behind her and the smile fell off her face. Kendra realized as well what her mother was doing and silently prayed that it was not true. The two girls stood motionlessly as Paula walked over to Peri and took the headphones out of her ears.

They saw Peri look over at them with a look of horror and knew it was hopeless. Paula was going to try to end the feud. Peri stood up and followed Paula over to Damia and Kendra. The four looked around, but Aideen was nowhere to be seen. Paula called to her husband Dan who was just leaving the house, "Dan! Is Aideen in there?"

Dan paused and looked back through the window. He turned to his wife and shook his head. Paula frowned, putting her hands on her hips, "Where could that girl have gone?"

Peri looked up at her aunt, "I threw the Frisbee over the fence and Aideen went out after it. That's the last I saw her."

"Over the-" Paula started. Then with panic in her voice, she asked, "How long ago was this?"

Peri shrugged, "Five, ten minutes?"

Paula rushed over to the entrance that led to the front yard. If what she thought was true, then her plan wouldn't work and she probably would never get the girls together again. They would avoid her at all costs after tonight if they didn't make up. "If I know Aideen, she probably is half way home by now!"

She reached the gate and pulled it open. Aideen stood there, surprised that the door she was about to open had been pulled out of her hands. She looked up at her aunt, who said, "Aideen! There you are! I thought you had left!"

"What?" Aideen asked. Then she realized she had had the perfect chance to escape and didn't even think of it. She rolled her eyes at her stupidity. "Sorry, Aunt Paula. No such luck."

Paula wrapped an arm around Aideen's shoulder and ushered her inside the gate. Aideen got the sinking feeling that she was being led down death row. She saw Peri, Damia and Kendra standing a few feet away and knew she should have made a run for it before the gate had closed.

Paula smiled at the four girls and said, "Grab a chair. Come over here."

The four girls did what they were told in silence. They felt like they were tiny kindergarteners who had been caught stealing each others' crayons and about to be scolded in front of the entire class.

From the moment Paula had made Peri take off her head-phones, everyone's eyes were on them. It was no secret that there was drama between the girls, and any drama in the family instantly became the entire family's business.

The four girls each took a green plastic chair and sat them in a row, facing Paula. They were about to sit down when Paula said, "No. In a circle."

The girls looked up at her, refusing to look at each other. She smiled and waved her hands, "I'm not going to be the one doing the talking! You are!"

The girls glanced quickly at each other, and all of them knew that none of them wanted to be doing this. Reluctantly they created a small circle, but refused to look at each other. Paula sighed, "Do you really want to spend the rest of your lives mad at the girls you spent your entire childhood with?"

Chapter Thirteen

The silence was unbearable. With every moment it grew louder and louder. They could feel it pouring into the spaces around them, trying to suffocate them. Trying to make it so that they would never speak again. They all knew that if this didn't work out, the silences would only get more awkward afterwards. They would only be reminded how they had tried to work things out but couldn't. There was only one thing worse than the silence.

The guilt.

Paula's last words to them felt like a kick in the stomach to a prized fighter already down and out. After eleven years of silent hate, they had forgotten all about the seven years before the summer of 1998. They realized that keeping their silence was to ignore the first seven years of their lives. To honor the memory of those years, they had to at least try to get along. The only problem was how they were going to start getting along.

So they sat in silence.

They tried to come up with conversation starters; college, boyfriends, bands, but they all seemed so unimportant. How would they get their friendships back in line by talking about college? They looked around, helpless. They began making eye contact, smiling feebly at each other, waiting for someone besides themselves to start the healing.

Damia tucked a piece of hair behind her ear and Peri gasped.

The others looked at her, and saw she was looking at Damia's wrist. She reached out and grabbed her cousin's hand. She flipped it over, looking at the two bracelets on her wrist. She recognized them both, but it was the string that interested her. Breaking the eleven year silence, Peri said, "I can't believe you still wear this! I forgot all about them!"

Damia shrugged, "I figured I would let it fall off on its own, but it never has."

"What is it?" Aideen asked.

"Our friendship bracelets," Kendra said, remembering how she had cut hers off right after the fight they had. "We made those the summer we stopped talking."

"Whoa," Aideen said. "You've had that bracelet on for eleven years?"

Damia nodded, "Both of them."

Peri frowned, "I wonder what happened to mine. I don't remember it falling off..."

Kendra smiled sheepishly, "I cut mine off right after I got home that summer."

Peri nodded, "I think I did too. I was so mad."

"Why? I can't even remember what we were fighting about," Aideen said.

"I have no idea," Peri said. "It was probably nothing; we just never let it go."

"What could make four seven year olds so mad at each other?" Damia asked.

"We were probably fighting over a toy," Kendra smiled.

Peri's eyes lit up, "No. It wasn't a toy. An imaginary friend."

"You're kidding," Aideen said. "I've never had an imaginary friend."

Damia laughed, "Yes you did. We all did. Prince Michael."

Peri nodded excitedly, "I remember him! He was my first boyfriend."

"Hmm..." Kendra said, a flood of old memories coming back to her. "I thought your boyfriend was Prince Peter. Prince Michael was mine."

Peri shook her head, "Prince Michael was most definitely mine. There was no way I would have given him up."

Damia smiled, "I remember Prince Michael. He was so gorgeous."

"Careful," Peri said to her. "That's *my* boyfriend you're talking about."

Aideen watched her cousins in silence, realizing the very source of their argument back in 1998. She wondered if anyone else would realize how obvious it was. She watched as the conversation, having been quite dead moments earlier, began to heat up very quickly. Aideen soon understood that her cousins had figured out the answer to why they had stopped talking without even realizing it. They were so wrapped up in it that they could not see it. She said, interrupting, "Guys! I think this Prince Michael is the exact reason why we haven't been talking for the last eleven years. We were fighting over this imaginary prince of ours."

The others looked at each other, grasping the concept. They couldn't believe how obvious it had been, and yet how they could never figure it out. Peri laughed, "You mean we, four eighteen year olds, have been fighting over a fake prince?"

Peri was soon joined by the others in her laughter. After a minute, the laughter died down, and the four cousins were again plunged into silence. They looked at each other, wondering how to keep this conversation afloat. Peri asked, "So does this mean we're friends again?"

"I don't know about *friends*," Aideen said, looking Peri over. "But I know I don't hate you as much."

Peri made a face at Aideen as Damia said, "I can't believe it's really been eleven years. We need to do some serious catching up… what has been going on with you?"

Kendra smiled, "My best friend and I started dating yesterday."

Peri looked over at her, a huge smile on her lips, "You mean Ryan McPherson?"

A look of confusion crossed over Kendra's face, "Yeah..."

"Oh my god!" Peri said. "Congrats! I cannot wait to tell Annie! You do realize that the entire school has been waiting for you two to hook up."

Kendra's face turned bright red, "Really? They have?"

Peri nodded. She took her cell phone out of her pocket and started typing away, "Annie is not going-"

She paused and looked up, "Oh yeah. I forgot."

"What's wrong?" Damia asked. They all saw the tears forming in the corners of Peri's eyes, as she set the phone down on the chair next to her.

Peri rubbed her eyes, "Annie is no longer talking to me." She gave a half-hearted laugh, "I stop talking to my three best friends and I meet my new best friend. My new best friend stops talking to me, and I make up with my three old best friends. What the hell is that?"

"Why aren't you and Annie talking?" Kendra asked in disbelief. "You two are joined at the hip."

"Apparently not," Peri said. "She wants me to break up with Joey, which I am *not* about to do."

"Why would your best friend want you to break up with your boyfriend?" Aideen asked, feeling bad that she had been mean to Peri earlier.

"I think she didn't think we would last this long, and now that we have..." she trailed off. "I don't know... she's mad at me."

"You'd think that your best friend would be happy that you're in a stable relationship," Damia said. "Maybe she's jealous."

Peri laughed, "The last thing Annie wants is a stable relationship. She even said so. 'Relationships are supposed to be two weeks long,'" Peri said mockingly. She then shook her head, "Annie and I haven't been getting along lately anyways."

"Well I guess we made up at the perfect time," Damia said. "We're here for you, Peri."

Kendra and Aideen nodded in agreement. Peri smiled, "Thanks, you guys. But please, can we change the subject?"

Damia bit her lip, "I got an acceptance letter yesterday...from Julliard."

"Damia! That's amazing!" Kendra said. "You are going, aren't you?"

"Of course!" Damia said.

"Wait," Aideen said. "For what? I didn't think you played an instrument. And I *know* you can't sing."

"You don't remember?" Peri asked, her tears were nowhere to be seen. "Dance! It was the only thing she could ever talk about. Dance this... First position that..."

"It wasn't the *only* thing I talked about," Damia said defensively.

"Yeah," Kendra said, with a smirk. "It was."

Damia frowned, "Well if I knew how much you hated it, I would have stopped."

"Its fine," Kendra said, realizing that Damia was hurt. "Julliard is impressive. I think you have a right to gloat about that."

"I wasn't *gloating*..." Damia said, looking away.

"So, Aideen," Peri said, changing the subject again. "What has been up with you?"

Aideen shrugged, "Nothing like Julliard. No boyfriends to report of either. My life is boring."

"Do you still draw?" Kendra asked. "I remember some of the things you did. They were wonderful."

Aideen smiled, "Yeah, I still paint. I'm working on this one right now. It's a sunrise, but there isn't a definitive sun in it, just a huge swirl of colors."

"Sounds..." Peri thought. "Abstract."

Aideen laughed, "Yeah, it sort of is."

Chapter Fourteen

"Oh my god, Paula. You did it," Dan said.

"They're talking. They're not even fighting…they're *laughing*," Frances added.

There was a huge smile on Paula's face, "I'm so glad their fight is *finally* over. Did you know it was over some imaginary guy? They were arguing which one he was going to marry."

The party erupted in laughter. Paula looked back and saw that everyone was either laughing or watching the four girls. It seemed that they had stolen the limelight. Their fight had grown bigger than the four girls had known. It had had the entire family worried about them. Now they saw that their worrying was over, and they were happy. Paula was glad she could have helped. She was glad that her daughter was back to being friends with her cousins. The last eleven years had been hard on her, even if she wouldn't admit it.

"So what are you going to do next?" Paula's brother-in-law Adam asked her. "Cure cancer?"

Paula laughed, "One miracle at a time."

She then stood up and walked over to her daughter. She waited for the four girls to finish laughing before saying, "Who wants to do cake and presents?"

The four girls followed Paula over to the rest of the family as Dan retrieved the cake from inside. After singing to Kendra and watching her blow out the candles, she cut the cake right down the middle with a large knife. She paused before pulling the knife out of the cake and asked, "Whose birthday is next?"

After a moment of silence, Paula said, "I believe that would be Aunt Karina."

Karina smiled and moved to take her place in front of the cake. As she paused to make a wish before pulling the knife out of the cake, a timeless family tradition, Kendra moved over to where Peri, Aideen and Damia were standing.

They were smiling uneasily and when Kendra reached them, Peri said, "Why is everybody looking at us? My mom's the one with the knife."

"They should know better than to give her that thing," Aideen said.

Kendra smiled, "Are you kidding? We just made family history!"

"What?" Aideen asked.

"Our little feud has been family gossip since it began. After eleven years we finally just ended it. They're all talking about that," Kendra explained.

Damia frowned, "I feel like we're under a spot light."

"You better get used to it, Miss Julliard," Aideen said with a smirk.

Damia laughed sarcastically, "You're hilarious, Aideen."

Aideen's smirk grew, "I know. Who else to balance out your bitterness?"

Damia's mouth dropped. Paula looked over at them before Damia could respond and asked quickly, "Presents?"

Kendra nodded and walked back over to her mother. Art and her father were now coming from the house with a pile of wrapped boxes and a pile of birthday cards. They set the gifts in front of Kendra, who smiled. Again her thoughts drifted to Ryan; she couldn't wait for him to come over later and help her make a list for her thank you cards. It was something they had always done, but this year would be different. She could barely contain her excitement.

After a large pile of clothes, a sweatshirt, three novels, a flash drive, two DVDs, one CD, $100 in gift cards and $250 in cash were all unwrapped and in a large pile at Kendra's feet, it was time to serve cake. The sheet cake was covered in white frosting and was decorated in pink, blue, and yellow frosting flowers. As pieces began to be removed, the strawberry filling was revealed. The four girls quickly got in line for their pieces, and once they were in hand, they drifted back over to their little circle of chairs.

The conversation flowed steadily now. They were surprised how natural it was to talk to each other. It was as if the last eleven years had not happened, and they were still the close friends they had been. True, there were some moments where the conversation got sticky and rude comments were made, but they moved quickly past those and the healing continued.

They spent the next hour sitting in those green plastic chairs talking. They updated each other on their lives, what had happened in the eleven years they had been absent for. They discovered that Kendra had a secret passion for singing, and that Peri had failed her first three road tests. Damia learned that Peri was just as obsessed with Harry Potter as she was, and Kendra found out that Aideen shared the same passion for the TV show One Tree Hill as her.

They were discussing other TV dramas when Kendra noticed Aideen could not stop fidgeting in her seat. Kendra looked at her, "Are you okay?"

Aideen responded quickly, "Yeah. Why?"

"You look like you have to pee," Peri said.

Aideen shrugged, "I'm just bored of sitting." Her eyes got big, "Wanna play Frisbee?"

Peri shook her head, "Sorry. I have the worst aim ever."

Aideen doubted that, after seeing Peri throw the Frisbee into Mrs. Herburger's yard. She scowled, still wanting to get up and do something. Kendra then asked, "What about a walk? A couple times around the block?"

Aideen shrugged, "That sounds good. Better than just sitting here."

Damia smiled, "Why not. Peri?"

Peri sighed, "Okay, fine. Since everyone else is."

They stood up and Kendra ran over to her mother, who happened to be heading over to her at the same time. They met in the middle and Kendra asked, not failing to notice the camera in her mother's hands, "Can we go for a walk around the block?"

Paula frowned, "It's getting dark out…"

"I know my own neighborhood, Mom."

"Alright," Paula said, reluctantly. "But let me get a picture of you first."

She held up the camera and smiled. Kendra rolled her eyes and waved over her three cousins, who were waiting for her by the gate. "One second! My mom wants a picture."

The three girls groaned, and dragged their feet, but walked over to Kendra and Paula. Paula lifted the camera to her eye as the girls huddled together, their arms wrapped tight around each other. Paula smiled, "Say cheese!" and took the picture.

"Pepperoni!" came the response from the four girls, a tradition they had started when they were toddlers. They laughed, surprised that they all had said it. Paula rolled her eyes and said, "Thanks. Now don't stay out too long. People are going to start leaving soon."

Chapter Fifteen

"Oops. Okay, let's start heading back," Peri said.

The four girls were standing at the opposite end of a dead end street. They had started walking less than ten minutes earlier, in the brightly lit neighborhood around Kendra's house. Now the street lamps were beginning to turn on, and the sun had passed behind the houses around them. Kendra would never have admitted it to the others, but she didn't recognize this part of the neighborhood. The last thing she remembered that she recognized was the large lake in the center of the community, but that had been early on so it didn't help her at all.

She was about to agree with Peri, when Aideen said, "Oh, come on! It's a dead end. We can turn around once we reach the end."

"By the time we reach my house," Kendra said, "it will be dark. People are most likely waiting for us to get back so they can leave."

"Aww," Damia said with a smile. "It's just one more street. And we can see the end from here! No big deal!"

Peri smiled, "Alright. No big deal."

Kendra frowned and looked around. She suddenly had a bad feeling about this walk. Standing in between Aideen and Damia, she linked her arms with theirs, hoping the contact would ease her nerves. They looked at her and she smiled, "Let's go."

Peri noticed them linking arms and quickly linked her arm in Damia's. She smiled at her cousin before the four of them walked down the empty street. There weren't any cars on the road or in the driveways. All the house lights were off, not even a porch light was lit. Curtains were closed and the people were all safe inside their homes. It looked like they were expecting a storm.

The four girls walked in silence, looking straight ahead at the large cement wall in front of them. There had once been a road there, but once the highway went up, the road was useless. Then houses started spreading out, farther and farther from the city and the families who bought these huge houses didn't want to look at an old abandoned road and the old abandoned houses on it. So there was a wall built to hide them.

It took just a few minutes to reach the wall, but to the girls it felt like half the night had passed. They stopped when they got there and Aideen laughed, covering the slight anxiety she felt, "That wasn't so bad, now was it?"

Kendra smiled, "No, I guess not."

"Alright. Now can we go back?" Peri asked.

"Yeah," Kendra said as they turned around. "That's a good idea."

They had only taken two steps when something made them stop. The streetlamp nearest to them flickered for a second, before going out. Their immediate surroundings fell dark. Then the rest of the streetlamps on the dead-end road went out, one by one. It happened so fast that for a second the four girls weren't sure anything had happened, except for the fact that they could not see an inch beyond their noses.

"Dumbledore?" the others could hear Peri ask weakly. "Is that you?"

Her question was met by silence, and then suddenly they heard a loud crack: glass shattering somewhere in the distance. Lots of glass, like a car or house window. Before anyone could react properly, the street lit up again. Relief washed over the four girls, until they realized it was not the streetlamps the light was coming from. The light was casting long shadows of them in front of them.

The light was coming from behind them.

Standing in the middle of the street, they immediately believed it was a large truck or semi coming at them. However, the light was too small to be the headlights of a semi-truck, and the road behind them was completely blocked by the large brick wall. The only reason why the girls could see the small light was because the entire street in front of them was pitch black. They looked behind them, to the source of the light, and saw it was coming from a house on the other side of the wall.

The house was an old Victorian, one that had been built long before the suburbs reached this part of the city. It stood on its own, with no neighboring houses and only the trees to keep it company. The girls could easily tell it was abandoned, and had been abandoned for some time.

"Wait a minute," Kendra said. "I know this house, but it's impossible. It's only a myth. A story at school."

Peri laughed, "You are *not* talking about the Trac house are you?

"Yeah, I am," Kendra said quickly.

"You're crazy. I know the guy who made that story up," Peri said.

"But look at it," Kendra said. "An old abandoned house hidden on a suburban block by a brick wall. What else could it be?"

"A coincidence?"

"Wait a second. Slow down," Aideen interrupted. "Not all of us go to Placoid."

"Oh, right. Sorry," Peri said. "Kendra here is talking about a stupid story that was going around freshman year."

"What was it?" Damia asked.

Peri sighed, "It was stupid. The seniors made it up to scare us."

"It was about a family who lived here in the sixties. Aldan and Rose Trac, with their six kids. By the time the kids all had kids of their own, Rose got really sick and died. Alan got re-married about a year later, to a Dorothy Rhed. His kids were convinced that she poisoned their mother to get Aldan to marry her. Dorothy had a kid of her own, but I can't remember his name. But anyways, one day, the entire family disappeared. Aldan, Dorothy, all seven kids and grandkids."

"Even the next-door neighbor was never seen again," Peri said, getting into the story.

"For the next five years, anyone who went into that house disappeared. And lots of people went in, troops of people at a time. Anyone who went in, never came out," Kendra continued. "They think Dorothy Rhed did it. Killed the entire family, and then everyone else."

Aideen let out a laugh, "That is stupid. Just the seniors trying to scare you."

"Thank you!" Peri said, throwing up her hands.

Kendra frowned, "Then why does that house look like the Trac House?"

"Because they probably saw this one and made up the story because of it," Peri said. "Probably brought some poor freshmen out here too."

Damia quickly shook her head and said in a low whisper, "I don't think so, Peri. Look!"

She pointed up to the house, to where the light was coming out of an upstairs room. In the frame of the window was the dark shape of a person. It didn't move when it saw the girls looking at it.

"Stop pointing at it!" Kendra hissed, grabbing Damia's arm. "Do you want her to kill us as well?"

Damia screamed and ducked behind the wall, out of view from the house. The others hid as well; all starting to feel their walk was a very, very bad idea. "I want to go home," Peri whispered.

"Are you kidding?" Aideen said, a huge smile forming on her face. "Let's go check out that house!"

"No!" Peri yelled. "There's someone in there! It's Dorothy Rhed! She's gonna kill us!"

Aideen laughed at Peri's panic, "Are you telling me you're buying into this? That can't be Dorothy Rhed! She'd have to be ninety years old by now! Are you afraid of a ninety year old woman?"

"A mass murdering ninety year old woman? Yes!"

"You're assuming she's still alive," Damia said, panicking. "That could be her ghost up there."

"Now you're telling me you believe in ghosts?" Aideen asked with a disbelieving smirk.

"Yes!" Kendra said, trying to get Aideen's attention away from the house. "Now let's go!"

"You can go," Aideen said. "But I'm getting a better look at that ghost."

Kendra groaned and Damia said, "Aideen, please. Let's just get out of here."

"See you back at the party," she said with a smile and a little wave. They watched as she turned to face the brick wall behind them. She gripped one of the bricks and began climbing. The others watched in silence until she was straddling the top of the wall. Aideen looked down at them triumphantly.

"That's very funny, Aideen," Kendra said. "Now come back down. We have to go back, and my mom will kill me if I leave you alone out here."

"Then I guess you're coming with me," Aideen said as she swung her leg over and dropped down the other side of the wall.

Kendra sighed and said, "Fine. My mom can yell at you when you come back alone. I *am not* going into that house."

Kendra started walking away, but Damia and Peri were hesitant about leaving Aideen alone to face a mass murdering ghost.

"Kendra, wait," Damia said. "I don't feel comfortable with leaving Aideen alone. I'm going with her."

Kendra stopped and looked around at Peri while Damia quickly climbed over the wall and disappeared. "Come on, Peri. Let's go."

Peri shook her head, "Do you really think Damia is going to be able to handle this?"

"Do you think you can?" Kendra snapped.

Peri frowned, "No, but I guess there is strength in numbers."

Kendra watched as Peri climbed up the brick wall too. She jumped down, and landed next to Damia who asked, "Is Kendra coming?"

"I have no idea," Peri answered.

"Of course she's coming," Aideen said from where she was crouching low behind a bush. "She can't help but come now, knowing that the three of us need adult supervision."

"That's right," Kendra said, appearing at the top of the wall. "You're gonna get yourselves killed, and I'll be the one to save you."

She jumped down off the wall and looked up at the large house hidden in the trees. Now, of course, it wasn't as hidden as before. The girls could see the overgrown front yard, with crabgrass and dandelions sticking out of the tall grass, which spilled over onto the pathway leading up to the front porch.

The porch was made with the same neglected, rotting wood as the rest of the house, with matching blue paint peeling off. As they walked closer to the old house, they could see that all the windows were broken, littering the porch and surrounding grounds with broken shards of glass.

"That must have been the glass we heard," Kendra said.

"Can ghosts break glass?" Peri asked.

"It's probably some stupid freshmen trying to see the ghost," Kendra said. "I bet that's who we saw in the window. Can we go now?"

"Are you joking?" Aideen asked. "We haven't gone inside yet!"

"You never said anything about going inside," Peri wailed. "I don't want to go inside, even if it's just some freshmen! That house is creepy!"

Ignoring her, Aideen crept closer to the house, keeping low to the ground, out of any ghost or freshmen's sight. Kendra sighed and followed after, knowing she was the most susceptible to danger. The two girls, with Damia and Peri close behind, crept up to the porch. When no ghosts started moaning, and no freshmen started yelling, the four girls walked up the front stairs, over the broken glass and to the front door.

Aideen twisted the doorknob, but the door wouldn't open. "It's locked," she said, the disappointment evident in her voice.

"Well, maybe that's because Dorothy Rhed doesn't want visitors," Peri said. "Maybe all those people disappeared because they disrupted the ghost. Do you want to disappear too?"

Aideen shook her head, "We're not going to disappear. I'm going to show you that Dorothy Rhed does not haunt this house."

The three girls then watched as Aideen walked over to a broken window and started to clear out the small amount of glass left on the inside of the window frame. She then lifted herself onto the windowsill and climbed through to the front room of the Trac house.

Aideen had expected the wind to stop blowing so hard once inside the house, but she was surprised to see that it had picked up significantly. She was even more shocked to see that it looked like a tornado had ripped right through the living room. It was clear that it was not high school boys who had done this. Something much bigger had happened, like the murdering of an entire family.

Aideen could see a couch standing on its side, pushed against the wall next to the window, and a coffee table flipped upside down against another. Photos were on the floor in shattered frames. The bare nails in the walls were the only clue to where they had been before tragedy struck. She picked up one of the pictures and saw that is was a family portrait.

A couple in their late forties was the focal of the picture, with their children and grandchildren spread out around them. Aideen instantly knew the couple had to be Dorothy Rhed and her husband, Aldan Trac. All five of Aldan's children were in the picture, along with their spouses and children. The oldest grandchild could not have been more than two years old, a small little girl with brown curls.

A strange feeling washed over Aideen as she studied one of the other grandchildren. Another girl, this one had to be less than six months old. She was staring right at the camera, staring right at Aideen. She could not shake the feeling she was having, like she had seen this child somewhere before.

Aideen noticed that Dorothy Rhed's hand was on the shoulder of one of the grandchildren. Aideen hadn't noticed him at first, but now he was sticking out like a sore thumb. He was clearly much older than the other kids, roughly three or four years old, but that was not what made him stick out. Unlike everyone else in the picture, this little boy had platinum blonde hair.

"Who's that?" Damia asked, looking over Aideen's shoulder.

"I think it's the Trac Family," Aideen said, trying not to show the fear she had felt for a split second, thinking that Damia was Dorothy Rhed, ready to murder her where she stood.

"Look at the back," Damia said, oblivious to Aideen's thoughts. "My mom always dates pictures. Maybe Dorothy did too."

Aideen arched an eyebrow at Damia, but did as she was told. She slid the picture out of the broken frame and flipped it over. To her surprise, Damia had been right. Along the bottom of the photograph it read:

October 1st, 1949. Richard, Gloria and Peri Vavia, eleven months. Robert and Kathleen Trac. Lois Trac. Aldan, Dorothy and Kenneth Rhed, four years. Helen, Charles and Aideen Dehann, ten months. Walter, Frances and Kendra Trac, eight months. Evelyn, Arthur and Damia Neimann, one year.

"It *is* the Trac Family," Aideen said, quickly finding the names Aldan, Dorothy and Kenneth together. "Kendra, you were right."

Kendra nodded, "Okay. It's the Trac house, can we go now?"

"Please," Peri added quickly.

"My mom's got to be wondering where we are by now," Kendra said.

"Nope," Aideen said. "We still haven't seen the ghost."

"Aideen, come on," Kendra started, but was interrupted by Damia, who had taken the Trac family portrait from Aideen.

She said, "Guys, look at this."

"What is it, Damia?" Kendra asked.

She pointed at the four toddlers on the front of the photo, "Those kids are cousins, okay."

"So?" Peri asked.

"Look at their names," Damia said, flipping over the picture for them to read Dorothy's label.

"Peri Vavia, Aideen Dehann, Kendra Trac, and Damia Neimann," Kendra said in a whisper.

"Oh my god," Peri said. "Those are *our* names."

"What the hell does that mean?" Aideen asked.

"Oh come on," Kendra said. "It's got to be a coincidence. Two people can have the same name."

"But two sets of cousins? And it's not like our names are Jane, Sally, Mary and Sue. Our names aren't a coincidence."

"I repeat: What the *hell* does that mean?" Aideen said.

"You don't think it could be us in that picture, do you?" Peri asked, thinking out loud. "Is that even possible?"

"No," Kendra said. "We'd all be sixty-five years old."

"No wrinkle cream could make us look this good," Aideen said. "Those kids aren't us."

"I really don't like this place anymore," Peri said frantically. "Can we go *now?*"

Aideen sighed, "Yeah, fine. This place is starting to give me the willies."

"Good. Let's go," Kendra said, directing everybody over to the window they had crawled through earlier. They were just about to climb through when the wind, which had settled down to a not so gentle breeze, jumped back up again, as if It was protesting their leaving. It started blowing wildly, even more so than when Aideen had first climbed through the window. If the furniture hadn't already been pushed against the walls, it would have been moving all over the room. However, before the girls could get to the safety of the night, their only exit was blocked. The couch, which had been standing upright next to the window, fell, almost crushing Peri in the process.

She screamed and clutched Damia, who screamed and buried her head in Peri's shoulder. Aideen looked at them in disbelief. She said, "Stop screaming! It's giving me a headache!"

Damia and Peri looked at her and Peri snapped, "Well I'm sorry I almost died. I'll try to remember your headache the next time Dorothy Rhed tries to kill me with a couch."

"Thank you," Aideen snapped back, which caused both Damia and Peri to glare at her.

Kendra interrupted, "Guys, we have a problem."

The three girls looked to where Kendra was, trying to push the couch away from the window. They realized that the high back of the couch was now blocking their only way out, and the wind wouldn't let the piece of furniture move. After trying in vain to move the couch, Peri said, "What about the front door? Maybe there isn't a couch in front of that exit."

They quickly found the front foyer, and at the end of it was the front door. All four girls were relieved to see that no large pieces of furniture were blocking this escape route. The only thing that had been stopping them from using the front door to get in was a deadbolt that had been thrown years before the girls had even been born.

Kendra quickly unlocked the door and a large gust of wind blew the door wide open. Without a moment's hesitation, Kendra ran out onto the front porch with Peri close on her heels. Damia and Aideen were not too far behind them, but as they were stepping over the threshold, they heard something come from deep within the house. They paused for a second and looked at each other. Aideen's eyes grew wide and her hands turned to fists.

"Aideen, don't," was all Damia could say before Aideen turned around and bolted towards the noise. Damia ran onto the porch to see Kendra and Peri were waiting for them at the end of the pathway.

"Where's Aideen," Kendra asked.

"We heard a noise. She went after it," Damia answered. Kendra and Peri were back on the porch in seconds.

"I don't know how we were ever friends. I can't wait to go back home and never see her again," Kendra muttered to herself as she ran into the house after Aideen.

"What kind of noise did you hear," Peri asked, almost afraid to know.

Damia looked over at her, "Laughter."

~*~

"Aideen, where are you? Get back here, we have to go! Aideen!" Kendra shouted, walking into the home. She started with the kitchen of the abandoned house. She was surprised to see how unabandoned it looked. True, it looked like it hadn't been touched in forty years, but Kendra could tell that before that, it had been loved. The cupboard doors were swinging loosely in the wind, and Kendra was able to catch a glimpse of many different cooking ingredients and spices. There were the basics: flour, sugar, baking soda, but there were also many things Kendra could never name. Those were stacked in clear masonry jars. She wondered if it was Dorothy Rhed who was the cook, or perhaps it was Kendra Trac.

She shivered, trying to thinking up reasons why she and her cousins shared the same names of the Trac cousins. She hadn't mentioned it when they were looking at the picture, but even before Damia showed them their names, Kendra had thought one of those toddlers had looked a strange amount like her. She even noticed that the man holding the toddler Aideen Dehann had the same reddish brown hair as her own cousin Aideen, unlike either of her actual parents. Kendra's stomach was twisting into knots. There was something going on here, something she didn't like.

We have to get out of here, she thought, the knot in her stomach rising into her throat.

"Aideen!" She yelled, turning out of the kitchen, and back into the foyer. She stepped out just in time to see Peri and Damia running up the stairs to the second level of the house, both shouting Aideen's name. Kendra quickly followed behind them, wondering what was going on.

They reached the top of the stairs to see Aideen pushing against a closed door. She was trying to jimmy the door open, but it would not budge. She saw her cousins watching and said frantically,

"I saw her! I was on the stairs, and I saw her out of the corner of my eye! She's in here!"

The three girls eyes immediately went to the door, and the bright light that was pouring from every crack in it. They also noticed that the wind, which had been increasing steadily for some time, had picked up even more, and seemed to be centering around the room Aideen was trying to get into.

"Aideen, get away from that door," Kendra said. "You don't know what's behind it!"

"Yeah, I do!" she said excitedly. "Dorothy Rhed!"

As soon as she spoke the ghost's name, the door she was holding flew from her grip, slamming open and filling the dark hallway with a bright light. Aideen shielded her eyes and looked into the room. Kendra, Peri and Damia quickly reached her side, ready to drag her by hand and foot away from whatever was inside that room. However, once they saw what was inside, they completely forgot about running.

The light they had seen through the cracks in the door was coming from the wall to their right. The entire wall was lit up, and the four girls could see it was moving. The wall looked like it had liquified, and every so often a ripple would go through it, causing the entire wall to wave.

Ever since the street lamps had gone out on the girl's walk, the wind had been getting stronger and stronger around them. Now they realized that the wind had been originating from the wall in front of them. Standing in the same room, the wind was now blowing so violently that the girls had to hold onto the doorframe to keep from falling over.

However, the wall was not the only thing in the room that caught the girls' attention. Standing across from them, back toward them, looking out a window was not Dorothy Rhed at all. It was a man. He slowly turned around, unaffected by the wind blowing around him, or by the bright light that made his pale skin look translucent. He faced the girls and smiled.

"I presume you are the Keepers."

He was an old man, with grey hairs on his balding head and whiskers on his chin. His eyes were the darkest the four girls had ever seen; they could see no distinction between the irises and pupils in them. His clothing was something they had never seen before. His shirt was light brown and looked to be made out of cheap linen, with sleeves that tied at the wrists and neck. His pants stopped just below his knees and he wore leather boots. The thing that was strangest to the four girls was the tights he wore between his boots and breeches. It looked like this man had time traveled to them from the seventeenth century.

"The what?" Peri yelled, trying to hear the man over the wind.

"The Keepers!" He answered. "Protectors of Beindor, lost for eighteen years!"

"I don't know what you're talking about!" Aideen said. "But we don't protect anything!"

"I'm afraid you're wrong," he said, unaffected by the loud screeching of the wind. "You protect all of Beindor and every creature who lives there."

"What is Beindor?" Damia asked.

"Beindor is a great country older than the land we are standing on!"

"What did he say?" Kendra asked.

"He said we're supposed to protect some old land!" Peri said.

"Oh!" Kendra said. She paused and then added, "Why?"

"Because," the old man said quietly, taking a step closer to them. "It is the Keepers who protect the humans of Beindor from the creatures that wish to harm them."

"Creatures?" Peri asked. "What do you mean by creatures?"

"Vampires...cyclopes...werewolves," the old man listed. "You are the chosen ones! The Protectors of Beindor!"

The girls quickly exchanged glances. All of them were wondering the same thing: which crazy hospital he had escaped from, and who would call the police. Aideen spoke up, "Okay! I think it's time to go back. NOW!"

Kendra nodded, just before they turned around and sprinted down the stairs and out of the house. They reached the wall and frantically climbed over it before racing down the dead end street and made a left onto the closest road. They ran for a few more minutes, until they realized that the part of the neighborhood they were in had working streetlamps and cars in the driveways. They slowed down and looked over their shoulders, half expecting the crazy old man to be chasing them down with stories of vampires and werewolves.

They made it back to Kendra's house easily enough. It turned out that they had only been a few blocks over. They raced up the driveway and collapsed just inside the gate of the backyard. Paula was instantly there, coming to tell them that people had been waiting to say goodbye before they left. She was about to tell them, but she realized they had been running. She could see that the terror on their faces was real, "What is it? What happened? You look like you've seen a ghost."

"If only it *was* her," Peri said with a nervous laugh.

The others looked at her, not sure what to say. There was no denying that that wall had been moving like liquid, and that the old man had recognized them immediately as these Keeper people. He had not seemed senile, but what else could explain what he was saying, and what he was wearing?

After that night, the girls started to drift apart again. They didn't ever mention what they had really seen that night of Kendra's eighteenth birthday party. Kendra never even mentioned it to Ryan, who came over later that night. The two of them spent the rest of senior year in bliss. But once college started up they slowly began to drift apart. They met again at their ten year high school reunion, and were married three years later. They had two kids together, Lisa and Bryan. Peri and her boyfriend Joey broke up a few weeks later when Peri found her ex-best friend Annie and Joey making out in an empty classroom at the Spring Fling. Peri went on to become a school teacher at Placoid, but she never was able to make herself go into the room she found Joey and Annie in.

Damia went to Julliard the following year, and after graduating, became the prima ballerina for the Modern American Dance Company. After a nice long career with MADCO, Damia returned to Seattle to run the dance studio where she had spent her childhood. She took over the studio when Miss Diana passed away. After graduating high school, Aideen moved to Austin, Texas where she got a bachelor's degree in Fine Arts. She co-founded a company that supported local artists with a fellow classmate, which eventually became nationwide and made Aideen Morris a household name.

At least that is what would have happened had the old man not intervened.

Chapter Sixteen

"You are the chosen ones! The Protectors of Beindor!"

The girls quickly exchanged glances. All of them were wondering the same thing: which crazy hospital he had escaped from, and who would call the police. Aideen spoke up, "Okay! I think it's time to go back. NOW!"

Kendra nodded, and the girls even had their backs turned to the wall but they were never able to run back to Paula's house. With one flick of his hand, the four girls were sent hurtling backwards, towards the liquid wall. They realized they were flying backwards, and anticipated falling right out the second story window. The braced themselves for the impact that would most likely crush their skulls and break their spines, but it never came.

~*~

Paula found herself pacing. Back and forth, in front of the gate that led out of her backyard. It was a half hour since the girls left on their walk, and they still hadn't come back. It was way past dark, and all the streetlamps were on. Something was wrong. Paula knew Kendra would never go walking this late, especially if there were people waiting to say goodbye to her.

She had tried her daughter's cell phone, but when she saw the phone vibrating on one of the green plastic chairs the girls had been sitting on earlier, she hung up. She got the other three girls' phone numbers, but they all seemed to have left them in their purses, seated at the side of the other plastic chairs. Paula wondered if they had even noticed that they didn't have their phones with them, of if they did it on purpose.

She glanced over at her husband, Dan, who gave her a questioning look. She shook her head and his expression fell. She watched as he turned to her mother-in-law and said something. Frances looked over to Paula who smiled weakly at her mother. Frances got up and walked over to her second oldest daughter, "Aren't they back yet?"

Paula shook her head, "It's been a half hour since they left."

"I don't want to worry you, but should we send someone out to look for them?"

Paula sighed, "What could've happened to them? It's not like we're downtown! This is the safest neighborhood in Seattle!"

Frances put an arm around her daughter, "I'll ask Matt and Art to go around the block."

"Thanks," Paula said. "I hope they're okay."

"They probably just lost track of the time," Frances said.

~*~

He knew instantly. There was no mistake this time. He had spent so much time searching, gaining information he did not have the last time they met. He was also creating a group of supporters among the enemies, turning key players to his side. He spent the last eighteen years interrogating captured enemies, trying to find where the four pieces had been hidden. He had found the locations, and was getting ready to retrieve them, and then everything changed.

The door had been opened.

He got there within seconds, and saw the one thing he had dreamt of controlling ever since the first time he had passed through it, the door that led to Earth. He wanted so badly to just step through and destroy them. If what he had found out was true, they were all eighteen again and without any memories of what had happened so long ago. They were the most vulnerable they would be for a long time, but he knew they could be useful to him. They could do something that he could not.

He felt his body shifting, changing its shape almost instantly. When he opened his eyes, he was much lower to the ground. He took a breath and stepped through the door. He found himself in a place had had not been for over forty years.

Earth.

"I presume you are the Keepers," he shouted in a raspy voice that was not his own.

He felt like he had traveled back in time, rather than across the planes. Standing in front of him where the four girls who discovered Hecate in 1965. He paused, realizing that they were not the girls he had grown up with. They were different, and he could tell now by the way they reacted to him. They were scared, unlike his nieces, who had been excited, and eagerly stepped through the door. These four were about to run away.

He frowned, not about to let them escape him. With a flick of his finger, he watched as the four girls were hurled through the door. They disappeared and he was alone. He again felt the urge to stay and conquer, but knew that once the door closed he would be stuck on Earth and the Keepers would be stuck on Hecate. Being able to jump from Hecate to Earth was vital to his plan, and now that the Keepers were back, so were they.

Across the large community, in the manmade lake that sat in the center of the houses, four figures bobbed up to the surface. The figures floated face down in the shallow waters, their hair swirling around their heads.

He took in a deep breath of the air around him, savoring the old smells he had forgotten about. He opened his eyes and looked out the window of his childhood home, scanning the horizon one last time before stepping through the door after the Keepers.

Chapter Seventeen

Instead of crashing through the window, the four girls found themselves landing on something soft and prickly at the same time. They didn't have a chance to see what happened before gravity pulled them tumbling down a steep hill. They did not stop rolling until the ground leveled off, ending in a heap of arms and legs. They untangled their bodies and sat up, surveying their new surroundings.

The first thing they noticed was the smell. They covered their faces with their hands and looked around, wondering where the stench was coming from. It smelled like unwashed bodies and manure, pollution and food rotting in the sun. They noticed a large city was about a mile away with a fog looming over the top of it and spreading out to the surrounding homes and farms.

The city was like no other city they had seen before, especially not Seattle. There were no metal skyscrapers; in fact the tallest buildings looked to be only a few stories high. All of the buildings in the center of the city were made of brick, covered in plaster and the surrounding buildings used uncovered bricks. The poorer homes moving away from the center of the city were not built with bricks; instead they used mud, manure and wood. They were sturdy but could not hold as much heat as the brick homes.

Farther out, the homes became fewer and fewer, with more land in between them. There were at least two acres between the homes, which were either being used to grow wheat and corn or raise cattle and other livestock. The roads that ran into the city were made up of dirt and mud, and farther into the city, they became brick. Carts traveled these roads, full of barrels and baskets which held merchandise ready to be sold.

The girls then realized that it was bright out, and the sun was high over their head. It was no longer a cold February night. It felt like a warm June day. Too much in shock to remove their winter coats, the girls looked around, not sure what to do.

Peri was the first to speak, "Where are we?"

"Welcome to Beindor, Keepers!"

They four girls looked up to find the old man standing at the top of the hill, looking down at them. Aideen felt a sudden surge of anger and she pulled herself up the side of the hill towards the old man. Her cousins quickly followed her and by the time they reached the top, Aideen was towering over the man, "First off, we are not keeping anything for you, and second, what the *hell* did you just do?"

The man smirked, not at all afraid of this explosive little girl. He said, "I simply gave you the push you needed. It was obvious you would not have come with me any other way."

"Damn right we wouldn't have come with you! You need to be put back in the loony bin you escaped from," Aideen shouted.

The others quickly jumped between Aideen and the old man, moving Aideen away from him before she did something she regretted. Kendra turned to the man and asked, "Where exactly are we?"

"Hecate!" The man said. "It is a planet similar to Earth. Specifically, we are in the country of Beindor, and that is the city of Canhareth behind you. The Keepers settled it when they first came here from Earth when they were eighteen. That was forty-four years ago."

"Wait," Peri interrupted. "We're not on Earth?"

The old man shook his head, "Far from it."

The girls stood in silence, trying to wrap their minds around what that meant. Damia spoke next, "And who are these Keepers?"

The man smiled, "You are the Keepers. When they died eighteen years ago, they made sure that their souls would go to four girls capable of continuing their work."

"So," Damia thought. "We are these Keepers reincarnated?"

He nodded, "Exactly. And when the youngest of you turned eighteen, the door between Hecate and Earth was able to open again."

Aideen rubbed her hands together, "So how do we open it again? It's time for us to go back."

The man's face fell, "Why would you want to go back? The Keepers belong in Beindor."

"The others might have belonged here," Kendra said. "But we certainly don't."

Peri nodded, "I want to go home."

"I'm afraid that's not something done over night. In fact, it could very well take years," the man said.

Chapter Eighteen

Thomas and Chelsea Pierce continued to jog around the neighborhood, despite the darkness that had crept upon them. Tom was required to jog five times a day for a half hour each time to get ready for an annual marathon in the spring. He had made it to second place last year, and he was determined to get first place this year. Chelsea, his golden retriever, came along to keep him company.

"Come on," Tom said to Chelsea. "Only two more miles and we'll be done for the night."

Chelsea looked up at him with a grin that said, "I'm going to beat you home."

Tom laughed, "Alright, we can race until the lake, then the next mile we can walk."

Chelsea responded, like she did every night, by speeding up her pace just a tiny bit. She was now about three feet ahead of Tom, looking back at him, waiting for him to start running harder. He smirked and sprinted at his full force. Chelsea was soon at his heels, never going more than a few steps ahead of him.

They raced like this until they reached the road facing the manmade lake that was in the center of the community. Chelsea jumped off the road and ran head first into the water. Tom stepped off the side of the road, and watched as Chelsea's head popped up from the water. He laughed and started to call her back when he noticed what she was swimming next to.

He gasped and ran into the water, pulling at the closest body. He couldn't believe what he was seeing. There were four bodies in the water... all of them were face down, floating in the still water. He turned the closest body, afraid he recognized the short brown hair as his friend Peri Andes. With some difficulty he flipped over the bloated body, and drew back from it in horror. Her make-up was running down her cheeks, and he knew he would never be able to get the image of her terror-filled eyes out of his head.

He then felt something brush against his back. He spun around and saw it was another body. He didn't dare touch it, but recognized the auburn hair and jacket of the girl with the Frisbee. He scrambled away from the four bodies with Chelsea right behind him. He crawled onto dry land and vomited up his last energy drink.

He continued to vomit until he was bringing up nothing but air. He looked over at the floating bodies, his mind racing about what he should do; what had happened to the poor girls. The terror in Peri's eyes suggested some sort of foul play, but he had no idea what could have caused all four of them to drown. He had been barely waist deep where they were, they should have been able to just stand up, unless they hadn't drowned at all.

Chelsea nudged his arm and he realized that he was shaking violently. The water had been ice cold, and now he was in the freezing night air. He stood up and took off, away from the lake and the girls. He would have called the police instantly, but he didn't have a cell phone on him. Running was the one time he didn't have a cell phone; his sweats didn't have any pockets to put it in. Instead, he ran straight for Kendra Dodson's house, knowing she had been in the water along with Peri, the Frisbee girl and the fourth he did not recognize. Cynically, a thought crossed his mind as he raced down the empty streets: If he had run this fast last year, there would have been no doubt of his coming in first place.

Chapter Nineteen

"What do you mean 'years'?" Peri said, her voice raising an octave as she finished her sentence.

"While you were able to open the door by yourselves just now, I'm afraid you won't ever be able to again," Kain, the old man, explained. "The first Keepers were only able to do it once, and I can safely assume the same goes for you."

"So now what do we do?" Kendra asked. "They were able to open it other ways, right?"

Kain nodded, "With the Amîr Crystal. The Crystal had been created for the sole purpose of opening the door between Earth and Hecate."

"Great," Aideen said. "Now where can we find this crystal?"

Kain's face fell, "I'm afraid this is the troublesome part. Before the Keepers were killed, they split up the Amîr Crystal into four parts, and spread them across Beindor."

"Wait," Damia interrupted, he voice wavering. "The Keepers were killed?"

Kain frowned, "Yes. The Keepers were killed. They were killed by the most powerful man in Hecate, with more powerful magik than the Keepers. He wanted to take control of Beindor, Hecate, and then Earth, but the Keepers made it their job to stop him. They split up the crystal so that if they did not succeed in killing him, then Tárquin would not get to Earth like he so longed to do."

"Where is Tárquin now?" Kendra asked.

"He has not been seen since the day the Keepers died," Kain said. "It has been assumed that they killed him before dying themselves."

"So," Aideen thought. "It wouldn't be a big deal if we got this *mirror* crystal back together, would it? I mean, Tárquin's dead."

Kain cringed at Aideen's mispronunciation and said, "*Amîr,* and no, I don't believe it would be a *big deal.*"

"So where are these four pieces," Kendra asked. She could feel her stomach turning in knots as she thought about what was happening. They were in a world that was not Earth, about to cross a foreign country to find four pieces of crystal. With a sinking feeling in her stomach, she realized she wasn't going to be seeing Ryan later that night.

"They are in the four corners of Beindor," Kain said. "Each Keeper gave one piece of the Amîr Crystal to their most trusted allies. Keeper Damia gave hers to Queen Bryndis of the Elvin in Taurëfor, the Forests of the North; Keeper Kendra gave hers to King Valin of the Merpeople in Aearad, the Seas of the South; Keeper Aideen gave hers to King Sheng of the Dragons, in Imladun, the Caves of the East and Keeper Peri gave the final piece to the High Priest Kiros of Vavia in Orodun, the Mountains of the West."

While Kain began describing where the four pieces of the crystal were, Peri began to realize the position they were in. *Years,* she thought, taking a deep breath. *Years.* It seemed to be the only thing that she could concentrate on. She tried listening to Kain, even when he mentioned her name, but she couldn't. She tried to focus on her breathing; she tried to control the urge to scream. She felt her hands begin to shake with the effort to stay calm and closed her eyes.

What was she supposed to do? She couldn't just get up and leave her life. She had to finish high school, go to college and live happily ever after with Joey. She stopped breathing. *Joey.* She was about to spend *years* away from Joey. She would be surprised if he stayed true to her after her Houdini act. He would probably wait a few weeks, and then with no word from her, start dating again. She couldn't bear to see him with another girl when she finally got back home. She would rather *die.*

That's when she realized she had to get home *now*. If she waited years it would be too late. She had to get home right now or else she would lose Joey forever. Her eyes flew open and she said in a high pitched voice, cutting Kain off mid-sentence, "We can't do this! We have to get back *now*!"

Kain shook his head, "That's impossible. The only way is to get the Amîr Crystal."

Peri cried out, "But what about Joey? I can't lose him! If this takes more than a few days, then he'll move on! Forget about me! I can't handle that!"

She crumbled to the ground, "What if we make it back home and he's with someone else? What am I supposed to do after that? We were perfect. I'd never be able to get over him."

Kain looked at the girl at his feet, unsure what to do. He had never seen someone pathetically hopeless. Keeper Peri had never been this disgraceful while she was alive. Kain could barely look at what she had become, this selfish little girl collapsed at his feet. For a second he wished that she had never been reincarnated, that her memory could not be tarnished by this spoiled brat.

However, he kept his mouth shut and let her cousins handle her. Kendra picked Peri up off the ground and said, "Don't worry about that now. Take one step at a time. We're going to go as fast as we can to get these crystal pieces, I promise. We all want to get home."

Peri nodded and wiped the tears that had fallen down her face. She was still having some difficulty controlling her breathing, taking in big gulps in quick succession. She let go of Kendra's arm and stood on her own. Another tear fell down her face, but she ignored it.

Kain continued.

He pulled a parchment out of a hidden pocket on his person, and handed it to Damia, the closest of them to him. She took it from him and unrolled it. After a second she gasped and the others came around to look at the piece of parchment over her shoulder. It was a map of Beindor.

They could tell it was old, as if drawn over a hundred years ago. The lettering on the map was in a small slanted calligraphy but still easily read. The detail of the map was amazing, the mountains on the right side of the page were numerous and none of them looked the same. The trees at the top of the parchment were similarly drawn in such great numbers, and yet each tree top distinctive and original.

They saw that Canhareth, the city they could see off in the distance, was in almost the exact center of the map; the center of the country. By the size of the picture on the map, Canhareth was much bigger than the other cities and towns labeled on the map. Some cities, such as Vavia and Nérand had small pictures of cities along with the lettering, while others such as Moorel were nothing but the names and a small black dot where they were.

The four girls looked up toward Kain and Kendra said, "This is amazing, thank you so much."

But Kain had disappeared. They looked around the hill top, and down the sloping sides, but he was nowhere to be found. "That was odd," Aideen said.

Damia frowned, "I still had a question for him."

"What?" Peri asked, wiping her eye.

"He kept mentioning magik. The Keepers had magik...Tárquin had magik...does that mean we have magik too?"

The girls looked at each other, wondering if it was even possible for magik to exist. "I wouldn't be surprised," Aideen said. "We're not even on Earth, after all."

The girls stood in silence, trying to wrap their heads around all that had just happened. They were the new Keepers, 'Protectors of Beindor'. They might have magikal powers, and they have to travel across Beindor in search for four pieces of a crystal.

"I hope my mom isn't too worried," Kendra said.

"Maybe Beindor is like Narnia," Aideen suggested. "When we go back it'll be like we never left."

Peri smiled, "I like that idea."

Aideen smiled at her, glad she could have helped.

Kendra then said, "Come on, let's get going."

"Where?" Aideen asked. "Which piece are we getting first?"

"We can figure that out too," Kendra said, staring down the hill where they had fallen down earlier. "I meant to Canhareth. We need supplies and food. Possibly a cart or horses...we can't travel across the country on foot."

~*~

His throat still burned from when he threw up everything he had eaten that day, but that as nothing compared to what he was feeling in his feet and legs. They had prickled when he started running the half mile to Kendra Dodson's house, and had gone numb about half way there. Now they were completely without feeling, and Tom Pierce wasn't sure he was even running anymore, except for the speed of which the houses were moving past him.

He looked down and saw that Chelsea was keeping good speed with him. She wasn't as effected as he was; she had her winter coat to protect her. However, he knew that if he didn't get her dried off soon that she would start to freeze as well. Unfortunately, that wasn't the main problem at the moment. Four dead girls, floating in the lake, was.

He didn't know how he was going to tell Kendra's mother. To find out that your daughter is dead, that isn't light news. He didn't want to be the one to send her into a massive mental breakdown. But knowing he had no choice, he pushed on.

Finally he saw the house.

He remembered when Chelsea had picked up that girl's Frisbee. She had been so full of life; ready to explode with her emotions. Now she was dead. Tom shivered, but he wasn't sure if it was because of the cold creeping up his body or the image of the dead girls. He pushed the picture out of his mind as he ran up the driveway. He rang the doorbell multiple times with his stiff hand. When no one answered, he pounded on the door with his fist.

"Hello?"

He spun around to see a woman looking at him from the entrance to the backyard. He remembered what the Frisbee girl had said; they were having a birthday party back there. He ran down to the woman and stuttered, "Mrrsss. Dododsssson?"

The woman's face fell, and Tom knew she had figured out what he had come to tell her. "Yes?" she replied, her grip on the door tightening.

Tom took a breath and said, "K-Kenndrdra a-an-nd P-Periii,"

Mrs. Dodson cut him off, "The girls? Have you seen them? What's happened to them?"

Tom continued to shiver; his entire body beginning to shake. Ignoring the rattling of his teeth, he said, "D-d-drrownn-wned i-inn th-the l-la-akkkee."

Mrs. Dodson let out a wail and collapsed to her knees. Tom looked behind her and saw others of the party coming closer to them. He recognized Peri's mother, Mrs. Andes. She came over to him, "Thomas? What happened to you?"

She looked down at her sister, whose husband had come over to comfort her. Tom could hear him asking what he had said to her. Mrs. Dodson was now sobbing uncontrollably, but managed to say, "Dead! They're all dead!"

Mrs. Andes looked up at Tom, who nodded, wrapping his arms around himself. Chelsea brushed against his leg and he looked down at her. She sat down and looked up at him, obviously concerned for the strangers in front of them. Tom looked back up at Mrs. Andes, whose eyes had begun to well up. With a quiver in her top lip she said, "Matt, could you get Tom here and his dog inside and dried off. Get the other kids inside too."

Matt, who had been about to demand of Tom where his sister was, clenched his fists. He opened his mouth to protest, but saw the look his Aunt Karina gave him and nodded. He looked at Tom and said in an ice cold tone, "Come on. I'll get you some towels."

He then shouted over at Art, who was keeping David occupied, "Get David inside!"

Art, who had been trying to listen to what was happening at the front gate, nodded and quickly followed Matt, Tom and Chelsea inside with David on his hip. Once they were all inside, Dan asked his wife, "Where are they?"

"In the lake," Paula replied, barely above a whisper.

Dan nodded and ran out to his car, which was in the driveway. Others piled in with him, including Karina and Kelly, while Frances and Melissa stayed behind with Paula. None of them were prepared for what happened next, and none of them could understand why. Just like Tom had realized, the water was barely hip deep on the girls. How could they have all drowned in such shallow, harmless water?

It would be a long time before they got the answer.

Chapter Twenty

What would it look like if all fashions, all cultures, all time periods were mixed together in a salad bowl and tossed into the street?

This, Peri thought, answering her own question.

The four cousins could not believe the sight before them. Not only did it look like they had traveled back in time, it looked like they had traveled back to all the times at once. The clothes were early seventeenth century, with corsets and skirts, breeches and leggings. The buildings of the inner-city looked to be in the Georgian style of the late 1700s of England, and the outer-city buildings seemed to employ a wattle-and-daub technique, which was wood weaved together and covered in dried clay, a method used throughout history, but most notably in the Dark Ages.

Other things about the city seemed strange to the four girls. Besides the phonograph playing in one window and the kids playing with a hand-woven ball on the other side of the street, there were things that weren't from Earth at all. They saw an Orsina, for instance. The Orsina is a giant cat-like creature with purple fur that swam to Beindor across the Rómearya Sea from the country of Úrdor. There were other creatures that the cousins did recognize, but never thought they would see, other than in a Hollywood movie.

There were Elvin, trolls, pixies, Cyclops, satyrs, and the occasional phoenix. They all walked or flew among the humans, as if they were all okay with each other being there. There was no shock on one shopkeeper's face when an ogre came up to her to buy some earrings for his wife. Everyone seemed to be living in perfect harmony.

After people watching for a while, Kendra began searching shop names, "We need to find a place to sleep tonight. Some sort of hotel or inn if possible. I don't think any American money we have will work here, so we might need a backup plan as well."

They searched for only a few minutes before finding The Dancing Bear, a tavern on one of the more populated streets of the inner-city of Canhareth. They walked in and saw that it seemed respectable enough. They knew they wouldn't have to worry about pickpocketers and other lowlifes in this tavern.

There was a steady flow of people, but not so much to call the place crowded. About half of the tables were occupied and so were the chairs set up at the long bar that filled up the back wall of the large front of the tavern. The air in The Dancing Bear was smoky, due to people's smoking at all hours of the day, and the lights were dim. The atmosphere was light. Relaxed. Music came from the fingers of the piano man and floated gently over the heads of The Dancing Bear's patrons.

The girls walked over to the bar and stood in an opening between two men. One of them was an older gentleman, who was nursing a large draft beer. His head was sunk low and his shoulders were hunched over. He did not look up at the cousins as they approached. The other man was much younger. He looked to be about twenty years old, and was casually sipping a smaller drink, looking around as if waiting for someone. He immediately looked over at the girls when they came to a stop next to him, and did not look away.

The man was not hiding the fact that he was staring at the four. In fact, a very audible noise came from deep within his throat. He sounded both terrified and in awe that the four girls had appeared next to him.

The four girls were caught off guard by the man now gaping at them. Aideen refused to look over at him, even though she wanted to yell at him for staring like he was. Damia blushed and concentrated solely on the wall behind the bar; trying not to picture what the man looked like with his mouth hanging open.

Kendra bit her lip, also refusing to look at him. She was trying not to think of the vile things he was thinking. Peri was the only one who continued to stare back at him. She glared at him for a second, and when she realized he was not about to look away she opened her mouth to make a snide remark.

Before she got her chance, however, Mahak the bartender came up to them with a large smile on his face. He seemed oblivious to the man sitting next to them, blatantly staring. Mahak asked, with a booming voice, "How can I be of service, tonight?"

Kendra spoke up for herself and her three cousins, "We would like a place to stay for the night."

Mahak smiled, "We have many rooms available. Two hundred and eighty Denas a night."

Kendra glanced over at her three cousins, as if to tell them to start thinking of a backup plan. They had no idea what a Dena was, and assumed that there was no American currency exchange. Kendra looked back at the bartender, noticing that the man sitting next to them was now listening to their conversation with an unsettling interest. Kendra frowned, "Well, you see, we aren't from..." she hesitated, not sure what to say. She wasn't sure if Denas were used only in Canhareth, all throughout Beindor or on an even larger scale like the Euro, "...around here."

Mahak's smile did not falter, "We also accept Úrdos and Talis here."

Not knowing what those were, Kendra smiled sadly, "We don't have any of those."

Mahak looked confused, as if he couldn't understand there being a possible fourth type of currency. "Well, what do you have," he asked.

Not seeing any harm in telling the truth, Kendra pulled out her wallet and took out a single dollar bill. She handed it over to Mahak, who looked even more confused than before. Peri glanced over at the man watching the encounter and saw a look of recognition on his face. Unlike the bartender, he knew exactly what American money looked like.

Mahak's eyebrows knotted together, creating folds in his forehead. He turned the bill over in his hands and looked up at the four girls. He asked, "Green paper? That is your money? What about gold or silver? How is this paper worth anything?" He then laughed, taking a stray napkin from off the bar, "Can you buy a drink with this in your country?"

Kendra sighed, not really wanting to go into the explanation of paper money to this man. Instead, she took back the bill and said, "We have no other way to pay, so I think it's best not to waste anymore of either of our time."

Mahak suddenly turned serious, the smile falling off his face. He was losing four customers, and he had no idea how to stop them from leaving; all they had was fake green money. He nodded and went back to serving his paying customers. The four girls looked at each other and Aideen asked, "Now what? Where are we supposed to go if we don't have any money?"

"We could always go back to that hill outside of town," Damia suggested. "It didn't look like it was going to rain or anything."

Peri's face fell, "You want me to sleep outside? I'll die! There are bugs and snakes and mosquitoes out there!"

"Do you have a better idea," Kendra asked. "I doubt anyone will be nice enough to let us stay with them for free. And anyone who does shouldn't be trusted."

"Excuse me."

The four girls looked at the man sitting next to them, the one that had been staring earlier. A smile was forming at the edge of his lips as he said, "I don't mean to be eavesdropping, but I don't think sleeping out on some hill is a wise thing for the Keepers to do. Especially if someone is willing to pay for their room."

Both Aideen and Kendra started talking at once, while Damia and Peri looked at each other in silence. Aideen flipped out, demanding, "How could you possibly know we are these Keepers? We haven't said a word about it!"

Kendra on the other hand, responded to the latter part of his statement, "Why would you offer to pay for a room for us?"

The man smiled, answering Aideen first, "The Keepers were easily recognizable when they were older, but I was lucky enough to be acquainted with them well before they became the Saviors of Beindor. My family was among the first to respond positively to their discovery of Hecate."

"But how?" Peri asked. "You can't be any older than twenty-five. Kain said that the Keepers discovered Hecate in the 60s. That was fifty years ago!"

He just smiled, "I am truly flattered by your assumption, but I am hardly twenty-five years old."

He then went on to answer Kendra, who was glaring at him. She did not trust a man who offered to pay for four strange girls' hotel room. He said, "I am offering to pay for your room because, like I said, I was good friends with the Keepers before they..." he hesitated, glancing quickly over at Damia, "disappeared. I can only assume you would return after such a long time for a noble mission, and I could not imagine you spending just one night sleeping outside when there is a large city just down the road."

Nobel mission? Aideen thought. *Were these Keepers some sort of saints?*

She glanced at her three cousins, and could tell they all had the same thoughts running through their heads. They weren't sure if they should tell this man their mission. Would he not pay for their room and board if he found out their mission was less than noble?

Kendra again spoke for the group, "That is very kind of you."

"It is nothing," he said, standing up. He turned to the bartender of The Dancing Bear and said, "Please, a room for these four ladies."

Mahak looked up from where he was across the bar and looked between the man and the four cousins. He gave the four a concerned look, no doubt wondering why they were suddenly letting a strange man pay for their room. He did not hover on the thought though, because he walked over to them and accepted the two hundred and eighty Denas from the man. He handed him a small brass key, who then turned it over into Kendra's waiting hand.

She smiled and said, "Thank you. Seeing that you know very well who we are, I suppose it isn't rude to ask who you are and how you knew the Keepers," she paused and added, "sir."

The man flashed them some teeth, amused by Kendra's curt question, "My name is Kynton and I was first introduced to the Keepers through Keeper Damia. We had some common interests, and happened to meet while she was exploring the Tauröfor Forests."

Kynton quickly looked at Damia, who again blushed. She glanced away and turned her attention to Kendra, who had also turned to look at her, understanding the subtle meaning behind his stare. Kendra quickly turned back to Kynton, upon seeing Damia's blush and asked, "Were you close with the Keepers?"

Kynton nodded, "My mother was one of the few who helped the Keepers build Canhareth and build some respect around Beindor."

Kynton paused and combed his fingers through his curly hair, pulling it down below the bottoms of his ears. He glanced around and said, "Before you ask any more questions, would you like to get a table?"

The four girls nodded, a little bit in shock that they had gotten such a break in The Dancing Bear. This man, who they just happened to come to stand next to, not only knew the Keepers first hand, but was also friendly enough with them to offer their replacements a room at his expense. The four were excited that their fortune was so good that night, but in the back of their minds they wondered if their encounter with Kynton was more than chance. They silently agreed that maybe questioning the man would enlighten them to this strange coincidence.

Kynton picked up his drink and led the four to a nearby table. He sat down and motioned them to sit as well. They took the four seats facing him, and he suddenly felt like he was on trial. He looked away; thinking about all the things that he had done that would have made the original Keepers really put him on trial, especially Damia. He knew that no matter the cost, the Damia in front of him could not find out what he had done.

Meeting the Keepers at the Dancing Bar that night was a gift from the Fates, Kynton realized. He was being given a second chance; a fresh start without the weight of how things turned out last time pushing down on either his or her shoulders. He noted happily that there was no fifth guest this time, no nosy neighbor that would ruin everything again.

He glanced at her again, quickly because she was watching him with judgmental eyes. He couldn't believe how young she looked, just like she had when they first met. Of course her hair was styled a different way and the clothing styles of Earth had obviously changed, but there was no doubt that this was the woman he had fallen in love with forty-four years ago.

His hands shook, he was so nervous about being around her. He felt like he was a teenager in love all over again, and by the way she was watching him, glancing quickly between him and her cousins, he could tell she could feel something too. He tried to concentrate on the questions as they were asked, but he found himself looking over at the eldest of the Keepers as if he was an insect and she was the soft glow of a lamp.

She was the only thing he could concentrate on, and the light was bringing him closer, closer to the feelings he had let consume him for the better part of the past half of a century. He had spent so much time mourning her, so much time wishing she had chosen a different path, that the years had flown by in a way he could never have imagined. Suddenly thirty years had passed and he was still acting like she had left him the day before.

He moved away from his home, and started traveling around the world. He did everything that could put her in his past, but everywhere he went he was reminded of the Saviors of Beindor. There was no escaping the monuments, the holidays, the praise that was given to them. Every word, every sight that reminded him of her felt as if a piece of his heart was being ripped from his chest, leaving a gaping hole.

He quickly discovered that traveling had not helped in the slightest. He was about to turn back home when a man approached him. This strange man had given Kynton something that he could hold on to, a mission that did not involve the Keepers. That is, until he sent Kynton to The Dancing Bear, and the first ones to get even close to him where the ones he had spent such a long time trying to get away from.

Again Kendra was the first one to say something when the five of them sat down at the table. She asked, "Why did you call the Keepers 'the Saviors of Beindor'? The man who brought us here called us the "Protectors of Beindor' as well. What did the Keepers do that was so amazing?"

Kynton almost laughed, "Everything they did was amazing. They were the first humans to set foot on Hecate. Every single human here was brought over from Earth. The people around us are only the first and second, even third generation of humans on Hecate. The Keepers were their rulers, their saviors and their celebrities. They were the ones everyone came to with their problems, they were the ones who settled Beindor, inspiring others to settle the other countries of Hecate. They used their magik to create a safe haven away from Earth."

"Magik," Damia asked in surprise, remembering that Kain had also mentioned magik.

"Yes, magik," he held her gaze for a second longer before looking back at the others. "The Keepers were rewarded by the Council of Hecate with magik of the oldest kind. Magik that set them apart from other humans, and even the other creatures of Hecate."

"You mean magik powers," Peri stated excitedly.

"Yes," Kynton said with a smirk. "Magik powers unique to each one of them. These powers were crafted around the titles that the Council of Hecate gave them."

"Titles," Kendra said, wondering what more titles they could have had besides 'The Keepers,' 'The Saviors of Beindor,' 'The Protectors of Beindor,' and Kain had even said 'The Chosen Ones.' That seemed like enough titles for four girls to last a life time.

Kynton nodded, and looked at each of the girls respectively, "There was Aideen, Keeper of Fire; Peri, Keeper of Air, Kendra, Keeper of Water, and Damia, Keeper of Earth."

"The elements," Aideen said in surprise. "Their powers were about the elements?"

"Wait," Peri said. "I don't understand. Those aren't elements. There are one hundred and seventeen elements, and those are nowhere on the Periodic Table."

Aideen rolled her eyes, "Fire, Water, Air and Earth were the very first elements, Peri. Long before your precious table, the Greeks said that the entire world was created out of the *four* elements. Fire, Water, Air, and Earth."

Peri thought about that for a second and asked, "How come I didn't know that? I should know that."

Aideen shrugged, "Maybe you skipped that day of kindergarten."

Peri huffed, but Kynton continued, used to the bickering between the four. He was glad that is was happening; it reminded him of a time when they all had gotten along, and were happy. He never wanted to leave. He then said, "I hope this is helpful for your mission. It wouldn't be wise for you four to try to save anyone, or arrest anyone, if you didn't even know that you had such abilities like you do."

Peri was about to ask what sort of abilities came with being the Keeper of Air, but Damia beat her, saying, "We haven't been telling you the entire truth, Kynton."

Ignoring the pounding sound in his ears as she said his name, he turned to her and asked, "What are you talking about? You are the Keepers, aren't you?"

She smiled, "I believe so, but that isn't what I mean. I'm talking about our 'mission.' I'm afraid it isn't this noble thing you think it is."

Chapter Twenty-One

Kynton's eyebrows knotted together, wondering why Damia would say something as strange as their mission wasn't noble. "Any mission the Keepers are on is bound to be a noble one," he said.

Kendra, Peri and Aideen looked at Damia in shock. She was about to tell him what they were really about to do, and that could mean trouble. True, he had already given the key to their room to Kendra, but that didn't mean he couldn't make a scene, demanding it back. He could even expose them as the Keepers. After hearing some of the things that they did, or were even called, they knew there would be a riot. They would never be able to find the crystal pieces in peace. Damia seemed to be oblivious to what harm her actions might cause, and the others knew exactly why.

Kynton hadn't been very subtle about how he felt about Damia. It seemed they even had a relationship before she died. Now he was making eyes at her, and she seemed to have been taken in by it. Maybe she was just flattered that he was paying so much attention to her, or maybe she actually was starting to have a little crush on him as well. The others had no idea, but they did know that it was strong enough that she felt compelled to tell him what they had decided not to tell him.

"Our mission," she said, "isn't noble at all. We're going to find the Amîr Crystal so we can go home."

"The Amîr Crystal?" Kynton asked, surprised to hear that word. It hadn't been the first time he had heard someone tell him they wanted the crystal that would open the portal between Earth and Hecate. The man who had helped him after they left had always talked about the Amîr Crystal, and how he wanted to go to Earth. What a coincidence that the man had sent Kynton to the bar that the Keepers would pick to stop in for the night.

Then another part of her sentence hit him.

"Home?" He asked, more urgently than he had asked about the crystal. "What do you mean?"

"Home," Damia said. "As in Earth. We didn't plan to come here, and we want to go back."

"You want to leave Hecate?" Kynton asked, realizing that he would lose her all over again if he let them go through with this. "You can't. The people of Beindor need you. You are their protectors. Without you there would be no Beindor."

"They've gotten along without us for the past eighteen years," Kendra said. He knew, so why not help explain. He seemed to be handling the news half way decently. He wasn't yelling at them yet, at least. "And if we do this right, they won't even know we've been here."

"So that's it?" Kynton asked. "You're just going to sneak out under everybody's nose?"

"You make it sound like we're some common criminals," Peri said. "It wasn't our choice to come here. We should at least get to choose if we want to stay or not."

Kynton frowned, not being able to argue with her logic. He turned back to Damia and said, "If you stay, and let everyone know you're here, you can do so much good. You can save innocent people, and convict the guilty. You can continue your reign and no one would think worse of you."

Damia's lip quivered, "This isn't want I want to be. My life doesn't include reigning over anything. I want to go home. I said some awful things to my mother, and I need to apologize."

"Please," Kynton said, looking at all of them. "You can't leave again."

The four girls looked at each other, not sure what to tell this man. He seemed so passionate about their staying in Beindor, and his reason was good enough. He didn't even mention himself, and how his life already seemed to be brighter because of them. He talked about the people of Beindor. They need their Saviors, and who were they to take that away from them?

Then Peri shook her head, "No. We can't do this. We have to go home. We aren't meant to be here, and we need to leave as soon as possible."

The three others looked at her and in doing so realized that she was right. They can't get sucked into something they don't want because they feel guilty. They don't want to stay in Beindor, so they don't have to. While they thought along those lines, Kynton felt himself starting to spin.

He felt like he was spiraling down towards a place he did not want to go back to. The Keepers couldn't leave, if only for his sanity. He couldn't handle watching them disappear twice, and knew he had to do something to stop them. He thought about what they had said, they needed to find the Amîr Crystal, and supposedly they had broken it up into four pieces before they died eighteen years earlier.

That meant they would need to find four crystals before they could leave. Maybe Kynton could convince them to stay before they got the fourth piece. He realized that he needed to go with them, and this was why they had come to stand next to him in the bar. He had to convince them to stay in Beindor, for the people. He had to convince her to stay, for him.

"Alright," he said. "I won't fight you against it. You want to leave your people, fine. It doesn't affect me."

Kendra's eyes narrowed, noticing the anger in his voice. Damia smiled, "Thanks. I'm glad we told you."

Kynton smiled back at her, but before he could say anything, Aideen let out a huge yawn. The four looked at her and she smiled sheepishly, "I'm sorry, did I interrupt something?"

Kynton laughed, "No, you should really get some sleep. The next few weeks are going to be busy for you."

He stood up, and the four girls agreed. When they stood up, Kynton looked down at the clothing they were wearing. It was nothing like what he was wearing, or the other people in the tavern. He noticed that others sitting around them looked at the girls with questioning eyes. They were standing out, and that wasn't something they should be doing, if they didn't want anyone to notice that they were the Keepers. Luckily it was only half lit in the tavern, and anyone who cared to notice was already intoxicated.

Kynton stopped the girls from leaving the table, "Wait."

"What?" Kendra asked, pulling on the coat she had taken off when they sat down at the table.

"You're going to need some better clothes before you start on your way," Kynton said.

The four looked down at their own clothes, then at each others. They then noticed what he was wearing, a tunic and breeches, and what everyone else in the tavern was wearing. They looked at each other and Peri gave a little sigh, "I like what I'm wearing."

"Well you can wear it, fine by me," Kynton said. "But if you don't want to bring attention to yourselves, then I suggest a quick change."

"Where are we going to find clothes before tomorrow?" Kendra asked.

Kynton shrugged, "I know I good place, but it's closed now. We'd have to go in the morning. It might delay the trip a day or two."

"Do we have any other choice?" Kendra asked.

The others shook their heads and Kynton led them to the back of the tavern, where a staircase led the way up to the rental rooms on the second floor. They walked silently down the long hall, until Kynton stopped in front of a small door that had the number seven etched into the wood, "Well, this is my room."

"Which one is ours?" Peri asked.

"It should say on the key," Kynton said, pointing to the key in Kendra's hand. She lifted it up and saw that there was a small four painted in black on it. The girls searched the hall for the number four, and saw it was on the opposite side of the hall as Kynton's, two doors down. They said goodnight to him before unlocking the door and walking in.

The room wasn't as small as they had thought it would be. There were two large beds on the left wall, and a window on the wall across from the door. There was a small closet on the remaining wall, and a table in between the beds. The beds and table were made out of the same dark wood as the door and the door to the closet. There were cream colored linen sheets on the beds and an oil lamp on the bedside table.

Aideen went over to the table next to the beds and found a box of matches next to the lamp. She lit a match and removed the chimney on the oil lamp. Once she lit the wick, she replaced the chimney and blew out the match. She looked around the room and saw that it was now filled with a warm glow from the lamp, instead of being in the semi darkness of the night.

As Aideen had turned on the lamp, Peri went over to the window and threw it open. She let in a deep breath of fresh air and felt as a breeze entered the room. She turned around to see that Damia had taken up the bed closer to her, while Kendra sat on the edge of the bed next to Damia.

Damia took out the map that Kain had given her, and laid it out on the bed in front of her. She studied it for a moment, remembering where Kain had said the four pieces of the crystal were. She pulled out a small notebook and pencil from her coat pocket and wrote down what he had said:

Taurëfor - Queen Bryndis of the Elvin
Aearad - King Valin of the Merpeople
Imladun - King Sheng of the Dragons
Orodun - High Priest Kiros of Vavia

She then found the four places from her list on the map, and realized that they made a circle around Canhareth, with Taurëfor above, Aearad below, Imladun to the left and Orodun to the right. Traveling in a circle would make the trip a lot easier, instead of jumping around Bcindor in no particular order. Of course it wouldn't be a full circle, since they were starting in the middle. She wondered if there was a part of Beindor that they wouldn't want to travel through; a part of the land that would slow them down or a long stretch between cities.

She spotted the Loicrea Marshes in the upper left hand corner of the map, and knew marshes would be hard to travel through. Other than that, there was the Talanno Plains, the Taurëfor Forests and the Orodun mountains. Traveling through the Orodun Mountains and the Taurëfor Forests were inevitable, seeing as two of the pieces of the crystal were there. So that meant that the marshes were the only real part of the country they could avoid. Having decided which way the four of them would travel around Beindor, she flipped the page in her notebook and rewrote her list so that they were in order:

Imladun - King Sheng of the Dragons
Aearad - King Valin of the Merpeople
Orodun - High Priest Kiros of Vavia
Taurëfor - Queen Bryndis of the Elvin

Kendra was watching her and asked, "What are you doing?"

Damia looked up and said with a smile, "Trying to figure out which way we should go to get this Amîr Crystal."

"And which way is that?" Peri asked, coming to sit down on the bed across from Damia.

Damia looked at her notebook and read off the second list. Aideen laughed, "Where did you get the pen and paper?"

Damia shrugged, "I always carry it around with me. Just in case."

"Just in case we get sucked into a black hole where they don't provide us with any?" Aideen continued to laugh.

Damia smiled, "Yes. And we did, so why are you laughing?"

Aideen stopped laughing and frowned at her. Kendra rolled her eyes at the two of them and said, "Alright, alright. Guys don't start. We should get some sleep... we should get an early start tomorrow. Find some better clothes and get some supplies. Then we need to be on our way," she paused, "Imladun, right?"

Damia nodded and Kendra continued, "Then let's get to sleep."

"Wait," Aideen said. "Who's sleeping where?"

The others looked at her, wondering what she meant. Kendra and Damia were already on the one bed, so that meant she would sleep with Peri in the other. Aideen knew this was what they were thinking but shook her head, "I'm not sleeping with her! She kicks!"

Peri's mouth dropped, "I do no- How do you know that?"

"I remember having a *huge* bruise on my leg after every sleepover because I got stuck sleeping in the same bed as you. I am *not* going to do that again."

Damia and Kendra looked at each other and tried not to laugh. Damia said, "I'll sleep with Peri."

Damia then rolled up the map and set it down on the table next to the lamp and moved over to the bed that Peri was sitting on. Aideen took Damia's place on the other bed next to Kendra. The four girls then got under the covers, but not before Aideen blew out the oil lamp. They lay there in silence, thinking about what had happened to them that day.

Now, in the silent darkness, the day's events seemed to weigh down on them more than ever. In the dark night, traveling through a mysterious world with three strangers seemed less like an adventure, and more like an escapade down into the lowest levels of Hades' realm.

Peri wiped away a tear, hoping that Damia didn't notice she was crying again. Damia did, of course, but didn't say anything because she was crying as well. In the bed next to theirs, Aideen sighed and turned over onto her stomach. She buried her face in the pillow and did not come up again that night. Kendra curled up into a ball with her back facing her three cousins. She wrapped her arms around herself and begged for the nightmare to be over.

Chapter Twenty-Two

Carr Faal knew something was up the moment his twin sister sat up in the bed she shared with their little sister, Sara. He had been thinking about the boy Trey DeLuca who lived a couple blocks east from them. Carr had always hated Trey; hating the DeLuca family was one of Carr's first memories. This time Trey had said something about Carr's mother, and Carr was having trouble sleeping. All he could think about was pounding Trey DeLuca's face into the ground.

He watching in silence as Kassidy walked out of the room without a noise. He was shocked that she had moved about so easily. The floorboards hadn't been replaced in years, and it was impossible for any one of the five person family to walk about the house without stepping on at least one loose board. Her silence was what intrigued Carr; she had obviously done this many times before.

He waited until he heard the door of the small two room house close before he threw off the blanket he was under. He got up off the mat on the floor which served as his bed and tip-toed out of the room, praying that his parents didn't wake up. Every time he stepped, his foot hit a noisy floorboard.

He quickly reached the door that led outside and opened it. He saw that Kassidy was already at the end of the street. Before she turned the corner, she glanced back at the house. Carr ducked out of the way, hoping she didn't see him. When he looked again, she was running again, turning right at the corner.

He closed the door behind him, and sprinted down the street after her. By the time he reached the end of the street, she was already making another turn. He ran as fast as he could to catch up to her, but made sure she did not know she was being followed. He wanted to see where she was headed.

He barely was keeping track of where she was taking him, but if he had, then he would have recognized the neighborhood immediately. There was only one neighborhood in the city that Jedrek Faal forbade his kids from going to, and it was this one. The one where Rico DeLuca and his family lived, including his sons Ciro and Trey.

Only when he saw Kassidy running along the edge of the house, with her head bent below the bottom of the windowsills, did Carr stop and take in what she was doing. He recognized the house immediately, having snuck over himself many times with his cousins to vandalize it. They'd broken windows, stolen doorknobs, and toilet papered it. Of course Rico DeLuca knew exactly who had done these things to his home, but he let Trey and his brother handle it; just as his father had let him handle Jedrek Faal and his brother Kegan.

Carr's mind started racing with questions. What would make Kassidy sneak over to the DeLuca house in the middle of the night? Was she spying on them for him and his cousins? Or was it something worse; something Carr didn't even want to think about. He watched as Kassidy found what she was looking for, a small window into the basement of the DeLuca house. She opened the unlocked window and slid inside.

Carr waited for something to happen. Maybe she was stealing from them and would be back out in just a few minutes. Then, a light turned on in one of the first floor rooms. Carr watched as a figure moved into his sight. A wave of panic went through Carr as he recognized it as Trey Faal. He must have heard Kassidy come into the house, and would no doubt kill her if he found her in there.

Then Carr saw someone else was in the room and his heart fell to the ground. It was Kassidy, and she was talking. She was talking to Trey DeLuca, and she didn't even look scared or angry. She looked more at ease than she did when she was with Carr and her own family.

Carr ran silently towards the house, closer to it than he felt comfortable. He snuck up to the window where Kassidy and Trey were, and peeked his head up so he could see what they were doing. He could now also hear what they were saying through the window, though it was slightly muffled.

Kassidy was saying, "I just hate sneaking around like this. I'm sick of it."

"What else can we do? Go public?" Trey asked sarcastically. "I don't know about you, but I want to keep living."

Kassidy sighed and sat down on the edge of the bed that was in the room. Carr could only assume they were in Trey's bedroom. And what did he mean by 'go public'?

Trey came and sat down next to Kassidy. He took her hand in his and said, "Kass, I'm sorry. I'm fed up too. I wish we really could tell our families. But-"

"I know, I know," Kassidy said. "They won't understand. They can't see past that stupid feud of theirs."

She then sat a little taller, and asked excitedly, "What if we ended the feud? Then they'd have no reason to hate us being together."

Trey laughed, "Do you even know what the feud is about?"

Kassidy frowned, "No."

"Neither do I. I don't even think our fathers know. It's just something that's been bred into us. How can we stop something that we don't even know about?"

Kassidy put her head on Trey's shoulder, "I can't loose you, Trey. I don't want this feud to ruin us."

Trey ran his hand through Kassidy's long red hair, "It won't. Just as long as we still love each other. Do you love me, Kass?"

Kassidy picked her head up off his shoulder and smiled, "With all my heart."

"See?" he asked, running the tips of his fingers down her cheekbone. "We have nothing to worry about."

He paused, bringing his head down closer to hers, "I love you too."

He then closed the distance between them and kissed her. She eagerly kissed him back, feeling all her doubts being washed away. She knew she wanted to be with Trey forever, no matter what her family said. She would deal with them when the time came. Now all she wanted to do was enjoy her time with Trey.

A small yell broke them apart, and they looked to the window to find Carr Faal staring at them in disbelief. Both Trey and Kassidy stood up. Kassidy looked frantic, "I thought he was still asleep!"

Carr stumbled backwards, away from the window. He looked around frantically, wondering if anyone else had seen what he had just witnessed. Kassidy Faal and Trey DeLuca...*in love*? There was no way it could be possible. The two were sworn enemies. Trey was *his* sworn enemy, and his twin sister had gone and fallen for him!

He then turned around and started running. He had to get his father. He had to tell him what was going on. Maybe Jedrek could talk some sense into his daughter; and knock some sense out of Trey De-Luca. He hadn't gotten very far when he heard a window open behind him. He didn't dare turn around to see what was happening behind him. He just had to get home.

Suddenly there was a hand on his shoulder and he was spun around. He looked into the face of Trey DeLuca, who looked both pissed off and anxious at the same time. "Carr," he started. "I know we've had our troubles in the past, but please-"

Carr cut him off with a punch in the nose. Trey let go of Carr and grabbed his nose, "What the hell was that for?"

"Don't you dare touch my sister again," Carr spat.

Kassidy reached them at this point and said, "Really, Carr? Must you be so immature?"

Carr spun on his sister, "And you! What do you think you're doing? Trey DeLuca? Anyone else, Kass! Anyone else but him!"

"It's a little late for that," Kassidy said.

Carr groaned, "Please. Don't say that." He started to turn, ready to run back home and wake up his father. He *had* to know about this.

"Carr! Wait!" Kassidy said. "Please don't tell anyone!"

Carr looked at Kassidy in disbelief, "You really expect me to stay quiet about this? How long have you been involved with this scum?"

Trey's hands curled into fists. Just because he was in love with Kassidy Faal didn't mean that he didn't still loath Carr Faal.

"That's none of your business," Kassidy replied.

Carr scoffed, "You still think I'm going to keep your little secret?"

"Carr, wait," Trey said. "I promise that I won't attack you or your family ever again, even if it means blowing my cover."

Carr glared at Trey, not sure if he could believe him. The offer was very enticing. Then Carr thought of all the stuff he could get away with, holding this over Trey DeLuca's head.

"You have my word," Trey added, seeing Carr's doubt.

Carr looked at Kassidy for a second and saw the pleading look on her face. How could he not do what she asked? The two of them always had each others backs. Carr couldn't even begin to count the number of times Kassidy had saved his butt. The number of times she has lied to their parents for him. He sighed and said, "Alright. Fine. But *please*. I do *not* want to see or hear about this *ever* again."

Kassidy let out a sigh of relief and threw her arms around her brother, "Oh, Carr! Thank you so much! You don't know how much this means to me!"

"Yeah, yeah," Carr said with a glare at Trey. He then pulled away from Kassidy and said to her, "Alright. It's time for us to leave."

Kassidy smiled at him, very aware of how uncomfortable he was with the whole situation. She let go of him and turned to Trey. He looked down at her and said, "I'll see you around, okay?"

She nodded, before pecking him on the lips. Carr made a very audible groan behind them, but Kassidy ignored him. She smiled up at him and whispered, "I love you."

He whispered back, "I love you too."

Carr moaned, "Let's go, Kassidy! Before I throw up!"

Trey laughed and let Kassidy slip out of his arms. She took Carr's hand in hers and led him down the street. Before they turned the corner, she turned to Trey and blew him a kiss. He waved to her before watching them turn the corner. He turned around and climbed back into his window, wondering if his life would ever be the same again.

Chapter Twenty-Three

Aideen let out a little sigh and rolled over in bed. She opened her eyes and saw that the sun was shining in her room. She panicked for a second, wondering why her alarm hadn't gone off. Then she realized that it was Sunday and there was no reason for her alarm to be set. Aideen then looked around the room, and realized she wasn't even in her own bed.

Again she felt the panic, wondering what she had done the night before to end up in a strange bed. She looked around, and saw that there was a body in the bed next to her, fast asleep. The panic rose like bile in her throat, until she realized it was Kendra sound asleep next to her.

She relaxed and took another look around the room. Memories of the previous day flooded into her head like a dam had just been broken. She remembered how she had been on Earth yesterday morning, and on Hecate last night. She remembered meeting Kain, and meeting Kynton. She remembered being told she was the Keeper of Fire.

She rubbed the sleep out of her eye and mumbled, "Toto, I've a feeling we're not in Kansas anymore."

"We must be over the rainbow!"

Aideen looked around and saw that Damia was standing in the doorway of the small room. Kynton was standing behind her, looking very confused at what the two of them just said. Aideen gave Damia a questioning look, "You can quote 'The Wizard of Oz'?"

Damia nodded, "I love Judy Garland. And don't look so surprised. You just quoted it too."

Aideen gave a small laugh, "I guess I did."

Peri groaned from where she was lying on the bed next to Aideen, "Why are we being so loud?"

Damia laughed, and Aideen noticed that she was already dressed and looked very wide awake. She had even done her hair, which was now in a long braid hanging over her shoulder, instead of frizzy and sticking out everywhere like her hair normally was in the morning. Aideen asked her, "How long have you been up?"

Damia shrugged and glanced down at the small watch on her wrist, "Maybe about two hours."

Aideen looked around, "What time is it?"

"Nine o'one," Damia answered quickly.

Peri groaned again, but didn't bother complaining. Damia glanced at her before looking back at Aideen, "I came up to let you know that we're about to have breakfast, if you want to join us."

Aideen grumbled and lay back down, with her arm covering his eyes, "Wake me up again in two hours. Then we can talk about food."

"I agree," Peri mumbled, unmoving.

"Sorry," Damia said. "But we really have to get started."

She glanced back at Kynton before whispering to the others, "Apparently, you can't just pick out clothes here. You have to get them special made. We'll be lucky if we get out of here tomorrow, at this rate."

Neither Aideen nor Peri moved, or even reacted to what Damia had said. She wondered if they had fallen back asleep as she was talking. She glanced over at Kendra, who had been out cold the entire time. She quickly walked over and shook her gently, knowing she could get the others up, "Kendra, I'm sorry. Please wake up, it's nine o'three already."

Kendra was laying face down with her head half way under the pillow; her hair was fanned out around her, the obvious result of her moving around a lot when she slept. She lifted her head slightly when Damia shook her and looked around. She saw that everyone was looking at her and asked groggily, "What time is it?"

"Nine o' three," Damia said agitatedly, as if the wasted minutes were a wasted lifetime.

Kendra grumbled, but sat up anyways. She ran her fingers through her hair and sighed, "We better get a move on. We still have to get clothes and figure out how we're getting from Canhareth to Imladun."

Kynton stepped into the room, after hanging awkwardly in the doorframe. He listened to what Kendra said, and got an idea. He smiled to himself, but kept quiet. He knew exactly how they would travel, by horseback. He had certain horses in mind too, but he couldn't let the Keepers know that. They would know exactly what he was if they figured out where he got their horses. And the last thing he wanted was for them to figure out what he was.

Kendra glanced at Kynton, very aware of how he was now standing in their room while three of them were still in bed. She pushed the thought from her head, and tried to convince herself that Kynton could be trusted. He knew the Keepers, after all. The Keepers had trusted him, so why couldn't they?

But Kendra couldn't help but distrust Kynton. There was something about him that seemed off. He was hiding something from them; possibly more than one thing by the way he was acting around Damia. Kendra didn't trust people who had something to hide.

She then looked at Aideen and Peri, both of whom had not moved an inch since she sat up. Damia sighed, "I tried getting them up, but they just ignored me."

Kendra leaned over and started shaking Aideen, similarly to how Damia had woken her up, but with more force. Aideen grumbled and moaned, "What the hell? I'm up! I'm up!"

She rolled over to look at Kendra, "Was that necessary?"

"Apparently."

Kendra then got up out of bed and walked around to where Peri was still asleep, or at least still pretending to be asleep. She be-

gan to shake her as well, with a little less force than she had with Aideen. In a loud, cheery voice she said, "Rise and shine, Sleepyhead!"

Peri moaned loudly and refused to open her eyes. Instead,
she flipped over so she was lying on her stomach, with her face in the
pillow. Kendra put her hands on her hips and said in a voice that was
scarily close to her mother's, "Peri Karina Andes. You get up out of
bed this instant, before I start yelling."

After a moment Peri flipped over and blinked her eyes open,
"Jeesh. You didn't have to pull out the middle name. I've been up
since these two started quoting Dorothy Gale."

Kendra gave Aideen and Damia a questioning look, and Aideen stood up, "Don't ask."

Peri stood up as well and Damia smiled, "Well we'll let you
get ready, and see you downstairs. There's a bathroom down the
hall. The water's a little hard, but" she motioned to her calm and un-
frizzed braid, "if I can do this, then you three should be fine."

She then half skipped and half danced across the room and
out the door. Kynton quickly followed her out without a word, glad
to have an excuse to leave. Kendra, Aideen and Peri looked at each
other, none of whom had half the amount of energy Damia had at
that hour of the morning. Aideen grumbled, "Who wants to use the
bathroom first?"

Peri moaned and flopped back down on the bed. Kendra
quickly grabbed her hand and pulled her up again, "Oh no you don't.
We're trying to get out of here, remember? The more time we waist,
the more time we are away from home."

Peri's eyes flew open and then they fell to the floor. "Home,"
her voice cracked. Suddenly her arms flew around Kendra and Peri
pulled her into an embrace. Peri sobbed into her cousin's shoulder,
"What are we doing, Kendra? Hecate? *Beindor?* A crystal that opens a
portal to another world? Magik powers? Ever since I was little, I
know I wanted to be like Hermione Granger and be able to use magic

and go to Hogwarts and have a magic wand. But is this actually possible?"

Peri paused, and cried into Kendra's shoulder. Kendra, not expecting Peri's sudden break down, had awkwardly wrapped her arms around her cousin and started rubbing her back. Aideen had been just as caught off guard as Kendra, but since she seemed to be out of the loop, she just sat down on the edge of the bed and looked away. She quickly wiped away a tear that was forming in her eye.

Kendra was about to say something, anything, to comfort Peri when Peri said with a said attempt at a laugh, "I thought we fell out the window, but that's impossible, right? We were too far away. And that guy was in the way," she paused. "Well, maybe we really did fall. Maybe we're dead right now and this is whatever comes next. Maybe we're being punished for not spending more time with each other. We've been damned to an eternity of trying to make up for the past eleven years."

Aideen looked sharply over at Peri, whose eyes were closed, buried in Kendra's shoulder. Aideen wondered if what Peri said could be possible. Were they really just dead? Were they being punished for something? Was there no such thing as Beindor, and magik and dragons? But Aideen knew better. She knew that whatever came after dying, this could not be it. They weren't aimlessly wandering around; they had a mission, a goal. They were going to get home, and that's what made Aideen believe that they weren't dead. The drive she felt to find the Amîr Crystal was what was keeping them alive, if only in her mind.

Kendra shook her head, "No, Peri. I don't believe that."

Peri looked up at her, and asked weakly, "You don't?"

"No. Maybe we are being punished for not spending the last decade together, but we aren't dead," Kendra said. She believed it with all her heart. She had to. If she gave into thoughts like that, then where would they be? They would give up and possibly never find the Amîr Crystal; never get home.

She continued, "We've been given a second chance. That's what I think. We have the chance to make up for what we've done to each other. We're about to set out on a great adventure that could very possibly take years to accomplish. We can't fill our heads with thoughts of death, we have to stay positive. We're alive, Peri, and we are going to see Earth again."

Peri smiled softly, wanting to believe what Kendra said. She wanted to, but couldn't. She hated having such a depressing outlook on the whole situation, but there was no other way for her to look at it. Her life had been going great; Joey was just as amazing as ever, she had finally stood up to Annie, she had actually made up with her cousins. Now her entire life was shattered. She wasn't going to be able to finish high school, unless by some miracle they found all four pieces of the stupid crystal in the next week, which she highly doubted.

She wasn't going to be able to see Joey for a long time, and her nightmare would come true. He wouldn't cheat on her, though; he would do something much worse. He would move on. He would forget all about Peri and the four years they had spent together. He would marry another woman and have her kids, not Peri's. They would buy a house together and get old together, all while Peri was stuck in another world trying to find pieces to a crystal. She might as well be dead.

Peri took a breath, gathering herself, and then smiled, "Thanks, Kendra. You know, you're really good at the whole pep talk thing."

Kendra laughed, glad that Peri was returning to normal. At least she wasn't crying anymore, "Thanks. But we really should get going. Damia and Kynton are waiting downstairs for us."

"Yeah," Aideen said. "And we shouldn't leave those two alone for too long. Who knows what they could be doing."

Peri laughed, wiping the last of her tears from her face, "You noticed that too?"

Kendra smiled, hiding the fact that she wanted to vomit, and changed the subject, "Who wants to use the bathroom first?"

~*~

"I wonder what's taking them so long," Damia said, glancing down at her watch. "It's already nine twelve."

Kynton watched her, amused that she was getting stressed out over the small amount of time her cousins were wasting getting ready. To him, the nine minutes Damia was so worried about seemed like half a millisecond. Time was very different for him. He had experienced a lot more of it than Damia ever would, and knew that there was no point for him to stress out like she was over half a millisecond; he would have many, many more.

"Calm down," he said with a smile. "They just woke up; it's going to take more than ten minutes for three girls to get ready in one bathroom."

Damia sighed, "We should have set an alarm or something last night. I know my phone has one, but I left it at Kendra's house last night. Of all the times we could have left our phones behind."

Kynton laughed, and Damia looked over at him. She looked at him as if she had forgotten he was there. She bit her lip, realizing he was laughing at her. "I'm sorry," she said. "Was I rambling?"

"It's fine," Kynton said. "You're just anxious to get home."

Damia didn't miss the hurt that flashed across his eyes, and she felt her heart go out for him. She gently touched his forearm, which was resting on the table they were sitting at. They were at one of the only occupied tables in the large room. A family of four was sitting at a table a few feet away from them, and was eating their breakfast in relative silence. There was also a man sitting at the bar that Kynton recognized as the man who had been sitting next to him the previous night when the Keepers walked in. It seemed that he hadn't moved since Kynton last saw him.

"Kynton, you have to understand. We don't belong here. How can you expect us to want to stay somewhere where we don't belong?"

Kynton thought of his home as she said that. He thought of home, where his parents refused to help the Keepers on their last quest. He remembered watching his mother silently accept what Keeper Damia gave her, and did not try to protest. He remembered how he yelled at his mother for letting her go. She had answered him, "You don't belong here, Kynton. You are too young to understand. Damia, and the other Keepers, must do this to save Beindor."

Kynton had run away then, in search of Keeper Damia. He had to tell her everything, had to let her know how he truly felt about her. He couldn't lose her…

"Kynton? Are you okay?"

Kynton blinked, resurfacing from his memory and looked at the girl sitting next to him. It was her. It was Keeper Damia. He hadn't lost her after all. Even after all these years, his emotions had not died down. Instead, as he looked at her, they grew stronger. He knew without a doubt that he had been given a second chance at a life with her. He couldn't lose again.

"You do belong here, Damia," he said softly. "With all my heart, I know you belong in Beindor. Why else would you open the portal?"

Damia unconsciously touched the end of her braid, and said, "I don't know. Kain said it was because we were the Keepers reincarnated, but just because we have the same souls as them doesn't mean we have to repeat their lives."

"But think about it," Kynton said. "Normally with reincarnation you don't know who has had your soul before you unless you ask a Seer. You have a completely different face, voice, temperament. *You* on the other hand, look exactly like Keeper Damia, talk exactly like her and even have the same name. If that doesn't mean you're supposed to be the new Keepers, I don't know what does."

Damia looked away from Kynton, considering what he had said. It gave him some hope, knowing that she was considering the fact that she was meant to stay in Beindor. Maybe it wouldn't take years to convince her to stay, after all. He had practically done it in one day.

Saying that Damia was confused would be an understatement. She had no idea what to think. She knew for a fact that she wanted to go home. It hadn't been three days since she was accepted into Julliard, and that wasn't something you pass up. Her dreams were coming true. Then, all of a sudden, she was given a responsibility that she wasn't expecting.

Protector of Beindor? She knew being a Keeper would be more than just a police officer protecting the streets of Canhareth. She got the feeling that the Keepers, the Saviors of Beindor, were more like the President of the United States, or the Parliament of England. She remembered Kain also saying that the Keepers were the founders of Beindor; similar to the Founding Fathers of America, they were the Founding Mothers of Beindor.

Damia had to smile at that one. At least sexism wasn't as dominant in Beindor as it was in the United States. The people of Beindor seemed fine with the idea that they were under the rule of four women, which was more than Damia could say for the United States, which still couldn't see a women as President.

But could she be the President of Beindor, or at least the equivalent Keepers? She had no idea. Just the thought of ruling a country made Damia queasy. She was glad that if they ever even considered taking the place of the Keepers, she wouldn't be alone. She had her three cousins with her, and they would be with her all the way. She knew that with their four very different styles, they could be excellent rulers of Beindor.

Damia frowned; she didn't want to imagine herself as ruler of anything. She couldn't let thoughts of being Keeper of Earth distract her from the goal at hand, which was to get the Amîr Crystal and get home. Maybe by the time they have all four pieces, she might have changed her mind, but she couldn't now. Now she had to give getting home a chance.

Aideen, Peri and Kendra walked down the stairs into the tavern a couple of minutes later, all looking fresh and wide awake. They walked over to where Kynton and Damia were sitting, and sat down as well. Damia smiled, "Awesome. Now we can get some food."

As if on cue, Mahak the bartender came over and asked, "How can I be of service, this morning?"

"What's for breakfast today, Mahak?" Kynton asked.

Mahak smiled and listed off plenty of choices for his five hungry customers. When he was done, Aideen ordered a side of toast, not really in the mood for food so early in the morning. Peri ordered a Western Omelet and a side of pancakes, Kendra got a grilled ham, egg, and cheese sandwich, and Damia and Kynton both ordered country fried potatoes and toast.

Mahak had their meals out to them quickly, and after only a few bites the girls assumed that he had been one of the best short order cooks on Earth in a previous life. They finished off their meals in a hurry, anxious to continue on their way. Once Kynton paid Mahak for the meal, the five of them left the quiet tavern and walked into the busy streets of downtown Canhareth.

Chapter Twenty-Four

Even though it was nine-thirty in the morning on a Sunday, the streets of Canhareth were packed with people and creatures of all different shapes, sizes and colors. Before stepping out of the tavern, the girls had momentarily forgotten about all the creatures they had seen the day before wandering around Canhareth. Now they looked around in awe.

Kynton laughed at their stunned faces, and said, "Come on, Ophelia's is this way."

They followed Kynton as he weaved through the people on the street. He suddenly took a right hand turn down a street that was even slightly larger and busier than the one The Dancing Bear was on. They continued down the street for less than a minute, and then Kynton stopped and said, "Here we are. Clothing by Ophelia."

A bell rang over the door as they walked in. The tall ceiling and white walls made the shop look ten times as large as it was, but clothing in piles, clothing on racks, sewing instruments, fabrics, patterns, and mannequins filled up the rest of the space, making the shop look quite small. A woman appeared in the doorway on the back wall of the shop, and looked over to see who had just entered. She smiled at the group and walked quickly over to them.

Ophelia was a woman in her late forties, with her dark black, graying hair tied up in a tight bun at the nape of her neck. She wore a simple dress, made even less attractive when she came to stand next to one of the display mannequins with a large ball gown on. Over her dress, she wore a smock and on her head was a pair of reading glasses.

"How may I help you?" she asked in a singsong, salesperson's voice.

"We need clothes," Kendra said, not exactly what they were going to need for their journey. She hoped Ophelia would be able to help them.

Ophelia's eyes traveled across the clothing the four girls were wearing and her mouth formed a small O shape. She took a step forward, professional curiosity getting the better of her. She reached out and touched Kendra's dark blue sweater. Her eyes then flitted over to Aideen's jeans. She bent down and touched them as well. As she circled around the girls, she asked, "Where in Beindor did you find these clothes? And in such *good* condition? Denim is such a rare fabric. It hasn't been seen in over a thousand years!"

Peri gave her cousins a very confused look. *Over a thousand years,* she thought. *That's impossible.* The Keepers didn't even bring the first humans over until the sixties. That was fifty years ago, not a thousand. Peri saw that her cousins had come to the same conclusion she had, and Kendra was about to say something when Ophelia said, "Oh, I'm sorry! You want clothes! Of course, of course. You can't go around wearing denim, after all!"

Ignoring the woman's strange last sentence, Kendra said, "We are going to be traveling around Beindor. Sight-seeing, and all that. We just need clothes for the trip. Nothing fancy, but it has to be durable."

Ophelia smiled and said, "I have some patterns you may look at, and fabrics you can choose from."

"Is it possible to get these done today?" Damia asked. "We're on a very tight schedule."

Ophelia's smile faltered, but it did not fall. "Today?" she asked. "Four dresses in one day?"

"Please," Kendra said. "It's very important."

Ophelia let out a staggered breath, but then nodded. "It can be done. I will have to rearrange my appointments, but it can be done. I close at sunset. They will be done by then."

She ushered them over to a large sewing table, and brought to them a stack of papers. The girls started looking through them, and saw that each piece of paper had a different dress pattern on it. The four girls quickly realized that they had no idea what they were supposed to be looking for. They read words like overskirts and underskirts, poplin skirts, corsets and cumberbunds. They were glad there were pictures, because otherwise they wouldn't have known what to do.

They couldn't tell Ophelia this, of course. Ophelia assumed that they, like all the others in Hecate, were brought up wearing clothing similar to those in the patterns. Telling her that they had no idea what a cumberbund was would surely give them away, if their jeans hadn't already.

While the four girls pretended to know what they were looking for among the patterns, Ophelia tried to engage them in some small talk. She wanted to know where they had gotten their denim, and why they would make it into something as atrocious as pants! What could they have been thinking? Four women with denim pants? Where could they go with those? Now if they had been smart and made it into skirts or dresses, then they could flaunt their denim at a ball or gala. For women who could afford denim, there were always balls and galas coming up.

"So where around Beindor are you traveling to? Vavia?" she asked.

The girls nodded, and Damia said, "That's one of the stops we're making."

Ophelia nodded, and asked another question, "Are you from around Canhareth, then?"

"No," Aideen said. "We're just visiting."

"Then where are you from? Nérand? No, you look more like northerners...Talania, maybe?" Ophelia asked politely, handing a pattern she thought would look lovely on Peri to her.

"We're actually not from Beindor," Peri said.

"Oh," Ophelia said, realizing that they wouldn't be. Denim was the rarest in Beindor, but in Úrdor and Ohtalie it was much more common. "Where then, are you from?"

"Ohtalie," Kynton said, knowing that none of the Keepers could remember what the other countries were called. They had been dead for eighteen years, after all. No one could be expected to recite the names of all the countries in Hecate after being dead for such a long time.

Ophelia nodded, thinking about a cousin she had up in Othalie. Perhaps he could find some denim for her…

"So, are we going to get these dresses?" Aideen asked.

Ophelia snapped out of her daydream, where she was making herself a beautiful denim ball gown, and looked over at Aideen. For a moment she looked like she had no idea who they were, then the recognition came and she remembered that she was trying to sell these good people clothing. "Oh, yes! My apologies!"

She then clasped her hands together and asked, "Have you each found a pattern for your dresses?"

The girls nodded and handed Ophelia four separate patterns. Ophelia looked them over for a second before smiling and exclaiming, "Ah! What taste you have! All of these patterns are treasures in my shop. They are based on the clothes the very Keepers themselves wore when they were alive, bless their souls. What a sharp choice for those about to discover the secrets of Beindor as the Keepers did, bless their souls."

The four girls remained silent as Ophelia led them to another part of the store, where there were rows upon rows of fabric. What a coincidence it was, for the four of them to pick patterns based on the clothing of the Keepers. And what a bizarre coincidence, at that. It seemed everything they did since coming to Beindor could reflect back on the first Keepers.

Ophelia let the four girls and Kynton browse through the fabrics, while her mind wandered off to the moment when she would
be wearing a denim dress at a very important gala. Kynton stayed
close to Damia, almost afraid to let her leave his sight; lest she disappear like she had so many years ago. And Damia used Kynton's
knowledge of travel to pick out the strongest fabric they could find.
Aideen and Kendra were walking through the rows of fabric, not really looking as well as they should have been.

Their minds, similarly to Ophelia's, were off in a distant daydream. Kendra was thinking about Ryan McPherson, wondering
what he was thinking about her disappearance. She wondered if he
could ever fathom what had happened to her in the twenty-four
hours since she had last seen him.

Aideen, on the other hand, was thinking about what she and
her cousins were about to do. She tried to picture the four of them
riding on horseback in medieval clothes. That was the easy part of
the picture she was trying to create. The part she couldn't see was
the part when they all became best friends. She feared that their
years spent separated would hold them back from getting closer. She
also feared that if their friendship ever failed, then it would most
likely be impossible for them to find the Amîr Crystal and get home.

Peri was walking through the rows of fabric like she was
walking through a large library. She scanned the material quickly,
looking for something that would catch her eye. She walked slowly
and quietly, as if her steps would distract fellow readers among the
bookshelves. She reached the end of one row without success, and
was about to turn down another when something new caught her
eye.

It wasn't a fabric, like she was supposed to be looking at, but
was so beautiful that she couldn't bring her mind back to the task at
hand. She walked quickly over to the mannequin, which was stand-

ing on a pedestal, with her hands behind her back, as if she couldn't trust herself to get close to it without touching it.

The dress Peri stood before was like nothing else in the shop. There was not a hint of the seventeenth century style that influenced almost every other piece of fabric in the store. This dress was just as modern as the Uggs on Peri's feet.

The pink of the dress was what first caught Peri's attention. It was a soft, almost white, pink so different from the browns and blacks and other dark colors that filled up most of the rows of fabrics. The second thing that Peri noticed about the dress was how much it resembled the prom dresses she had always fantasized about wearing. It was strapless, with a formfitting bodice reaching all the way down to the mannequin's thighs. The fabric of the entire bodice was ruched together, with silver appliqué flowers falling from the bust, down the front of the bodice, gathering over the left thigh and then just beginning to trickle down the skirt.

The skirt was made by layered tulle. It wasn't as wide as a classic prom dress, but it definitely gave the dress some volume. The top layer of tulle was cut shorter than the other layers. The cut wasn't as jagged as if someone had taken scissors to it randomly, but it wasn't as neat as a drape over the longer skirts.

The dress made Peri think of a ballerina, or a faerytale princess. She ran the tulle fabric through her fingers and sighed, knowing that she was not a princess, and that she could never have this dress. Despite this, she found herself imagining what she might look like in it, walking down a large staircase somewhere. Somewhere where hundreds of eyes were on her, and her alone.

She walked slowly, trying not to concentrate on all the faces turned up to watch her. Her back was held up straight, and she looked straight ahead. The dress felt like air, floating around her as she walked down. Then she reached the bottom of the stairs, and a man was there, with his arm out for her to take.

She smiled at the blonde haired mystery man, and slipped her arm gracefully into his. He smiled down at her, and she smiled back up at him. The two of them looked like they were remembering a secret, a secret from a past lifetime that only they would find amusing. They walked out into a large open space in the middle of their audience, and were joined by three other couples. Once all four couples were in position, music began to play, and they began to dance.

"This here is one of my finest creations."

Peri blinked, and the ballroom image faded from her mind. As she looked up at the dress, she tried to recall the face of the blond haired man in her daydream. She knew it wasn't Joey she had fantasized dancing with, because he had his mother's dark brown Italian hair. This man's hair was as blonde as Joey's was dark.

There was something about Blondie that Peri found to be troublesome. She couldn't put her finger on it, but there was something familiar about him. The others in the fantasy had been familiar too. She remembered recognizing them, but couldn't remember them now, back in Ophelia's shop.

Peri looked over to see that Ophelia was standing next to her, looking up at the dress as well. Her eyes were bright, as if recalling the moment she had designed the dress Peri still held in her hand. "It's beautiful," Peri gushed, unable to hide her true feeling about the dress.

Ophelia smiled at her, "Thank you."

Peri looked back up at the dress, unable to turn away from its beauty.

"Oh, Peri! It's beautiful! You must try it on!"

Peri turned to see Damia and Kynton emerge from one of the rows of fabrics. Damia's eyes flew between Peri and the pink dress and she rushed forward. She stood next to Peri and said to her, "Please try it on. I know you'll just look gorgeous!"

Aideen laughed, coming to see what the commotion was all about. "What happened to getting on our way as fast as possible?"

Damia looked back at her and shrugged, "We're going to be spending the day here anyways...we might as well enjoy ourselves!"

"By trying on dresses?" Kendra asked, coming to stand next to Aideen.

"Not just any dresses!" Damia exclaimed. "*The* dress."

It was Peri's turn to laugh, "You can't be serious, Damia! I couldn't..."

"Why not?" Damia asked. "You know you want to."

And Peri did want to. She was using all her willpower not to give into what Damia was suggesting. She knew that the moment she put that dress on, she wouldn't ever want to take it off. She was just that kind of shopper, and this dress was calling to her. She had to do everything in her will not to answer.

"Alright. Fine," Peri said. So much for her willpower. And her self esteem, for that matter. She knew as soon as she left the store without the dress, her whole day was going to be ruined. But at least she'd have five minutes of heaven when she puts the dress on.

Ophelia's smile grew and she quickly and expertly took the dress down off the mannequin. She motioned Peri to follow her, and led her into the back rooms of the store. While Ophelia helped Peri into the pink ball gown, the others continued to look for fabrics for their new clothes. They picked out fabrics and set them down on the table on which their patterns still lay.

A few minutes later, Ophelia stepped out of the backrooms. Her cheeks were rosy, as if she were watching her daughter's first chorus concert and her lips were pressed together to keep from smiling. She motioned for the others to come closer, and when they did, they saw Peri emerge from the dressing rooms.

She blushed as she walked forward, and when she saw the looks on her cousins faces she felt the blush creep down her neck.

When she reached the spot where her cousins were standing, they were speechless. She looked down, and ran her hands over the appliqué flowers, "I look terrible, I know."

Kendra shook her head, "No, Peri. That dress was made for you."

Peri smiled, "Really? You think so?"

Damia nodded, "It's tremendous."

"Too bad we don't have any parties to go to," Aideen said.

Peri sighed, "I know. I wish we did. Just so I could wear this."

"Well there is prom," Damia said quietly, "if we make it back in three months."

The other three looked down at the dress, wondering if they were going to be back on Earth in three months. By the sinking feeling they got in the pits of their stomachs, they knew they wouldn't be. Aideen then smiled, "I have an idea! When we get back, whenever that is, we should throw a party. A big fancy party where you can wear this dress."

Peri's eyes got big, "You would do that? Just so I could get this dress?"

Aideen shrugged, "Why not? I've a feeling we're all going to need a party."

Kendra shook her head, "But we can't drag that dress everywhere we go. That's not very practical."

Ophelia then said, "I will hold it for you."

"Can you do that?" Peri asked, excitedly.

Ophelia nodded, "I do own the place. Besides, I don't think I could sell this dress to anyone else, after seeing you in it."

"Oh!" Peri exclaimed, throwing her arms around Ophelia in a hug. "Wait until Joey sees me in this!"

~*~

A half hour later, Aideen, Peri, Kendra, Damia and Kynton were again walking down the streets of Canhareth. There were many different shops lining the streets, some as common as a butcher or a baker's shop, to the ones that could not be found any place on Earth. Those were the ones filled with creatures that the four girls could not even begin to name.

One shop was called 'Dragon's Treasures' and claimed that all the gold and jewelry inside was stolen from real dragons' caves. Another one was run by a mermaid who could change her tail into human legs. Her shop contained all the secrets of the sea, including a seashell that whispered the name of your true love when you put it to your ear. When Kendra listened to the seashell, all she could hear was a low vibrating 'nyheeeeehn' sound.

When she told the mermaid what she had heard, the mermaid's eyes went big for a second. Kendra wondered if there was something about what she had heard that the mermaid wasn't telling her about. Maybe her one true love's name was Nyheeehn, and the mermaid knew who he was. Kendra didn't like the fact that nyheeehn sounded nothing like Ryan. She pushed Ryan away from her thoughts, not wanting to think about him and how so very far away she was from him. How they had only started dating the day before she disappeared. It seemed the Fates didn't want them together, after all.

Kendra remained silent for a while, while the others explored the shops nearby. By the time they had all come over to her, sitting on a bench outside the mermaid's store, she had managed to hold back most of her tears, and successfully stop thinking about Earth and the people whom she had left behind.

Peri sat down next to Kendra, and wrapped an arm around her. Peri noticed the look on Kendra's face immediately, especially because she had the same look on her face the day before when she realized that she wouldn't be seeing Joey for a very long time. Instead of bringing attention to Kendra, however, Peri asked Kynton a question that had been nagging her since she first saw the pink ball gown in Ophelia's shop.

"Kynton, why is everything so miss-matched here? The clothing is all seventeenth century Europe, but then there is that ball gown. There's running water and toilets in the bathrooms, but horse and buggies are as far as transportation seems to have gotten. You have phonographs but no radio or movies. The Keepers came here in the 1960s, yet there are homes that look like they are from the Dark Ages," Peri said.

Kynton thought about what Peri had said, and wondered what seventeenth century Europe and the Dark Ages were. Not wanting to look stupid in front of the Keepers, he didn't dare ask. Instead, he said, "When the Keepers brought humans over from Earth they decided that they didn't want to make a replica of Earth, over here on Hecate. There were some things about Earth that they didn't like, like the transportation."

"They didn't like cars?" Aideen asked in disbelief.

"They are a terrible invention," Damia said. "All that pollution they emit into the atmosphere."

"Could you stop being a hippie for just five minutes?" Aideen asked her with a shake of the head.

Kynton continued, pretending he knew what a car was, "So when they saw that they had the chance to start over, with only the best from Earth, they did. The erased all memories of Earth, making the people's old world seem like a faerytale. No one actually believes there is an Earth; they just think someone made it up as a bedtime story. Just like elves and dragons and merpeople for the humans on Earth are faerytales."

"So," Kendra said. "The Keepers erased the memories of their people?"

"Only to protect them," Kynton said, seeing that the girls weren't liking this side of the Keepers. "They did what was best for their people. Besides, they only got rid of the Earth part. They still have all their memories; they're just altered so that they think they grew up on Hecate."

"Is that why Ophelia said something about denim not being seen in thousands of years? Because she really thinks humans have been in Beindor that long?" Aideen asked.

Kynton nodded, "They think that the Keepers created Canhareth just over two thousand years ago, instead of fifty."

"But people here are over fifty. How do they explain being around two thousand years ago?" Peri asked.

"They don't," Kynton said. "They don't remember coming from Earth and settling Canhareth. They don't realize that the stories they tell their kids about their ancestors coming from a mythical land called Earth are really about themselves."

"That's so sad," Damia said.

"Not really," Kynton said. "They don't know what's happened. They live peaceful lives, and are content."

"What about you?" Kendra asked. "How do you know all this, when the Keepers erased *everyone's* memories?"

Kynton almost panicked, almost. He had said too much and the Keepers were on to him. He had used the word human too loosely. They knew he didn't come from Earth with the Keepers. Then he remembered what the Keepers did to a select few humans, including their family and *her* husband. He explained, "The Keepers let a choice few keep their memories. Those who were closest to the four women, and who they felt would not give away their secret."

After a moment, Peri said, "Tárquin was in that group, wasn't he?"

"Yes," Kynton said. "Regretfully."

"That's how he still knew what Earth was, and that he could go back," Peri said. "The Keepers let him keep that knowledge."

"The Keepers might have survived if they erased his memory of Earth, along with all the other humans," Kynton said.

Aideen then thought of something she noticed in Ophelia's shop, "Ophelia kept saying 'bless their souls', as if the Keepers were some saints. From what you just said, they weren't saints at all. They were manipulative and power hungry."

"The Keepers were the best people I have ever known," Kynton said, anger flashing in his eyes. "Don't you *ever* disrespect them like that again. What they did might be questionable, but their reasons never were. They only had the good of their people in mind, in whatever they did. They sacrificed their lives to save these people."

The silence that followed was almost unbearable for Kynton. As soon as his voice got higher, as soon as he got angrier, he knew it was over. They wouldn't want him to come along with them, and they wouldn't let him get the chance to try and convince them to stay. All they would see was an explosive stranger who couldn't be trusted.

Kynton was right, about one of the girls at least. Kendra didn't trust Kynton one bit. They had barely known him one day, and how could anyone be trusted after that short of a period? But the others didn't see him like that, especially not Damia. She saw a man who had lost the people he held closest to his heart, and now that they were back, all his old scars were opening up again.

As Damia reached out to take Kynton's hand, Aideen said, "I'm sorry. I didn't realize."

Kynton shrugged it off, unable to trust his own voice. Peri was the one who broke the awkward silence that followed. Her forehead crinkled as she thought of something Aideen said. Out loud she thought, "If Ophelia kept blessing the souls of the Keepers, doesn't that mean she was blessing us?"

Aideen and Damia laughed, realizing the truth in Peri's words. Kendra just shook her head at her three cousins and said, "Come on. Let's keep walking."

Chapter Twenty-Five

He knows.

Trey DeLuca was pacing in his room. Images of the top half of Carr Faal's head peaking over the side of his windowsill kept replaying over and over in his head.

Everything is ruined now because her idiotic half-brained good-for-nothing brother knows.

As soon as he had seen Carr, Trey felt himself standing on the edge of a cliff. His toes hung over the edge. He hadn't even known he was walking on a cliff until he had met Kassidy. Before her, he had been strolling down a large open plain. As soon as he saw her, as soon as they first met, he realized that the path he was walking was headed for a cliff, a sudden drop off.

It had been after one of his brawls with Carr Faal. Trey didn't even know what they had been fighting about. Sometimes they didn't even need a reason. They would just see each other and start fighting. This time, when the fight stopped, Trey was covered in blood. Carr had busted his lip and broken his nose.

He would have gone home, except that Ciro was there and would demand an explanation. He could not let his brother know that a Faal had made him look like this. Ciro would no doubt tell their father, and then Trey would never hear the end of it. So, instead, he walked around trying to find a place where he could wash his face.

The first place he saw was a tavern called The Dancing Bear. As he approached it, the door swung open and a large man teetered slowly out. His eyes were glazed over, and he had a crooked smile on his face. From behind him, Trey heard someone say, "Let's go, Father. Mother is worried sick about you."

When the man passed, Trey got his first glimpse at Kassidy. Her hair shimmered like fire in the lamp light of the dark street. She was half the size of her father, and twice as gentle. She walked with a lightness that no man could achieve, and the apologetic smile she sent Trey's way almost knocked him to the ground.

He went back to that same tavern every night after that, hoping to see her again. When he did, he managed enough courage to approach her. Soon they were talking and laughing like they were childhood friends. It only took a few meetings for them to figure out that they were a Faal and a DeLuca.

The silence that followed almost tore them apart, but then Trey suddenly said, "I don't care what your last name is. I love you, Kass."

From that moment on, Trey began looking at his life from a very different perspective. While he still continued to fight and quarrel with Carr, he was beginning to realize how pointless it all was. He didn't really want to spend the rest of his life pitted against Carr and the Faals, but by the looks of his father, and his grandfather before him, it was inevitable.

So he continued his day to day life, dreaming about the day when he and Kassidy could run away from Canhareth together. He dreamed of the day he could look at his father and tell him he is no longer a DeLuca. Every time he thought of being included in the DeLuca family, Trey cringed. He knew he was going to have to get away, and now that Carr was in on his secret, he knew it was doomed.

Carr Fall wouldn't be able to hold this secret in for long. He would have to tell someone, soon. Trey prayed that Carr wouldn't tell his father, because Jedrek Faal was one person Trey knew wouldn't understand. All Jedrek would see would be his daughter with the son of the man he hated most. Just like Carr, Jedrek wouldn't be able to understand.

"What are you brooding about?"

Trey looked up to see his brother Ciro standing in the doorway of his bedroom. Ciro was just ten months younger than Trey, but ever since they were little it was Ciro who had the same hatred and quick temper of their father. Trey, as the oldest son was always the favorite, but Ciro was the more promising of the two, especially in recent months.

Trey didn't answer and Ciro laughed, "What'dya do? Eat the whole fuckin' lemon?"

Trey rolled his eyes, "At least I wasn't like you and eat the whole watermelon."

Ciro glared, "Shut up. I was six."

Trey laughed and Ciro came in and sat on the bed. He said, "I heard Faal is at the Scorpion's House. Wanna go spit on him?"

Trey couldn't stop himself from laughing. "Spit? Is that the worst you've got?"

Ciro grunted, "We could just kill him."

Trey spun on Ciro so fast, Ciro thought he was going to hit him, "We can't *kill* Carr!"

Ciro's mouth dropped, he had never seen Trey defend a Faal before. Trey paused, realizing the mistake he had just made. Quickly he recovered and said, "What the hell would we do afterwards? *Spit?*"

Ciro chuckled; no longer worried that Trey had gotten soft for the Faals, "Good point. We'd be so *bored*."

Trey let out a quick sigh, sensing that he was out of danger. He had to watch how he acted around Ciro. He had actually *defended* Faal. But the ease of which Ciro mentioned killing him scared Trey. He wondered if he had been like that before meeting Kassidy. He hoped not; Ciro was a monster.

Chapter Twenty-Six

Aideen was walking a few paces in front of the others, look-ing at the shops around them in awe. Every time she looked at a new store, it seemed to amaze her more than the previous one. There were so many different things on Hecate, Aideen had to fight the urge to stay and explore the whole world.

While she was walking, Aideen spotted a certain shop that seemed to drawn her right over to it. The others followed, at first protesting, but then they seemed to be drawn in by it as well. It was hidden in the shadows of the buildings around it, and no one walking by seemed to be giving it a second thought.

In the window display case there were things like crystal balls and Tarot cards and a set of Runes. The group couldn't see much past that, though, because the windows were covered in a layer of dirt. It seemed that whoever owned this little shop didn't want to bother to clean up after whatever had caused the dust and dirt inside. On the window, painted in bright colors were the words, 'Korinna's Magikal Shoppe'.

They walked inside and saw that the tiny store was filled with magikal trinkets, from love potions to amulets to rabbits' feet. They were able to drift around the store for only a couple minutes before they heard a woman's heels clicking their way towards them. They looked up in time to see her smile at her new customers.

Her hair was violent orange in color, and cascading over her shoulders like a waterfall of waves and curls. A small amount was pushed out of her face and clipped to the side of her head with a small white feather. She was wearing a simple dress, but it wasn't as plain as Ophelia's. This tunic dress was light blue and giving her an empire waist was a light brown cumberbund. Around her neck was a pendant in the shape of an owl, whose eyes were made out of celes-tite gems. Her eyes were a color that matched her tunic, but it wasn't just her irises that were light blue, but her entire eyes that matched the color of the sky, though she was not blind.

Clio stepped forward and said, "It is an honor to have you in my shop once again, Keepers."

Aideen groaned, "Is the word Keeper written on our foreheads, or something? How come everyone can tell who we are?"

Korinna chuckled, "There is nothing written on your forehead, dear Aideen. I am the Seer Korinna, and I have been waiting for you to come."

"You're a Seer?" Kendra asked. "What does that mean?"

"It means that I Saw the Keepers coming into my store today. I also Saw how you came to be in Hecate," Korinna said.

"You can see the future?" Peri asked.

"Yes," Korinna said, looking at her. "And so can you."

"What?" Peri asked in disbelief.

"Yes," Korinna repeated. "One of you is a Seer, one a Healer, one an Empath and the last is a Traveler, each an Opulian."

The four girls looked at each other, not expecting this when they walked into Korinna's Magikal Shoppe. Damia then asked, "Is that our magik powers thing?"

"Part of it," Korinna said with a chuckle. "There are a great many *powers* that the Keepers possess. Being an Opulian is only the beginning."

"What is an Opulian?" Peri asked.

"Special creatures who have magik powers that are traditionally not genetic. Anyone can be an Opulian, humans, merfolk, ogres. It is one of the sole magiks that transcends species."

"What about you?" Peri asked. "Are you more than a Seer?"

Korinna smiled, "I possess knowledge in all forms of magik, unfortunately I am not as gifted as the Keepers."

"How do you See things?" Peri asked, wanting to learn all she could about her sudden gift. "Seeing the future, I mean."

"For me, all I have to do is think of what or whose future I want to See, and I can See it. My first visions were dreams, and then I had to be touching the item of which I was Seeing the future."

Peri immediately thought of the ball gown, and how she had had that daydream of a large gala where she was wearing it. She had thought it was just a daydream, but then why would the man from her dream be in her daydream, and not Joey?

Then Peri realized that her dream wasn't a dream at all. Korinna just said that her first visions were in the form of dreams, so that meant the dream she had of Joey kissing a strange girl wasn't just a dream... it was the future. And the man who had hugged her was in her future as well, as her date or boyfriend to the big ball from her vision from earlier that day. Peri made a mental note to look out for gorgeous blond haired, green eyed men who might ask her to a ball.

Thinking about the ball in her vision, she also remembered who else she had been dancing with. It was Aideen, Kendra and Damia. They had been the other guests of honor. Did that mean that the ball Aideen had suggested would really come true? Would they reach Earth and be able to celebrate their return home? That thought gave Peri some hope, as she tried to erase the vision of Joey kissing someone else from her head.

Peri still felt something nagging her about her vision of the ball. There was someone else there she had recognized. One of her cousins' dance partners. She immediately thought of Kynton, but knew that Damia had been dancing with a tall, dark haired man, not lean and lanky, brown haired Kynton. Then she thought of her other vision, and how Kendra had showed up in that one as well, with a man by her side.

That was where she had seen him before. The man who had been dancing with Kendra in the second vision was the one singing with her in the first one. Peri had seen both of these men twice in her visions, she wondered if that meant anything important. Were these men important to their journey across Beindor?

Korinna's smile got wider as she read the expression on Peri's face, "It seems you have already had some visions of your own."

Peri nodded. Damia gasped and asked excitedly, "What did you see?"

Peri looked over at her cousins and said softly, "I dreamt that Joey cheated on me."

Damia's hand flew to her mouth and Kendra said, "Oh, Peri. I'm so sorry."

Peri shook her head and said with a smile, "It's okay. It hasn't happened yet."

"How do you know?" Aideen asked, with a frown.

"Because I catch him, and there is someone with me who I haven't met yet."

Damia reached out and pulled Peri into a hug. Peri wiped away a tear from her eye, and Damia did the same. Damia said, "That's an awful way to start seeing the future."

"The second vision was a lot better," Peri said.

Damia smiled at her, "What was that?"

"I was wearing that dress to a party. It looked like a huge ball. You were all there, and the four of us, with our dates, were dancing."

Damia's smile widened and she quickly glanced over at Kynton. He smiled back at her. Peri didn't have the heart to tell Damia that it wasn't Kynton who she saw Damia dancing with. Aideen laughed, "I guess I didn't have to tell you that we should have a party. You already knew."

Peri smirked, "I didn't know it was a vision. I thought I was just daydreaming."

"So who were we dancing with?" Kendra asked with a sly smile. "Did you see?"

"Yeah, but I didn't recognize who you were dancing with. Sorry."

Kendra frowned, trying to think back. Had Peri ever met Ryan McPherson? Kendra hoped she didn't, and that's why she couldn't recognize him in her vision.

"I can tell you about your loves," Korinna interrupted. "If you are interested in your dates to this ball."

The girls agreed most readily. Korinna was a gifted Seer, they could tell. They knew that whatever she Saw was bound to be the truth. They wondered if she could even tell them the name of their true loves; their soulmates. Kynton was a little less excited about this proposition. If Korinna was a gifted Seer as she said she was, then she would be able to See into his past as well as future. The past was not something he wanted to revisit, especially not with Damia anywhere near him.

"Follow me," Korinna said. "We will be much more comfortable back here."

They followed Korinna into the back of the store, where she had emerged from earlier. There was a small round table, only a foot or so off the ground, with large pillows thrown around it. The table was covered in a white cloth, and on top of the cloth sat a small black caldron, with four white candles standing next to it. Korinna lit the candles and motioned for the five to take a seat around the table.

Once the four girls were seated, with Kynton standing a little ways behind them, Korinna asked, "Who would like to go first?"

Peri volunteered and Korinna closed her eyes. They waited in silence as they watched Korinna's eyes move behind their lids. Korinna then said in a soft voice, "You are very much in love right now, but his heart has been shattered. You will see him again, but by the time you do, you both will have moved on. The one who follows is someone you hate. The hate is mutual, but slowly it turns to love." Korinna smiled, "He is the one you see in your visions."

Peri kept going back to one word, *shattered.* Why would Joey's heart be shattered? What could Peri possibly have done to shatter his heart? Then she realized Korinna had said something else. She had mentioned Blondie, the one Peri had seen in her visions. He was her next love. She just wished she knew who he was.

Korinna opened her eyes for a moment, just long enough to see that Aideen was sitting next to Peri. She closed her eyes again, this time focusing on Aideen and her future. "You find love quickly and easily on your travels, but it is not true. You will be blinded by your passion, and will make a terrible mistake."

"That's just great," Aideen said with a roll of her eyes.

Korinna opened her eyes suddenly, as if Aideen's words had wakened her from a deep sleep. Korinna smiled, "Do not worry, it will all end well."

"Damia," Korinna said, closing her eyes again. "I see many obstacles ahead of you. You must go through many trials to prove that your love is true. Those around you will fight you, telling you you can't love such a man. Some will even die because of you."

Damia gasped and asked in a stricken voice, "Die? Because of me?"

Korinna slowly opened her eyes this time and said, "Just because one path is the easiest, does not mean that it is the wisest."

Kendra looked at Damia, and saw the tears coming. She looked at Korinna, whose eyes had closed again. She tried interrupting, "Umm... I don't think I want to know what happens to me. Thanks."

Korinna didn't hear her, though, and continued anyways, "Your path is the smoothest of all I've seen today. From the moment you see each other; you know that it's meant to be. There is one fleeting moment of uncertainty, but other than that you have a blissful life, unless you're trying to help the others with their problems."

Kendra almost laughed. Hers was going to be the easiest of the four? What a relief that was... but then she realized that she hadn't met him yet, and that meant that he wasn't Ryan. She wasn't going to end up with Ryan. The crush that lasted almost six years had turned into a two day fling. So that's why the laugh that Kendra almost had was caught in her throat.

Korinna looked up at Kynton, who just like Kendra started to tell the Seer not look into his love life. And again, Korinna ignored him. She closed her eyes, and Kynton watched, horrified, as Korinna's eyes started moving faster and faster under their lids. Her face twisted into a look of horror, like she had been betrayed. After a moment, she gasped and her eyes flew open. She glared up at Kynton and said, "I think it's time you left."

Korinna then looked back down at the Keepers and smiled, as if Kynton wasn't even in the room. Quickly she stood up and unconsciously wrapped her hand around the owl pendant resting on her chest. "My apologies, Keepers, but it is time Korinna got some rest. All these visions are giving her a headache."

She ushered them all out of the backroom, and out towards the door. They tried their hardest not to trip over each other as she literally pushed them out her door. They were about to walk away, not sure what else they could do, when Korinna suddenly grabbed Damia's wrist and pulled her back inside the door. In a low whisper Korinna said to her, "Be careful of him. He may seem innocent, but he is holding secrets from you. The Water Keeper is wise not to trust him."

Korinna then let Damia go and gave Kynton one final glare before slamming her door closed. The five of them watched her retreating back in shock. She had seen something in Kynton's future that she did not like. Kynton felt very self conscious, and wondered when the Keepers would turn on him. Aideen was the first.

She turned to look up at Kynton, with her hands resting firmly on her hips. With a judging glare, she asked, "What the *hell* was that about?"

Kynton shrugged, trying to act calm and collected, "I don't know. It's in my future, right?"

Aideen snorted, and her hands fell from her hips. She studied Kynton for a second more, "Good point. I guess we can't hold that against you."

I can, Kendra thought. The Seer's reaction to Kynton's future only sent Kendra's mind into full force, trying to figure out what he would do that sent her into such a frenzy, even to start talking about herself in the third person. Kendra knew there was something off about Kynton; she just wished she could figure out what it was. Not being able to figure it out was putting her in a mad mood, and she did not like being in a mad mood.

What could he not want us to know? She thought as they walked away from Korinna's Magikal Shoppe. She knew that was the wrong question. They weren't just strangers he met yesterday to him. They were the Keepers. *What could he not want the Keepers to know? Does he think they would try to stop him if they found out?* Kendra was beginning to not like where her thoughts were going...*Is he going to try and hurt us? Is that what Korinna saw in her vision?*

Kendra looked up ahead of her, where Kynton was walking next to Damia.

What did Korinna say to Damia? Does Damia know what Kynton is going to do? If she does, she doesn't seem too worried about it.

Kynton said something and Damia laughed. She was walking close next to him, and even from behind Kendra could tell that she was blushing. *It can't be too terrible if she's still okay with him hanging around.*

"Hello... Kendra!" Aideen waved her hand in front of Kendra's face. "Are you wake?"

Kendra blinked and looked over at Aideen, "Huh? What?"

Aideen smirked, "You weren't responding."

Peri added, "I asked if we should go see Ophelia now. It's almost sunset."

"Oh, yeah," Kendra said, looking to were the sun was starting to disappear behind the buildings.

Up ahead, Damia laughed again. She felt like she was walking on air, after spending the whole day with Kynton. Korinna's warning to her about Kynton was a bit unsettling, but Damia figured that if Kynton was keeping a secret from her, then he had good reason to. It wasn't like he knew everything about her life, either.

And Korinna had also said that the Water Keeper didn't trust him. That was Kendra, if Damia remembered correctly. She wasn't surprised that Kendra didn't trust him. He was a strange man who had rather suddenly latched himself on to the Keepers. They had no way of knowing if he was telling the truth or not. But Damia got the feeling that he wasn't going to do anything to harm them, in fact she had the feeling that he was happier with them than he had been in a very long time.

She felt bad about suddenly appearing in his life, and then disappearing just as quickly. She felt that he wasn't too excited about them leaving him, either. She could tell he wanted to come with them on their journey to find the Amîr Crystal; it was written all over his face. She wondered if it was such a bad idea, for him to come.

It would be useful for them to have someone as knowledgeable as Kynton come along. Damia got the feeling that they weren't going to understand everything they encountered, and it would speed up their trip if they could have their own personal guide book coming along with them. At least, that's what she would say to convince the others to let him come along. Damia had her own reasons why she wanted to keep Kynton close.

"Hey, you two!" Peri called, running to catch up with Kynton and Damia. "Wanna go see what Ophelia has for us?"

Damia's eyes brightened, "Oh, is it sunset already? This day went by so quickly!"

Kynton laughed, "I bet you haven't had this much fun back on Earth."

It took them less than ten minutes to find Clothing by Ophelia. The bell rang again when they opened the door, and they all piled inside. Ophelia looked up from where she was working, hunched over the large sewing table. Her hair, which had been in a neat bun this morning, was now coming apart, with long strands of hair sticking out. There were also many pins sticking into the bun, and on the sleeves of Ophelia's dress. She looked like she had a lot less fun than the Keepers had that day.

She forced a smile when she saw them and straightened up, "Welcome back! You're just in time. I was fixing up the last stitch now."

The four girls walked eagerly over to her, trying to catch a glimpse of their new clothes. Ophelia gathered the pile of clothing up in her arms and said, "Come, you can try them on in the back."

The four followed Ophelia into the back of the shop, leaving Kynton alone for the first time since he had met Damia in the hall of The Dancing Bear that morning. He found a seat near the door to the back, and waited for the five women to come back out. He had the sinking feeling that the Keepers were deciding his fate, now that they were alone without him for the first time.

He had no way of knowing what they were going to decide. He hoped that Damia had gotten attached to him enough to convince the others to let him come along. She was the only real reason why he wanted to go with them anyways. If she didn't want him there, then there was no point in sticking around. He'd go find a cliff and jump; if only that could kill him.

Automatically, his fingers found the piece of string wrapped around his left wrist. He picked at one of the two knots that kept it to his wrist, deep in thought. He was worried that the Keepers were getting suspicious of him. The Seer Korinna hadn't helped his case by looking into his love life, and seeing what had happened eighteen years earlier. Now the Keepers probably thought he was going to kill someone, or worse, them. He knew that Keeper Kendra didn't trust him; she didn't hide her emotions very well.

But he couldn't blame her. He also wondered if it was more than a coincidence that he happened to be at The Dancing Bear at the same time as the Keepers. He wondered if everything he was doing, wanting to stay with the Keepers, falling back in love with Keeper Damia, was all part of the plan. He wouldn't be surprised if it was. The nameless man who had enlisted Kynton's help was a genius; Kynton had no doubt of that. If somehow he knew that the Keepers would go to The Dancing Bear, and sent Kynton there to accidentally bump into them, then Kynton knew that he was supposed to go with them on their journey. The nameless man would want exactly that, and Kynton could not disobey.

Chapter Twenty-Seven

Aideen looked like a fish, as if sucking in her cheeks would help Ophelia fasten the corset around her stomach. She watched as Damia did the same thing for Peri, and Kendra tied up the front of her blouse. It was a strange feeling to see them in these seventeenth century clothes. It was strange to be in these seventeenth century clothes.

Aideen glanced at herself in a mirror. She looked like she belonged in a period movie or renaissance festival. Seeing herself in these eccentric clothes made the fact that they were no longer on Earth even more real. At first she liked the feeling of being in a different place, with new experiences ahead. She had always longed for adventure, and now she had the chance to go on one. It would be a lie to say that she wasn't excited.

But she also wished that she were back in Seattle. As odd as that was for her, Aideen missed her home. She missed her little brother, David and she missed her parents. This was the first time she had done anything truly without them. They weren't remotely close to her; not even in calling distance. She wondered how long it would be before she could see them again. She hoped it would be soon. She wanted to give each of her parents a big hug, and apologize for being mean to them in the past.

"There!" Ophelia exclaimed, and Aideen let out the breath she was holding in. Again, she turned towards the mirror, this time with her cousins standing next to her. They fidgeted with their new costumes, wondering if they could ever get used to wearing them and not their normal jeans.

Aideen was wearing a white long sleeved tunic blouse and black knee length skirt, with a deep red corset over the blouse. Peri also had on a similar blouse, with a navy blue vested, knee length dress over it. Damia was wearing a green skirt similar to Aideen's, and a white blouse with a light brown cumberbund over it. Kendra was wearing a fitted light blue baby doll dress with a white blouse underneath.

Ophelia was radiant, standing behind them. She clasped her hands together and said, "Aha! I told you I could do it! Four dresses in one day! Not even the Keepers, bless their souls, could do that!"

Aideen chuckled, "No, I don't think they could."

"Come! Let's go show your friend," Ophelia said, gesturing towards the door, but not before gathering up their discarded clothes. She gently picked up each pair of denim pants and folded them, aghast at how the girls had just left them on the floor.

"Oh," Damia said and Ophelia paused. Damia continued, "Could you give us a few minutes first?"

Ophelia smiled before walking out to the storefront, with their clothes still in hand. Once she had disappeared, Damia looked at the others and said, "I was thinking...and I figure it would be a good idea if Kynton came with us."

Aideen snorted, "Well we all knew that was coming."

Damia blushed, but said, "I mean that he knows a lot more about Beindor than we do, and we might need that knowledge to get the Amîr Crystal."

Kendra did not like this idea at all. She wanted to be rid of Kynton as soon as possible. Maybe sneak out in the middle of the night if necessary. She was about to disagree when Peri said with a smile, "I think that's a great idea. He could come in handy."

Peri then gave Damia a wink that turned Damia scarlet.

Aideen added, "Plus he's the one with the money. Unless we get a job of some sort, I don't see how we're going to pay for anything."

The three girls then turned to look at Kendra. She knew that her vote was the deciding one, even if she was out numbered. She could say no, and that would be the end of it. If either Peri or Aideen had said no, then Damia would have turned to Kendra for help. She would ask Kendra to defend her. Even though Kendra knew she had this power; that with one word she could get rid of Kynton forever, she just couldn't say it.

If she refused, the look on Damia's face would guilt her into changing her answer. The look on Damia's face now was guilting her into her answer. Kendra could tell that Damia wanted Kynton to come along with them for more than just his knowledge, and frankly, Kendra was repulsed. Was she the only one who remembered that he had to be well over *forty* years old?

But she just couldn't say no. Not only because Damia liked him, but because both Peri and Aideen were backing her. If Kendra said no, then she would be the only reason, and they all would resent her. She would become the odd man out in their group, and if they were possibly going to be spending at least the next year with each other, she did not want to be the odd man out.

Kendra shrugged, "Sure. Why not?"

Damia, knowing very well that Kendra didn't want Kynton to come along with them, threw her arms around her cousins and said, "Thank you so much! You don't know how much this means to me!"

Moments later, the four girls emerged from the back. Damia couldn't hide the smile that seemed to be plastered to her face, and Aideen and Peri exchanged knowing looks. Kendra sulked in the background, fuming at her own incapability to stand up against her cousins.

Kynton smiled when he saw the four of them walk over to him, "Anyone who sees you will think you four were born right here in Beindor."

Ophelia interrupted them, asking, "Will you be needing your old clothing?"

The four girls looked at each other, and Kendra shrugged, "Not really."

Damia added with a smile, "You can keep them. I know how much you want the denim."

Ophelia's eyes got wide as she touched the topmost pair of denim pants, "Oh, thank you very much. I shall make a beautiful gown out of this denim."

Aideen had to hold back a laugh. Ophelia wanted to make a *ball gown* out of *denim.*

"How much do we owe you?" Kynton asked, stepping forward.

Ophelia tore her eyes away from the denim, which she now was holding up in the air. She focused on Kynton, as if he was a new customer. Then she smiled and said, "Four dresses...Four hundred and eighty Denas."

Kynton handed Ophelia eight coins and Ophelia smiled, "It's been a pleasure doing business with you."

She then turned to the four girls and said, "Thank you again, for this denim. It will be put to very good use."

~*~

It only took them ten minutes to get back to The Dancing Bear, and since it was still rather early, Kynton said, "I'm going to have a drink. You're all welcome to join me."

Peri was the first to respond, "That sounds like a great idea. What do you think, Aideen?"

Aideen nodded, but she wasn't looking at anyone standing in front of her. Peri followed her gaze over to a group of men sitting around a table in the corner of the tavern. They were playing cards. Aideen looked back over at her cousins and said, "I'm going to go check out that card game."

She then smiled at Kynton, "Can I borrow a couple of coins? I promise I'll have them back to you."

Kynton agreed and handed a handful of coins over to Aideen, knowing that he didn't have to worry about how much money he had. He had brought his entire fortune along with him, which was much more than the Keepers ever needed to know about. Even after traveling for so long, there was still a huge pile of Denas sitting in his room upstairs. He had a feeling that he might never run out, even if he gave most of his money to Aideen to gamble with.

Peri looked between Aideen, Damia and Kendra, and the table of men playing cards. She wondered if she was the only one who thought Aideen was crazy to approach a group of strange men while they were deep in their game. Forgetting about a drink with Kynton, Peri said, "I think I'll come with you."

The two of them walked over to the card game, leaving Kendra alone with Damia and Kynton. The three stood in silence for a moment. Damia could feel the hatred pulsing off Kendra, and how afraid Kynton was of that. Damia wondered what Kynton was afraid of. Kendra was harmless.

They continued to stand in silence until Kendra suddenly turned on her heel and walked away. Damia and Kynton watched as she walked over to the piano man, and stood next to him, listening to him play. Damia turned to Kynton and said, "Sorry about her. I don't know why she's being so cold."

Kynton shrugged it off, even though Kendra's rude behavior was more troubling than he let on. Keeper Kendra had always been the leader, the most influential of the four women. He knew that if Kendra didn't warm up to him soon, she would start poisoning Damia's mind, even without saying a single word against him. Keeper Damia had always looked up to Keeper Kendra; they all had. Kynton knew that if he wanted to have a successful relationship with Damia, he had to be very careful not to get on Kendra's bad side.

Kynton then said, "I guess it's just you and me, then."

Damia blushed, "I guess so."

Together, they walked over to the bar and sat down. Mahak the bartender quickly walked over to them and asked, "What can I get'cha, tonight?"

"I'll have a pint of your finest," Kynton said. He looked over at Damia, "What would you like?"

"Oh," Damia paused. "I don't drink."

"You don't?" Kynton asked. "Why not?"

"Well, mostly because I'm underage," Damia said.

"Underage?" Kynton asked, not sure what that meant at all.

Damia smiled, "I guess the Keepers didn't like that rule either. It means I'm too young to drink alcohol."

"Too young?" Mahak asked. "I've never heard such a thing. I'll get you something. Don't worry, sweetheart."

"Thank you," Damia said with a small laugh.

Kynton looked down at her, still in shock that she was actually sitting next to him. He couldn't begin to count the number of times he had dreamt of this happening. He had spent twenty years of his life, as short as that is, begging with the Fates to bring her back to him. He had come up with all possibilities of how she could come back, too. They had never actually found their bodies, so that could mean all sorts of things: They had snuck away for a much needed vacation; they had lost all their memories in the fight, and just got up and walked away; they were being held prisoner in Tárquin's fortress...

All of these possibilities had helped Kynton keep his sanity, but as time went on and the Keepers didn't reappear, he knew that he had to accept their fate. They had died and they weren't coming back. Tárquin had won, after all.

But it seemed that the Keepers had one last trick up their sleeves. They had managed to guide their souls into four women who could continue their work. Kynton was at a loss as to why they would do that. Was it just in case Tárquin survived and they didn't? Had

Peri looked into the future and saw that he survived and was grow-ing more and more powerful every day? Kynton didn't know, and he didn't really care. All he knew was that she was back and that he had her all to himself.

Chapter Twenty-Eight

"Come on, please."

"Nope."

"Just one."

"Never."

"For me?"

"Alright."

"Plea-" He stopped, "Really?"

Kendra laughed, even though she couldn't believe she was agreeing to this. She had walked over to the piano man just because she wanted to get away from Kynton. She knew she shouldn't have left Damia alone with him, but she did not want to spend the evening with him. So instead, she walked away. She saw the man playing the piano and came right over to him, to listen to the soft blues number he was playing.

After a moment, he looked up at her and asked, "Do you sing?"

Kendra shrugged, thinking of the all chorus concerts she had been in, "I have."

"I bet you're real good," he said with a smile.

Kendra laughed, "I doubt it."

"Oh, come on. How bout you sing one for us?"

After a few minutes, Kendra gave in. She could feel the butterflies in her stomach as she said yes. She was about to make a complete fool of herself. She had never done more than sing in the back of the chorus concerts. She had never had solos, and she most certainly never sang in front of a crowd of complete strangers. And yet, here she was, about to sing in a completely different world. A world where the only people she knew were the three people she had refused to talk to for the past eleven years.

"Alright," the pianist said with a smirk. "Now we're talking. Pick a song. Just tell me the tempo, little lady, and I'll be playing in no time."

Kendra searched her mind, wondering if there was a certain song that she was really good at. A song that she knew she couldn't make a fool of herself with. Then she thought of a perfect one, and said with a small smile, "Okay, I know just the one."

It took him just a few minutes to get the correct rhythm going. He started the introduction, and Kendra took in a staggered breath. She closed her eyes, and listened to the melody. The song was by one of her favorite blues artists, Michael Bublé. It was perfect, and Kendra hoped she could get through it.

She focused only on the music, letting all other noises fade away. She no longer could hear the clink of glasses on tables, Damia's laughter coming from over at the bar, Aideen's conversation with a group of card playing men in the other corner. She couldn't even hear the soft tap of the pianist's foot. All she heard were the soft notes floating up to her, caressing her.

Then, when she had successfully blocked out all the sounds of The Dancing Bear, she began to sing. She sang about Earth, and how much she missed her family, her house, her boyfriend. She put all the energy she had into the song, as if singing with all her soul would help her return home again. Kendra looked around the tavern as the last notes of the song faded away. Everyone was silent, staring at her, mouths hanging open. She felt the blood rush to her face. *I knew it! I've made a fool out of myself!*

She was about to run away, up the stairs, into her room and not come out again until they left Canhareth for good. Then, the entire tavern came to life. It was filled with noise so loud that it startled Kendra. They were applauding. A small smile broke out across Kendra's lips as she realized that they didn't hate her at all.

The piano man's face turned into a large smile as he said to Kendra, "Whoa. You ever need a job, little girl, you have one. The Dancing Bear. Don't forget."

Kendra laughed and thanked him for the song, before she was surrounded by Aideen, Peri, Damia and Kynton, all of whom were talking at once. Kendra was glowing. She knew she could sing, but she never expected a reaction like that.

~*~

Aideen had spotted what looked like a Texas Hold'em game almost as soon as she walked into The Dancing Bear that night. She had also seen it the previous night, but much bigger things were on her mind then. Tonight, since she had nothing better to do, and her inner gambler was itching to go play, she had walked over to the game.

With Peri following, hoping that Aideen wasn't about to get herself in trouble, Aideen approached the table. She watched from a few feet away, quickly calculating her chances against them as she watched their skills. They were good, but after years of Sunday Texas Hold'em nights with her grandmother, Aideen knew she could beat them.

The first one to notice Aideen and Peri was a boy about their age. He looked up at them and asked, "Can we help you, ladies?"

That was when the other two men looked up as well. The one closest to Aideen and Peri was the oldest, with black hair similar to the boy's, but with grey streaks running through it. He was large, with burley arms and thick fingers. The third man was just slightly younger than the second, with his black hair only sprinkled with grey. He wasn't as heavy set as the other man.

Aideen smiled, "I was wondering if I could join you."

The three men chuckled; obviously no one has ever asked to join in their game before. It was the second man, the one with the thick fingers, who said, "Certainly, if you can keep up."

Aideen smirked, "Oh, I don't think that will be a problem."

The man's eyebrow arched, but the smile did not disappear from his face. He said, "Pull up a chair; we were just about to deal."

Aideen and Peri quickly found chairs, and the three men made room around the table for them. The man with thick fingers held out his hand to Aideen, "My name is Jedrek Faal."

"Clio Morris," Aideen said.

Peri glanced over at Aideen in surprise. Aideen looked back over at her, *Fake names. Our real names are the Keepers names. It won't be long before this entire world knows who we are.*

Peri's mouth dropped. Aideen's mouth hadn't moved, but yet Peri had heard every word she had said.

Aideen's eyebrows knotted together, *What is she gapping at?*

She did it again! Peri thought excitedly, her mind racing to figure out what was going on.

Then it was Aideen's turn to look at Peri in surprise, *Did she just...Was that her thoughts?*

Aideen! Peri thought, *Can you* hear *me?*

Aideen nodded slowly, *What the hell is going on?*

*It must be another one of our powers...*Peri shrugged. *We need to tell the others!*

"Hello?" Jedrek Faal asked, noticing that the two girls were giving each other very strange looks, nodding heads and shrugging shoulders. He wondered if all the lights were on upstairs, if you know what I mean.

Aideen turned back to him and said with a smile, "And this is my cousin, Thalia Andes."

Later, Aideen said, the inner gambler getting more excited. *I want to play first.*

Peri waved hello, and Jedrek Faal introduced the others, still wary of the two girls. Motioning to the older one and then the younger one, he said, "This is my brother, Kegan Faal, and my son, Carr Faal."

Kegan and Carr Faal nodded their hellos and Jedrek said, "Shall we begin?"

"Yeah," Kegan said as he added two coins to the pot, followed by Carr, who was the dealer, then Jedrek put in one more. Aideen said, "I'm checking."

The group looked to Peri, who shook her head, "I'm not playing. Just watching."

Carr nodded and flipped over three cards in front of them. Each player looked at the cards and compared them to their own, thinking about the potential matches they could make. Peri tried to keep up as the games went on, but her understanding of poker was just about as great as her understanding of the giant purple Orsina cat and the fur trade it sparked when it swam to Beindor from Úrdor.

After another round of betting, Kegan folded, choosing instead to watch the game with Peri, but with a little more understanding. He had bought an Orsina fur hat for his wife just the past week. Now the pot contained eighteen wooden coins and Carr flipped over another card. All three of them checked, keeping the pot the same amount and Carr flipped over the last card to be played.

They all judged the cards again and Carr ended up folding his hand. Then it was between Aideen and her new friend, Jedrek. They had increased the pot to twenty-six coins and they flipped over their cards. After the three guys, Aideen and Peri studied the cards; Aideen laughed and pulled the pile of coins in front of her, "Told you I can play."

The three guys looked at each other astounded and yet amused. Jedrek shook his head with a small laugh, "Didn't think you really could. Care for another round?"

"Of course," Aideen said as they started to play all over again.

Peri sat back in her chair with a thud, "I am *so* confused."

The four continued to play, with Peri watching and trying to understand, until a soft voice reached their ears. The voice was almost magikal, luring its listeners closer to it. The three men Peri and Aideen were sitting with turned towards the voice with their eyes wide and their mouths forming small O shapes. Peri and Aideen looked up in surprise, recognizing a small undertone of the voice. They looked over to the source, and saw that is was Kendra singing, even though the voice sounded like it should be coming from a sea siren.

The song she sang was about home, and the lyrics brought tears to both Aideen and Peri's eyes. They recognized the song as Michael Bublé's, but they had never heard it sung with such force and with such passion before. They also sat, entranced by her voice. Then, when the song was over, it was met with silence. Peri, Aideen, and the Faals sitting next to them were not the only ones who had to pull themselves out of the trance Kendra had put them in.

Then, as Aideen and Peri started to look around, the entire pub started applauding Kendra. Both men and women alike where standing, clapping their hands together and demanding encores. Kendra turned an interesting shade of red, and Aideen turned to the Faals, "Excuse us."

They let them go, Aideen with her winnings. She figured that they wouldn't be able to play for a few minutes anyway. They looked like they had just woken up with a hangover. Aideen and Peri rushed to meet Kendra, and Damia and Kynton were right behind them.

"Kendra!" Aideen said. "I didn't know you could sing like that! Why didn't you tell us?"

"Because she's always been too scared," Peri said. "I've seen you in the chorus concerts. You've always had the best voice, but you never had the guts to audition for a solo."

"You knew I was in the chorus?" Kendra said, shocked.

"Are you kidding?" Peri said. "Everyone knew after you stole the show last year."

"Stole the show?" Kendra started, very confused, but Damia interrupted, "That was amazing, Kendra. What a perfect song."

Kendra smiled, "I thought so too."

Kynton didn't agree, but he didn't say so. He was still trying to get on Kendra's good side. So instead of voicing his opinion, he said, "Why don't we get a table? Instead of standing here, blocking traffic?"

The others agreed and they quickly found a table. Aideen counted out fifteen coins, and handed them out to Kynton, "Thanks! Told you I would get them back to you!"

Kynton laughed, "There's no need to pay me back. You need that more than I do."

"Seriously?" Aideen said, her smile growing.

"Yeah," Kynton said. He glanced over at Damia, then Kendra who was giving him a suspicious look. "That is all the money the four of you have. And you'll be needing money when you go on your trip around Beindor."

Chapter Twenty-Nine

Damia looked over at her cousins, figuring now was as good a time as any. Kendra could almost read Damia's mind, and she shrugged, not wanting to be the one to say it. Damia would want to do it anyway. Aideen smiled, while Peri nodded her head enthusiastically. Kynton looked at them, wondering what they were up to. He was about to ask, when Damia said, "Kynton, we've been thinking. We would like you to come with us, on our little quest around Beindor. We could really use your help, since you know so much more about this country than we do. Plus, I -uh, we- think it would just be nice if you came along."

Damia blushed, but Kynton did not seem to notice her mistake. He was too ecstatic to care, anyway. They wanted him to come with them! They needed his help, at least. That was a start. But Kendra had agreed to let him come, that was a good sign. He could warm up to her; she could learn to trust him. Then he would be in the clear with Damia.

Damia.

He turned to face her and a smile spread across his face. He took her hands in his and said, "I would *love* to come with you."

Damia's smile matched Kynton's as she threw her arms around him in a hug. When she pulled away she said, "I'm glad. This is going to be so much fun. I can't wait!"

Kendra had to hold back a groan as she watched the two gush over each other. She had to admit, Kynton was smart. He had picked the easiest of them to pretend to love. Damia was the most naïve out of the four girls, despite being the oldest, and would most likely fall in love with any guy who showed just a little bit of interest in her. If Kynton wanted to infiltrate the Keepers, for whatever ghastly reason, he was doing a magnificent job of it.

"So," Kynton said with a smile. "Since I'm apparently your source of all things Beindor, what would you like to know?"

The four girls looked at each other, wondering where to begin. They had so many questions about Beindor and about Hecate. All day long, they had seen things that they could not begin to explain. They wanted to know more about Denas, about the creatures of Hecate that were not on Earth, and about the ones that they had thought mythical creatures before ever stepping foot on Hecate.

"How could there be mythical creatures like mermaids and dragons here on Hecate, and none on Earth, when humans knew about them long before the Keepers ever discovered Hecate," Kendra asked. She wondered if Kynton could even answer all their questions.

Kynton frowned, "That's a really good question. I don't even think the first Keepers knew the answer."

Kendra sat back, a smug look on her face. The first question and he was already stumped. She wanted to give herself a pat on the back.

Then, Kynton continued, "I don't think anyone ever told them that Hecate was a safe haven for your so-called mythical creatures. They had all resided on Earth, but once humans got it in their minds that they were superior to all others, the mythical creatures had to go into hiding. The humans were hunting them, capturing them and forcing them into servitude. That was when the elf Tlacelel, the dragon Lóng, the mermaid Kalyn, and the faery Dareh decided to create a world hidden from the humans.

"So they put their magik together, and created Hecate. There was only one door in or out of Hecate, and it was invisible to the humans. A crystal, filled with each of their magiks, was created to fuel this door. The Amîr Crystal. First Tlacelel, Lóng, Kalyn and Dareh brought their people into Hecate. They settled the four kingdoms of Beindor: Taurëfor, Imladun, Aearad, and Orodun. Once their people were settled, they opened the door to the other *mythical* creatures. The door remained open for all of those who wished to pass from Earth to Hecate, and back. The creatures of Earth finally had their safe haven, Hecate.

"They lived peacefully for many centuries, without a second thought about humans. They let the humans take over Earth, knowing that they could never find Hecate. Then, one day all that changed. The door opened for four humans, and they passed through into Hecate. Not realizing that Hecate had been created to keep humans away from the creatures that settled it, the four humans brought their own people and created a city not far from where the crystal was kept.

"At first, the creatures of Beindor were outraged. They wanted to slaughter every human that stepped through their door and onto their sacred land. Again Tlacelel, Lóng, Kalyn and Dareh came together to figure out what to do. They called this meeting the Second Meeting of the Council. It was the elf Tlacelel who suggested that maybe there was a reason why these four humans had found the door to Hecate. He wanted to question the four humans, to figure out how they had gotten through.

"The other members of the Council agreed, and the four humans and the rulers of the four kingdoms met. It was obvious immediately to the Council why these four humans had been able to open the door and no others could. There was a magik in these four humans that no other humans could naturally possess. They were the Elementals.

"The Elementals, according to legend, were in essence, the four elements. Air, Water, Fire and Earth. It was common belief that the elements could manifest in four souls, which were called the Elementals. It had never happened before so the legend had turned to myth, but the Council saw that it had happened in their absence.

And that's why the door had appeared for these four. Their bodies were human, but their souls were that of the Elementals."

The smug look that had been on Kendra's face had disappeared. Instead, it matched the look on her cousins' faces. They were stunned. Hecate had been a safe haven from humans, and the Keepers had disregarded that. They had never even bothered to ask why Hecate was in existence. Just like all humans, they saw a new world and had to conquer it.

"So," Peri asked. "What happened to the Keepers and the humans after that? What did they decide to do with them?"

Kynton smiled, "Well, you already know that. The Council let the humans stay in Beindor, under one condition. That they never try to rise up against the others of the country. They must live in harmony, as one of the many species of Hecate, not as the superior one. The Keepers agreed, and the Second Meeting of the Council was ended.

"The Council did do one more things for the Keepers before they returned to their settlement. They gave these four humans, because that's what they were, a way to harness the magik flowing within them. They gave them their magik *powers,* as you call them, according to the element that their soul possessed."

"What happened to the Council?" Aideen asked. "Are they still around today? Maybe we can get their help to get the crystal back."

Kynton frowned, "I know for a fact that King Tlacelel, King Lóng, and Queen Kalyn have passed away. Queen Dareh is another story. She disappeared only a few years after the Keepers died. No one knows what happened to her. The faery race has all but died out in her absence."

"How do you know all this?" Kendra asked, rather suddenly.

Kynton looked at her, "My grandfather told me."

Kendra's eye narrowed. His grandfather? But Kynton had made it out to sound like he had come over to Hecate with the Keepers. He said that his mother was one of the first to accept the Keepers and to help them move the others into Hecate. It didn't fit together. How would his grandfather know things that the Keepers didn't even know? Kendra's mistrust of Kynton grew. He was hiding something, there was no doubt of that now.

"So, tell us what kind of adventures we can expect on our travels around Beindor," Peri said excitedly.

"Well, let's see,' Kynton thought, "We're going to Imladun first, right?"

Damia grabbed her notebook from a small brown canvas bag Kynton had bought for her during the day, and flipped it open to the right page. She nodded, "Imladun, Aearad, Orodun, Taurëfor."

"Imladun..." Kynton thought. "Oh, the Great War. That's what we will find there. The dragons and the dwarves have been fighting with each other for decades. Such a pity, too. They really make magnificent weaponry together."

"Why are they fighting?" Aideen asked.

Kynton shrugged, "It's been going on for so long, I doubt even they know anymore."

The four cousins looked at each other, remembering how just the day before they had been in that same situation. Kynton was oblivious to what he had said, and continued, "Aearad is the merfolk kingdom. They are having troubles as well. Pirates have been killing them and selling their tails. Apparently large fish tails are quite the rage in Nérand."

"Pirates?" Kendra asked, horrified.

Kynton nodded, "The Rámcírya and her crew are the most feared of the pirates down there. Her first captain was killed by the Keepers just a few months before they died."

"What about the captain now?" Damia asked. "Don't you think that he'd learn from the first captain's mistakes?"

Kynton laughed, "Pirates never learn. Besides, he's probably taking it out now on the merfolk, because the first captain was his father."

"That doesn't mean he has the right to harm the merfolk," Kendra said.

Kynton laughed, "Captain Torolf doesn't give a damn about merfolk rights."

The name sent shivers down Damia's back. She looked away, trying not to visualize the captain of those foul pirates killing innocent mermaids and mermen. She wondered what could ever make a man so cruel and so evil. Kendra, on the other hand, wasn't trying to figure out the captain's motives. She was trying to figure out a way that he could be stopped. If she did one thing as a Keeper, it was going to be to stop that Captain Torolf and make sure he is punished for what he has done.

"Anyway," Kynton said. "Where are we going after that?"

"Orodun!" Peri said excitedly.

"Well... there isn't much there except Anwelindo," Kynton said. "That's a test of true love that the Keepers made before Vavia was a city. Actually, Vavia was created around Anwelindo."

"What do you mean by test of true love?" Aideen asked.

"I'm not sure how it works," Kynton said. "I've never been through the door. It won't open for you unless you are trying to prove that you and your lover share true love. I've always wanted to see how to works."

Damia blushed, and said, "Lastly is Taurëfor. The Elvin, right?"

Kynton's fists curled, and he had to look away from the Keepers. When he spoke, his voice was low and it sounded like it hurt to speak, "There is nothing special about the Elvin. They deserted the Keepers in their greatest hour of need. They should all be ashamed of what they have done. They let her die."

Damia put her hand on Kynton's shoulder. She hadn't meant for him to get so upset. As soon as she touched him, he jerked away. "I have to go," he said. He stood up without another word and walked out the tavern door, into the night.

Something else had happened when Damia touched Kynton. She could feel his pain. She understood immediately why he was so upset with the Elvin. She clutched her stomach, as if his pain had become her own. Tears welled up in her eyes. *How could they have betrayed her like this? My own people!* she thought.

Noticing the pain Damia was in; the others demanded to know what was wrong. What was happening to her? "Kynton," Damia gasped. "He's...he's..."

"Well, go after him!" Peri said motioning to the door.

Damia nodded, and quickly followed Kynton out the door. The others looked at each other, very confused at what just happened. As soon as Damia touched Kynton's shoulder, her face twisted into the same look that had been on Kynton's face. It was as if she had felt his emotions just as he had, just by touching him.

Kendra glared at the closed door of the tavern, her arms folded over her chest in detest. "I'll give them five minutes," she said. "Then we're going out after them."

Chapter Thirty

The streets were dark and deserted. Canhareth looked very different at night. There were no traders, no one going about their day-to-day lives. The shops were all closed and Damia could see no friendly faces. She ignored her panicking conscience and ran after Kynton. She couldn't see him, and knew that he was not anywhere close.

She picked a street and turned down it, praying that she would eventually find Kynton, and hopefully not get lost. She was in shock about what she had just felt. One moment she was feeling bad for Kynton, the next she had an overwhelming hatred for her people, the Elvin. She wasn't even an elfe, yet for that split second, she had thought she was. For that split second, she had felt the hatred Kynton felt for his people as her own.

She couldn't believe how blind she had been. Of course Kynton was an elf. It explained everything. He had met Keeper Damia while she was in the Taurëfor Forests, he had known that Hecate had been a safe haven, even when the Keepers didn't. She wondered why he hadn't told her earlier about being an elf. Was he so mad at them that he was ashamed to include himself with them?

So many thoughts were going through Damia's head at that moment, that she didn't notice she had found Kynton. He had stopped at the base of a Willow tree. Damia was thrown off for a second. That Willow tree was the first tree she had seen since coming to Hecate. She looked up at it in wonder. She could tell it was old. Much older than the buildings around it. She figured that it had been part of the original blueprints for Beindor.

Kynton was pacing in front of the Willow. Damia watched as he ran his hand through his curly brown hair. As his fingers combed through his hair, Damia could see the anguish on his face. She realized there was much more to him than he was letting on, and her heart went out to him.

Damia took a few more steps forward and Kynton looked up at her, with a sad smile on his lips. She moved closer, so she and Kynton were almost touching. She gently touched his cheek and said, "There's no reason to be ashamed of who you are."

Kynton looked away. It was obvious he didn't agree, but he didn't push her away. He didn't want to admit it, but at that moment he wasn't ashamed. Just for a split second he was glad that he was an elf, because it had given him this moment with Damia. She would never have touched him otherwise. His heart leapt for a second, but then he remembered why he was ashamed in the first place. "I'm not ashamed of who I am. I'm ashamed of what my people have, and haven't done."

Damia took Kynton's hand in hers, "They did what they could. It wasn't their battle. Tárquin was the Keeper's enemy, not the Elvin's."

"But they could have helped!" Kynton said desperately. "The Keepers might have been saved. They might have lived."

Kynton's shoulders sagged, and Damia quickly wrapped her arms around him in a hug. She wanted nothing more than to comfort him, to make him feel better. A hug wasn't much, but Kynton didn't object. In fact, he wrapped his arms around Damia and held her close to him. Damia smiled and said into Kynton's shoulder, "I don't mean to sound selfish, but if the Keepers had survived, I wouldn't be here."

Kynton laughed, and said, "I think that's the only good thing that has come from this. I've miss you so much, Damia. I'm so glad to have you back."

Damia bit her lip. She realized that he wasn't talking to her. He was talking to Keeper Damia. She ignored it, though. She knew that it was tough for him. He had lost the love of his life, and now here she was, teasing him with an exact replica of that love. She pulled out of the hug and took a hold of his hand again. Without a word, she lead him over to the Willow tree. They sat down, leaning their backs against the trunk. Damia let out a small sigh, feeling the bark against her back. She closed her eyes, inhaling the smells of the ancient Willow tree.

The grip on her hand got tighter and she opened her eyes. Kynton smiled at her and said, "Thank you, for inviting me along with you. It means a lot to me."

"It means a lot to me too," Damia said softly, a soft blush creeping into her cheeks.

"I just wish that I wasn't so much trouble for you," Kynton said, looking away.

"What do you mean?"

He frowned, "I know what the others think of me."

"The others?"

"Kendra," Kynton said, looking up at Damia.

Damia frowned, "Oh."

"I know she doesn't like me," Kynton said.

"That's not true," Damia interrupted quickly. "She doesn't know you, so she's hesitant."

"Do you think you know me?" Kynton asked. "I can't help but think that Kendra's right to be hesitant. There are things about me, about my past that you have no idea about."

"And there are things about me that I have yet to tell you too," Damia said. "We've only known each other for two days, you can't expect us to know all of each other's secrets. And yeah, Kendra's probably the wise one, being hesitant, but that's her role. Not mine."

"Then what is your role?"

Damia shrugged, "I don't know yet."

Kynton smiled, "I know my role."

"Oh, yeah?" Damia asked slowly. "What's that?"

"To fall in love with you," Kynton said, running his fingers down Damia's cheekbone.

Damia blushed some more and looked down, away from Kynton. He ran his fingers under her chin, and she looked back up at him. She felt her heart pounding against the inside of her chest, and she vaguely wondered if her heart would be able to break through her skin, as it seemed to be trying to do. She had never felt such emotion for one person. Sure, she loved her parents, her brother, but the love she had for them was nothing compared to the love she felt at that moment. She wondered if she would ever be able to go back to her normal life after this, after feeling something so strong that she wasn't capable of thinking straight.

The kiss that came next was both so sweet and innocent and yet filled with such passion that Damia thought she had fallen asleep, and was now dreaming of Kynton wrapping his arms around her in a way that made her think he would never let go. She had never expected this to happen, she thought that it had been hopeless when she had left, *when she got married.* But now here she was, kissing the girl of her dreams.

Damia's eyes flew open.

She stopped kissing Kynton and sat up, her mind racing. She had just thought something, something bad. Something that was not her own thought. Damia's hands flew to her mouth; she had been thinking of herself! She had thought she was kissing *herself!*

What is going on? Damia thought, as Kynton opened his eyes, realizing that Damia was no longer in his arms.

First I think I'm an elfe. Now I think I'm kissing myself?

"Damia?" Kynton pulled away, seeing the confusion on her face. "I'm sorry. I should *not* have done that."

"Oh no," Damia said, quickly smiling again. "It's fine. I don't mind, really."

Kynton smiled, "I thought you were going to slap me again."

Damia couldn't recall slapping Kynton. She shrugged it off as a slip of the tongue and laughed, "I would never slap you."

"Promise?"

Damia nodded, and leaned forward.

This time their kiss was interrupted by a very angry cousin.

~*~

Kendra was able to wait about half a minute before she stood up so sharply that her chair fell over backwards. Not even noticing the looks people were giving her, not to mention Peri and Aideen's protests, Kendra stormed out of The Dancing Bear. Peri quickly picked up Kendra's overturned chair before she and Aideen followed her out of the tavern.

"Kendra, wait up!" Aideen said. "You said five minutes! Not thirty seconds!"

"Come on, she can't be too far ahead," Kendra said, quickening her pace.

Aideen sighed and looked over at Peri, "What is wrong with her?"

Peri shrugged, "How should I know?"

Aideen did not like this. Kendra was getting too much into Damia's business with Kynton. It wasn't such a big deal, bringing Kynton along with them. He was going to help them. He was going to be their personal bank and travel guide rolled all into one. And if Damia had a crush on him, then great! At least he won't think he's being used.

Aideen just didn't understand why Kendra hated Kynton so much. Was she not sharing something with the others? Had she figured out that he secretly wanted to kill them, or something? Or was it just Kendra being Kendra, and overreacting when a stranger takes an interest in them. Aideen hoped it wasn't the second one, or else she would have to have a talk with Kendra. *She needs to loosen up,* Aideen thought as she ran to catch up with Kendra.

"Stop it, Kendra!" Aideen said. "Damia can handle herself."

Kendra spun around and looked at Aideen and Peri, "We don't know that. And I don't want to have to find out!"

"What?" Peri asked. "You think Kynton…"

"All I know is that I don't trust Kynton. At all," Kendra said. "I don't think he should be coming along with us, and I don't think that Damia should get involved with him."

"Come on, Kendra," Aideen said. "Kynton knew the first Keepers. He can't be all bad!"

"Exactly! He knew the first Keepers! He met them *before* they became the Keepers! That was over forty years ago! He has to be at least sixty years old! Does that not creep anyone else out as much as it does me?"

Peri and Aideen looked at each other, never thinking about it that way. Peri asked, "Then why does he look so young?"

"I don't know," Kendra said. "But it can't be natural. Or good."

Before either Peri or Aideen could argue, Kendra continued down the road. She didn't really know where she was going, but she knew she had to get to Damia and Kynton before anything bad happened. She would not be happy if she found the two of them kissing or doing anything worse.

Not only did Kendra not trust Kynton, but she knew that any sort of romance would slow them down. How could they focus on the task at hand if they were too busy staring longingly into each other's eyes? And what happens when Kynton breaks Damia's heart? How would that affect the rest of them? Would he stay? Would the rest of their trip be spent in awkward silence? Or worse, what would happen if they stayed together? Would Kynton come back to Earth with them? Or would Damia stay on Hecate with him?

Kendra didn't like either of those ideas. She wanted Damia on Earth and Kynton on Hecate. That's why, when Kendra found the Willow tree, and the couple kissing underneath its branches, she felt her temperature rise.

"Damia!" Kendra yelled, storming over to her and Kynton. "What the hell are you doing?"

Kendra pulled Damia to her feet and said, "Come on, we're going back to the inn."

Damia pulled her arm out of Kendra's grip and demanded, "What was that for?"

Kendra glared at Kynton for a second, before looking at Damia, "It's late. We have to get going early tomorrow. We need to sleep."

Damia knew Kendra was lying. She knew that Kendra hated Kynton. She had figured earlier that Kendra didn't trust him, now she knew that Kendra loathed him. As soon as Kendra had pulled Damia to her feet, Damia knew that there was no hope for Kendra. She was disgusted by the image of Damia and Kynton's kiss, which was now floating around in her head.

Damia glared at Kendra, not understanding why she couldn't just be happy for her. But she also knew that Kendra was right. They did need to get to sleep, since they were starting early in the morning. Damia couldn't argue with that, she was the one who decided on the seven o'clock wake up call.

She nodded and looked at Kynton, "She's right. Seven o'clock is coming up fast."

Kynton agreed, and Kendra was satisfied. She hurriedly walked away, past Peri and Aideen and down the street. Once Kendra was gone, Peri said to Damia and Kynton, "We're sorry. We tried to talk her out of coming to get you. We tried."

Damia smiled, "No problem. She's a hard one to control when she's angry."

"I think that's a family trait," Aideen said before she and Peri turned around and started walking back to The Dancing Bear.

Damia looked up at Kynton, "I'm sorry about that. I guess we under estimated Kendra's hesitance towards you."

Kynton frowned, and despite his best interest said, "Maybe it's not a good idea for me to come along. I don't want to get in between you and your cousins."

Damia pulled Kynton's hands into her own and said, "Kynton, no matter what happens between me and my cousins, you will always be welcome with us. Never forget that. Not because we need your knowledge or your money, but because *I* want you to come."

Kynton smiled down at Damia. Even if Kendra didn't ever like him, he knew that Damia did, and that's all he could ask for. She was willing to put herself on the line, something that she never would have done for him eighteen years ago. He didn't care if this was all planned by the man who had saved him. He knew he never wanted to see him again. He wouldn't help him anymore. He had just what he wanted. He had Damia.

"Thank you, Damia," he said. "Hearing that from you is all I've ever wanted. *You're* all I've ever wanted."

He pulled her into another kiss, and after a moment, he felt her smile. She wrapped her arms around him and put her head on his shoulder. "Come on," she said. "Before Kendra comes back and starts yelling again."

She then took his hand, and together they walked back to The Dancing Bear.

~*~

Kendra stormed up the stairs of The Dancing Bear, not caring who heard her. She stomped over to the door with the number four sketched into it and opened it. Not caring how close behind the others were, she slammed the door behind her. Though she knew she was throwing a tantrum, she couldn't help it. It felt so good to slam doors and stamp her feet. She had wanted to slam a door since the moment she arrived in Beindor.

Kynton and Damia were simply the last straw.

Everything was happening so fast. Twenty-four hours ago, everything was normal. Now they were completely messed up. Ryan had finally asked her out, now she wasn't sure when she was going to see him again. If ever. She had been fine not getting along with her cousins, but now that they were sort of better terms, she knew it was too good to be true. There was no way it would last.

They hadn't been talking for eleven years. *Eleven years.* That isn't something easily forgotten. She knew that once they got back to Earth there would be no reason for them to keep their weak friendship going. It would crumble before their eyes, if it hadn't already. Kendra knew she wasn't doing a very good job at fixing their frail friendship, but she couldn't care less at the moment.

She sat down on the edge of the bed, but could not sit still. She began to pace the room, her fists clenched and her shoulders stiff with anger. Her breaths were coming in short bursts and her eyes were narrowed, focused on the door of the room. She watched as Peri and Aideen entered, both slightly scared of her. She wanted to scream at them, but knew she couldn't. She had to control herself.

She waited for Damia to enter, but after five minutes, she still hadn't shown. With each passing second, Kendra's anger grew more and more. Her fists were clenched so tight that her nails bit into her palms, but she didn't notice. She just stared at the door.

Peri and Aideen floated around the room, trying to steer clear of Kendra and her wrath. Aideen silently wondered if she looked as crazy as Kendra did when she got angry. She knew she had a quick temper, but she rarely got to see the other side of it. If she looked as crazed as Kendra did, she knew exactly why everyone at school was scared of her and her tantrums.

Aideen could feel her anger rising, as she watched Kendra pace. Kendra had no right to be pissed at Damia. So the girl had kissed Kynton? She had found a guy she liked and made a move. *Good for her,* Aideen thought. At least she wasn't sulking around, feeling sorry for herself like the rest of them. Kendra was in a sour mood because they had been thrown into this situation, and she was using Damia as a scapegoat.

Then the door slowly opened, and Kendra paused in her pacing. She crossed her arms and glared at the moving door. Damia slipped inside and immediately found Kendra's glare. Her face flushed and she looked over to Aideen and Peri, who had both taken a seat on the farther of the two beds. Damia closed the door without turning around and opened her mouth to say something, but nothing came out.

Kendra took her chance to pounce.

"What were you thinking, Damia?" she yelled. "Going off alone with him? Do you want to get yourself killed?"

Damia looked at Kendra in shock. "Kynton would never hurt me," she said.

"How do you know that?" Kendra yelled, beginning to pace again. "You can't trust him! You met him *yesterday*! He could be a psycho serial killer who lied about the Keepers!"

"He didn't-"

Kendra cut Damia off. It was obvious she wasn't going to listen to reason. "*How do you know?* He could be working with Tárquin! He could have been sent here to *kill* us!"

Damia's mouth fell open in shock. She had known Kendra didn't like Kynton, but she had never suspected this. Damia had thought Kendra just didn't trust him. She didn't know she feared him.

"You're overreacting," Damia said gently. "I talked to Kynton. He wasn't telling us everything, yes. But he isn't a killer. He's an elf."

The other three looked at Damia in shock. They hadn't figured it out like she had. They were completely floored by what she said. Peri gave a half laugh, "Well that explains why he doesn't look forty years old."

Kendra looked over her shoulder at Peri, then back at Damia. Her anger was nowhere near diminished because of this news. "Just because he's an elf doesn't mean he can be trusted. I have a bad feeling about him. Something isn't right."

"Just because your guy got left behind and Damia found one here doesn't mean he's evil," Aideen said.

Kendra spun around to face Aideen, "What?"

Aideen stood up, "You heard me. Just because your precious *Ryan* isn't here doesn't mean we can't have a little fun."

"This isn't about Ryan," Kendra said. "I just don't think it's a good idea to go falling in love with anyone here. We can't get attached. We get the crystal and leave. Nothing more."

"Oh, so you hated exploring the city today? Was that being too attached? Because you seemed to be enjoying yourself. And don't forget when you serenaded all those men downstairs. That seemed to be a little more than just getting the crystal and leaving."

"I didn't serenade-" Kendra started.

"You're such a hypocrite, Kendra!" Aideen yelled. "You don't want Damia to fall in love, but you can't stop thinking about your boyfriend! You don't want anyone to have fun, but you go and play karaoke in front of tons of strangers!"

Fire.

It was her name, so none of them should have been caught off guard by what happened next. But they were. Once it was over, Peri and Damia saw that they were the only ones left standing. Both Aideen and Kendra were on the floor. Unmoving. Not breathing.

Chapter Thirty-One

The room filled with heat, making it seem more like a sauna than a hotel room. But the heat did not bother any of the four who were in it. They weren't concerned with the sweltering temperatures, they were too wrapped up in the conversation to notice. Damia was the first to notice the abnormally high spike in Aideen's rage. One second it was just barely tolerable, the next, Damia was seeing white flashes, as if Aideen's anger was her own. She gripped the door behind her, afraid she might even lash out.

Aideen noticed it next because suddenly she could see nothing but fire. She felt the flames too. She felt their heat as they moved away from her body. She wondered for a second if there was a fire behind her, and it was blowing past her. But that didn't make sense, because there was no wind, and she felt no heat on her back. She saw the flames touch her skin, but it did not hurt. It felt like a cool breath, blowing gently on her. Then the fire consumed her body and she felt herself drop to the floor. After that, she saw nothing but the backs of her eyelids.

Peri let out a scream as she watched from the sidelines. She hadn't made a sound since Aideen and Kendra started yelling. Then, all of a sudden, there was a wall of fire between Aideen and Kendra. It seemed to push away from Aideen, heading straight for Kendra. Peri had no idea where it had come from, but she knew where it was going, and there was no way of stopping it.

It didn't stop, and the last thing Kendra saw was the fire. She had been listening to Aideen yell, with her fists clenched and her jaw tight when suddenly she was watching her death. She barely had time to register what had happened before it hit her. She felt the scorching heat seconds before the impact. She felt her skin blister and her hair burn. She felt her face melt right off the bone, the muscle burn into ashes.

She fell to the ground, the impact of the blast sending her over backwards. She felt the back of her head hit the ground, and the heat give way to a sudden coolness. She held her breath, wondering when the pain would come. She knew it would, she had felt her skin char. That would be enough pain to kill her.

But the pain never came.

Instead of feeling like she walked through a forest fire, she felt as if she had jumped into the ocean. She could feel the cool water run over her body. She felt like her entire body was being gently messaged by the waves of the ocean. She was floating along, just letting the tides take her wherever they wanted.

Then a hand suddenly plunged into the water and brought Kendra to the surface. She gasped for breath, and opened her eyes. Disorientated, she looked around. She was nowhere near an ocean, or any other body of water. In fact, she had never left The Dancing Bear. She had never left her room.

Damia was kneeling next to her, her eyes wide in shock. Her hand was on Kendra's shoulder, and she said, "Kendra! How did you-? You were dead two seconds ago!"

"What?" Kendra said. She didn't feel dead. In fact, she felt much better than she had in a while, besides a slight headache.

Damia had tears running down her face. "I saw it!" she said. "You were hit by a wall of *fire!* You were beyond recovery. I swear..." she paused. "Your face was gone. All I could see was bone."

Kendra frowned. She would have argued with such nonsense, except she had felt what Damia was describing. She had felt her face melt away, so how could she still be alive? And in one piece?

Damia was crying still, "Kendra, I thought you were dead. And the last thing we did was argue. I don't want that to ever be the case again. Please, I don't want to argue with you anymore. Can we just agree to disagree, and move on?"

Kendra sat up, about to respond when she noticed that she was soaking wet. Damia seemed to notice just then too, and asked, "How did that happen? You look like you just jumped into a swimming pool."

Kendra felt her hair, which was also dripping wet. She thought about the moments after she had been on fire, and how she had been floating in the ocean. She wondered if that had anything to do with why she was soaked now. She told Damia of these thoughts, and Damia said, "But that doesn't explain why there isn't a scratch on you."

At that moment the two girls heard a groan from across the room. They watched as Aideen sat up, obviously dazed. Peri was kneeling next to her, and said to her, "Are you okay?"

"What happened?" Aideen asked, holding a hand to the side of her head. She had a pounding headache, and she felt like she had been asleep for a month. All she could remember was being really mad. That, and fire. She had no idea why she remembered there being fire. The lantern in the room wasn't even lit.

"I think," Peri started, then hesitated. She looked over to Kendra and Damia, who were watching. "I think you set Kendra on fire."

"What?" Both Aideen and Kendra demanded.

Peri grimaced, "That's what it looked like to me. One minute Aideen, you're yelling at Kendra, the next she's on fire. What else could it have been?"

"How could I have set her on fire?" Aideen asked. "Sorry, but I left my Zippo at home."

"Aideen was the Keeper of Fire, right?" Damia asked.

Aideen's lips pursed together, "Are you saying I can just make fire appear, whenever I want?"

Damia shrugged, "It makes sense."

Kendra then asked, "But why didn't I die? I felt the fire on me."

"Maybe our powers don't work on each other?" Peri suggested.

Kendra rung out her hair, which was beginning to dry. "Then why I am soaking wet?"

"Well, you're the Keeper of Water," Damia said. "It could have healed your burns."

"Wait!" Peri said. She smiled, excited as she remembered something. "You're the Healer!"

"What?" Kendra asked, having no idea what Peri was talking about.

"Remember what Korinna said? One of us is a Seer, a Healer, an Empath and a Traveler. I'm the Seer and Kendra, you're the Healer!"

"It's a possibility," Kendra said, not sold on the idea. She thought back to how she had cut herself at the birthday party, when Ryan guided her right into a table. She still had the Band-AIDs to prove it. She looked down at her knee, where the bandage was. She slowly peeled it away, and gasped at what she saw underneath. Smooth, healthy skin. There was no bruise, no cut, no scab. It was as if it had never happened.

"But how come I didn't heal right away?" Kendra asked.

"Well, we weren't in Beindor yet. We didn't have any powers yet," Aideen said.

"But I had my first vision on Earth," Peri said. "I had my power then."

"Maybe our powers are growing. They started with Peri's visions, and as we go along, the more powers we'll have," Damia said.

"So my fire was like a growth spurt?" Aideen asked.

"And my healing was my body's defense against it," Kendra said.

Aideen bit her lip, "Sorry, Kendra. I didn't mean to hurt you."

"Good thing it was me you decided to point your uncontroll-able powers at," Kendra snapped. "If it was Damia or Peri, they wouldn't be so lucky."

"I wonder if you could heal us, though," Peri said.

"What?" Kendra asked.

Peri shrugged, and moved to sit down on the edge of one of the beds. "You're a Healer," she said. "I think you might be able to heal anyone."

"Well, I'd rather not test it out," Kendra said, standing up. "I think we've had enough excitement for the night."

Kendra moved past Damia, remembering again that she was mad. Damia saw this, and frowned. She stood as well, without saying anything to Kendra. She hoped that Kendra hadn't heard her when she suggested a truce, and that she could offer again in the morning.

Aideen saw the hurt in Damia's face and said to her, changing the subject, "So what do you think? You're an Empath or a Traveler?"

Damia thought about it and said, "I have no idea what those mean."

Aideen smirked, "Hmm...well I suppose an Empath makes paths... and a Traveler travels places."

Peri rolled her eyes, "That was so insightful, Aideen."

Aideen looked at her and shrugged, "What else can they do? A Seer sees and a Healer heals, right?"

Damia thought about what Aideen said. She wondered if she was the Empath or the Traveler. She had no idea what a Traveler was. Could she travel places instantly? She found that idea unlikely. She thought about an Empath, and what they might do as well. As she thought of the abilities of an Empath, Damia realized she knew exactly what an Empath did, for she had done it plenty of times since coming to Beindor.

"An Empath can feel another person's emotions as their own," Damia said.

The others looked at her, surprised. Aideen asked, "How do you know?"

Peri smiled, "Do you think you're an Empath?"

Damia nodded, "I think I've been an Empath for a while, actually. I never noticed it, it just sort of happened."

"How can you tell?" Aideen asked.

"Well, for one, I felt your anger right before you're little growth spurt," Damia said. "I felt it as my own. As if I was the one about to combust."

"Well, you were angry at Kendra too, right?" Peri asked. "Could it just have been your own anger?"

Damia nodded, "But I've never felt anger like that before. That was nothing I could come up with on my own."

"Hmm…" Aideen said. "I guess that means I'm the Traveler. I wonder what my special ability is."

"We already know *that* one," Kendra said, starting to pull down the covers on her bed. "But like I said before, I think it's time for bed."

Since when did you take charge?

Kendra straightened up and turned to look at Aideen, "Excuse me?"

Peri and Damia glanced at each other. Damia hadn't seen Aideen speak, but she had heard her. Peri, on the other hand, had glanced at Aideen just in time to see that her lips only moved into a frown as she spoke. She instantly remembered what had happened in the tavern, during the poker game. She tried to interrupt, but Aideen and Kendra ignored her.

"What?" Aideen asked, moving over to the other side of the bed she shared with Kendra.

"You know what," Kendra said, putting her hands on her hips. "I can't believe you just said that."

Aideen raised an eyebrow, "I didn't say anything."

"Yeah. You did," Kendra said. "You said, 'Since when did you take charge?'"

Aideen laughed, "I didn't-" her face then fell and said, "Oh my god. We completely forgot."

"What?" Kendra asked, glaring at Aideen.

"When we were downstairs," Peri said, stepping in, "Aideen and I discovered another one of our powers."

"And you decide to mention this *now?*" Kendra asked.

"We can hear each other's thoughts," Peri explained.

Both Kendra and Damia stared at the other two, trying to comprehend what that meant. Kendra looked at Aideen, "So you just thought that about me? You didn't say it?"

Aideen shook her head, "I would never say something like that out loud."

"I appreciate that," Kendra said, glaring at her. She silently lay down and closed her eyes. She pulled the covers up to her neck and opened her eyes again, "And I did not take charge. Good night."

She then quickly reached over and put out the lamp that was sitting next to her on the table, leaving the others standing in the dark. The others silently got into bed, hoping that Kendra would be in a better mood in the morning. She wasn't. But instead of lashing out at the others, she stayed quiet. She silently watched the others, knowing that her behavior wasn't helping, but she also knew that she couldn't help it. She was angry, and her anger wasn't something she easily forgot.

When Kynton met up with the girls in the morning, he pulled Damia aside and asked, "How did it go with the others last night? Is everything back to normal?"

Damia shook her head, "No. Kendra is still pretty angry. She hasn't said a word to me yet today. I doubt she's going to."

"So did she explode last night on you?" he asked.

Damia couldn't help but laugh at his choice of words. "Kendra wasn't the one who exploded. Aideen was."

Kynton waited for her to explain.

"Let's just say we are coming into our powers very quickly," Damia said.

Kynton's eyes widened as he realized what she meant. He quickly looked her over, asking, "Are you okay? Did you get hurt?"

Damia shook her head, but said with a smile, "No. Thankfully, Aideen's rage wasn't aimed at me last night. Kendra, however, wasn't as lucky."

As if she had heard her name, Kendra suddenly appeared and said her first words to Damia of the day. "Let's get a move on. We don't want to be in Beindor any longer than we have to, remember?"

Kendra gave Kynton the once over before disappearing again. Damia smiled apologetically to Kynton before taking his hand and following Kendra down the stairs and into the main area of The Dancing Bear. Peri and Aideen were waiting for them by the door, and the five of them headed out into the morning air.

"I sure am going to miss the city," Peri said as they walked along.

"Don't tell me," Aideen said. "The countryside isn't your thing?"

Peri shook her head, "I'm pretty much allergic to the countryside."

Aideen smirked, "I think I'm going to have fun with this."

Peri looked at her sideways, "Why do I have the feeling I am going to regret ever telling you that?"

Aideen shrugged innocently, "I dunno."

Up ahead, Kendra trudged on silently. She refused to look back at the others, still hurt about what had happened the night before. Against her better judgment, she kept silent. She knew that these were the few people she would be spending who knows how long with, and she wasn't letting things get off to a very good start.

Well maybe Damia shouldn't have dragged along the first guy she saw, Kendra thought bitterly. *Then we would have been blissfully unaware of Aideen's newfound ability.*

Damia and Kynton followed behind Peri and Aideen, wisely keeping a distance from the still seething Kendra. They walked hand in hand, talking in low whispers that could not be overheard. They did not want to give Kendra any more reason to snap at them.

The group was walking down one of the many streets they had explored the day before, when Aideen recognized it as a street more important than the others. It was the one Korrina's Magikal Shoppe was on. A grin found its way between her nose and chin and stuck there. She turned to Peri first, "Come on, we should go see if Korinna will give us another reading. Yesterday was *fun.*"

"If I remember correctly," Peri said, "Korinna kicked us out."

Aideen's grin did a twist, and turned into a frown. She looked over at Damia and Kynton, who had joined in their conversation, and said, "No, she kicked *him* out yesterday. The four of us can go in, and he can wait outside."

Damia protested, "That's not fair. How would you feel if we left you outside?"

Aideen replied, "Oh don't you bring our powers into this. I feel bad enough as it is for setting Kendra on fire."

Damia was about to respond when Kendra cut in, "We're trying to leave, remember? Stopping by Korinna's doesn't improve on this plan."

"It'll just be a minute," Aideen said. She turned to Kynton, "You don't mind waiting outside for a minute, do you?"

Kynton shook his head. Damia was about to argue, but he said, "It's fine, I don't care. Really."

Damia frowned, but didn't protest. She wanted to go see Korinna just as much as both Peri and Aideen did. Kendra shook her head, "We shouldn't do this. We should leave before we end up spending the week here."

Aideen smirked, "It'll just be a minute. You can come in with us...or you can wait out here with Kynton. It's your choice."

"I'm coming in," Kendra said without looking over at Kynton.

That was probably a good thing too, because Kynton couldn't control his eyes as they rolled around in their sockets. Damia smiled up at him, understanding exactly what he was feeling. He squeezed her hand and kissed her quickly, "Don't worry about me. I'm fine out here."

He leaned against the wall next to the shop and watched as the four girls went inside. Once they disappeared inside, he leaned his head back and closed his eyes. Beneath his lids he could see exactly what the future held for him. He was going to convince Damia to stay, and they would spend the next eternity together. They would get a house somewhere, maybe build one in Taurëfor, and have at least five kids together. They would be able to escape the responsibilities of the world. Escape into their haven of a cottage, and live happily ever after.

Kynton almost laughed at how childish and impossible that all sounded. There was no way Keeper Damia Neimann would be able to escape her duties, her responsibility to the humans and to her cousins. There was no way Kynton would be able to escape his destiny either. Ever since his sister had run away and gotten herself killed by a pirate, Kynton was now the one the family counted on. Not to mention the impending doom that was lurking around the corner. He wasn't really sure how he was going to bring that one to the Keepers' attention. They were all blissfully ignorant of the evil they were about to face.

Kynton, however, was not as ignorant as he would like to be on that subject. From the moment he saw the four Keepers standing right next to him in The Dancing Bear he knew exactly what was going on. It was no coincidence that *he* had sent Kynton there, where the Keepers just happened to show up. *He* had a plan; the first problem was that Kynton had no idea what that plan was. He only knew it involved the Keepers and the Amir Crystal.

The second problem was that Kynton wasn't sure he wanted to tell the Keepers. He felt bad for them, just starting off in a strange world. The last thing they needed was to hear that their archnemesis was back, and most likely exploiting them at that very moment. They barely recognized the power the Keepers held, barely understood the influence they had over everyone else in Hecate. How could Kynton expect them to comprehend the fact that their lives were in so much danger? Two days earlier they were nobodies; today they were the biggest celebrities, biggest political figures Hecate had seen since it was created. Of course, there would be danger.

He realized he didn't want to be the one to burst their bubble. He didn't want to be the one to tell them. He knew very well how they would react, how they would take it out on the messenger. Besides, with the mood Kendra was in now, he would most likely be kicked out to the curb. She wouldn't want him coming with them, and the others probably wouldn't either. He doubted even Damia could understand what he was going through.

~*~

The four cousins stepped into Korinna's Magikal Shoppe, and saw that nothing had changed since they were there the day earlier. Even the dust on the shelves and everything on them had stayed the same. It seemed that Korinna had more important things to do than clean.

It only took Korinna thirty seconds to appear, a smile spread wide across her face. Today her hair was a beautiful shade of midnight blue. "Welcome back, Keepers. I'm glad to see that I did not scare you away yesterday."

Aideen smirked, "We decided to leave him outside this time."

Korinna nodded, "Good idea. Now, what can I do for you today?"

The four girls looked at each other, not really knowing what they wanted. "Honestly," Peri said, "We just wanted to stop in."

Korinna nodded, "Then I know exactly what I can do for you. How would you like to look into your pasts? Into the lives of the first Keepers?"

"You can do that?" Damia asked excitedly.

"As I said yesterday, I know how to do all sorts of things," Korinna said.

Kendra frowned, "Will this take longer than ten minutes?"

Korinna looked at her, "It will take as long as you want it to."

Kendra nodded, "Okay then, let's do this."

Korinna smiled and ushered them into the back room, just like she had the day before. They sat around the little round table again, and this time Korinna said, lighting a white candle, "Close your eyes. Relax."

The four did as they were told, and Korinna began chanting. The girls listened closely to her words, until Korinna's voice got quieter, distant. Then her voice disappeared all together. They sat in silence for a moment, the words of Korinna's chant filling the voids of their minds. Suddenly her voice came from within their consciousness. It said in a soft whisper, "Open your eyes."

Chapter Thirty-Two

Kendra opened her eyes, just as Korinna said to do, but found that Korinna was nowhere to be found. In fact, neither were her cousins. Kendra was alone, alone for the first time in two days. She wondered where the others were, and why they had been separated. They were supposed to be seeing back into the Keepers lives, so why weren't the others with her?

Kendra heard voices shouting down the hall. She started to walk forward, but when nothing happened, she realized she wasn't standing. She was floating. She looked around, and realized she was submerged completely underwater. She touched her fingers to her lips, having no trouble breathing at all.

Her mind began to race, wondering how it was possible. It wasn't, and Kendra knew that. It was physically impossible for a human to breathe underwater, and even more impossible for people to be shouting so clearly. It was as if they weren't underwater at all, or as if being underwater came naturally. Then it hit Kendra, it was merfolk she could hear shouting. She swam quickly toward the voices, but soon realized that they were coming at her as well.

Before she could hide from the merfolk, they rounded the corner and started swimming down the hall. Kendra froze when she saw who it was coming at her. It was herself. For a moment Kendra thought she was looking right into a mirror, but then she realized that the woman in front of her was very different from herself.

True, they had the same basic features. The same eye color and the same shaped lips, but everything else was different. There were lines around this woman's mouth that only age could create, and the short bob of hair was exactly the opposite of Kendra's shoulder length locks, even in its graying color.

"What else could you *possibly* say to me?"

Kendra looked at the older version of herself in shock. It had been her own voice coming from the woman's lips, just aged a few years. Kendra was so startled that she gasped. Quickly she covered her mouth, fearing that they could hear her. They had overlooked her, but it was possible that that had just been a lucky break for Kendra. They were bound to notice her eventually.

But Keeper Kendra and the merman she was with did not notice her. They were too wrapped up in their conversation to notice that they had an audience. Kendra wondered, as she watched them, if they could even see her at all. She was there to watch, maybe that was all she could do.

The merman, with a tail maroon in color, was obviously chasing after Keeper Kendra. When she turned on him, he paused and looked at her with begging eyes. It was obvious to Kendra that these two had a long and complicated history together. But it was also obvious that, at least at that moment, it was not working out.

The merman found his voice, and reaching out to take Keeper Kendra's hand, said, "Kendra, I'm sor-"

Keeper Kendra cut him off, pulling her hand out of his reach, "Don't you dare. You are never sorry, and *yes*, you did mean to say those things. You don't ever say anything you don't mean, remember? Do you think I would forget that? Stop pretending you feel bad for me, and just *go away.*"

"Kendra," he started again.

"Rajan," she said, her ice-cold voice melting. Kendra could tell she was hurt. This merman had hurt her. She continued, "*Please.*"

Rajan's eyebrows knotted, but he did not say another thing. Keeper Kendra frowned and moved closer to him. "I wish we didn't have to end this way, I really do. You have to understand why I'm doing this. This is so much more than you and me. I am doing this to save my people, to save your people. Could you honestly tell me you wouldn't do the same thing?"

"You know I would," Rajan said, taking Keeper Kendra's face in his hands. "But that doesn't mean I can't be selfish."

Keeper Kendra smiled, but it did not reach her eyes. "Don't make this harder on yourself."

"It's too late for that," Rajan said just before he pulled Keeper Kendra to him. Kendra had to look away as they shared one last, very passionate kiss. She felt terrible spying on their last moments together, for she realized just when she had popped in on them. Keeper Kendra was about to go and stop Tárquin, and she was going to die in the process. She would never see Rajan, her lover, again. Kendra also realized that both of them knew this.

Keeper Kendra pulled away first and said, tears choking her voice, "I love you, Rajan. I always will."

"I love you too, Kendra. I always have," was Rajan's response.

Keeper Kendra, after one last kiss, swam away. Kendra and Rajan watched her go. Kendra looked at Rajan, and saw that he was now debating whether he should follow Keeper Kendra or not. It wasn't long before he decided he should. Kendra followed at his heels, not surprised at how fast he could swim.

She followed him out of the palace they had been in, and followed him out into the city. As Kendra looked around, she realized that she was in Aearad, the underwater kingdom of the merfolk. She wanted to get a better look at the city, but knew she couldn't lose Rajan. He led her straight through the city, and suddenly she found herself swimming across a great underwater desert.

At the other end of the large desert was a large rock wall. Kendra could only assume that that was Beindor, and the port city of Nérand. Rajan moved quicker now, with no buildings or other merpeople blocking his way to Keeper Kendra. Kendra looked ahead and saw how far away Keeper Kendra was.

Kendra watched as her counterpart swam up to the surface and disappeared. Rajan moved even faster as he saw that Keeper

Kendra had made it to land. Kendra tried to keep up with him, but she quickly realized that he was a much more powerful swimmer than she was, even though she had been on her high school's swim team all four years of high school. She watched as Rajan swam away from her, and she felt her heart go out for him.

Rajan loved Keeper Kendra, that was obvious. He loved her more than he had loved anything else in the world. Kendra wondered what happened to him once Kendra died. She wondered if he was still in Aearad, and if she could meet him. Perhaps he could tell her of Keeper Kendra and of how her life had been before Tárquin had destroyed it.

Kendra broke the surface when she could no longer see Rajan. She was surprised to see how close to the port city she actually was. She could see the people bustling down the waterfront, going about their daily lives. Ships were moving in and out of port, there seemed to be a hundred of them. Kendra looked at the closest one, which was moving away from the city, in awe. It looked like an old military ship of England, one made in the 1600s. The side of the ship was covered in windows for cannons and the huge masts were over thirty feet tall.

Kendra tore her gaze away from this magnificent ship and looked back to the city. Almost immediately, she found Keeper Kendra, moving through the parting crowds. Kendra was astonished to even see some people dropping to their knees before her. Keeper Kendra didn't seem to notice, though. She was running as fast as she could, trying to get away from her city.

There was shouting coming from behind Keeper Kendra, and Kendra looked to see Rajan chasing after her. The crowds didn't part for him, they were too busy looking after the Keeper. He pushed his way as far as he could, but he quickly lost pace with Keeper Kendra. Kendra looked back to where she had been moments before, only to see the city people staring after her in wonder. Kendra searched the heads for the Keeper's, but could not find it. Rajan paused, also having lost her.

Kendra watched as his shoulders sunk, his body almost folding on itself in defeat. He looked up and out at Kendra, doggie paddling in the water. She ducked down so only her eyes were above water, but then realized he could not see her. He was looking out at the water, not at her. She watched as he turned down a dock, only to pause at the end of the wooden platform. He raised his hands over his head and dove into the water.

Kendra ducked underwater and quickly found Rajan swimming towards her. His human feet had changed back into his maroon tail, and he swam deeper and deeper below the surface. She watched as he swam right underneath her, and that's when she started swimming after him. She knew she was supposed to be following Keeper Kendra and her life, but she was drawn to this merman. She had to see what happened next to him.

A shadow crossed over Kendra and she looked up. It was a ship. The ship she had seen earlier, she guessed. It was moving fast overhead, straight over Aearad. Suddenly Kendra heard something moving fast through the water. She thought of a torpedo, but then realized there couldn't be any such thing on Hecate.

She was about to turn around, to find the source of the strange noise, when she felt a strange tug at her chest. She looked down and saw that something was sticking out of her. She saw it was a rope, and it was moving. She followed the rope and saw that there was a harpoon attached to the long rope, still moving fast, as if it had never pierced Kendra. She then felt something she had not expected at all. Nothing.

She felt no pain where the harpoon had torn through her. It was as if no harpoon had touched her. Then she realized that it hadn't. To this world, she was just a ghost. Just like Keeper Kendra and Rajan could not see her in the hallway, the harpoon could not hurt her.

A chilling scream rippled its way through the water and Kendra looked down to the source, to Rajan. He was no longer swimming; instead, he was floating down to the ocean floor. To Kendra's horror, she realized that the harpoon that had passed right through her had been aimed for Rajan. It did not miss its target.

Kendra screamed, but no one could possibly hear her. She swam as fast as she could, but by the time she reached Rajan, he had hit the sandy bottom of Aearad, sending up a cloud of dust around him. She reached out to touch his face, and her fingers passed right through. She watched helplessly as Rajan's eyes fluttered closed.

"It's okay," Kendra said, feeling the prickling of tears forming, though none could be seen. "Someone will find you, and then you can go after Keeper Kendra and find her before she gets to Tárquin. You can tell her you love her and you two can live long and happy lives. It's going to be alright."

But Kendra knew it was not going to be alright. She already knew the ending of this story. Keeper Kendra would not live to see the end of the year, and by the look of Rajan, he was not going to see the end of the day. He would never say 'I love you,' to Keeper Kendra again, and they would not have long and happy lives together.

Kendra was ready to turn away, to go back to the present and forget all of what she had just seen. She made a move to leave, when Rajan's hand flew out and wrapped around her wrist. Kendra froze, knowing that it was impossible for him to do that. She wasn't really there, and just like the harpoon and her fingers, he should have passed right through her. Then Rajan's eyes opened and he looked right at Kendra. He gave her a weak smile and said, "I love you so much, Kendra. Please forgive me, for all the things I have done to you. Please remember me."

"Of course I will," Kendra said, still confused at how Rajan could see her.

"I love you," he said again, his eyes closing.

"I love you too," Kendra said, not knowing what else to say.

Rajan smiled at her words. Suddenly the two of them were not alone, as a large group of merpeople rushed around Rajan. The first to get to him was a mermaid who looked to be in her mid-twenties. She threw herself over Rajan and Kendra watched as she sobbed into his shoulder. The mermaid looked up at Rajan and said, "Brother! Don't worry; you're going to be okay."

Kendra could tell that this mermaid, Rajan's sister, did not believe her own words. That is, until Rajan's eyes fluttered open. "Kali?" he asked.

"Yes," the mermaid said. "I am here."

He wrapped his arms around his sister and said, "Tell her-tell Kendra that I love her. And that I'm sorry. Tell Father, and Ne-"

"You can tell them, yourself," Kali said, realizing that Rajan knew that he was not going to make it.

Rajan shook his head, and said to her, "I love you, Kali. I am so proud of you. You will make a great Queen."

Kali shook her head, her throat tightening. "No, Rajan. You will be King, just like you were meant to be."

Rajan smiled sadly at her, and said, "I'm afraid my destiny lies somewhere else."

Kali buried her face in her brother's shoulder and said, "I love you too, Rajan."

Kendra watched in horror as Rajan's eyes closed for the last time, but not before he looked right at her. Kendra took a step back, and watched helplessly as other merfolk rushed around the dead prince's body. Before they could start to mourn his passing, his body gave a sudden jerk. For a split second, Kendra hoped that he had come back to life. That he would get up and laugh at what a scene he had created.

Then Kali let out a horrified scream, and Kendra realized that Rajan was not moving on his own. The rope that the harpoon was tied to had gone taut, and was beginning to move backwards, back towards the ship that had sent it out. Kendra wondered if they realized whom they had just killed, and then a more chilling thought crossed her mind. She wondered if that ship knew exactly whom it had killed, and that they had killed him on purpose. She wondered if that ship that she had marveled at earlier was exactly the same ship that she had sworn to take down. If the Rámcírya had killed Prince Rajan.

Kendra watched as Kali and other merfolk struggled with the harpoon head. Soon, though, they were able to remove it and watched as the rope pulled the rest of the harpoon out of Rajan's body. Blood floated into the water and a merman standing near to Kali said, "We'd better get his highness' body out of the open. Before sharks come."

Kali nodded, but she didn't seem to realize what she had been nodding to. She was watching the retreating line that was the harpoon and rope that had killed her brother. She glared after it with a look of vengeance Kendra recognized; she had often it displayed herself. She hoped she would be able to meet this Kali, and that she would be able to help Kendra stop the pirates who had killed Rajan. Kendra knew that not much else would be occupying Kali's mind. Kendra watched as the merman who had spoken turned toward the body. He bent down to lift it up, and other merfolk around them helped. Together they swam back to the city, leaving Kali alone with Kendra.

Kendra watched Kali until the Princess turned away from her and followed after the group that had taken her brother. Kendra floated down to the sand, close to the spot where Rajan had fallen.

She turned away from the receding merfolk, and looked out at the underbelly of the Rámcírya. She wondered if Captain Torolf was on it now, realizing that his catch had been released.

She wanted to see him. She wanted to see the man she would destroy. She wanted to be able to recognize him the next time she was in Aearad. She wanted to know without a doubt who she was going to take down. She swam faster than she ever had before, and reached the ship in record time.

She broke the surface near the side of the ship. Keeping her head low in the water, she searched for a way onto the ship. Then she spotted a foothold carved into the side of the massive beast. She looked up the rest of the ship and realized that there were footholds similar to this one up to the top of the ship. She quickly swam over to them and started climbing.

It took her almost ten minutes to climb the side of the ship, despite the waves crashing up against her and the wind blowing madly around her. At first, she hesitated, wondering if someone would spot her. But then she realized that no one could see her and she climbed over the side. She found herself standing on the Rámcírya, unseen and unnoticed.

As she watched the men hustling around her, she noticed that they were all in a frenzy. They were running around, not entirely sure what to do. Kendra searched their faces, not caring about the crew. She only wanted to see the Captain. She wanted to see the man who was killing the merfolk. The man who killed Rajan.

"Captain, sir!"

Kendra watched the man who was walking quickly over to the Captain. He was leading her right to him. She saw who the man was talking to, and walked right over to them.

"Captain," the man started, but the Captain glared at him. He continued, not as confident as before, "Marv, sir. The harpoon hit its target, but the other fish must have seen it. The harpoon was released from the body. We lost it."

The Captain swore, and said to the man, "You are sure that it hit?"

"Positive," he responded. "It was not released until after we started pulling the fish up."

The Captain smirked, "Then we have done what we set out to do. We have successfully killed the King and his heir."

Kendra's hands clenched together in anger. This Captain had just assassinated Rajan, and from the sound of it, they had already assassinated the king. Unlike in the future, when he would just start killing all the merfolk, this attack had been personal. Kendra could tell that this Captain was an angry man, anger directed right at the merfolk.

She studied his face, and saw a fresh scar running across it. It started at the upper left corner of his forehead, traveled diagonally over his eye, his nose, and cheek and did not end until his right collarbone. It looked as if he had recently been in a knife fight. Kendra moved closer to him, wanting to punch him in the jaw. Though she knew it would do nothing, she could not fight the urge.

She was about to move when she felt something pass through her. She looked down and saw that a small boy had run right through her and had latched itself onto the Captain's legs. He looked to be about four years old, with dark brown hair and large steel grey eyes. "Daddy, Daddy, Daddy," he was saying.

The Captain removed the boy from his legs and knelt down, looking him in the face. The boy gasped, obviously not expecting his father to have the large scar on his face. "James, I am not your father. It's me, Marv. Remember?"

James frowned, but shook his head. "Where's Daddy?"

"Some very bad people took him away from us," Captain Marv was saying. "He isn't going to be coming back."

"Who took him?" James asked, his eyes going wide. Kendra was shocked to hear the little boy's voice ice over with hate.

"Some very bad people," Marv repeated. "The Keepers."

Kendra looked over at Captain Marv in surprise. It was the first time she had heard the Keepers called bad people. It was strange not hear praise for the Saviors of Beindor, but then Kendra had to remind herself that these people were pirates. Little James' father probably was a very bad pirate. Kendra stepped away, realizing she could not feel sorry for the tiny pirate. He had run to the Captain, assuming he was his father, which meant that the little boy was the previous Captain's son. If Kendra did the math right, that would make little James twenty-two years old in the present. She realized that this little boy was going to grow up into the Captain of the Rámcírya. This little boy was the Captain Torolf that was killing all the merfolk. This child was the man she was going to kill.

Kendra watched as Captain Marv picked up the little Captain Torolf and walked up to the poop deck. She watched as little Captain Torolf reached out and grabbed the large steering wheel of the ship. She watched the little boy laughing, turning the wheel as fast as he could. Kendra no longer felt sympathy for the child, for losing his father. She only felt hate for him, for killing the merfolk. Even though she was watching his childhood right now, she relished in the thought of killing him.

Kendra looked away, out over the ocean. She took a breath and steadied herself. She was getting way too far ahead. She still had to focus on getting the Amir Crystal, and that had nothing to do with Captain Torolf and the Rámcírya. They weren't even on their way to Aearad yet. They still had to go to Imladun and get Aideen's piece of the crystal.

Kendra took another breath and realized she no longer wanted to see the past. She was done watching little Captain Torolf; she was done watching merfolk die. She wanted to get back to the present and wanted to start on their way. She could do nothing in the past but watch. In the present, she could change the world.

The boat rocked violently to the side. Kendra lost her balance and tumbled to the deck. She grabbed her head, which was now spinning viciously. She closed her eyes, but that made the spinning only worse. She gripped the wooden deck as hard as she could, for fear of rolling off the side of the ship. Then everything stopped.

Kendra could no longer smell the sea. She could no longer hear the shouts of the pirates around her. She was no longer spinning. Instead, she felt herself lying on something large and soft. She could smell sweet incense, and could hear the steady breathing of her three cousins. She was back in Korinna's Magikal Shoppe. She was back in the present.

Chapter Thirty-Three

She could hear birds chirping, the wind blowing gently through the trees. She could hear the steady breathing of a nearby fox. Damia inhaled deeply, smelling the fragrance of the forest. She didn't want to open her eyes, afraid that she would be dreaming, and that when she woke up she'd be home in bed, the alarm waking her up to get ready for school.

She opened one eye first, hoping that the other could stay asleep. When she looked around and saw that she was not in her room, nor in her bed, she opened the other eye and realized she had not been dreaming. She really was in a forest.

The trees were wide and tall. Looking up, Damia could not see the tops of them for their branches created a canopy overhead. Everywhere Damia looked, she could see green. The ground was covered in grass and plants, while the tree trunks were covered in moss and the leaves were so bright green, Damia feared they would turn red at any moment. Damia stood up from where she was sitting, against one of the many large tree trunks and took a deep breath of the forest air.

Then, rather suddenly, her tranquil forest was pierced by a bone-chilling scream. Damia looked around frantically, wondering what could be making that horrid sound. She started running through the trees as fast as she could. She had to find the woman who was screaming, because that's what Damia realized it was. A woman who sounded scared for her life.

It barely took a minute for Damia to find this woman, but when Damia tried to talk to her, the woman wouldn't listen. Her front was covered in blood, but it didn't look like she was hurt. There was blood covering her hands and arms as well, as if she had been holding something else that had been bleeding.

"What's wrong?" Damia asked, yelling over the woman's screams.

The woman, however, continued to look straight ahead, and continued to scream. Damia tried to grab the woman's shoulders, to make her look at her, but her hands passed right through. Damia stared at the woman in shock, wondering if she was imagining her. She also wondered if this woman was a ghost, and trapped in some horrific time-loop.

Damia then looked around, and saw that she and the woman were standing to the side of a small clearing. There were others in the clearing, and they seemed to be just as panicked as this first woman was. Damia looked more carefully and realized that some of the people were fighting each other.

Damia had happened upon a battle. It seemed to be two different species fighting. One seemed human enough, except Damia had never seen humans quite as beautiful as these were. The others, however, looked to Damia to be walking corpses. They were bloated and their skin was stained dark, as if their entire bodies were bruised. Their hair was a deep red as well, and to Damia they looked just as beautiful as the others. She wondered if they had once been the lighter skinned species, but then some vile disease had turned them into what they were.

Of course, Damia instantly knew that the lighter skinned species were Elvin. She had no idea about the other species. She wondered if they were zombies, for they looked just like the undead. As if they had literally sat up in their graves and came to attack the Elvin.

The elfe that stood in front of Damia was about to run right through, off into the woods, when a sudden pair of hands grabbed her. Damia was startled by the new person, and was even more startled by who it was, Keeper Damia.

She was much older than Damia, looking to be in her early forties or late thirties. Everything else about her seemed to be almost exactly the same. They both had the same green eyes, and the same long curly brown hair. Keeper Damia also had the same concerned look on her face as she talked to the elfe. "It's okay. Don't scream. Vasska and the other vampires aren't going to hurt you."

The elfe looked wide-eyed at Keeper Damia and nodded. Tears started streaming down her cheeks, and she sank to the ground. Keeper Damia followed after and said, "You have to move. There are some more Elvin in hiding the trees nearby. They will protect you. Do you think you can make it over there?"

The elfe nodded again, as if all her energy had been spent on screaming. The elfe stood and she smiled weakly at Keeper Damia. Keeper Damia smiled back and said, "I'm so sorry about your baby."

More tears ran down the elfe's face and she turned away. Keeper Damia watched as she disappeared into the trees, where some Elvin were waiting for her. Damia continued to watch the older version of herself in awe. She watched as she battled the vampires with a vigor that Damia knew she did not possess. The way Keeper Damia was able to kill the vampires shocked Damia. She watched as she continued to behead vampire after vampire, alongside the Elvin.

Damia studied the vampire that Keeper Damia was fighting, surprised at how different they looked from what she had always imagined. They looked exactly like corpses, even down to the bloating and discoloration. There was nothing attractive or spell binding about them. They wore no cloaks and they weren't afraid of the sun. There was nothing Draculish about them. They didn't even have fangs. Damia was surprised to find that she was disappointed. These vampires were not in the least bit as romantic as she imagined. They were ugly and they were dead.

Damia realized that the vampire Keeper Damia was fighting was talking to her.

He was saying, "No matter how much you fight me, I will win. I will kill my sister and all the Elvin. Give up now, and I won't kill you as well. I can be merciful, Damia."

Keeper Damia snarled, "I will never give in to you, Vasska. No matter how much you talk, I know you were never merciful alive, and you're nowhere near merciful now."

Vasska laughed, "You know me too well, but I wasn't lying. I don't plan on killing you. I have something very different in mind."

"That was a long time ago, Vasska," Keeper Damia said. "My feelings for you have long since vanished."

"I don't believe that," he said, moving closer. "Why would you be here helping my sister if you didn't feel even the slightest thing for me."

"The only thing I feel for you now is hate," she said before lunging at Vasska, her blade piercing his stomach. He paused, a look of horror flashing across his face. Keeper Damia stood tall, not fooled by his act. Vasska stood as well, a smirk creeping across his face. "I cannot trick you," he said. "You know very well the only way to kill me is to burn my heart."

"I will rip your heart out of your chest with my bare hands," Keeper Damia said with a voice that shocked Damia. This woman was not who Damia thought she would be. Something had happened to change Keeper Damia from the loving, nurturing one of the group into a murderer. It scared Damia. She wondered if she would end up the same way.

Vasska laughed, pulling Keeper Damia's sword from his abdomen. He threw it to the ground a few feet away. Keeper Damia watched in horror as the steel blade shattered on impact. Vasska took a step forward and wrapped a hand around Keeper Damia's forearm. He stepped chest to chest with her and said, much to both Damia and Keeper Damia's disgust, "I don't think so, Keeper. The next time I see you, you will be mine."

Then he was gone. Damia had not seen where he went; she had been too caught up in what he was saying. Keeper Damia seemed to be having the same reaction. She looked around, dazed. She then saw her sword; millions of tiny little pieces scattered in the dirt, and sighed. A few moments later, an elfe approached Keeper Damia and gently touched her shoulder.

Keeper Damia looked up at the elfe, who said, "Thank you, dear Keeper. You have saved my life once again from my brother."

Damia looked around and realized that the vampires were gone. Only the Elvin were left, gathering the corpses together, vampire and Elvin alike. Damia watched as some Elvin started a large bonfire, and realized that they were going to throw the bodies on it. Vasska had said that the only way to kill him was to burn his heart. That is what they were doing to the vampires to make sure they did not come back and to the Elvin to make sure they did not become vampires themselves.

Damia looked back at Keeper Damia and the Elvin Queen. Keeper Damia put her hand over the Queen's hand on her shoulder and said, "I am glad I reached the Forests before he could do you any harm. However, I'm afraid that I will not be able to hunt him down like I promised. I am needed elsewhere, and only came to give you something."

Damia watched as Keeper Damia pulled an ornamental silver leaf from her hair. Damia had not noticed this piece of decoration earlier, thinking it was just like one of the many things she tended to put in her hair, leaves and flowers included. But now as she watched Keeper Damia hand it over to Queen Bryndis, she realized that there was one small jewel on the stem of the silver leaf. That one small jewel was the color of cream and jagged in shape. Queen Bryndis recognized it immediately, and so did Damia.

It was the Amîr Crystal.

Queen Bryndis refused, saying, "What are you doing? You know I can't take this."

"Please, Bryndis," Keeper Damia said. "It is very important that you do."

"What happened to it?" she asked. "Why is it so small?"

"We have broken it up into four pieces, and have entrusted each piece to four separate people. Without all four pieces together, the door to Earth cannot be opened," Keeper Damia explained. "You must not lose your piece. You must not let anyone steal it or give it to anyone. Not even me."

"This has to do with Kenneth, doesn't it?" Bryndis asked solemnly. "That's why you can't keep it yourself."

Keeper Damia nodded, "We are going to face him once more. We will be using *all* of our powers."

Bryndis sighed, "I was afraid of that. You know the risks, of course."

"Yes," Damia said. "We may not be able to come back. Our powers might turn on us."

Bryndis frowned, "I know you have Rohak. What about the others? Have they all found true love?"

Keeper Damia was confused with the change of subject, but knowing that Queen Bryndis was much wiser than she, responded, "Aideen and Kendra have, but they are much too complicated to call it true. And Peri, well," Keeper Damia looked away, "that is impossible."

Bryndis nodded, understanding something that Damia did not. She wondered what had happened with Keeper Peri and her love. She also wondered who this Rohak was. With a sinking feeling in her stomach, Damia realized that Bryndis had not said Kynton for Keeper Damia's true love.

Kynton had said that he had known Keeper Damia when she was alive, and that he was very much in love with her. Damia began to realize that maybe she hadn't been as in love with him as he was with her. She wondered if something had happened between them, and that was why Keeper Damia was not meant to be with him, but rather this Rohak.

Bryndis continued, pulling Damia from her thoughts, "Then I'm afraid to say that your mission might be unfeasible. True, you will be able to stop Kenneth, but without your true loves, you will not be able to stop your powers from overpowering yourselves."

Keeper Damia bit her lip, realizing that Queen Bryndis was telling her she was going to die. Bryndis then added, "But I do know a way to make sure that you will come back, and if Kenneth does happen to survive, then you will be powerful enough to destroy him."

Damia looked at this Elvin queen in shock. She was talking about what had made Damia an exact replica of Keeper Damia. Damia was about to learn why their souls had recycled their former bodies and not gone on to new ones. Damia listened in shock as Bryndis recited a spell for Keeper Damia. It had been a simple spell that made Damia exactly what she was. It was the spell that created her life.

Keeper Damia suddenly bowed and said to Queen Bryndis, "Thank you, dear friend, for all your help."

"It is an honor," Bryndis said with a little bow, "to be in acquaintance with such a magnificent person as yourself."

Keeper Damia's smile faltered and she rather ungracefully flung her arms around the queen in a bear hug. The Queen returned the hug and said into Keeper Damia's shoulder, "I will miss you, dear one."

"I will miss you too," Keeper Damia said, and Damia could tell that she was crying.

Keeper Damia removed herself from the Queen and bowed again, "I will see you again."

Queen Bryndis nodded, and slipped the ornamental leaf into her hair.

Keeper Damia turned away from her friend and walked past Damia as well. Damia turned and followed her counterpart into the forests. She watched as Keeper Damia wiped a tear from her cheek and sighed. She had paused, but was about to start moving again when both Damias heard someone shouting for them.

"Keeper Damia! Wait! Don't leave!"

Damia turned quickly at the familiar voice, excited to see Kynton was in this little day dream she was having. She wanted to walk over to him, but when she saw how Keeper Damia slowly turned towards him, with only a cordial smile on her face, Damia realized her fears were about to come true.

"Hello, Prince Kynton," Keeper Damia said.

Damia looked at Kynton in shock. *A Prince? Why wouldn't he tell me? He knows exactly where the Amir Crystal is! His mother has it!*

Kynton smiled nervously, "Please don't call me that. I told you, it's Kynton."

Keeper Damia nodded and said, "Then, Kynton, what have I told you about me?"

"To call you Damia," Kynton said sheepishly. "I'm sorry."

"Don't apologize," Keeper Damia said. "From now on we know not to use our titles."

Kynton's smile fell, as he remembered why he was chasing after her. "Is it true?" he asked. "Are you really going to die?"

Keeper Damia's cordial smile fell and she looked down, "I am starting to believe that it is very true."

"Why?" Kynton demanded, forgetting his nerves around the Keeper. He wanted nothing to harm her, and yet here she was, walking right into her death. "You don't have to do this!"

"But I do," Keeper Damia said, recognizing his anger. "The lives of all the humans on Hecate depend on the destruction of Kenneth. The lives of all the humans on Earth, as well. My cousins and I have found a way to destroy him, but it may destroy us as well."

"So you're willing to give up your lives for millions of people you do not know?" Kynton asked in disbelief.

Keeper Damia shook her head, "Not for millions of people I do not know, but for all of my people. The people who look up to me and the others to protect them. How can we protect them if we are afraid to get hurt in the process?"

"Dying is so much more than getting hurt," Kynton said. "Please Damia, don't do this."

Keeper Damia frowned, knowing that Kynton would never be able to understand what she was doing. He had moved a lot closer to her, their chests were almost touching. Keeper Damia took a step back and said, "I must go. I have done everything I have come here to do. The others need me now."

"Damia," Kynton whispered, taking another step closer. He put his hands on her forearms, "What about me? I need you too."

"Kynton," Keeper Damia's voice had turned to ice, just like it had when she had been talking with the vampire Vasska. "You know that we can never be. I am in love with my husband, and would never betray him. I told you all of this before. Please don't make my last memory of Taurëfor a bad one."

Kynton seemed to not have heard her, for in the next moment he leaned down and kissed Keeper Damia. Though he had a grip on her, she was much stronger than the elf. She threw him off her with such force that he flew backwards in the air. He hit a tree and fell to the ground, unconscious. "I am sorry," Keeper Damia said to him, though she knew he could not hear. "You know nothing good would come from that. We are not meant to be."

Damia watched the whole thing in horror. She wondered if anything Kynton had said to her had been the truth. He had said that he and Keeper Damia had been in love, but by this picture, Damia knew that only Kynton loved Keeper Damia, and not the other way around. Keeper Damia was in love with a man named Rohak, and Damia had no idea who that could be. She wondered if Rohak was another elf, or maybe a human that she had met in Canhareth.

Damia watched as Keeper Damia continued on her way, leaving Kynton unconscious on the ground. Damia wanted to stay and make sure Kynton was okay, but what she had learned held her back. She wanted to see Kynton's life, to discover why he said the things he did. But Damia also knew that she was there to watch Keeper Damia's life, not Kynton's.

Damia followed after Keeper Damia, and found that the Keeper of Earth had started to run through the trees. Damia was surprised to see how swiftly the woman could run, especially while dodging trees, plants, and other wildlife. Not once did Keeper Damia fall, not once did something on the forest floor catch her off guard. Damia realized that Keeper Damia knew every single tree in the forest, as if each were a child she had nurtured.

Suddenly Keeper Damia stopped, which allowed Damia to catch up to her. Damia didn't know the forest as well as Keeper Damia, and so it was not as easy for her to gracefully run through it. Damia watched Keeper Damia's face, and realized that Keeper Damia had become stiff, as if she were a deer sensing that she was about to be roadkill. Instead of running like the deer would have, Keeper Damia, in one fluid motion, removed the bow from her back and knocked an arrow on it.

"Who's there?" Keeper Damia shouted.

Damia watched as Keeper Damia searched the crowded trees around her, trying to find the presence that alarmed her. Damia watched as Keeper Damia closed her eyes for the briefest second. Damia panicked, knowing that Keeper Damia was vulnerable with her eyes closed like that. The predator that was somewhere in the trees could easily kill her without much effort.

Then Keeper Damia's eyes flew open and she said, looking at a single tree right in front of her, "What on Earth are you doing here?"

Damia watched as a man stepped out from behind the tree Keeper Damia had her bow and arrow pointed at. He was a good-looking man of forty-five years, with black hair that was starting to show the signs of his age. He had large brown eyes and all though he had an intimidating figure, Damia could tell that he held nothing but love for Keeper Damia. This was her husband, Rohak Moorel.

His hands were over his head in surrender, but a smile was playing at his lips, "Are you going to lower your weapon so I can kiss my wife?"

"No," Keeper Damia said, glaring at Rohak. "I told you not to come here. You were going to stay in Vavia with Thisbe." Keeper Damia's eyes grew wide, and her bow and arrow slackened a little as she asked frantically, "Where is Thisbe? What did you do with her?"

"Don't worry," Rohak said. "The munchkin is safe. I gave her to Kiros to watch over. She was having a ball playing with his little Briam."

Keeper Damia's eyes narrowed, "I don't like that boy. He's going to cause trouble. I can tell."

Rohak laughed, "He's an infant! Not a year old yet!"

Keeper Damia smiled, "I know, I guess I'm jealous. He gets to play with my daughter while I have to go save the world."

Rohak moved closer to his wife, and she replaced the bow and arrow in on her quiver. He reached out and ran a finger along her cheekbone, "You will have plenty of time to play with her after you save the world."

Keeper Damia's eyes filled with tears, "I talked to Bryndis. She's accepted the crystal, but she has just about as much faith in us as I do. She knows that it will be impossible to come back. We won't survive. I won't see Thisbe again."

"Yes you will," Rohak said, embracing Keeper Damia tightly, afraid that he might never be able to again. "You will watch your daughter grow old, you will see her get married, you will see your grandchildren born. And you will see all of this with me."

Keeper Damia looked up at Rohak and smiled, "Thank you, my love. You have always known what to say to make me feel better."

Rohak kissed Keeper Damia's forehead, "It is my pleasure."

Keeper Damia lifted herself onto her toes and caught Rohak's lips with her own. Damia watched with silent tears pouring down her face. She knew that Keeper Damia would not be able to see all those things that Rohak had promised her, and she knew that Keeper Damia must have known this as well. Damia hadn't realized what tragic lives the Keepers had; she wondered if their lives would be any reflection on what would happen to her and her cousins.

"Come on," Keeper Damia said, pulling away. She took Rohak's hand in her own and said, "We will go to Vavia. I will meet up with Peri there and together we can go to the Taurpíca Forests. Rohak," Keeper Damia paused. "You know you cannot come with us. This is one thing that we must do on our own."

Rohak twisted to face his wife, anger in his eyes, "You know I will not leave you four alone with *him.* Kenneth cannot be trusted."

"But he will kill you if you come," Keeper Damia said. "He knows what you mean to us, to *me.* He will kill you, leaving us vulnerable." Tears sprang into Keeper Damia's eyes, "Please, Thisbe cannot lose both parents to Kenneth."

Rohak hugged Keeper Damia again, "She won't lose either, but I will honor your wishes. I will stay in Vavia with Thisbe, and together we will await your return."

"Thank you," Keeper Damia said, kissing her husband again.

Damia watched as Keeper Damia and Rohak walked deeper into the forests. She did not follow them, knowing that she had invaded their privacy enough. Instead, she walked the other way. She thought of Kynton, lying unconscious in the trees and felt little pity for him. He had lied to her, and she did not know what to do about it. She knew she liked him, a lot. But was that enough to forget what he had done? Damia remembered Korinna's warning from the day before, "Be careful of him. He may seem innocent, but he is holding secrets from you."

She wondered if this was the secret he had been hiding from her. She had figured it was his Elvin origins, but that seemed trivial next to the fact that Keeper Damia did not love him. Korinna had mentioned more than one secret, maybe those were the two secrets he was hiding. *Or maybe,* Damia thought cynically, *he has even more secrets he is hiding from me.*

Damia realized that this was the first time since she first saw Kynton that she wasn't crazy about him. She only felt confused and pity for him. She was surprised to find that for the first time in a while, her emotions were clear and not a huge mixture. She wondered if being away from other people was the reason. She could not feel their emotions, so she only had her own to feel.

Then a more depressing thought crossed her mind. What if she hadn't felt her own feelings since the last time she was completely alone. She tried to think back, and realized the last time she had been completely alone was when she was getting ready to go to Kendra's birthday party, two days before. What if the entire time so far in Beindor she had been feeling other people's feelings? What if she wasn't in love with Kynton at all, but was confusing his emotions for her with her own?

Damia sat down, feeling like she had just been hit in the head with a purse full of bricks. As soon as she sat down, she felt the ground lurch to the left. She tumbled over, wondering what happened. However, when she tried to straighten up again, she found that the trees around her were spinning. She tried to focus on one, to make it stop spinning, but it only got faster and faster until she had to close her eyes.

Then the spinning stopped and she realized she was nowhere near the forests of Taurëfor. She was back in the magik shop run by the Seer Korinna. She opened her eyes to find that the others around her were doing the same. She wiped the tears from her eyes, wondering if she was ever going to feel her own emotions again.

Chapter Thirty-Four

Aideen could feel the heat beating down on her, and she inhaled deeply. She could feel the sunrays tickling her skin and she had never felt so at home. She wondered if her cousins were feeling this at peace at the moment. "Now this is what a vacation should feel like," she said. "No need to run around searching for a crystal. Just soaking in the sun."

Aideen waited for someone to either agree or disagree. Maybe Kendra would say something about Aideen calling their little adventure a vacation. She waited, but no one said a word. She opened her eyes and looked around, only to find that she was most definitely alone. The realization shocked her. She hadn't been this alone for a while now. It had been surprisingly easy to get used to the company of her cousins, and even after two days, a moment without them felt wrong.

Aideen was sitting at the base of a large grassy hill, but other than that, there was nothing around for miles. She looked out to the horizon and was surprised to see that it looked like the grassy plains went on forever, a few trees growing in random places the whole way. She had no idea where she was, and was worried that she might not even be in Beindor anymore. She was about to start walking through the grassy plains when she heard laughter come from overhead.

She looked up to the top of the hill, where the familiar laughter had come from and saw something large and red sticking out from the side. Aideen ducked down when she saw the bat like wing, which was easily over fifteen feet long. Then she realized exactly where she was, Imladun. And that thing she just saw was the wing of a dragon.

Aideen climbed up the side of the hill, wanting to get a closer look at the magnificent creature. She also remembered where she had heard that laugh before; she remembered hearing it come from her own mouth. It was Keeper Aideen laughing on the hill with the dragon. Aideen continued to climb the side of the hill, listening to the conversation Keeper Aideen and the dragon were having.

"What was that?" Keeper Aideen asked, after hearing a sudden noise coming from below them on the hill. Aideen looked down and saw that a small rabbit was chewing on a loose twig from the tree that sat on the top of the hill. The twig had snapped, causing Keeper Aideen to jump slightly.

The dragon looked over the side of the hill, and Aideen looked up at it in fright. She could see its large red eyes, like rolling balls of fire in their sockets, but she also noticed the red color quickly changing from yellow to white and back to red again. The dragon's diamond shaped scales also seemed to be changing color, but not from red to yellow. Instead, it looked like all the shades of red were on his scales at once. With just the shift of his muscles or the rise of his chest as he breathed, the vibrant fire engine red shifted to a deep burgundy and then back to a beautiful blood red.

The shape of the dragon's head reminded Aideen of a serpent, with a long nose and thin nostrils that flared up when he sniffed the air. His mouth was a thin line, but Aideen was not fooled. She knew that there were rows of razor sharp teeth behind those lips that were just waiting to tear her apart. On the top of the red dragon's head were multiple long horns that reminded Aideen of a crown. The horns became spikes as they traveled down the dragon's back, until they reached the tip of his long lizard-like tail.

His large bat-like wings were tucked closely against his body, but Aideen saw that they could be just as deadly as the dragon's teeth. On the ends of the wings were claws that could rip Aideen to shreds. The dragon also had large claws on the toes of all four feet, similarly to a large cat.

The dragon did not intimidate Aideen. In fact, she found him rather attractive, in a large beast sort of way. He looked over the hill not with anger or hate in his eyes, but with amusement and adoration.

Aideen then watched as the dragon opened his mouth. For a second she thought he was going to douse her in his fiery breath, ending her life instantly. But, to her surprise, he spoke to her, "It's just a little rabbit."

She watched as his head turned around on its snake-like neck to look back at the top of the hill. He continued speaking, "You're just too jumpy."

Aideen let out a breath she hadn't known she was holding. The dragon hadn't been talking to her, he was talking to the other Aideen, who had heard the rabbit break the twig. Aideen then realized that the dragon had said that there was just the rabbit on the hillside, when Aideen knew very well that there was more. She was also on the hillside, and the dragon had looked right at her. Hadn't he?

Perhaps he had looked at the hill, but not at Aideen. Perhaps he could not see her. She was watching a memory, after all. She wasn't playing an active role in it, so why would she be able to change the memory.

"I'm not jumpy," Aideen heard her counterpart say.

"Are you scared?" came the deep voice of the dragon. Aideen paused in her climb, it sounded like the dragon was teasing Keeper Aideen. Aideen knew that if she was anything like her, then teasing her would be a very bad idea.

"No!" Keeper Aideen said in offense. She then added, to her own defense, "I am *never* scared."

Aideen paused. Was it her imagination or was Keeper Aideen *flirting* with the dragon? She knew she had had weird crushes in the past, but a *dragon?* That kicked all her other crushes in the ass. Aideen continued climbing, wanting even more to see Keeper Aideen and this dragon...flirting.

She was almost there, almost to the top. She could see the top of the dragon's scaly back, complete with the spikes running down his spine. She could see the sharp claws on the tips of the wings. She could see the crown of horns on his head. She was almost there.

Then, rather suddenly, there was a large growling noise that shook the entire hill. Aideen quickly grabbed a hold of tufts of grass, praying she didn't lose her balance and start rolling down the hill. She had been discovered, they could see her after all. She closed her eyes, wondering if the dragon was going to kill her now. Maybe roast her and eat her. *Do dragons eat humans?* She thought to herself as she waited for the deathblow.

"Stop laughing at me!"

Aideen opened her eyes at Keeper Aideen's words. Laughing? That noise was *laughter*? If that was how the dragon laughed, she didn't want to see how it killed.

"I am sorry, little one," the dragon said in its deep voice, though the growling laughter continued to reach Aideen's ears.

"It's not *that* funny," Keeper Aideen said.

Aideen realized that Keeper Aideen had done something the dragon found rather amusing. Aideen could tell that he would find anything Keeper Aideen did amusing.

"Oh," the dragon said; the growling finally subsiding. "On the contrary. It was very funny."

Aideen reached the top of the hill just in time to see the look in Keeper Aideen's eyes. She barely had time to look at what she would be like at age forty, before realizing that she was in trouble. The look in Keeper Aideen's eye was one that Aideen knew very well. It was a look of mischief and conniving thoughts.

The dragon must have noticed the look as well, for he paused and looked at Keeper Aideen. Then Keeper Aideen stretched her arm out the short distance between her and the dragon's side, and pushed. Aideen assumed that the dragon would hardly feel the shove, but Keeper Aideen's strength must have grown since she turned eighteen for the dragon began to topple over.

Being a very large dragon, sitting on the top of a rather small hill, the only thing that could come out of being pushed by the Keeper of Fire was that he began to roll down the side of said hill. Not only did he start to roll down the hill, he started to roll down the side of the hill that Aideen was hiding on. She barely had time to scream before the dragon rolled over top of her.

She waited for the bone crushing weight. She waited, and waited. When she felt nothing, she opened her eyes and saw that the dragon was already below her. She looked at him in surprise, still rolling; scrambling to catch his claw in the side of the hill. She was pondering how she had survived the dragon's weight when she noticed his claw coming down on the section of hill where she was crouched.

She watched in horror as his claw come in contact with her exposed leg, and watched in awe as it went right through, and into the grass beneath her. She moved her leg, and watched as it passed right through the dragon. He didn't even notice she was there. She scrambled out of his way before he could test if the rest of her body was just as transparent as her leg. She watched as he climbed past her, and found herself staring at the diamond shaped scales on his side. They were changing colors even as he moved up the hill.

Not being able to resist, she reached out to touch one. She watched in amazement as her hand passed right through the scales. She kept her hand out, and as the dragon moved, her hand moved right through his side. It felt like she was sticking her hand into the water from a moving boat. The dragon didn't seem to mind having someone run their hand right through him, he didn't seem to even know it was happening.

Aideen watched as the dragon reached the top of the hill, and quickly followed after him. She nervously brought herself up to the top of the hill, waiting for one of them to turn on her. When they didn't, she sat down and watched them. She realized immediately that these two had much more than a crush going on. They looked like a match made in heaven.

"What was that for?" the dragon asked when he reached the top of the hill. He bent down so his eyes were level with Keeper Aideen's.

She smiled innocently, "If you hadn't laughed at me, you wouldn't have fallen down the hill."

"Oh that's not fair," he said. "You've laughed at me plenty of times and I can't just push you down a hill."

"Why not?" Keeper Aideen asked, putting her hands on her hips.

"You're a human girl, that's why," he said.

"Are you afraid I'd *break?*"

The dragon chuckled, realizing the mess he had just stepped in. The hill shook again, and Aideen grabbed a hold of the grass to steady herself. She watched to see how the dragon would worm his way out of this situation. She had seen men try to do it before, and with her, they always failed.

"Of course not," he said. "You're a beautiful human girl who wouldn't give a second thought to hexing me into oblivion. That, or set me on fire. Either way I don't think I win."

Both Keeper Aideen and Aideen laughed at his answer. "Nice save," Keeper Aideen said.

The couple sat in a comfortable silence for a few minutes. Keeper Aideen picked at the grass near her, while the dragon rested his head close by, his eyes closed but a smile playing at his lips. After a pause, Keeper Aideen looked over at the dragon, "Do you really think I'm beautiful?"

The dragon's eyes opened slowly, as if he were waking from a dream. His smile widened, "Of course I do. I wouldn't say so without meaning it. And I would never lie to you."

Keeper Aideen smiled, and Aideen realized that this relationship was much more fragile that she had thought. They had seemed so natural together that she had figured they had already gotten through these awkward first stages. But from the look on Keeper Aideen's face, she had gotten very nervous around her dragon friend. The dragon looked away, deep in thought. Aideen watched as his expression twisted in pain, and she was afraid of what he was to say next.

He didn't have a chance to say anything, though, because Keeper Aideen beat him to it. She said, in a voice so soft Aideen wasn't sure the dragon could have heard her, "I love you."

But when the dragon's eyes snapped closed, Aideen realized that he had heard her. He had heard, and wished he hadn't. He let out a sigh that sent a cloud of vapor into the air. He then looked at Keeper Aideen and said, "I love you too."

"There's a 'but' coming, isn't there," Keeper Aideen said, her voice filling with ice.

The dragon nodded, "But you know we can't do this. You know it's impossible."

"Because I'm a human girl?" Keeper Aideen said, using the dragon's words.

"Yes," he responded, looking down at Keeper Aideen. "And I'm a dragon."

The way he said it, with such disgust, Aideen turned away. She didn't really want to hear this. She didn't want to find out that her counterpart never found her true love, that she died thinking that she was alone in the world.

"So?" Keeper Aideen asked, standing up. The dragon's head followed her, keeping eye level with her. Aideen looked over at them.

Keeper Aideen's voice was so strong, but Aideen knew that it was just a mask to hide the hurt. She had worn that mask too many times to be fooled by it.

"So how are we supposed to make this work?" the dragon asked. "What are people going to say? A human and a dragon! It's absurd!"

"Since when have I cared about what people say?" Keeper Aideen asked, fire igniting in her eyes. "All I care about is what I feel for you, and what I know you feel for me. We don't need anything else but that."

She reached out to touch his face, but he moved away. He closed his eyes and said, "I'm sorry, Aideen, but I can't do this. Not if I can't have you, in the end."

Keeper Aideen bit her lip, to keep it from trembling. Aideen touched her own lip, realizing she had done the same exact thing. Keeper Aideen stood motionless as the dragon spread its wings. She and Aideen watched as the dragon jumped into the air and without a word flew away from the hill.

Keeper Aideen sank back down to the ground, tears now running freely from her face. "But you already have me," she whispered.

Aideen watched as the dragon looked back at the hill, at Keeper Aideen. She wondered if he heard what she had said. She wondered if he realized what a stupid mistake he had just made. She looked back at her counterpart, crying into her hands. She did not see the dragon look back at her, did not know whether he was feeling even the tiniest bit of remorse. All she knew was that the dragon had left her. Aideen stood up, anger stinging in her eyes. She did not want to see this anymore. She wanted to get away from this sad chronicle.

She started down the hill, stomping her way through the grass. She tripped and fell to her knees, scrapping them bloody. She didn't care. She just wanted to get away from this memory as fast as she could. She wanted to go home and curl up under her sheets, never to think of Beindor or dragons again.

How could he be so stupid? She yelled in her head. *She loves him! Isn't that enough?*

But she knew it wasn't. Despite all the hatred she was feeling for the dragon, she knew that what he said was true. They would never have been truly happy. There was no way a human and a dragon could make it work. They couldn't even hold hands, let alone spend the rest of their lives together.

A dragon could never live in a house, and a cave isn't suitable for a human. They would never be able to live comfortably. Aideen could not believe she was agreeing with the stupid dragon, but she had to look at it realistically. It would maybe last a month before they would drive each other crazy.

Aideen sat down in the grass where she had first woken up. She wiped away the last of her tears and laughed at the image of herself living with a dragon. She could barely live with other humans, how could she manage with fire-breathing creatures? She lied down in the grass and closed her eyes; thinking about herself and a dragon had given her a headache.

Although she had always found dragons enticing, the thought of being with one was making her head spin. Even with her eyes closed she could feel the world spinning around her. For a moment she wondered if the world had caught up with her situation, which was also spinning out of control. Not only was she supposed to be some savior to these strangers in this new land, she just found out she had been in love with a dragon in her past life. That was enough to make anyone's world spin.

But when the world started moving faster and faster around her, Aideen realized that it wasn't a metaphorical spinning she was feeling. She gripped the grass underneath her, praying she didn't fall off, and realized she wasn't gripping grass. She was gripping silk. She sat up and saw that she was no longer in her memory. She was back in Canhareth, in Korinna's Magikal Shoppe.

Chapter Thirty-Five

When Peri opened her eyes, she found herself staring up at a cathedral styled ceiling, white in color. Being used to the red clay and dirt buildings of Canhareth, Peri realized that she was nowhere near the first human built city of Beindor. She sat up and looked around the large room she was lying in. There was a large wooden table in the center of the room with many high backed chairs surrounding it. There were other chairs and couches pushed against the walls of the large room. Peri thought for a second that she was in the middle of an extravagant movie set.

Then she realized that there was another person in the room, and they seemed to have spotted her. The voice said, "Show yourself. I know you are in here."

Peri peaked over the side of the large wooden table, surprised to see herself staring back at her. She fell over backwards in shock. As she sat there, on the ground in this strange room, she realized that it was not a mirror she had peered into. It was the eyes of the other Peri, the first Keeper of Air. She peaked over the side of the table again, and saw that Keeper Peri had not moved. She was sitting in one of the chairs of the large table, looking straight ahead.

Peri watched as she said, still looking over Peri's head, "I am defenseless. I only wish to talk."

"Then talk," hissed a voice from behind Peri. She turned around, but found no one was there. She looked back at Keeper Peri, who Peri realized was in her early forties, in a moment that took place less than a year before she died.

A look of pain came to Keeper Peri's face as she said, "You will not show yourself even to me?"

The mystery voice spoke again, "Why should I honor a Keeper with my presence?"

"Today I am not a Keeper, Kenneth," she said, "but your wife."

Peri's mouth dropped. She had not known that Keeper Peri had married. She wondered who this man was, and why he was so mad at his wife.

Kenneth growled, "That was a long time ago, Keeper. Do not think I will hesitate in killing you because of it."

Keeper Peri nodded, "I am not asking you to spare my life. I am here to ask you to spare the lives of the people of Beindor, of Earth."

Peri's mind began racing. *She couldn't be married to* him, *could she? Why did no one ever mention this before? Why am I first learning of this now? Tárquin married to a Keeper is big news! And to my Keeper!*

Suddenly Kenneth appeared, as if he had stepped out from behind an invisible curtain. He stood close to Peri, looking at his wife over the table. His face was twisted into a snarl, but Peri could not help but find him attractive. He had white blonde hair and pale skin. Peri would have thought him part albino if not for his coal black eyes. With another growl, he said, "How typical of you, defending those disgusting creatures. You're just as bad as them."

"Kenneth," Keeper Peri said, reaching across the table. She placed her hand over his, "You are one of them, same as me. Same as the other Keepers."

"No, I'm not," Kenneth said, ripping his hand away from hers. "I am so much more than they are. We are so much more."

"Just because you believe yourself better than everyone else does not mean you are justified in wiping them out," Keeper Peri said. "You have to stop killing innocent people."

"Oh just like a Keeper to say that. To assume they are innocent," he said with a laugh. "I bet you think your grandfather was innocent too. That my mother was completely in the wrong. He was holding her back from her dreams."

"Whatever differences they had," Keeper Peri said, "they could have talked them out. Seen a shrink. Gotten a divorce. She didn't have to murder him!"

Peri's mouth fell open in horror. First off, she had been married to Tárquin. Secondly, her grandfather was married to his mother. And thirdly, his mother *murdered* her grandfather. *What a twisted family,* Peri thought.

Then a thought came to Peri like a flash of enlightenment. She remembered the Trac House, and the picture they had found inside with the set of cousins with the same names as her and her cousins. There had been a Kenneth in there as well. Peri realized that the house they had found belonged to the first Keepers, and that Kenneth's mother, Dorothy Rhed, when a murderer after all. Just like in the story.

Kenneth's lips curled, "But murdering her was okay?"

Keeper Peri sighed, it was obvious they had gone over this before. "We did not murder her," she said. "She was tried for murder, found guilty, and hung."

Kenneth obviously saw it differently. He sighed and said, "No matter what, you and your cousins have always had it in for me and my mother. It will always be the Tracs versus the Rheds."

"Kenneth," Keeper Peri said softly. "If I had it in for you, would I have married you?"

Kenneth shook his head, "Like I said, that was a long time ago. Don't think I don't know what you and your cousins are planning. You're going to kill me, just like my mother."

"I don't want to kill you, Kenneth," Keeper Peri said. "I want to save you. That's why I'm here."

"I thought you were here to save the people of Beindor," Kenneth hissed.

"No," Keeper Peri said with a smile. "The Keepers want to save the people. I want to save my husband."

Kenneth shook his head, "You are the one who needs saving, Peri. From your cousins. They have corrupted you. Twisted your mind into thinking that what I am doing is wrong."

Keeper Peri's smile fell and her hands dipped underneath the table, onto her lap. "My cousins have done nothing to me. I have always believed that killing innocent people and massacring towns is wrong, even before you picked up the habit."

Kenneth took a step backwards. Peri watched as something completely washed over him. She was surprised to see it looked like defeat. His shoulders slumped and his head bowed forward slightly. His hands, which had been up to this point in fists, uncurled and hung limply at his sides. "What are we supposed to do now?" he asked. "How are we supposed to go forward? We will never be able to see eye to eye. Your cousins will never accept me. Beindor will never accept me."

"But Kenneth," Keeper Peri said with a smile, "they will. We're giving you a second chance. We want to meet. All five of us. To discuss what comes next."

Kenneth frowned, not sure how to take this news. He didn't want to meet with the Keepers, knowing that nothing good would come out of that. But he did want to work things out with his wife. If he did anything, that was what he wanted to do. "Okay," he said. "I will meet with your cousins."

"Good. Six weeks from today," Keeper Peri said, "we will meet you in the Taurpíca Forests."

Kenneth nodded, knowing exactly where in the forests she was talking about. "Six weeks," he said.

He turned to leave, but Keeper Peri put out a hand, "Wait."

Then Keeper Peri moved for the first time since Peri woke up. She watched as the woman stood, very slowly, never taking her eyes off her husband. Peri's eyes instantly traveled down the woman's body, and to the large bump that was coming from underneath her dress. Peri's mouth dropped, realizing that Keeper Peri was pregnant with Tárquin's child.

Peri looked back over at Kenneth, who also noticed the slight change in Keeper Peri's appearance. His face had gone pale, paler than it had been before. The little color that Peri could see was gone. It drained out of him, along with all his contempt for his wife. Peri watched as he processed what was going on. She watched as the corners of his lips pulled up into a smile, and his eyes brightened as he looked up into the face of his wife.

"You're-" he said, moving closer to her.

"-Eight months pregnant," Keeper Peri finished with a smile.

"What have your cousins said? I'm sure they've wondered about this, and who the father is," Kenneth said. "You didn't tell them about us, did you?"

Peri looked at the couple in shock. That was why no one knew about this relationship. They had never told anyone. They must have known how wrong it was for a niece and uncle to fall in love, even if they were the same age and not blood related. She wondered if the other Keepers ever figured it out.

Keeper Peri shook her head, "I've been casting a concealment charm on my stomach. They do not suspect a thing."

Kenneth nodded, still looking at his wife's very pregnant stomach.

Keeper Peri said softly, "I trust you will do the right thing, Kenneth. For me. For our child."

Kenneth looked up at Keeper Peri and he hesitated. The smile fell from his face. Peri watched in disappointment as his face went from happy and proud to be a father-to-be to terrified that everything about his life was going to change. She could see the panic start to set in as he realized that his life just flipped upside down.

He took a step backwards, away from Keeper Peri. He shook his head and said, "Six weeks. Taurpíca Forests. I will see you there, Keeper."

He then disappeared just as quickly as he had come. He vanished without moving a single step, without a wave of his hand or a whisper of a word. Peri watched as Keeper Peri covered her mouth with her hand, trying to soften the sobs coming from between her lips. She gripped the arms of her chair and slumped down into it. Tears poured down her face, and it was obvious to Peri that she had hoped for a different reaction from her husband.

Peri wanted to reach out and comfort this woman, but when she went to touch her shoulder, Peri's hand passed right through her. She looked at her hand in shock, wondering what that meant. Perhaps Peri was just a ghost to this world, and not really a part of it. She was there to watch, after all, not to comfort the Keeper of Air.

Keeper Peri then stood up and wiped away her tears. She took a deep breath and stood tall. Peri smiled sadly, recognizing what she was doing. She was trying to act strong, trying to fool herself into thinking that everything was going to be okay. She was convincing herself that Kenneth would be coming back to her. To her and the baby.

Peri gasped. If Keeper Peri died in six weeks, and was eight month pregnant now, that meant that either she died just about to give birth... or died just after giving birth. There could be a little Peri running around Beindor! Peri wondered if the child even knew who his or her parents were. If they had been raised to hate their father, not even knowing Tárquin was their father. She realized that she could pass the child on the street, and not even know they were there.

She had to find out if Keeper Peri's child was alive. And if so, who they were. She wondered how many eighteen-year-old orphans there were in Beindor. There couldn't be a huge amount, and if she used her Keeper authority, it would be easy to figure it out.

Peri was pulled from her thoughts when Keeper Peri placed a hand on her large stomach. Peri watched in amazement as the bulge under her dress started to shrink until there was nothing left. Keeper Peri no longer looked like she was pregnant. Peri realized it was the concealment charm she had mentioned earlier. She had lifted it to show her husband, and he flew from her.

Keeper Peri walked past Peri and out the door. Intrigued, Peri quickly kept pace with her pregnant counterpart. She followed her down the hall, around a corner and into a bedroom. Peri was surprised to see Keeper Peri walk over to a small girl sitting on the large bed, playing with a life sized doll.

The girl turned to look up at Keeper Peri and her face lit up. With a large smile she said, "Auntie Peri! Can we go see Briam now?"

Keeper Peri laughed, "If I didn't know any better, Thisbe, I'd think you have a crush on that boy."

Thisbe's cheeks turned a dark shade of red and she frowned, "Auntie Peri! He's just a baby! And I'm six years old! I should be dating men by now!"

Keeper Peri covered her mouth, "Men! But they're so yuckie!"

Thisbe giggled, "How can you say that? Don't you like men?"

"Sure," Keeper Peri said as Thisbe got down off the bed. Peri followed the two out of the room, and down the hall. Keeper Peri continued, "But men can be so *annoying*. Why would we want to date them?"

Thisbe shrugged, "I don't know. That's what Priya said."

"Priya said that, huh?" Keeper Peri said with a small shake of her head.

Thisbe nodded, "She also said that she is going to marry Pritam."

"Who's Pritam?" Keeper Peri asked, looking down at her niece.

Thisbe blushed again, "He's the boy who lives over the wall."

Peri smiled at the little girl who was walking next to Keeper Peri. She was such a cute little thing, Peri wondered who she belonged to. She kept calling Keeper Peri 'Auntie' so Peri knew she couldn't be the mother. It had to be one of her cousins. Peri wondered which one of them was luckily married, or if they all were and she was the only one that got left out. Figures she would be the one to fall in love with their archenemy.

Who does that, anyway? Peri thought as she followed Keeper Peri and little Thisbe into a new room. It was very similar to the room that Keeper Peri had met with Kenneth in, except instead of a large dining room table in the center, there was a group of couches and a smaller coffee table in the center. Sitting on one of the couches was a couple about the same age as Keeper Peri. Kiros and Leda Middlen. They stood when she and Thisbe entered the room. Keeper Peri shook her head, "Sit back down, you two. You know you never have to do that for me."

The couple smiled and sat back down. Leda laughed, "What are you talking about? We bow for everyone who enters the room."

Keeper Peri sat down on the couch across from them, and Peri sat down next to her. She looked at the couple in front of them, and realized that they were very much in love. She wondered how much it hurt Keeper Peri to see them together, when her own marriage was in ruins. The large smile on Keeper Peri's face didn't show an ounce of that pain, but Peri knew it was there.

Thisbe, who had been silently following her aunt since mentioning the boy Pritam, upon entering the room, forgot all her shyness. She rushed over to where a blanket had been laid out on the floor, and a baby placed on his stomach on it. The couple's gaze immediately followed her over, and Peri watched as their eyes brightened when they found their baby boy.

Kiros looked over at Keeper Peri and said, "We're trying to get Briam to crawl. He'll be six months a month from today."

Keeper Peri smiled at the mention of the date. She said, "It will be an important day for all."

The couple exchanged glances, not entirely sure what the Keeper of Air meant by that. Leda then spoke, "Keeper Peri, you said there was reason for this visit. A very important reason." She hesitated, "Is everything okay?"

Keeper Peri sighed, and looked away. Peri watched as she stood up and moved over to Thisbe, who had the baby Briam in her lap. "May I?" she asked of Thisbe.

Thisbe nodded, and held up Briam to Keeper Peri. Keeper Peri picked up the small baby and brought him back over to where she was sitting before. She sat him on her lap and started playing with him. He laughed and Peri could see a few teeth starting to peak through his pink gums. She smiled; babies always made her feel better.

But Peri also noticed that Keeper Peri wasn't answering the couple's questions. They were watching her play with their son, but they were waiting for an answer. Peri could tell that whatever Keeper Peri had said earlier had been bothering them. They wanted to know what was going on, but since they already asked once, they didn't want to push the Keeper.

Keeper Peri finally looked up from the baby, and at his parents. She said, "No, everything is not okay. The situation with ...Tárquin is not going as planned. I'm afraid my cousins and I are going to have to use a dangerous amount of magik to stop him."

"I'm sorry, Keeper Peri," Kiros said. "But what does this have to do with us?"

Keeper Peri looked down at Briam again, who was now chewing on his fingers. When he saw Keeper Peri looking at him, he smiled and held his arms up towards her. She smiled, but it did not reach her eyes. She tickled Briam's stomach and his laughter filled the room. Thisbe came to sit next to Keeper Peri, and she started tickling him as well. Keeper Peri looked down at her, and realized that what she had to say was not for Thisbe's ears.

"Thisbe, why don't you go see if Priya wants to come over for dinner? Maybe even stay the night?"

Thisbe's eye lit up, "Really, Auntie Peri?"

Keeper Peri nodded, and said with a smile, "Sure, why not?"

Thisbe jumped off the couch, and ran out of the room, "Thank you, Auntie Peri!"

Realizing what Keeper Peri just did, the couple sitting on the couch across from her knew that Keeper Peri was about to trust them with a secret that not even the daughter of a Keeper could know. "The magik that we have to use," Keeper Peri said. "There is a very good chance that it will kill us in the process."

Leda gasped, and Kiros stood up, "No! Keeper Peri, I must insist you do not do this. Destroying Tárquin is not worth your life!"

Keeper Peri smiled, "Thank you, Kiros, for your concern, but we have already decided. Destroying Tárquin is worth our lives five times over. He should not be able to continue what he is doing."

Peri watched Keeper Peri as she said this. She could tell that not too far from the surface, this woman was protesting every word she was saying. Peri realized that Keeper Peri did not want to hurt her husband, though she knew it was the only way to save many innocent people's lives.

Kiros sat back down next to his wife. He said, "You are a great leader, Keeper Peri. There are not many who would give their lives for strangers."

"I still do not understand what this has to do with us," Leda said.

Peri watched as her counterpart reached around her neck, and untied a hidden necklace that was there. As Peri watched Keeper Peri place the necklace in her hands, she realized what was on the end of that chain. It was her piece of the Amîr Crystal.

The small crystal was milky white in color, almost like a pearl, and had small jagged edges. Peri wondered how the four Keepers had separated it into four pieces. If they had used a pickax or magik.

Keeper Peri looked up at the couple, who did not recognize the Amîr Crystal as Peri had. She said to them, "I need you to do something for me. A favor."

"Anything, Keeper Peri," Leda said. "You know that."

Keeper Peri nodded, "Yes, but what I am asking is much greater that watching over the Door. What I am asking you to look after needs to be looked after with your lives. It can never leave your sight. You can never give it to another person to look after. You can never let another person touch it. No one must know you have it. Do not give it to your son. Do not give it to Tárquin. And most importantly, do not give it to me."

The couple looked at each other in shock. Kiros then looked at Keeper Peri, "What are you talking about?"

Keeper Peri reached over baby Briam, and handed Kiros her necklace. She and Peri watched as the couple inspected the small crystal. "Is this-? It can't be," Leda said.

Keeper Peri nodded, "It is one fourth of the Amîr Crystal, and I am asking you to be its keeper now."

"One fourth?" Kiros asked. "Where are the other three pieces?"

"I cannot tell where, except that each of my cousins have entrusted them to people who will protect them just as I trust you will," Keeper Peri said.

"We cannot accept this," Leda said. "This is your responsibility, Keeper Peri. Not ours."

Keeper Peri shook her head, "I have only one last responsibility. That is to destroy Tárquin."

Keeper Peri stood, and the couple could not argue with her. They stood as well, and Leda took baby Briam from Keeper Peri. Kiros nodded his head, "We will help you Keeper Peri, because we know you are doing what you believe is right for this country, and for your family."

Kiros looked at Keeper Peri's stomach with a face that made Keeper Peri cover her stomach defensively. Lena put a hand on her husband's forearm and said hesitantly to Keeper Peri, "There are some things you simply cannot hide."

Keeper Peri smiled at them, with a glow in her eyes that made Peri realize she was glad to have someone else know about her secret. Lena then said, "Your cousins should know about this. It isn't right to keep a secret from them."

Keeper Peri nodded, as a tear leaked from her eye, "I know. I am just scared of what they will say. If they will accept the baby."

"Of course they will accept the baby," Lena said in shock. "They are not as cold and unloving as Tárquin."

Keeper Peri gave a sob and covered her mouth. Lena's eyes grew wide and her hands went to her mouth as well, "Oh my..."

Keeper Peri sat back down on the couch, and Lena quickly came over to comfort her. She rubbed the Keeper's back and said, "You should not travel when expecting. Especially when it gets closer to the delivery. How far along are you?"

"Eight months," Keeper Peri said, wiping her eye.

"Eight months?" Lena said in shock. She then laughed, "Honey, you look amazing for a woman eight months pregnant."

Keeper Peri shook her head, "I've been casting a concealment charm on myself."

Lena nodded, and said, "Well then I insist all the more if you are so far along. You must stay here for the duration of the pregnancy. Tar- um, everything else can wait until afterwards."

"What?" Keeper Peri said, starting to get back up. "No, I have to leave. Damia is meeting me here *tomorrow*. We are leaving to meet up with Kendra and Aideen in Neared. Then we are going to face Kenneth."

Lena laughed, "You expect to fight when you are expecting? Honey, you'd kill the baby."

Keeper Peri's face twisted into a look of horror, "I've never done this before. I have no idea what I'm doing."

Lena smiled, and looked over at Kiros, who held Briam on his hip. She looked back at Keeper Peri and said, "Well you're in good hands. I've got five months experience."

Keeper Peri looked up at Lena and smiled, "Thank you. You have been a dear friend to me." She looked over at Kiros, "You both have."

Kiros smiled, "You should probably get some rest."

"Wait," Keeper Peri said. "What about the others? I can't just leave them."

"They can all stay here," Lena said. "One big family reunion before you give birth."

More like before you all die, Peri thought as she watched them talking. The Keepers were on their way now to meet Tárquin for the last time. This would only delay the meeting for a little bit, but she still knew it was inevitable. They were all going to die very soon. The same thought must have come to Keeper Peri, because she then said,

"If I don't make it, for whatever reason," she added because Lena started to protest, "I want you to take the baby."

Peri's eyes light up. If Kiros and Lena Middlen took her baby, then she knew exactly where to find the child. However, a less excited look came over Kiros' face. Keeper Peri saw it and shook her head, "No. I don't want you to raise my child. I want you to find another family to raise him or her. I don't want Kenneth to be able to find his child. I don't want him to have any power over the baby. No one can know that I have a child. No one can know who he or she is."

Kiros nodded, "We can do that."

Lena took Keeper Peri's hand in hers, "Come. You should lie down. I will take care of Thisbe."

Keeper Peri nodded and followed her out of the room. Kiros followed, rocking baby Briam on his hip. Peri sunk back down on the couch in utter defeat. *Great,* she thought. *Now I will never find that baby.*

She wondered if this Kiros and Lena couple would remember to whom they had given the baby. She was going to have to find them and ask. But first she had to get out of this memory/daydream thing. She had been there for a while now, and she wasn't sure if she was going to be able to get out. Korinna had never mentioned where the exit was. She wondered if she had to open a certain door or say a certain phrase. She wondered if 'Abracadabra' could do the trick.

She was about to go open every door she could find when she was suddenly hit with a splitting headache. She pressed her palms to her temples, but it did not help. The room was starting to spin around her. She closed her eyes and prayed for the headache to go away. Then, suddenly, it did. She sat up straight and looked around, wondering if anyone was going through the same thing.

She was surprised to see that there were others. Her cousins. They were sitting up from where they had fallen asleep on the cushions around Seer Korinna's small table. Aideen closed and opened her eyes, and said, "I guess the cushions have a reason after all."

Korinna smiled, "Welcome back, Keepers."

"How long have we been out?" Kendra asked. "I feel like I've been asleep for a week."

Korinna shook her head, "Not that long. Only the day."

"The day!" Kendra said in horror.

Korinna nodded, and looked out a window. The others followed her gaze to find the sun setting behind the buildings of Canhareth.

Chapter Thirty-Six

The Scorpion's House was a small club in the heart of Canhareth. It was originally thought an upper class restaurant, with even the Keepers stopping in for dinner. A man called Tedros 'Teo' Jorrin ran it. However, when Teo's son, Abner Jorrin took over after his father's untimely death, the higher-class restaurant became a hangout for the slum of the city.

With low class management and even lower class customers, The Scorpion's House became ground zero for all sorts of gang fights. The first large fight that broke out at the Scorpion's House was between Rico DeLuca and Jedrek Faal. It was a fight for the record books, with chairs smashed, tables overturned, bartenders injured and drunken onlookers encouraging every swing. After that, the DeLuca/Faal rivalry became epic, and many people went to the Scorpion's House just to witness another fight. Rico and Jedrek were two of the most legendary customers of the Scorpion's House, and once their sons were old enough to visit the club, they were revered as legends as well. All were expecting the fights to begin again.

They weren't disappointed.

"I love the Scorpion's House," Ciro DeLuca said to his brother, Trey. They were walking down to the club with a few of their cousins and friends. "There is always something entertaining."

"Have you ever noticed how the entertainment seems to revolve around us?" Trey asked.

Ciro smiled, "Yeah. Isn't it great?"

Trey rolled his eyes, "Can we just relax tonight? I don't feel like saving your ass, like every other time we step into that place."

Ciro looked over at Trey, anger in his voice, "Are you kidding me?"

Trey looked away, and Ciro added, "Since when do you save my ass? I thought I was always rescuing you."

Trey laughed, covering the fear he had just felt. He shook his head. Ever since Carr discovered him and Kassidy together he started acting very jumpy around Ciro. He was afraid that Ciro would find out as well, and he wouldn't accept it as easily as Carr had. "You couldn't rescue me," he said. "You can barely rescue yourself from some of the situations you get into."

"Whatever," Ciro said and kept walking.

Trey followed close behind. The DeLucas walked in relative silence for a few more minutes, until Ciro suddenly stopped walking. "Well, look who we have here," he said.

Trey came to stand next to his brother, and followed his gaze. He saw that Ciro was looking at a small girl, about five or six years old, walking down the street towards them. There was a small covered basket in the crook of her arm, and she was playing with a daisy in her small hands.

Trey recognized her almost as quickly as Ciro had. It was Sara Faal, the little sister of Carr and Kassidy Faal. They watched as she continued towards them, oblivious to the gang of boys watching. She didn't look up at them until she noticed they were blocking her way home. Her eyes grew wide as she saw Ciro and Trey DeLuca, but her jaw clenched in anger. She wasn't afraid of them, or at least wasn't going to show them that.

"What'cha got in the basket?" Ciro asked in an obviously fake tone.

"None of your business, DeLuca," she said, keeping her ground.

Ciro and the other boys laughed. Trey kept silent. He didn't want to hurt the little Faal girl, but he didn't want his brother to know that. So, he just kept his mouth quiet and listened to his brother taunt Sara Faal. There was nothing wrong with harmless taunting, after all.

"You know," Ciro said, stepping forward. "There are lots of wolves out this late at night. You wouldn't want to be snatched up by one of them. They'll eat you alive."

Sara took a step back, "Leave me alone."

Ciro laughed, "We just want to make sure you get home safely, Sara. That's all."

He reached out to grab her, but she was too fast for him. She turned around and ran the other way, letting out a bloodcurdling scream. Ciro and the others chased after her, cursing at her to stop. Trey followed, suddenly aware that Ciro wasn't planning on harmless taunting. He wanted to hurt the little girl.

Chapter Thirty-Seven

Aideen stepped out of Korinna's Magikal Shoppe and looked to the horizon over the tops of the buildings. She couldn't believe it was already sunset. They had gotten up before sunrise to get on their way, and they still hadn't made it past the city boundaries. Pushing the memory she had seen aside, Aideen said, "I can't believe Korinna kept us that long! We've wasted the entire day!"

"At least we had fun," Damia said, trying to stay optimistic. However, none of her cousins could agree with that statement. She wasn't even telling the truth. None of them had fun in their daydreams. None of them had seen a happy memory, none of them had seen their previous selves at a happy time.

"Speak for yourself," Kynton said, walking up to them from across the street. He had found a bench to lounge on as he waited. "I've been waiting out here for almost eleven hours now."

"Why didn't you go do something?" Damia asked.

"Because I had no idea when you'd be back. I didn't want to miss you, and then be unable to find you again," he said, wrapping an arm around her.

"Alright," Kendra said. "Let's get a move on before we lose the rest of the daylight."

"Wait, you don't want to leave *now*, do you?" Peri asked, stifling a yawn. She wasn't the only one who was exhausted from the magik done that day.

"Yeah," Damia said. "I think we should head back to The Dancing Bear, and get an early start tomorrow. Traveling at night really isn't the smartest thing to do."

Kendra sighed, "Alright, fine. But no more distractions! We've wasted enough time here already."

She started backtracking, walking the same path back to The Dancing Bear they had taken that morning. With every receding step, her anger began to grow. She was also oblivious to what was happening to one of her cousins right behind her.

At first it felt like she was nervous about walking down the dark streets alone, but Damia knew that she wasn't alone. Then the feeling grew into something worse. She was scared; she could see her hands shaking at her side. She could feel her stomach twist into knots, and she had the sudden urge to flee. She stopped walking, knowing something was not right. Knowing that she was in the safe company of her cousins, Damia realized that it was not her own feelings she was channeling.

Tears sprang into her eyes and her breathing became jagged. Kynton, Aideen and Peri noticed her pause and looked back at her. Peri was at her side in seconds, "Damia, what's wrong?"

Kendra paused at Peri's words and turned around to see Damia about to have a nervous breakdown. She sighed and walked over to Aideen and asked, "What happened?"

"Don't look at me," Aideen said. "She just started hyperventilating all of a sudden."

"Damia," Kendra said, walking up to her. She pushed past Kynton and took one of Damia's hands, "What is it?"

Damia looked at Kendra and whispered, "She's so scared."

"Who is?" Kendra asked.

Damia shook her head, having no idea. Kendra looked at her cousins, "What is she talking about?"

"She's channeling someone's feelings," Kynton said. "It's one of her powers."

"We know Empathy is one of her powers, thank you," Kendra said. "Why is this happening now?"

Kynton was about to respond when Damia suddenly gasped. Before Kendra could ask what was wrong, the quiet night was torn apart by a hair-raising scream. Damia's eyes brightened as she turned and ran back down the street they had just come from. "It's her!" she yelled as she turned the corner. "We have to save her!"

"Damia!" Kendra yelled. "Come back here this instant!"

"Who are you, her mom?" Aideen asked as she and Peri followed after.

"I don't like this," Peri was saying. "We should go back. We have no idea what's happening."

"Do you want to leave Damia alone then?" Aideen asked.

"No, of course not," Peri said.

"Then we have to follow her."

Kynton glanced at Kendra, who still had not moved. He had started to follow after Damia, but turned back to her, "Kendra, come on. You know they can't do this alone."

"Do what?" Kendra asked as she followed Kynton. "Save some screaming girl? We don't do the whole saving thing! There's barely even a 'we'!"

Damia was running fast through the streets, only following the fear she could feel from the girl. She couldn't tell where she was, or how deep into the city she was getting. She didn't even know if the others had followed her. All she knew was that the girl was in trouble, and that she was going to save her. There was no way she was going to let another little girl suffer like she had.

Peri was moving a lot faster than Aideen, and was able to follow the exact route Damia was taking through the city. It was like she had lojacked Damia's brain, and was able to tell exactly where she was going. Aideen, however, was not as lucky. Not ever being a fast runner, she quickly lagged behind and lost sight first of Damia and then Peri. Soon she found herself running alongside Kendra and Kynton.

"What's happening?" Kendra asked her.

"Besides my sides splitting apart? Nothing much. Last I saw, Peri was chasing Damia who was chasing a scream. How are things back here? You two getting to know each other?"

Kendra gave Aideen a death glare and Aideen smiled innocently back. Kynton bit his tongue to keep from laughing. He continued to run silently beside the two Keepers, knowing he could go faster, but not wanting to out shine the Keeper of Water. He knew she would hold it over his head eventually.

~*~

"Damia! Wait up! Do you even know where you're going?" Peri yelled after her cousin, almost toe to toe with her.

"Peri, we have to save her," Damia said. "She's hurt and scared. I never want to feel like this again. It's awful."

"Don't worry," Peri said. "We're going to find her."

Damia nodded and they continued to run toward the mysterious girl. It only took a few more minutes before they rounded a corner and saw why Damia was feeling so scared and in pain. At the other end of the street, a gang of boys was beating up a small girl, one who couldn't have been more than seven years old. They could see a basket abandoned by the side of the road, a few yards from where the boys were. There was a crumpled flower a few feet away from the basket.

"What are we going to do?" Peri whispered. "We can't take on the Jets!"

"I have an idea," Damia said. "You distract them, I'll sneak around and grab the girl."

"Distract them?" Peri asked, panicking. "How should I distract them?"

"I don't know! You're smart. You can figure it out!" Damia said as she quickly ran down to a street parallel to the one Peri and the Jets were on.

As soon as she was gone, Peri stepped closer to the gang. "Hey," she yelled. "Quit picking on her! What did she do to you?"

The boys stopped kicking and taunting immediately. They fell silent and slowly turned toward the voice that had interrupted them. They saw it was a girl they had never seen before, and laughed. They could easily tell she was no threat to them. It was obvious she wasn't very confident in herself, probably never stood up to someone in her life.

"What? Are you going to teach us a lesson, then?" one of the larger boys yelled.

Peri backed up a step, but her fists curled tight and she said, "Just leave her alone and no one will get hurt."

The Jets looked at each other and couldn't control the laughter that followed. The large boy started coming at Peri, "Oh, I think it's a little too late for that."

Peri tried to stand her ground, but when the other boys started running at her as well, she felt her heart drop to the floor. She screamed and started running in the other direction. *Happy now, Damia? I distracted them!*

~*~

As soon as Damia left Peri, she started running at her top speed. She moved as fast as she could down the side street, trying to distract herself from thoughts of doubt. *Peri can handle herself. Those guys wouldn't do anything to her. She's smart. She won't let them hurt her.*

She turned the corner and slowed down until she reached the street where she knew the little girl was. She peaked around the side of the building, and saw that the gang of boys was approaching Peri. They were laughing, but walking slowly, so Damia knew Peri was still safe. She crept over to the small form she knew to be the girl, and reached out to her. She instantly stiffened, and Damia sighed, knowing she wasn't dead. The little girl peaked up at Damia with a tear streaked face and Damia whispered, "It's okay. I'm going to get you out of here."

The girl wrapped her arms around Damia's neck, "I want my daddy."

"Okay. But first we need to leave. Be very quiet, okay?" Damia asked, picking the small child up in her arms.

Damia felt the girl nod into her shoulder and she started to head back the way she had come. She froze when she heard Peri's scream. She looked over her shoulder to see the gang of boys was now chasing Peri. *Happy now, Damia? I distracted them!* she heard Peri say in her head.

Run to Kynton and Aideen. They'll help you, Damia said.

Fine. But you owe me big time for this, Peri thought back.

Damia turned to run the opposite way, when she almost crashed into a figure standing behind her. She jumped back, thinking she had been cornered by another one of the gang members, when she realized it was Kynton standing there. "Are you okay?" he asked. "What happened?"

"Go help Peri," Damia said quickly.

Kynton looked behind her and Damia watched as his face dropped in horror. He ran past her, and she spun around to see what had made him look like that. Then she saw that the gang of boys had caught up with Peri, and were now using her as a punching bag, similar to what they had been doing to the little girl. Damia watched as Aideen ran past her to join Kynton in saving Peri.

Damia wanted to go help them, but didn't want to abandon the little girl. She could feel the girl's arms wrap tighter around her, and felt her begin to sob into her shoulder. Damia felt tears spring into her own eyes, and knew she couldn't leave her unprotected. Just then, Kendra came to a stop beside Damia and said, "I see you've found the girl."

"Yeah," Damia said, without taking her eyes off the scene in front of her. "And the gangs of Canhareth."

~*~

Aideen reached the gang of boys attacking Peri only seconds after Kynton. She watched as he grabbed one of them and hooked him in the side of the jaw. She quickly followed suit and grabbed another one of boys. She jabbed him in the stomach and he doubled over.

"You bitch. Who the fuck do you think you're dealing with?" he asked, looking up at her.

"Just some snot nosed brat who thinks he can pick on anyone he wants," she answered, punching him again, this time an uppercut to the jaw.

He lost his balance, but quickly gained it again and glared at her. "You'd better stop, before you regret it. I'm not afraid to hit a girl"

Aideen smirked, "I don't think you realize who *you're* dealing with."

She then went to jab him again when he caught her fist and twisted her arm until it was at its breaking point. Aideen gasped, and closed her eyes, fighting the sudden anger she was feeling. She knew the last time she had allowed herself to get this angry, she had almost killed Kendra. Then she thought that it wasn't a bad idea, using her powers against this asshole. She just hoped that Kynton and Peri could get out of her way quickly enough.

She sucked in a deep breath and kicked the boy holding her in the groin. He instantly let go of her. She spun around and opened her eyes. She couldn't see anything but fire, couldn't hear anything but Peri screaming and many male voices swearing. She did manage to hear one of the boys say, "Shit, Ciro! That's Keeper Aideen!"

Then the fire faded into black.

It only took Aideen a few seconds to wake up, and she found that she hadn't even fallen to the ground this time. However, when she did open her eyes, she saw that many things had changed since she had closed them. She wondered if more time had passed than she thought, because Kendra was standing next to her, holding her arm. Everyone else had disappeared.

"Aideen, what the hell was that for?" Kendra yelled as soon as she saw that Aideen's eyes had opened. "Peri was right there!"

"What? You think I did that on purpose?" Aideen yelled back. "I have no control over it."

"Well then keep your eyes closed next time that happens. Maybe you'll only burn yourself," Kendra said back.

Aideen wanted to say something back, but there were more pressing matters at hand. "Where are the others?" she asked.

Kendra just scoffed, "Thanks to your uncontrollable power, they recognized us as the Keepers. They grabbed Peri and ran. Kynton and Damia went after them. I stayed behind to watch you and Sara."

"Sara?" Aideen asked. It was then that she saw a small blonde haired girl clutching Kendra's legs. Kendra patted Sara's head and said to her, "Don't worry. We'll get you home as soon as the others come back."

Sara didn't respond and Aideen raised an eyebrow, *Is she okay?*

She just got beat up by a bunch of overgrown boys, what do you think? Kendra asked back, rolling her eyes. Aideen watched as she reached down and picked up Sara in her arms. Sara quickly wrapped her arms around Kendra's neck and buried her blood and tear stained face in the crook of Kendra's neck.

"So we just have to wait here until they come back?" Aideen asked.

"Do you know how we can track them?" Kendra asked. "Apparently Elvin have some sort of tracking gift, because he said it was no problem for him to find her."

Aideen frowned, and together they waited for Kynton, Peri and Damia to reappear. They waited for less than a minute before Damia and Kynton reappeared at the end of the road. Aideen and Kendra immediately started for them. "Where's Peri?" Kendra asked.

Damia was crying. She looked away when Kendra spoke, and Kendra suddenly felt light headed, as if she had stood up too fast. *This cannot be happening*, she thought to herself.

Kynton shook his head, "I lost them. We got about five blocks, and then they must have crossed the market place, because I couldn't find where they went next. There were too many other people around today for me to be able to find them. They got lost in the crowds."

"Are you crazy?" Kendra yelled. "You just lost our cousin! Maybe this isn't important to you, but it is to us! We can't just stop looking for her! She's been kidnapped in a foreign city! In a foreign country! We *cannot* lose her!"

Sara looked up at Kendra with wide eyes, "Are you going to take me home now?"

Damia immediately took the little girl away from her yelling cousin and said, "Yes, we are. Sara, can you do me a favor?"

Sara nodded and Damia asked, "Did you recognize those boys? They've taken my cousin, and we need to find her. Do you know where they would have taken her?"

Tears sprang into Sara's eyes, "Those were the DeLucas. They are an evil family, and we've hated them forever. They're always bullying my brother."

"Okay, thank you," Damia said. "We'll take you home now. Which way is it?"

Sara pointed down the street and Damia started following her directions. Kynton walked by her side, with his arm wrapped around her waist. She looked up at him and smiled weakly, "Thank you for helping me look for Peri."

"Of course I would," he said. "I would do anything for you."

She leaned into his side, trying to forget the memory she had witnessed earlier that day. *That was a lifetime ago. He has to be over her by now.*

Following behind them, Kendra said to Aideen, "We have to talk to Sara's family. Her brother might know where those DeLucas live. They'd most likely keep her there."

"Kendra," Aideen asked. "Why would they take Peri? What is the purpose of that?"

"I don't know," Kendra responded. "They panicked? For ransom money? I have no idea."

It took less than ten minutes for them to reach Sara Faal's house. It was on a small residential street near the outskirts of town. All the houses were the same, two room buildings made out of mud and wood. Each one had only one door, facing the street with a small window beside it. Under the window of Sara Faal's house was a beat up old bench, covered in chipping purple paint. On the bench was a flowerpot, filled to the top with dirt and one small green sprout sticking out.

Kendra stepped up and knocked loudly on the door to Sara's house. She had barely finished before the door was thrown open and a tall woman with dark red hair said frantically, "Sara? Is that you?"

She then saw that there were four strangers standing on her threshold. She looked startled at them, "Oh, I'm sorry. Can I help you?"

"Mommy!"

The woman found Sara in Damia's arms and her hands flew to her face. She recovered quickly, just in time for Sara to reach out and switch from Damia's grasp to her mother's. The woman wrapped her arms tightly around her daughter and kissed the top of her head, "Sara, are you alright? What happened?"

Sara looked up at her, and in a voice that held no seven-year-old innocence said, "The DeLucas jumped me."

Her mother gasped and called over her shoulder, "Jedrek! Carr! Kass! Get out here, *now!*"

The cousins and Kynton, still standing in the doorway, watched as a man and two teenagers walked through the only door off the main room. Aideen's mouth fell as she recognized the guys instantly from her poker game the night before. Carr recognized her as well, but Jedrek's attention was completely on his wife and daughter. Kassidy Faal moved over to her mother's side, eyeing the four strangers cautiously.

Jedrek rushed over to them and took his daughter into his hands. He touched her face, assessing the wounds. She had a cut on her cheek, a split lip and her left eye was starting to bruise. She didn't seem to care, glad to be in her father's arms. She threw her thin arms around her father's large neck and buried her face in his shoulder. He held her tight, and looked from his wife to the four standing awkwardly in the doorway.

"Who are you?" he demanded, his grip on his daughter tightening.

"They brought Sara to us," Fay Faal said to her husband. She turned to them and smiled, "Thank you, so much, for saving our daughter's life."

"Wait a minute," Jedrek said, looking at Aideen. "I know you. Clio, right? From The Dancing Bear last night."

Fay's eyes narrowed and Carr stepped in. With a laugh, he said, "That's right! You're the one who wiped us all clean in that poker game! Are you here to give us our money back?"

Fay raised an eyebrow at her husband, who just shrugged innocently back.

"Actually," Kendra said, stepping in, "We need your help."

"What's wrong?" Jedrek asked.

"Our cousin, Thalia, was kidnapped by the same people who attacked your daughter," Kendra explained. "She mentioned that you knew them. We were wondering if you could help us get her back."

Carr glanced over at his twin sister, Kassidy, who gave him a very small panicked look. He then looked at his father, whose eyebrows had knotted together at the mention of the DeLucas. Carr nodded, "Of course we will. You saved Sara, we will help you save Thalia."

"Thank you," Kendra said. "Can you show us where they've taken her?"

"The DeLuca house, no doubt," Carr said. "They love to torture people there."

Damia looked over at her cousins, her face showing all the emotions, the horror they were feeling. Kendra looked back at her and then at Carr, "Torture?"

"That's probably not the right word," Kassidy Faal said.

Carr laughed, "You've never been there, remember? I have. They are terrible."

"What are they going to do to Thalia?" Damia asked, her voice wavering. Kynton took her hand in his, seeing it was shaking at her side.

Carr shook his head, "I have no idea. They've never taken a girl before. I doubt Ciro and Trey have much of a problem beating them up as well."

Jedrek held his youngest daughter closer to his chest, "The DeLucas are a bad family. You don't want to go in there unprepared. If those boys don't kill you, their father will."

"Well we can't sit around and do nothing. Thalia is there now. We have to get her, before she gets killed," Kendra said.

"We can handle ourselves," Aideen said, thinking about the power that got them in trouble in the first place.

"No," Fay said. "I will not let four teenagers go on a suicide mission in the middle of the night. Not when the DeLucas have guns and more manpower than you'll ever have. You'll all be killed."

"We can handle ourselves," Aideen repeated, glaring at the woman. She didn't know who she was talking to, and Aideen wished she could tell her, just so she would shut up and listen to her.

But Fay was just as stubborn as the Keeper of Fire, and shook her head. She glared right back and said, "I will not let you. You will come in the house, have dinner with us, and we will talk like civilized people. I will not have my son lead you into this fight unprepared. Then you will go back to where ever you came from and wait for the DeLucas' next move."

Carr nodded, "They're going to find you, no matter what. It's what they do. It'd be better to play by their rules."

"We're not going to sit around waiting for them!" Kendra shouted. "They could kill Thalia or worse while we're sitting around here, eating dinner."

Damia looked at Kendra, "They're right. If we try to rescue Thalia now, they'll be expecting us. We'll be on their terms, in their house. We can't do that. We're not good enough, not organized enough. The Faals are. They've done this before, they know the De-Lucas. We need to trust what they say."

"Your cousin will be okay," Kassidy said. "Trust me."

Kendra glared at Kassidy, but said nothing. She looked at Aideen, who seemed to be her only ally in this, but she was losing her fast. Aideen looked back at her, "I think Damia is right. We need to cool down, figure this out like civilized people."

Kendra refused to look at Kynton, knowing he was already on Damia's side. "Alright, fine." Kendra said. "We'll talk, but you'd better talk fast. I'm not wasting more time. Who knows how much time Thalia has."

~*~

A yawn came from the corner of the dining room table. The Faals, the Keepers and Kynton all were sitting around, eating a large meal that Fay Faal had put out for them. Jedrek and Carr were discussing the DeLucas very animatedly, telling the company all the stories of them. How they relentlessly tormented them, picking fights over nothing and everything. The only thing they couldn't explain was how the feuding had begun.

"It's been going on since the days of Earth," Jedrek said, which got a laugh from his family. Everyone knew, of course, that there was no such thing as Earth.

However, the conversation ran long, and soon the smallest at the table was ready for bed. She let out the loudest yawn she could muster, and then proceeded to rub her blurry eyes. Jedrek picked up his youngest child in his arms and asked, "Has someone had a long day?"

Sara nodded, "I wanna go to sleep."

"Okay," Jedrek said, standing up. "Say goodnight to our new friends."

"Good night," Sara said as her eyes began to droop. As Jedrek walked toward the bedroom door, Sara perked up a tiny bit, "Can you tell me a story, Daddy?"

"Of course, Sweetheart. What story do you want to hear?"

"A Keepers story!" Sara said, excitedly, just as Jedrek expected her to say.

Damia, Kendra and Aideen looked at each other in surprise. They knew that the Keepers had a great impact on the lives of the people of Beindor; they were the ones who brought them here, after all. Nevertheless, they hadn't expected to be the subject of bedtime stories. They wondered what sort of stories were told before bedtime, and if they had any sort of truth in them. They wondered if they were going to hear something about their past lives that they had not heard before. Panic also set in as they wondered if any of the Faals would be shrewd enough to figure out that the subjects of the story were sitting at their dining room table at that very moment.

Jedrek had given up protesting Keeper stories a while ago, and laughed. Instead, he asked, "What kind of Keepers story would you like?"

"Any story, Daddy," Sara said, too excited to care.

"Okay then," Jedrek started, thinking of a good story. He waited for Sara to crawl into bed, and sat down on the bed next to her. She looked up at him expectantly and he smiled, "Long before Vavia was the city it was today, it was a small group of huts on the side of a mountain, all situated around the Door of Anwelindo. There were many cliffs and plateaus around the small gathering, and one day a young man found himself standing on one of these cliffs, watching the sunrise over the waters of the Rómearya.

"Keeper Peri, always an avid sunrise watcher, came over to stand next to the man and to watch the sunrise together. However, the cliff was not made to support the weight of more than one person, and began to crack. It didn't take long for the cliff to split com-

pletely from the side of the mountain, and before the sun had finished rising off the ocean, Keeper Peri and the man were plummet-
ing to their deaths.

"Or at least, that's what they had expected to happen once
the cliff gave way. Instead, they were holding on to each other for
dear life, unmoving in the spot where there had been a cliff moment
before. 'What are you doing?' Keeper Peri shouted, still panicking.
'Me?' came the man's response. 'You're the Keeper! Not me!' And
that's how Peri learned of her power of flight."

Sara giggled, "Keeper Peri's funny."

Jedrek smiled, "Yes, and now it's time for bed. I'll tell you the
rest of the story tomorrow night."

"The rest of the story?" Sara said, excitedly.

"Oh yes," Jedrek said. "Just because Keeper Peri could fly
didn't mean she knew how. They were stuck up there for a good
three days."

Sara laughed, and Jedrek leaned in to kiss her forehead,
"Night, kiddo."

"Night, Daddy."

Jedrek turned around to see Clio, Terri and Polly standing in
the doorway. Terri had tears in her eyes, Clio's hand was over her
mouth, trying to keep from laughing, and Polly's mouth was hanging
open."Three days," Clio asked with a laugh.

Jedrek nodded, "Have you never heard that one before?"

The three girls shook their heads. Polly said, "We have heard
very few stories of the Keepers. Each one amazes us even more."

"I don't know," Clio said. "I'm still trying to get over the first
one."

Jedrek was about to ask which story she was talking about,
but Kynton quickly interrupted. "Come on, girls. I think it's time we
head back to the inn. Long day ahead of us, tomorrow."

Polly nodded and the girls said their goodbyes. They and Kynton then made their way out of the Faal house and into the cool night.

"What a cool power," Aideen said. "I wish I could fly."

"We don't know that Peri can," Kendra said. "That was just a bedtime story."

Kynton shook his head, "Keeper Peri definitely flew, and that story was true. I'm surprised that man knew it so well."

Kendra silently glared at Kynton, wishing he wasn't such a know-it-all when it came to the Keepers. Especially because they knew so little, and they were the Keepers. "And how do you know it so well?"

"Keeper Damia told it to me," Kynton said, as if it was an obvious answer. Damia smiled at him and took his hand in hers. Kendra saw this and quickly walked ahead of them. Aideen chose to ignore both of her stubborn cousins, and walked between them. She said, to no one in particular, "I wonder if I have any cool powers."

Chapter Thirty-Eight

It came the very next morning. Aideen, Kendra, Damia, and Kynton were leaving The Dancing Bear when Mahak the bartender called them over. He silently handed it over to Kendra, and without another word, went back to work. When they asked who had given him the letter, he simply shrugged his shoulders.

> Keepers,
>
> You will get your cousin back when we get what we want. Ten thousand Denas. You have one week. Meet us by the Willow Tree at dusk on Tuesday. If we get our money, no harm will come to her. If we don't, then I'm afraid to say we can't guarantee her safety. We are not afraid of you, Keepers.
>
> Sincerely,
>
> *Ciro and Trey DeLuca*

"Oh my god," Damia said. "They're holding her for ransom? How did they even figure out who we were?"

"Aideen's little stunt kind of gave us away," Kendra said. "Not everyone can make fire appear on demand."

"Who said anything about my fire being on demand?" Aideen snapped.

Ignoring Aideen's comment, Kendra reread the letter. She was beginning to panic. It was their fourth day in this world, and they were already getting into major trouble. What did that say about the rest of the journey, if they got through this, that is. They hadn't even begun, and they were already being kidnapped and held for ransom. "Where are we going to get ten thousand Denas?"

"Gringotts?" Damia asked. "They've got Knuts, Sickles, and Galleons. Maybe they have Denas too."

Aideen shook her head, "Seriously? At a time like this, you just have to bring up Harry Potter. You are such a nerd."

"Oh, like you weren't thinking the same thing," Damia said, glaring at Aideen.

"Guys," Kendra interrupted, but not to agree with Damia that she had been thinking the same thing. Instead, she said, "Focus. We have a serious problem."

She then glanced at Kynton, and so did the others. He looked up at them, as if coming out of a day dream. He shook his head, "Ten thousand Denas. I don't think you realize how much that is. One Dena would be like," he paused, trying to remember what the Keepers had decided, "one half of an Earth dollar."

"So they want five thousand dollars?" Aideen asked. "That's not so bad. I think we might be able to-"

"Wait, no," Kendra said, realizing they forgot something. "The Keepers made the Dena in 1965, right? So that means the Dena was fifty cents in 1965. With inflation, fifty cents today would be about three dollars. So today, three dollars times ten thousand Denas is thirty thousand dollars."

"Oh my god," Damia said again. "Thirty thousand dollars? In one week? That's impossible!"

"Wait a second," Kynton said, putting a hand on Damia's arm.

"Oh great, more bad news," Aideen said. "Don't tell me. There's an interest rate. Oh no, maybe a tax we have to figure in. Everything is taxed nowadays."

"I have eight thousand Denas in my room right now," Kynton said. "It's everything I have, but there is no way I am going to let Peri get hurt."

A huge smile formed on Damia's face. She reached up for Kynton's face and pulled him down into a kiss. Even though he wasn't expecting it, Kynton quickly responded, wrapping his arms tight around Damia. It only took Kendra half a second to interrupt with a loud clearing of her throat. Damia pulled away, a dark blush creeping into her face. Kynton looked dazed.

"So that means we need to get two thousand Denas," Kendra said, "by next Tuesday."

"Maybe the Faals can help us," Aideen said.

"No offense to them," Kendra said. "But I don't think they have two thousand Denas just lying around."

"They might be able to tell us where we can raise the money," Aideen explained. "Maybe some high stakes poker games I can get into."

Damia raised an eyebrow, "Why are you so good at poker, anyway?"

Aideen smirked, "Why should I tell you? I don't want any competition!"

"Oh my god, Aideen," Damia said, putting her hands on her hips. "You don't cheat, do you?"

Aideen laughed, "Why would I need to do that when I am so amazing at playing by the rules?"

"Seriously, guys," Kendra said. "We need to focus. Am I the only one concerned for Peri right now?"

"Of course not," Aideen said. "We're all very worried about her."

"But there isn't much we can do," Damia said. "We have to focus on raising the money. That's the safest way to get Peri back."

"I know," Kendra snapped. "So stop talking about poker and Gringotts and let's start getting that money!"

"But how?" Aideen asked. "Since poker was so rudely put down."

Damia ignored Aideen's comment, and Kendra looked around The Dancing Bear, hoping to get inspired. She saw Mahak wiping down the long bar while a woman, most likely his wife was handing out platefuls of food to customers. The piano man walked down the stairs and slowly headed over to the piano on the other side of the room. Kendra watched as he grabbed a piece of toast waiting for him on the piano. As she watched him, she realized she knew exactly how they could raise the money. They would get jobs at The Dancing Bear.

~*~

It was a barren bedroom, but to Peri it felt like a prison cell in Alcatraz. The only two things decorating her cell were a mattress on the floor and a wooden chair pushed up against the far wall. She sat on the mattress, with her knees pulled up to her chest and tear stains on her cheeks. She sat there all night, too tired to try to escape; too scared to close her eyes and rest.

She had awoken midflight, as the boy Ciro tossed her onto the mattress. That's when her brain kicked in and she remembered trying to save a little girl with Damia. She also remembered being chased by a gang of boys, and a bright flash of light. That was it. That was the last thing she remembered. She wondered if the gang of boys had gotten away in that flash of light. She wondered if they had been successful in saving that little girl.

She quickly sat up and looked between the two boys in front of her. Her two captors. The one, Ciro, was watching her with pure hatred and joy at the same time. Peri could see the wheels turning behind those grey eyes. The other boy, Trey, however, had a different look on his face. True, there was hatred there, but instead of his brother's joy, Peri saw disgust.

She couldn't help but wonder what she had done to deserve such hatred. Sure, she had stopped these boys from hurting someone they hated, but did that justify kidnapping?

The joy on Ciro's face broke out into a smirk as he turned to Trey and said, "Who would have thought our night would go so well? Not only did we get to beat up a Faal, but imagine what kind of ransom we can get for a Keeper!"

Peri's mouth fell open, *That is what this is about? Ransom!*

She looked at the boy in shock. While she had always thought it would be fun to star in a movie, like Marilyn Monroe, or do something noteworthy, like climb Mount Everest, she never thought that her life would turn out to be such an adventure. She never thought she would be held for ransom.

"How do we even know she's a Keeper," Trey asked as his eyes narrowed. He glared at Ciro for a second before remembering what he was doing. He relaxed and turned to face Peri, a look of total boredom spread across his face. He looked Peri over, "Shouldn't they be like a hundred years old? And a little more powerful?"

Of course, Peri knew the answer to that question, but she wasn't going to help these idiots out. "What's your name?" Ciro asked her, but she only narrowed her eyes at him.

He laughed and said, "Peri, right?" She looked at him in shock and he added, "I heard the other ones call your name."

Peri frowned, but refused to confirm his question. He continued. "Of course the one who tried to set me on fire was Aideen, and the two watching were Damia and Kendra." He paused, and then laughed, "The guy you were with, that must be Rohak; the Keepers' trusty sidekick."

Despite the seriousness of the situation, Peri found herself laughing. She forgot her composure and that she was not trying to give anything away about her and her cousins. However, the thought of Kynton in tights was just too comical.

Ciro watched Peri's burst of laughter, and was caught off guard. Then he was offended; first, the silent treatment and now she was laughing at him. He wanted to slap her, make her stop laughing and start respecting her superiors.

Trey also saw this as no laughing matter. She did not know Ciro like he did, and he knew that laughing at him would have consequences. He could see the anger in Ciro's face, how his eyes got wide and his jaw grew stiff. Trey wanted to yell at the girl for laughing, she was causing more trouble for herself than necessary. Ciro's temper was not a good thing to be on the short end of.

Peri noticed her mistake almost immediately. She covered her mouth and looked between the two boys. Ciro looked about to explode, and Trey looked annoyed. Peri pursed her lips and said, "Kynton is no tight wearing sidekick. More like our tour guide."

"What?" Ciro asked. "You mean you don't even know your own city?"

Peri's mouth snapped shut, as she realized she was about to give away more secrets. She glared silently at Ciro and Trey, and they glared right back. Finally, Ciro gave up, "Fine. You don't have to talk to us. You can sit in here all by yourself for the rest of the week."

Ciro made a move toward the door, "Come on, Trey. We have a letter to write."

Trey followed Ciro out, and that was the last Peri saw of them that night. She didn't move off the mattress until the first rays of sunlight made their way over to her. She blinked in surprise, wondering what a strange city she must be in. Sunlight was never able to pass through brick walls on Earth. She immediately looked over to where the sunlight was coming in, and found herself looking down one of the many residential streets of Canhareth.

She quickly got up and walked over to the window, cursing herself for not noticing it before. She pressed her hands against the cool glass and pushed gently. She was surprised to find that the window opened easily. It was unlocked and the ground was only a small jump away. She pushed the window up slowly, afraid that someone might hear. She placed her foot on the windowsill, about to escape captivity, when she realized she was not alone.

She looked over her shoulder to see Ciro DeLuca sitting in the wooden chair pushed against the wall across from the mattress on the floor. She paused, wondering if he could reach her before she made it out the window. She was almost halfway there. Her foot was still on the window. She gripped the windowsill, screaming at herself inside her head. *Do it! You're almost there! Make a run for it! Get to a busy street! He'll never be able to catch you then!*

"I wouldn't do that if I were you," Ciro said. He hadn't moved, but she could tell he was ready to jump. He was relaxed in the chair, leaning back, with his arms folded across his chest. His legs were stretched out in front of him, crossed at the ankles. He looked bored as he watched Peri's failed attempt to escape.

Peri studied him, and realized she would never make it. As soon as she swung her leg out, he'd be there. He'd just grab her other leg and pull her right back in. She wouldn't even be able to make it out the window. She sighed and set both her feet firmly back on the ground. She then closed the window and turned to face Ciro, "What do you want?"

Ciro smirked, "Good choice. Besides, Trey is down the street, and would have grabbed you. If you even made it that far."

"What do you want?" Peri repeated, folding her arms across her chest.

Ciro nodded to the mattress on the floor, "Just thought I'd be nice and bring you some food."

Peri looked over to the mattress, where a small plate of pasta and sauce was sitting. She walked over to it and picked it up. Sitting down on the mattress, she swallowed a fork-full and said, "This is good."

Ciro shrugged, "It's just leftovers from last night. My mother's Spaghetti Carbonara."

"Tell her I say it's wonderful," Peri said, with a mouthful of the pasta.

Ciro gave a laugh, "My mother has no idea you're here, and we're going to keep it that way."

Peri arched her eyebrow, "You mean your parents have no idea you kidnap and beat up people? What a shock they're in for."

Ciro shrugged, "Not really. My father practically does this for a living. To him, it's no big deal that you're here."

Peri's lips curled, "You do this on a regular basis?"

Ciro laughed, "It's not like I get my kicks kidnapping Keepers and holding them ransom."

"But you do enjoy beating up seven-year old girls," Peri said, setting her plate down.

"That wasn't just any seven-year old girl," Ciro said, his laughter fading. "That was Sara Faal."

"And what? She beat you up before and you want revenge?"

"She's a Faal," he spat. "That family is the scum of the earth. They sleep on maggot infested beds and eat dirt for breakfast."

Peri raised an eyebrow, "Why do I doubt that?"

Ciro's eyes flashed with anger, "The DeLucas and the Faals have never gotten along. We never will, either. It's just who we are. We beat each other up and try to kill each other. You just stepped into a mess that wasn't your problem."

"Why do you hate each other so much?" Peri asked. Sure, she had hated her cousins, hated Annie, but never this much. Ciro was fuming, leaning forward in his chair, with his fists curled into tight balls. He was willing to kill this family, but for what?

"I need a reason to hate them?" Ciro almost yelled. "They've insulted my family, insulted our name. They think they are God's gift to us all. They deserve to die. They deserve to be wiped off the planet."

Peri sat back, realizing Ciro had been right. They had stepped into a mess way bigger than they were ready for.

Chapter Thirty-Nine

"Well hello there," Felton the piano man said, looking up to see the girl from two nights earlier standing next to him. He smiled, "Are you here to sing another ballad for us?"

Kendra blushed, "Actually, I was wondering if that offer was still open?"

Felton's eyes got wide, and he nodded, "Of course it is. Our business will quadruple with your musical talents bringing every available bachelor in a five-mile radius through those doors."

Kendra laughed nervously, but said, "So when can I start? And how much does it pay?"

"You can start now," Felton said. "And as far as pay goes, I can't pay you much. How does three Denas an hour sound? And we'll split the tips 50/50."

Kendra nodded, knowing she probably couldn't get much better than that. She held out her hand and Felton shook it. He smiled, "Welcome to The Dancing Bear team."

On the other side of the room, a similar conversation was happening between Mahak Baer, Damia, Aideen and Kynton. He looked between them and said, "I would love to hire all three of you, but I can't afford to pay three more people. I'll take two of you, a waitress and bartender. I'm sorry," he said, looking between Aideen and Damia.

Aideen and Damia looked at each other, wondering who would take the job. Aideen then looked at Mahak and asked, "How often is poker played in here?"

Mahak laughed, "Every night there are at least three games. Plus once a month I hold an all-day tournament. That'll be the end of the week. Saturday."

Aideen smiled and turned to Damia, "That's okay. You take the job."

Damia narrowed her eyes at her younger cousin, "You're not thinking what I think you're thinking, are you?"

"I don't know," Aideen responded. "How good are your mind reading skills?"

"Clio! You can't just play poker! What if you lose all your money? Then we'll be short and won't be able to-" Damia paused and glanced at Mahak before continuing, "-go see that play!"

Aideen laughed, "Have a little more faith in me, *Terri*."

Damia glared at Aideen a second longer before turning to Mahak and saying, "When do you want us to start?"

Mahak looked around, noticing that in the few seconds he had taken out to talk to these people, the entire tavern seemed to fill with customers. "Now," he said.

"And what about pay?" Kynton asked. "Is there an hourly rate, or daily?"

Mahak looked both him and Damia over, "I can give you five Denas an hour for bartending, and three Denas an hour for waitressing." He then added, "Plus whatever my wife asks help with. You know how to change bedcovers, yes?"

Damia smiled and nodded her head, "Of course."

"Good," Mahak said with a smile, then handing Damia a pile of menus. "Give these to that table over there, and take their orders."

Damia nodded again and quickly walked over to the waiting table. Mahak then turned to Kynton and ushered him behind the bar. "Good luck," he said before going to wait on another table. Kynton shrugged to Aideen before approaching a man who had just sat down a few stools away.

Aideen looked around and sighed. *I guess ten in the morning is too early for poker, anyway.*

She moved away from the bar, wondering what she was going to do until the poker games started up later that night. She knew that she wasn't going to just sit around while the others worked their butts off all week. She had to get a job, even if it was sloshing out the horse stalls at the local feeding trough.

A few minutes later, she waved Damia down, who walked up to her. Aideen was surprised to see how quickly she adapted to her new job. She was balancing a tray of food on her hip and carrying a stack of menus in her other hand. "What," she asked quickly, obviously wanting to get back to work.

"I'm going to see if I can find a job somewhere in the area," Aideen said. "I don't want to just sit here all day."

Damia nodded, obviously liking the idea. She wasn't afraid to hide the fact that she didn't think poker was going to be enough for Aideen to earn her part of the two thousand dollars. "Try Ophelia's or Korinna's. Maybe one of them will need some help."

Aideen agreed and let Damia get back to her job, before she was fired on her first day. She headed out the door and into the morning light.

She slowly made her way across the marketplace, retracing their steps from the day before. She was the only one of them without a job, and since poker wasn't up to the standards of Kendra and Damia, she began job-hunting while on those busy streets. Damia had mentioned Korinna or Ophelia, but Aideen wasn't too eager to work for the denim-crazy seamstress or the potion-heavy Seer. While they were the most probable to give her a job, she wasn't sure if she could handle being around those women for too long before going just as insane as they were.

She stopped at some food stalls on the street, hoping they needed another salesman or even someone to pick out the bad merchandise. After two ignored her, one yelled at her, and another spat at her, Aideen realized that she no longer wanted to work in food. She walked around the marketplace for another hour with very little luck. The only person who had offered Aideen any sort of job was a man with a thick accent holding a fish in one hand and a bear trap in the other.

Aideen quickly walked away from him, realizing there was only one last option: seek out the Seer or the seamstress. Never having been a fashion-forward person, Aideen was hesitant about asking Ophelia for a job. Plus the thought of her working with sharp scissors and needles worried her. She knew that was an accident waiting to happen. So, Aideen soon found herself standing in front of Seer Korinna's Magikal Shoppe.

She walked inside and immediately her nerves calmed right down. She took a deep breath of the air thick with magik and approached the front counter. Seer Korinna was standing there, her hair currently short, spiked and pink. In her hands were many empty glass bottles, flasks and containers. The counter in front of her was covered with them as well. They were all shapes and sizes. No two bottles were a like, not even the colors were the same.

Korinna smiled at Aideen and said, "These are my potion bottles. I need you to arrange them according to shape, size and color. They are very fragile so please do not drop any. You can put them in that cupboard over there. When you are done, come find me. I have some bloodstones that need cleaning."

Korinna smiled and handed over the bottles in her arms to Aideen. Aideen watched as the Seer started to walk into the back room. "Wait," Aideen called. "Does this mean I'm hired?"

Korinna laughed, "Of course! I'll pay you at the end of the week, and don't worry! He's going to be just fine."

"He?" Aideen asked.

Korinna's smile fell a little, "David. Your brother, remember? He's going to grow up to be a very powerful man."

Aideen's mouth dropped. She hadn't even thought about David. Now that she was gone, he was left with just their parents. She shuddered at that thought. They could barely take care of themselves, let alone a five-year-old boy. As Aideen began to organize the potion bottles, her thoughts kept drifting to Earth and her little brother who was there all alone.

~*~

Peri had never been good at staring contests; she always got distracted by the things around her. She tried to focus, looking straight into his eyes, his dark, unmoving, hate-filled eyes. She glared, narrowing her eyes so that there was nothing to look at but his eyes. Her own began to itch as she stared, but she did not blink. She watched him, and saw that he was much better at this than she was. He had had practice a few more times, with a few more prisoners, while the only practice she had ever had was with her mirror.

She watched as his lips twitched, once, twice, and then turned into a frown. Ciro blinked and said, "You're not going to give up, are you, Keeper?"

Peri shook her head, but did not blink, nor look away. She refused to talk to this boy. She would not give away any more secrets. She was sitting very still on the mattress of her prison room, focused on Ciro, who was sitting on the wooden chair across the way. Normally, he would sit in the chair to interrogate his prisoners, but this one was the most stubborn of them all. True, his normal prisoners were all teenage boys who Ciro could easily bully, not at all like the Keeper of Air.

"That's what I thought," Ciro said. "I wouldn't expect anything less from a Keeper."

Peri gave a slight nod, showing that she was still not going to speak.

"But I really had expected more of a fight, not just a hunger strike. The Keeper of Air," Ciro shook his head. "I always thought you had the coolest powers... Seeing, reading people's thoughts, control-ling people's thoughts and actions."

Peri couldn't control the look of surprise that spread across her face. She tried to cover it up, but it had been too late. Ciro saw the whole thing. He smirked, "What? You didn't know you could do that? Control people's actions? Yep, Keeper Peri was all about the mind. But, you should know that already..."

Peri glared at Ciro. She bit her tongue, hoping her face would not give away anything she was thinking.

Ciro looked her over, "So what? You're obviously not the same Keeper Peri that was around so long ago. You'd be at least a hundred years old, right? And a little more powerful. What happened to you, after your last battle with Tárquin?"

Ciro laughed, "I bet he killed you. I bet some random man with a few magik powers was able to kick all of your butts into the next life. "

Peri's eyebrows furrowed, not happy with the way this boy was talking about her and her past life. Ciro saw this and paused, "That's it, isn't it? He killed you, and this is your next life. You're the Keepers, after all. Why wouldn't you be able to control what your next lives would be?"

He leaned back in his chair, "Man, that has to suck. Starting all over again. It's like the past hundred years don't even matter. You can't even pick up where you left off. You have to learn everything over again. You have to figure out everything. That's why you have a tour guide; you don't know what the hell you're doing."

Peri frowned, and looked down at the mattress. Ciro was right, she had no clue what she was doing. What she was doing sit-ting here with him, in Canhareth, in Hecate. She wanted to be home, in her own room, sitting on her own bed, listening to her iPod, doing her nails or reading a book, or talking to Joey on the phone. She wanted to be worried about her homework, not worried about closing her eyes to sleep, fearing that she would never wake up again.

Ciro watched as the Keeper suddenly turned from the strong woman that he had always thought she was, into the scared little girl sitting before him. He watched as her shoulders began to shake, as she tried not to cry in front of her captor, but it was too late. Ciro stiffened in his chair, not ready for this at all.

"Keeper Peri?" he asked, off guard.

Peri looked up at him with puffy eyes and for the first time in two days, spoke. "You're right," she said, her voice cracking. "I have absolutely no idea what the hell I'm doing. I haven't known for a long time now. At least a week ago I knew where I was, what I wanted to do, who I wanted to be. Now," she shrugged, "everything's changed. I'm no longer a senior in high school trying to get into college, I'm the ghost of a once important person, trying to get back home. I don't know whether I want to stay here and be who people think I should be, or go back and be who I thought I wanted to be. Everyone calls us their Saviors, their protectors, but we haven't done anything. I'm pathetic. I can't even make up my mind about who I want to be. I have all these new powers, and I'm scared of them. I'm scared of who I'm becoming, because it's not who I thought I wanted to be. I know I want to go home, I know I want to see my family, but what if I miss this when I'm back on Earth? What if I start to wonder what would have happened if I stayed? Could I live with my choice, either way? I don't know, and I don't really want to find out."

Peri looked at Ciro expectantly, as if he would have all the answers to her problems. She watched as the stunned look on his face turned to one of great confusion. He looked out the window, thinking about what she had said. After a moment, he said, "I know exactly how you feel."

"You do?" Peri asked, off guard. "You seem so confident, you look like you know this is where you belong."

Ciro laughed and looked at her, "And I thought the same thing about you."

"I guess we're both messed up," Peri said, feeling only slightly better after her small rant to this stranger.

"So you really are from Earth?" Ciro asked.

Peri nodded, "I really am."

"What's it like?" Ciro asked, unable to stop himself. "Is it any better there?"

Peri shrugged, "I don't know. I've only seen a little bit, but I know I want to go back. This world is so weird to me. There aren't any creatures on Earth, just humans and all the standard non-magikal animals."

"That sounds boring," Ciro said. "You don't have any magik there?"

Peri laughed; which felt weird after crying so intensely moments ago, "It's not, and we've managed pretty well without any magik. We humans are handy on Earth. There's stuff that Beindor will probably never see. We have movies, television, airplanes, cars, CDs, DVDs, electricity, air conditioning, central heating, computers, iPods, cameras and so much more."

"I would like to see it," Ciro said, thinking about Earth. "I've never been out of Canhareth, never been past the city limits. I've never really wanted this life, just following Father's orders. I want to have my own adventures, do what I please. Explore unknown lands. Earth seems like it's a very different place. I have no idea what any of what you just said was. I like that."

Peri smiled, "I could never tell my cousins this, but I think I'm excited to see Beindor. I've never been here before, and this is all very different to me. Dragons and pixies and Elvin are just faerytales on Earth. Just like Earth is for you."

Ciro paused and looked straight at Peri. He frowned and said, "I would give anything to be you, to be able to travel across the country with people you actually enjoy being with. You see yourself as such a failure; I don't get it. You've lost all hope in yourself, and you've just only begun your adventure."

Ciro shook his head, and repeated, "I would die to switch places with you, and you're just sulking in here like a little girl. You're the Keeper or Air, you can do anything. You could escape, if you really wanted to. You're not a commoner, you can power through anything I do to try to stop you. "

Ciro then stood and said, "You just don't want to."

Peri watched as he walked out of the room. She wiped away the tears rolling down her cheeks. *He's wrong,* she thought. *I do want to get out of here. I want it more than anything else in the world. I just can't do it. The DeLucas would kill me for just trying. I'm not sulking... I'm trying not to get killed. But if he wants to see what I can do, he can bet I'll show him.*

Chapter Forty

Damia was in shock at how busy the small tavern got during the day. She had assumed it would be slow, if not completely dead until the nightly regulars came in to drink and play poker until three o'clock in the morning. What she was seeing during the day was completely different. There were families gathering for lunch, old friends reminiscing and couples whispering intimately over forgotten food.

It wasn't until after the dinner crowd cleared out that Damia began to see the bar fill up more than the dining room. She watched as Mahak and Kynton hurried around, filling drink orders. She listened as Kendra began singing more frequently and much different songs than the family-orientated songs she had been singing at lunch and dinnertime. Damia then realized Josephine, Mahak's wife, was watching her.

Damia quickly walked over to one of the only tables in the entire place that had people, and started taking their orders. She glanced over at Josephine again, and this time saw her shaking her head. Damia began to panic, wondering what she had done wrong. She saw Josephine making her way over to her, and as soon as Damia stepped away from the table, Josephine waved her over.

Once Damia was standing in front of her, Josephine not-so-discreetly looked her over and clucked with disapproval. Damia looked down at herself, wondering what was wrong. Did she have a food stain or something? When Damia saw her brand new clothes were spotless, she looked back up at Josephine, who was saying, "While your Sunday-school look is great when our customers are all two-year olds and their mothers, that's not who we serve after nine."

Josephine then reached out, untied the front of Damia's blouse, and pulled it down. Damia watched as she exposed a lot more skin than the shirt had originally been designed to show. Damia laughed and said, "Please tell me you're joking."

Josephine narrowed her eyes at Damia, obviously not in the mood for a good joke. Damia's smile fell and her face immediately turned bright red, "I can't wear this! There are people here!"

Josephine gave her one last disapproving look before heading off in the opposite direction. As soon as her back was turned, Damia pulled her shirt up and started to tie it back together. However, it seemed that as soon as she touched the fabric, Josephine turned around and narrowed her eyes even further at Damia.

Damia sighed and put the shirt back how Josephine had left it. As soon as Josephine disappeared into the kitchen, Damia pulled the shirt up slightly. It wasn't were Damia would have liked it, but it was better than where Josephine wanted it. She walked away before Josephine could come out and glare at her again.

Damia sighed, and went back to work. Her face turned bright red every time someone noticed the slight change in her wardrobe. She tried to ignore the heat that was rising in her chest and creeping into her face, but that proved impossible when she noticed a certain somebody watching her as she took the orders of three older men sitting close to the bar. She smiled up at Kynton, and he quickly looked away from her.

She laughed and approached the bar, the three men's order in her hand: three large pints of the best beer in the place. She handed the order to Kynton, and watched as he poured the drinks. He glanced over at her, and said, suddenly shy, "Wow. You look- you look amazing, Damia."

Damia laughed at Kynton's discomfort and said, "All she did was untie the top. I've been wearing this same outfit for three days now."

"I know," Kynton said, obviously embarrassed. "But- wow. You just- here."

Kynton held out a tray with three drinks on it and as soon as Damia took it, he moved to the other end of the bar to take another order. Damia watched him for a second longer, caught off guard by the sudden dismissal. She then smiled happily and brought the drinks over to their waiting recipients.

Now that all her customers were happily eating, drinking and playing poker, Damia was able to get a break and rest her feet. She started back over to the bar, and noticed someone waiting for her, a nasty look on her face, her arms folded tightly across her chest. Damia walked up slowly to Kendra and sat down on the stool next to her. She looked up at her and asked, "What's wrong? You seem upset."

"Of course I'm upset, Damia," Kendra said in a harsh whisper. "I was sitting by the piano, minding my own business when I glanced over and find myself looking at a one woman peep show!"

Damia crossed her arms over her chest, "Don't go yelling at me! Josephine was the one who wanted me to do this!"

"And why do I get the feeling that you didn't give much of a fight?" Kendra asked, glancing over at Kynton, who was trying not to overhear the entire conversation.

"I can't believe you, Kendra!" Damia said, tapping into Kendra's anger. "Always assuming the worst in people! Why don't you give him a chance?"

"He's still here, isn't he?" Kendra snapped, not even noticing the jump in the conversation.

"Yeah, on my invite," Damia said. "But I know you want him gone. You don't trust him. I just want to know why. He hasn't done anything against you, or any of us. We'd be starving on the street if it hadn't been for him."

"No," Kendra said. "We'd be on our way to Imladun if it hadn't been for him."

Damia shook her head, "You know that's not true! Give me one good, factual, reason why he shouldn't stay with us. Just one."

"I don't trust him," Kendra said. "I'm only looking out for you, Damia."

"Oh my god," Damia said, feeling a sudden flare of jealousy from Kendra. "You're jealous of me? Why? Is it because your boyfriend is who knows how far away and I have Kynton? You hate him because you miss your boyfriend?"

"That's not true," Kendra said quickly, her face going slightly red. "Of course I miss Ryan, but I wouldn't hate Kynton for it."

"Yes you would," Damia said. "You already hate him. It's too late for that. I'm sorry about Ryan, Kendra. I really am. It sucks, not knowing when you are going to see him again. I couldn't even imagine having that feeling all the time. But that doesn't mean you have to take it out on Kynton. He's a good guy, and I trust him."

Kendra shook her head, "I don't. No matter if I'm jealous or not, I still don't trust him."

Damia frowned, "Then where do we go from here?"

Kendra shrugged, "I honestly don't know. Now, if you'd excuse me, I have to get back to work."

Damia nodded, and watched as Kendra stood up and walked over to the piano. She listened to the song Kendra began to sing, Damia quietly slid off her stool and walked around the bar until she was standing next to Kynton. She wrapped her arms around him, and buried her face in his chest.

Kynton had heard most of the conversation, and was unsure how to feel. It did not look like Kendra was going to accept him any time soon. He knew all too well that he was causing a rift in the cousins' very frail relationship, a relationship that should be unbreakable. He wondered if he should stop being so selfish, and let Damia heal her relationship with Kendra before he tried to get any closer to her.

Damia then pulled him closer to her, and he suddenly could smell the shampoo she had used that morning. She smelled like apples, freshly picked apples from the apple trees that grew about a mile from where Kynton had grown up. She smelled like home, and Kynton realized that she was his home. Without her, he had been lost and confused. Now, she was back and he felt at peace. He could not let that get away from him again, could not let her get away from him again.

~*~

Aideen stumbled into The Dancing Bear and fell into the first empty chair she saw. She let out an exhausted breath and watched as Damia glanced over at her as she took the order of a man and a significantly younger woman. As soon as she was finished, she hurried over to her cousin.

Aideen smirked, "Nice shirt."

"Shut up," Damia said quickly. "Did you get a job?"

Aideen sighed again, "Yes, mother, I did. I spent the day organizing bottles for Miss Korinna the crazy Seer."

"Wonderful," Damia said with a smile. "Now what are you going to do? Kynton, Kendra and I are going to keep working for a while."

Aideen's smirk crept across her face again, "Do I get a discount for being family?"

Damia frowned, "Depends how much you're tipping."

Aideen glared," Alright, fine. Now tell me, who has the best game going?"

Damia laughed, "You really think I can tell?"

As Aideen stood to find the poker game she would join, the door to The Dancing Bear opened. Damia and Aideen watched as Carr and Jedrek Faal walked in from the dark street. Upon seeing the girls standing near by, Jedrek's face lit up, "Just the people I was looking for!"

"Hello, sir," Damia said with a smile. "It's good to see you."

Jedrek nodded, "Is your cousin around? I would like for all of you to hear this."

"Is it Thalia?" Damia asked, panicking. "Did you hear from the DeLucas? Is she okay?"

"I have heard no more than you have," Jedrek said.

"I'll get Polly," Aideen said, and in less than two minutes, the three cousins, Carr and Jedrek Faal were sitting at a table together.

"What is it?" Kendra asked, worried about Peri.

"My family and I have given this a lot of thought," Jedrek said. "We would like to give you some money to get Thalia back. Three hundred Denas."

"We can't take your money," Kendra said.

Jedrek nodded, putting a small sack of coins on the table between them. "You saved my daughter's life. It is the least I can do to help save your cousin's."

"Thank you," Damia said, tears springing into her eyes. She stood and hugged Jedrek, then Carr. "This means the world to us."

Jedrek laughed, "We are happy to have helped."

Aideen smiled, "I know another way you can help."

Jedrek raised an eyebrow, "How's that?"

"Can you stay for a round or two? Texas Hold'Em? Seven Card Stud?"

Carr smiled, and reached into his pocket, "I brought the cards!"

Aideen laughed, "You rock."

Kendra rolled her eyes. "I have to get back to work. You too, Terri. Thank you again, Jedrek."

Kendra then walked over to the piano, where Felton was playing a low melody of his own hand. Damia left as well, and headed over to the bar. Kynton was waiting for her, hoping to hear what Jedrek had to say, and what had made Damia cry.

The rest of the night moved along smoothly. Kendra continued to sing until three in the morning, when the bar closed and all customers without a room in the inn were kicked out. Jedrek and Carr had left around midnight, when Aideen had wiped them both clean. By three thirty, Aideen had won all the money of two more tables and called it quits. Damia and Kynton stayed until four, helping Mahak get the dining room ready for breakfast the next morning.

At five o'clock, there was a knock on the girls' door. Damia answered it, still bleary eyed to see Josephine standing there with a frown on her face. "Time to make breakfast," she said, leading Damia back downstairs. At seven, Kendra dragged Aideen out of bed and got her awake enough to go back to Korinna's again. Kendra met Kynton on the stairs, and together they went downstairs to start the day. At ten, Damia helped Josephine clean rooms, until the lunch rush at noon, and they began the same routine they had done the day before.

Chapter Forty-One

The sun was shining brightly, without a cloud in sight to frighten it away. The streets were busy with excitement, another day was starting and there were people of all shapes and sizes to sell to. Damia walked down the street, and despite the guilt of Peri's kidnapping, the stress of raising enough money to get her back, and the weight of the idea of not reaching home for a very long time, she was having a good day.

She was with Kynton, in search of fresh eggs for The Dancing Bear. Arm in arm they searched the street vendors for the cream color of their prize. They walked up and down the many streets in the heart of Canhareth, talking as they went. "So tell me what you did for fun back on Earth, Neimann," Kynton said, picking up an apple as they passed a fruit stand. He handed the vendor a coin and continued down the street.

"Well." Damia said with a blush. "I dance. I've just been accepted into a dance school in New York City, a city even bigger than Canhareth."

"Dance?" Kynton laughed. "But you're so clumsy!"

"I am not," Damia said, frowning up at Kynton.

Kynton nodded, "You are the only person I have ever seen fall over her own feet."

"When have I ever," Damia started, but Kynton interrupted, "Here we are."

They were standing in front of a small stand full of hens, roosters, and their prize: eggs. They bought twelve dozen eggs and started back toward The Dancing Bear, balancing their trophies very carefully in their arms. Kynton laughed, "I remember this one time, you were talking with Queen Bryndis. You were discussing boarder problems with Othalie, when all of a sudden your feet went out from right underneath you..."

Damia watched as Kynton was reduced to hysterics thinking about this memory of her. A memory she could not remember. She knew she had never met the Queen Bryndis, and she had never discussed Othalie. She wasn't even sure what that was. She smiled though, realizing that Kynton was getting her confused with the first Keeper Damia. She wondered if her new nickname, Neimann, had anything to do with her. She had worried this would happen; he had been so in love with her that it was almost expected.

She watched as the pile of eggs in Kynton's arms tilted slightly forward. She caught the basket before any of the eggs could come tumbling out, and said, "Okay Kynton, pay attention to what you're doing. You almost spilled all the eggs in the dirt. No one wants to pay for a mud omelet."

~*~

Peri was bored. She was sitting in the same spot that she had been sitting that morning. She also had to pee. She wondered if Ciro would let her go to the bathroom, or if he didn't even trust her to do that. She didn't think he had a reason to distrust her. She had only tried to escape once. That's about as much as you could expect from a hostage with a full bladder.

She wondered what the others were doing. They hadn't tried to get her back yet, as far as she could tell. She wondered if they were trying to raise the money, or if they had just left without her. She couldn't blame them, she had been pretty emotional earlier.

Peri shook her head, trying to get those thoughts out of her head. Of course they hadn't left her. Of course they were trying to get her back, despite her emotional rollercoaster lately. They were playing by the rules, and that meant getting the money and going to the exchange on Tuesday. Peri sighed. It was only Wednesday. She still had six days before she could get out of the DeLuca house. Then she panicked. She wasn't going to make it six days without going to the bathroom!

Knowing that panicking was only going to worsen the problem, Peri closed her eyes and took a deep breath. Trying to calm down, she started to think of a peaceful memory. The first thing that came to mind was a memory of when she was eleven years old. Her parents had taken her mountain climbing for her birthday. At first, she was scared, not being able to see the top of the mountain; it was so far up.

But then her father had taken her hand and led her over to the mountain side. Together they started to scale the rock face. It didn't take Peri long to get accustomed to the weightless feeling as she climbed up the side of the mountain. All she could feel were the ropes pulling at her harness and the warm rock under her fingers.

Knowing that her father was by her side the entire time helped too. He stayed close to her, just in case she panicked and wanted to get back on solid ground. But that never happened. They reached their destination with ease, and Peri quickly wanted to climb the rest of the way to the top. Peri remembered turning to her father with big eyes and hands clasped in front of her, begging to go higher. She could see his face clearly, his eyes full of laughter and his brow sweaty from the climb.

She watched as he took a step closer, coming over to unhook her harness and set up the picnic they had brought along. Then, as he reached down to Peri, his face changed. It was no longer filled with joy, but turned to a look of sorrow. The sweat on his forehead turned to tears on his cheeks, and his harness and climbing gear turned to a black suit and tie.

He reached out in front of him, and wrapped his arm around his wife's shoulder. Peri watched as she leaned onto him, burying her face in his side. They weren't standing on the side of a mountain, but in their large kitchen. Peri recognized it instantly, the Viking stove and oven, the marble counter tops and the large island where her parents now stood.

She frowned, not able to remember this memory. The only time she had seen her parents in these clothes was when her Great Uncle Aaron died, and neither of her parents had been this torn up about it. In fact, this was the first time she had seen her father cry, and it was upsetting her.

She stood up and walked over to her parents, trying to comfort them. She tried to wrap her arms around them both, but her arms went right through them. She tried again, she tried to put her hand on her mother's arm, tried to comfort her and tell her everything would be okay. But her parents didn't even see she was there. They didn't hear her talking to them, didn't see her standing almost on top of them. It was like she wasn't even there.

Peri could feel a lump forming in her throat as she watched her parents helplessly. They were so close but she was unable to touch them, unable to talk to them. It was all she had wanted since falling into this adventure. It was all she wanted and it was the one thing she couldn't have. With a small scream of disgust, Peri turned her back to her parents. Her body was trembling and she quickly pushed away the tears forming in her eyes.

For the first time since coming to Beindor, Peri wanted to go back. She hated seeing her parents like this and wondered what cruel Fates would make her watch this. She took a step away from her hopeless parents and toward the breakfast table. There was a large bouquet of flowers in the middle, lilies. There was only one reason why lilies would be in the house, and her parents would be dressed in such black clothes, but whose funeral would they be having? And why couldn't Peri remember it?

Then Peri saw the five pictures also decorating the breakfast table. She recognized two of them, though she had only seen one of them before. It was her Senior picture, along with Peri's, Damia's, and Aideen's. In the middle was the picture of the four of them that Aunt Paula had taken on the night of Kendra's party. The one they took right before they went on the walk that led to the Trac house.

It took less than a fraction of a second for Peri to figure out what that meant, but it took even less time for her to be woken from her vision. She looked around, startled by the red walls of her prison of a room. It took her a moment to focus on her new surroundings, and the person who had woken her.

She watched as Ciro's furrowed brow turned into a smirk on his lips. He sat back in the chair across from Peri and said, "You just had a vision, didn't you? What did you See? Your cousins saving you and locking me and Trey in jail?"

Peri shook her head, thinking of her breakfast table, and what had been on it. "No," she said, looking up at Ciro. "I saw my funeral."

"Well that's morbid," came Ciro's remark. "How'd you go? Did a Cyclops eat you? Or maybe a dragon. Didn't watch where it was stepping, huh?"

Again, Peri shook her head, "My parents think I died. When my cousins and I came here, they must have thought something happened. I don't know why they would stop looking for us. It's not like they found our bodies."

"Or did they," Ciro said, arching an eyebrow. "What if you did die and this is heaven."

"Some heaven," Peri frowned. "First, I get kidnapped, and then my kidnappers refuse to let me use their bathroom."

Ciro frowned, "You need a bathroom?" Peri nodded and he chuckled, "I keep forgetting The Keepers are human just like the rest of us."

Ciro stood, and motioned Peri up as well," Come on, human-just-like-me. Bathroom's this way."

"Are you going to stand guard?" Peri asked.

"Either that or come in with you."

"Ew. Gross! And watch me pee?"

"Something like that," Ciro said with a quick smirk.

Peri's eyes narrowed, "Pervert."

Ciro laughed and opened the door before leading Peri down the hall and toward the bathroom, much to her relief.

Chapter Forty-Two

It was a slow night at The Dancing Bear. Only a few men sat at the bar, and even less sat around the tables scattered throughout the dining rom. Damia sat at the bar, watching the people around her, waiting for a customer, any customer, to wave her over. Kynton stood behind the bar, glancing at Damia occasionally as he wiped the wood down with a rag. "Slow night?" he asked casually.

Damia sighed and looked over at him, "Yeah. I have no idea how we're going to get Peri if there's nobody here to give us money."

"Hopefully Aideen will keep winning," Kynton said, looking over to where Aideen was playing a game of poker with some unhappy looking men.

Damia smiled, "I don't know how she does it, but thank the heavens she's doing it. She'll probably raise the two thousand Denas herself."

Kynton laughed, "I'm hoping she gets all ten thousand Denas. That way we don't have to come out of this completely broke."

Damia's smile fell, "I didn't think about that. We might have to work a little more before leaving. Just so we have enough money to buy food and rooms."

"Or we could just let everyone know who you are, and we'll never have to pay again."

Damia laughed, "I don't think so. We'll just have to work like normal people."

Damia suddenly stopped laughing and turned around to face the dining room. She watched as two hooded figures walked through the door and over to a secluded table along the far wall. They were the only two in that part of the room, and Damia had a feeling that's exactly how they wanted it.

But something was troubling her. For a second, as the two walked in, Damia thought she recognized one of the figures. She couldn't see their faces, but there was something about them that had made Damia turn around. She started to walk over there, anxious to see their faces and confirm that she didn't know them.

However, as soon as she got within hearing range, one of the figures turned to her and waved her away. He said, "No thank you, we're not eating tonight."

Damia watched as the other figure turned the other way. She looked back at the first one, who had just dismissed her. She paused, taken aback by his face, by his voice. She recognized him, but was having trouble placing him. She also didn't want to leave without seeing the other person's face. That was the person she had sensed as they entered the inn. Reluctantly, Damia headed back over to the bar and sat down with a huff.

Kynton chuckled, "They didn't want anything, huh?"

"No," Damia said, dejected. She continued to watch the two, hoping that if she could remember the one man's face, she would know who he was with.

"What's wrong, Neimann?" Kynton asked.

"I recognized that guy," Damia said.

"You recognized him?" Kynton asked, surprised. "How? You know like five people in the whole world."

"Exactly," Damia said. "And the other one wouldn't even look at me, like they were afraid I would recognize them."

Damia continued to search the past couple days for the face, the voice. She knew he had never been in The Dancing Bear before, at least not when she was working. Could he have been a street vendor who sold her something? Or just another person she passed on the street?

No.

She knew he had been more important than that. But where else could she have seen a teenage boy in Canhareth?

"Go help Peri," Damia said quickly.

Kynton looked behind her and Damia watched as his face dropped in horror. He ran past her, and she spun around to see what had made him look like that. Then she saw that the gang of boys had caught up with Peri, and were now using her as a punching bag, similar to what they had been doing to the little girl. Damia watched as Aideen ran past her to join Kynton in saving Peri.

"Shit, Ciro! That's Keeper Aideen!"

That was it. The voice. That is where she had heard him before.

The night Peri was kidnapped.

Damia paused, *Could he be a DeLuca? But why would they come here? They know The Dancing Bear is where we're staying! Do they want something from us? The ransom money?! But it's only Friday! We still have four days! And why won't that other DeLuca look at me?* Unless it wasn't a DeLuca at all...

"Peri?" Damia whispered, standing up.

Kynton looked over at her, wondering what she was thinking. He watched as she started over to the two hooded figures again. One was standing, the one who had waved Damia away. Damia watched as the DeLuca reached out and took the other person's hand. Damia's heart swelled as she saw the small delicate hand of a girl slip into his.

It was Peri. There was no doubt of it now.

As soon as the DeLuca left The Dancing Bear, Damia rushed over to Peri and sat down in the DeLuca's chair. She couldn't believe this was happening.

~*~

Escaping is easy, Peri thought as she snuck through the DeLuca home.

There had been no one standing guard at her door, no one standing guard at the end of the hall. Alcatraz had been replaced with Switzerland. Peri was beginning to wonder if the DeLucas had forgotten she was a Keeper. She walked slowly down the empty hall, fearing Trey or Ciro would jump out from behind a corner at any moment. She knew that if either one of the brothers found her, she would be dead in an instant. She had seen the DeLuca temper before, and knew even she wasn't immune to it.

 She reached the end of the hall, but her celebration was short lived. She could now hear voices coming from a nearby room, and they sounded angry. She listened in.

"Do you really think I'm that stupid?" an older man said, who Peri assumed was Mr. DeLuca, Trey and Ciro's father. "I taught you everything you know! You use my methods! You don't think I would notice when you're holding someone hostage?"

Peri covered her mouth, hoping that her gasp of surprise wasn't audible in the other room. Not only were they talking about her, but also it seemed that Ciro had lied to her. He had said his father knew of her, but now Peri knew differently. Maybe she didn't have to escape, after all.

"Yes, Father," Trey said, emotionlessly. "We do have someone here against their will."

"But you're going to like who it is," Ciro added.

"Is it a Faal," Rico asked, excitedly.

"No," Ciro said quickly. "Better."

"Better?" Rico laughed. "What could be better than having a Faal hostage?"

"Having a Keeper hostage," came Ciro's reply.

Even though Peri couldn't see him, she knew a smirk had formed across Ciro's face. She shuddered at the image, but it quickly was replaced with the conversation in the other room. They were talking about her, and suddenly Rico DeLuca wasn't as livid. In fact,

Peri was beginning to think he wasn't going to let her go. He sounded excited to have a Keeper hostage in his house.

"What the hell are you talking about?" Rico said quickly. "The Keepers have been dead for twenty years now. Even when they were alive, you could not possibly have kidnapped one. Keeper Peri could kill with just a thought."

"But she is the one we have," Ciro said, and Peri could hear the satisfaction in his voice.

Rico then let out a terrifying laugh, one that made Peri freeze in fear. She wasn't sure if he was amused or about to lash out at one of his boys. He said, "That is impossible. Keeper Peri would have killed us all by now. You cannot be telling me that you've kept her in that room for the past couple of days. She could stroll past us right now, and none of us could stop her."

"She has changed," Ciro said, excitedly. "She's eighteen years old, at most. Not powerful at all. I don't even think she has all her powers yet."

"Now you're just trying to make me look a fool," Rico said, anger in his voice. "First you want me to believe she is alive. Next you want be to believe she has shed forty years and all her powers?"

"It's true," Ciro said. "Come have a look for yourself."

"Alright," Rico said, ready to prove his sons insane.

Peri's heart jumped into her throat. They were coming her way. They were going to check on her, and they would find her in the hall. If Ciro didn't kill her, Rico most certainly would. She had to get out of there. She had to find a place to hide. She refused to go back in that room. As soon as she did, she would never get up the courage to leave again. It was either now or never. Unfortunately, the only way out was through the room where the DeLucas were. It was either that or take a chance and hide behind one of the random doors in the hallway.

"Wait," Trey interrupted, not having spoken since admitting to Peri's presence earlier. She was startled to hear him, forgetting that it wasn't just Ciro and Rico in the room. "Mother will be putting dinner on the table now. Let's eat first, then check on our guest. Afterwards we can discuss what to do with the ransom money."

Rico let out another laugh, and Peri heard his voice fading into another room, "A good idea, son. I think I might want a summer home in Nérand..."

As soon as the voices faded away, Peri closed her eyes and let out a sigh of relief. She opened her eyes back up, and almost blew her cover, even though it was blown sky high. Trey covered her mouth before she could scream. He pushed her against the wall and whispered, still with his hand over her mouth, "What the hell are you doing? Stay in your room and behave! I promise, if you do, that you will be returned safely to your cousins. I can't be responsible for my brother's actions when you break the rules. He wouldn't be as forgiving as me."

Trey then let go of Peri and glanced down the hall, "Now go back, before anyone else notices you hanging out in the hallways. Go!"

Peri looked at Trey DeLuca, bewildered. Were her ears deceiving her, or did he sound like he was helping her? It sounded like he was actually concerned for her wellbeing. Why would her kidnapper be concerned for her wellbeing?

It didn't make sense.

But, then again, none of the DeLucas made sense to Peri.

She walked down the hall, slowly. She glanced over her shoulder, and saw that Trey was standing at the other end with his arms folded over his chest. She felt like a child being scolded, not a maximum-security prisoner. She opened the door to her cell and took one last look at the DeLuca boy watching her.

It was in that moment that she realized there was something different about Trey. He didn't fit in with the other DeLucas. He barely ever lost his temper, not once had he seemed interested in the ransom, and the only time he ever showed any interest in Peri was when he was rescuing her from Ciro and Rico.

Something was up. Peri just had no idea what it was.

Chapter Forty-Three

Kassidy Faal stood outside The Dancing Bear, stamping her feet with dual purpose. The first was simple, it was a chilly night and she was wearing little more than what she had worn to bed. The second was a much more secretive cause, she had been told to wait outside The Dancing Bear at midnight that night by an unsigned note given to her brother to give to her. Though the note and its writer were supposed to be a mystery, it was not worth a second of Sherlock Holmes' time. Not only could Kassidy recognize the handwriting on the note, but Carr's grumbling of, "I never signed up to play messenger for you," gave it away.

So here she was, standing outside of The Dancing Bear, stamping away the cold, and stamping out her anger that it was ten after midnight and Trey had yet to show his face. She watched the few people walking along the road, hoping one would turn to her and be Trey, holding out his hand to her, asking her to run away with him. Her heart began to beat faster as one man, about Trey's height, came toward her. She looked away when she realized it wasn't him, but just another man going into The Dancing Bear. She blushed; embarrassed that she was getting so excited over Trey. She had forgotten she was still very mad at him. Not only had he not tried to contact her in over a week, but also he had done nothing to help Thalia get back to her cousins. Kassidy had a sinking feeling this was why he had wanted to meet with her, not so that they could run away together.

She glanced over at the man she had mistaken for Trey and watched as he opened the door to The Dancing Bear. He paused before entering and looked over at Kassidy, at least she thought he was looking at her. The hood he was wearing cast a dark shadow over his face. He gestured for Kassidy to go inside, and that he would hold the door open for her.

She smiled and shook her head, "Oh no, thank you. I'm wait-ing-"

"-Kass,: he interrupted. "It's me. And why aren't you wearing your hood? What if someone saw you?"

Kassidy frowned, but put her hood up anyway, "What is going on, Trey?"

"Shh..." he said. "Wait until we're inside."

Kassidy sighed and walked inside The Dancing Bear. She saw Terri talking to Kynton at the bar, and quickly turned towards the farthest corner of the room. As soon as they sat down, Kassidy asked, "What's going on, Trey? Why did you want to see me?"

Trey frowned, "I can't ask you to see me at midnight without a reason?"

Kassidy pursed her lips, "No, you can't. What is it?"

Trey leaned forward and took Kassidy's hand in his, "I just want to apologize for not being able to see you this past week. Mak-ing sure Ciro doesn't hurt the Kee-"

He stopped talking when he realized Keeper Damia was ap-proaching. As Kassidy turned her head the other way, Trey waved Keeper Damia away. He said, "No thank you, we're not eating to-night."

He watched as Keeper Damia turned away, a very confused look on her face. He waited until she was out of hearing range before continuing, "As I was saying, making sure my brother doesn't hurt our visitor seems to be a full time job."

Kassidy frowned, "Is he really being that terrible to her?"

Trey shrugged, "He's been acting weird lately, I can't tell what he's thinking. All I know is that he's been hanging around her room a lot and he's too much of our father's son for that to be a good thing."

Kassidy nodded, "Her cousins have been working around the clock all week to get the money he's asking for. I honestly don't know if they're going to make it."

Trey sighed, "Ciro wanted to make it more, but I was able to talk him down to what it is. Truthfully, I don't think he expects to get any of it. He wants to go public and humiliate them."

"Why would it humiliate them? They aren't wealthy or famous, how could anyone expect them to raise that kind of money?"

Trey opened his mouth, wondering what the hell she meant, when Kassidy cut him off, "I'm sorry, Trey. I can't stay any longer. My parents are bound to notice I'm gone."

Trey nodded and rose from his seat. He reached down and kissed the back of Kassidy's hand, "I hope the next time we do this, it won't be so far away and so secretive."

Kassidy nodded her agreement, "Until then, I suppose."

"Until then," Trey said, moving away. He was almost gone when he turned around and added, "Oh, and tell your father that when I see him, I will have a question for him."

Kassidy looked at Trey like he was uttering gibberish, and he smirked. She watched as he disappeared before she could question what sort of question he had for her father, and why he would tell her. She knew she could never tell her father that, and she knew Trey knew that as well. So what sort of question could he want to ask him? Immediately she thought of a marriage proposal, but would Trey really do that? Would he ask a man who hates him for his daughter's hand? Kassidy prayed the answer was yes, for she knew that was exactly what her answer would be.

Kassidy was pulled from her daydream as someone sat in the seat across from her. As soon as she saw Terri's very confused face, Kassidy leapt up and started for the door. Damia put her hand on Kassidy's arm and said, "If you go out that door, I'm going to have to ask Jedrek what that was about. I'd rather you tell me, Kassidy. Why were you talking with one of Peri's kidnappers?"

Kassidy sighed and sat back down. "He has a name, you know. It's Trey DeLuca."

Damia's eyebrows arched, recognizing the name from the ransom note they had received earlier in the week. Trey DeLuca wasn't just one of Peri's kidnappers, he was one of the ringleaders.

"And you don't have to ask my father," Kassidy said. "I'll tell you."

"Good," Damia said with a smile.

"Trey DeLuca and I have been talking for a while now," Kassidy said, her chin pointing a little higher than usual.

"Talking?" Damia asked with a laugh. "That's not what I gathered. To me it felt like you two are madly in love, way beyond *talking*."

Kassidy frowned, "How could you have guessed that? All he did was kiss the back of my hand. That's not something two people madly in love would do."

Damia shrugged, and said, "I thought we were talking about you."

"Well now we're talking about you, Terri," Kassidy said with narrow eyes. "Answer me this: why is Ciro DeLuca *so* interested in you and your cousins? You're not the Royal Family of Úrdor, are you?"

Damia laughed nervously, realizing her plan to get the truth from Kassidy was failing. "Of course we're not *the Royal Family* of Ur-whatever."

Kassidy arched an eyebrow, "Do you even know what Úrdor is?"

Damia bit her lip, "A country?"

"The largest country in Hecate," Kassidy said. "And I'm pretty sure you're not too familiar with Beindor either. Even though it is your home, *Terri*."

Damia glanced at the bar, where Kynton was watching her curiously. "Where else would I be from?" she asked.

Kassidy's eyes got large and her smirk fell into a gaping hole in her face. "Oh my gods," she said. "You're from Earth, aren't you? That explains why the DeLucas are so interested in you. The only other people from Earth are the-"

She cut herself off and looked Damia over. Her head then snapped over to where Kendra was standing next to the piano. Then to where Aideen was playing poker, and finally back over to Damia, sitting before her. "The Keepers," she finished. "You're the Keepers. Back from the dead. How did that happen?" Her face fell, "How could a Keeper get captured by a gang of boys?"

Damia frowned, "Yes, we are the Keepers, but we're not back from the dead. We're the Keepers reincarnated, the same souls, near identical bodies. We came to Beindor seven days ago. Before that, we were ordinary cousins living ordinary lives."

"And Ciro is going to tell everyone you're back if you don't give him the money."

"And he'll hurt Peri," Damia said.

"I don't understand," Kassidy said. "Why not tell the world you're back? Why not become the leaders you were?"

"Because we're not leaders. We may look like the four women who ruled this country, we may sound like them and have their powers, but we are not them. They died eighteen years ago."

"But you can take their place. That's what you're here to do, right?"

"No," Damia said. "We're going home. Earth. We are going to go back to our ordinary lives. That's why we can't tell the world we're back. They'll never let us leave."

Kassidy frowned, "Well if you won't tell them, I will."

"Kassidy," Damia said quickly. "You wouldn't."

"Oh, I would. It's about time the Keepers made their comeback."

"Fine," Damia said, sitting back. If you tell the world my secret, I'll tell them yours."

Panic etched its way onto Kassidy's face. "Alright, okay. I won't spill your secret." Then the panic disappeared off her face, and a smile replaced it. "But I think you could do me a favor."

Chapter Forty-Four

"I would never hurt you, you know that. I love you more than anything else on Earth," Joey said, wrapping his arms around Peri.

Peri leaned her head on his shoulder, "I love you so much."

"I love you too."

Peri looked up to see Ciro looking down at her. He smiled and touched his hand to her cheek, "I see who you have become, and it disgusts me. You're not worthy of the title Keeper."

Peri stood up, getting away from Ciro. "You're wrong," she said. "I am. I will be a better Keeper than the Peri before me. I'll prove you wrong."

She turned away from him, only to find a new pair of arms wrapping themselves around her. For an instant, she thought it was Joey again, but when she looked up and saw it was Blondie, she almost wasn't disappointed. He said, "Don't worry. Soon this will all be just a bad dream."

Peri nodded and buried her head in Blondie's shoulder, letting him hold her tighter. She wished what he said was true, that she could just wake up and be back on Earth, where Joey was still madly in love with her and Annie was still her best friend. She wanted to forget about Blondie, Ciro, the Keepers, everything about Beindor, everything about her cousins. She wanted life to go back to what it had been: normal.

"So *this* is the great Keeper Peri? No wonder you were able to kidnap her, she's just a kid."

Peri wanted to keep her eyes closed. She wanted to go back to dreaming about Joey. She would even settle for dreaming about Ciro or Blondie. Anything was better than what she knew she would see when she opened her eyes. It wasn't Earth, that's for sure.

She also knew that she didn't feel comfortable being so defenseless against Rico DeLuca. She had no idea where he was, how close he was, if he had a gun pointed to her head or not. Knowing she wouldn't be able to fall back asleep with Rico DeLuca in the same room as her, she opened her eyes. She was relieved to see he wasn't pointing any sort of weapon at her and was still a safe distance away.

Ciro and Trey were also in the room. Ciro stood tall next to his father, and Peri could see how similar the two men looked. Just an inch or two shorter than his father, Ciro puffed out his chest slightly, as if that would create more height. They had the same dark brown hair and the same twisted grin plastered to their faces. Trey, on the other hand, was leaning against the wall behind his brother and father with a look on his face that made Peri think he was not at all interested in what was happening around him.

Peri thought about the moment just a few hours earlier when he was in a very different mood. Not only had he cared, but he had cared about her. Enough that he had stalled his father from seeing her and giving her the chance to return to safety. It had been the only time Peri saw any real emotion cross his features.

Looking at him now, she also noticed that he wasn't only emotionally different from the rest of his family, but physically as well. He was much taller than Rico and Ciro DeLuca, with long lanky limbs and bleached blonde hair, something neither of the other men had. His dark eyes were a surprising contradiction to his light hair and pale skin.

Rico took a step forward, and Peri looked back at him. He smirked, "Well, I see Sleeping Beauty woke up from her cat nap."

Peri flinched as Rico spat his words at her. She slowly stood from her seat on the mattress and for a second saw terror flash through Rico's eyes. Knowing she could never escape from a room with all three DeLucas in it, she pushed herself up against the wall, hoping to stay as far away from them as possible.

The fear in Rico DeLuca's eyes quickly faded when he saw he had the upper hand, and he took another step forward. He laughed when he saw Peri was, in fact, defenseless against him.

"Who would have thought," he asked, turning to face his sons, "that the great and powerful Keeper of Air would be so sad and pathetic. And that she would be scared of me. *Me*, Rico DeLuca, the son of a pharmacist."

Peri was surprised they even had pharmacies in Hecate.

Ciro smirked, "I told you, Father. Not at all the woman who could kill with a thought. She doesn't even have any powers."

Rico turned to Peri, "Is that true? A Keeper without powers?"

Peri was too afraid to move. What would happen if she said yes? She didn't really feel like getting beat up like that poor little girl they had saved from these people. But if she said no, then she would have to show them, and she could not do that. They only powers she knew she had were to see the future and talk with her cousins telepathically.

"Speak, girl!"Rico yelled, taking another angry step forward.

Peri bit her lip, not missing the panicked look Trey had given her when his father seemed to be about to hit her. Standing behind the others, she had been the only one to see it, and he quickly regained his composure, leaning back against the wall and looking out the window on the other side of the room.

Peri nodded her head; worried Rico DeLuca would really hit her. She did not say a word, but he seemed satisfied with her answer. He laughed again, seeing his power over a Keeper in action.

He looked back at Ciro and Trey, and his delight quickly turned to disgust, "I can't believe you've been hiding this from me. A Keeper in our house? You knew I would find out!"

"We were going to surprise you," Ciro said, seeing his father had turned against him. Peri could not see the look on Rico Deluca's face, but the one on Ciro's made her realize she was glad she couldn't see it. Trey stood up and came to stand next to Ciro, realizing they were both about to be yelled at.

"What were you going to do with the ransom money? Were you ever going to tell me about that? Or were you going to keep it for your greedy little selves?"

Rico took a step in their direction, and both boys flinched. Ciro then looked past his father at Peri. He was about to say something, but Rico cut him off, "I don't care if the Keeper sees me punish my sons." He suddenly turned and approached Peri, "If anything, she should be warned. If I *ever* catch you trying to sneak out and escape, these two boys will be the least of your problems."

Peri remained motionless, hoping he would turn back to Ciro and Trey. She pushed against the wall behind her, praying she could melt into it and never have to deal with Rico DeLuca or his sons again.

"Do you understand me, girl?" he yelled, grabbing Peri by the shoulders and shaking her violently. "Or are you just as deaf and dumb as the idiots I've been raising for the past twenty years?"

He let go of her and she fell to the mattress he still stood on. She closed her eyes, fighting back the tears that were about to come. She couldn't let him see them, couldn't let him know how much he truly frightened her. She listened as he turned around and yelled at his sons, "Next time you kidnap someone, anyone, you tell me! You understand?"

"Yes sir," came their harmonized response.

Peri then heard the sharp smack of skin striking skin, and then the same noise again. She opened one eye to see that Rico DeLuca had left, leaving two red-faced boys in his wake. As soon as he was gone, both boys relaxed, their shoulders slumping and their breath returning. Trey touched his red cheek tenderly, a frown on his face. Ciro's lip curved into a snarl as he said, "Some thanks we get for doing all the god damn work."

"What did you expect?" Trey asked. "A trophy?"

"A warm hearted, 'good job, sons,' would've been nice," Ciro answered. He huffed and walked out of the room, "I wonder if Mother's pie is ready yet."

Trey started to follow, but hesitated. He turned to look at Peri, who was still trying to get the room to stop spinning. He frowned, "I told you you didn't want them finding you out in that hall. They would've murdered you on the spot."

Peri blinked and looked over at Trey, but he was already gone.

She slowly lay down on the mattress and closed her eyes, wondering if there was any possible way to get back into that dream she had been having. Even an imaginary Joey was better than her real life right now.

~*~

"No. No way. I'm not helping you."

"You know you will," Kassidy said with a smile. "Not only do you have to, or else your secret's out, but it's written all over your face. You want to help me."

Damia bit her lip, "It's not my place. They've been fighting since before Canhareth was even a city, before any human came to Hecate. I'm not messing around with that."

"Please," Kassidy begged, taking Damia's hand in hers. "This isn't just about Rico DeLuca and my father. This is about Sara and Carr, Ciro, me, and even Trey. I don't want Sara to grow up knowing only hate for Trey and his family. I could never convince my father of this, but you can. He'll believe you, he'll trust in you."

"He's your father," Damia said. "You should be the one telling him of you and Trey, not me."

Kassidy frowned, "I wish I could, but only the Keepers could ever have the power to make him see reason when the DeLucas are involved."

Damia sighed and looked over at Kendra, who was still singing with Felton. If only she could make the Keeper of Water see reason when Kynton was involved. She watched as he poured a tall glass with an amber colored liquid and handed it to a small man sitting a few seats away from where he stood. The man passed him a few gold coins and Kynton nodded his head to the man.

Damia looked over at Kynton and smiled. She watched as he continued to serve the steady flow of customers walking into the bar, and realized that she would do almost anything for the person she was in love with, and she would hope a stranger would help him too. Coming from Kassidy's point of view, she would want her to do all that she could to help. How could she not say yes to that? To such pure love?

Damia sighed again, this time in defeat. She looked up at Kassidy and said, "Alright, I'll help you."

Kassidy grinned, "Thank you, so much, Keeper Damia!"

"Oh," Damia said. "One more thing. This stays between us. All of it. I'm still Terri to you and Trey is still the enemy to me. Got it?"

Kassidy's head bobbed up and down in excitement, "Understood."

"Good. Now get home before both our covers are blown."

Kassidy nodded again and quickly stood up. She thanked Damia again before disappearing into the night. Damia closed her eyes, *What have I done?*

~*~

Ciro strolled confidently into Peri's room and sat down in his usual chair. Peri straightened up in surprise at his sudden appearance, but was not alarmed. "I have a question for you."

"Shoot," she said, watching him with wary eyes.

"Why did you save the Faal girl?"

"What?" Peri asked, focusing on Ciro.

"Why did you feel the need to follow a stranger's screaming in the middle of the night and face a group of boys much stronger than you in order to save someone you had never seen before?"

Peri frowned, "It was the right thing to do."

"Obviously not." Ciro said, raising his hands to their current surroundings. "You're being held for ransom because of it. Your biggest secret is about to be made public, and you're being put very behind schedule on your hunt for this Amîr Crystal."

"But we saved a little girl's life. That's worth it all," Peri said.

Ciro leaned back in his chair, and Peri watched as a small smirk fought to make its way across his serious face. Peri leaned forward, "Why do you care?"

"You said that you're not sure you want to be Keeper, that you're not fit for it. Well I see differently. Out of instinct you saved that girl. If you were anybody else, you would have run in the opposite direction. There's no fighting it, Peri," he said, standing up and moving closer to her. "You are exactly who you were destined to be: The Keeper of Air."

"Why are you doing this," Peri asked, caught off guard by Ciro's sudden interest in her well-being.

Ciro looked her over, and Peri felt a sudden chill go down her spine. She wondered what he was doing, leaning in so close to her. Was he being serious, or just trying to make a fool out of her. She was about to ask when Ciro responded. "Because," he said in a low voice. "I love proving people wrong."

He then walked away from Peri and over to the door. He looked over at her and said with a laugh, "Don't look so flustered. I do it to everyone."

Peri wasn't flustered. She was about to have a panic attack. Replaying the last few moments over again and again in her mind, one part was jumping out at her: when her stomach twisted into a knot and her heart started pumping extra hard, when Ciro moved in close, and for a fleeting second she thought he was going to kiss her.

It wasn't the fact that he was going to kiss her that triggered the panic attack, it was the feeling of disappointment when he didn't. Peri had felt like this only once before, and that was with her Earth-bound boyfriend, Joey. She couldn't believe that she was already having feelings for someone else. It had been eight days since she left Earth, since she last saw Joey.

Then Peri couldn't help but wonder if Ciro had any remotely similar feelings, or if he even realized what he had done to Peri. She wondered what would happen if he did. Would he give up his life of crime to follow Peri across Beindor? And what about Joey? Would Peri just forget about him, her boyfriend of four years? She shook her head, it would take more than an almost kiss to make her forget about Joey Montgomery.

Peri just hoped it would take far less for her to forget Ciro DeLuca.

Chapter Forty-Five

Another day had come to an end, the Saturday before the trade-off, and the three girls were anxious to get their cousin back. They had finally reached their goal of two thousand Denas. It had happened earlier that day, thanks to a very happy man who had practically fallen in love with Kendra and her voice. Since his tipping tipped them over their target amount, there was no need to stay up late working.

Once Damia and Kendra's shifts in The Dancing Bear were over, they planned to go to bed and get a full night of rest before seeing the DeLucas the next day.

As soon as Kendra finished her last song, Blackbird by the Beatles, and Damia served her last customer, the group headed up toward their rooms. Damia naturally walked over to Kynton, and took his hand in hers. He reached over and kissed the top of her head, "We've done it, Neimann. Peri will be back with us in no time."

Damia closed her eyes, controlling the sudden heat in her chest. She stopped walking and called to her cousins, already starting upstairs, "Kynton and I will be just a minute. You go on without us."

Kendra made a move to walk back down, but Aideen put an arm on her shoulder. She smiled down at Damia and Kynton and said, "That's fine. We'll probably just see you tomorrow. I think I'll be asleep before I even make it to the room."

Damia smiled and nodded, "Night then."

"Night," Kendra said with a glare, not thrilled at all to leave Damia alone with Kynton. Now she doubted she'd get a wink of sleep until Damia was back in the room with them. Aideen pulled her up the rest of the stairs before she could turn around and drag Damia up with them.

As soon as her cousins were out of sight, Kynton pulled Damia close to him and with a sly smile asked, "What was that all about?"

Damia pulled away from him and walked over to an empty two-person table on the other side of the room. Not entirely sure what to expect, Kynton slowly followed. He sat down across from Damia, and waited for her to tell him what she was thinking. She looked down at her hands, which were folded together on the table between them. She sighed, and looked up at Kynton, "I've been trying, Kynton, I really have been, but I don't think I can do this anymore."

"Do what? We have all the money. Peri will be back tomorrow."

"No," Damia said, cutting him off. She took a breath, hoping to control her feelings and make sure Kynton's didn't somehow seep in. If that happened, then what she was about to do would never work. She bit her lip, which was quivering slightly. Kynton reached out to touch her, and Damia immediately moved her hands out of his reach; touching him would guarantee his feelings would overpower her emotions.

Kynton looked as if Damia had just told him that she hated him. His mind instantly went back to the moment she had done this before, eighteen years ago in the Taurëfor Forests. He watched as a tear slipped out of Damia's eye and asked, "What is going on?"

"When I first met you," Damia said, "You said that you were good friends with the Keepers, one of the first to welcome them to Hecate."

Kynton nodded, wondering if this didn't have to do with her lack of love for him, but rather her desire to get back home. The first was an impossible obstacle, but the second was one that he knew he could get around. He knew that he could convince her to stay with him by the time they got all four pieces of the Amîr Crystal.

Damia continued, "Well, I also believed that you were romantically involved with Keeper Damia."

Kynton looked away, realizing what was about to come next.

"I've since found out that she was no more in love with you than Ciro DeLuca is with Kassidy Faal. In fact, you led me to believe you two had been a couple, when in reality she had a husband and a family that had nothing to do with you. She didn't even know you liked her until-"

"Please," Kynton said, his anger rising as he was forced to recall that horrible night eighteen years ago. "Where is this going?"

"There has not been a second since the day we first met that you have been in love with me," Damia said, her voice wavering slightly. "It was all her. You've told me yourself that you've loved her every moment of those eighteen years since she died. You didn't suddenly stop loving her after all that time and fall in love with me. For some insane reason you've convinced yourself that I'm her."

"But you are her," Kynton started.

"Yes, we share the same spirit," Damia said. "But this is my body and my mind."

She held up her elbow and pointed to a small white scar, "Did your Damia have this? No, I don't think so. I got this when I was five years old, falling off my dining room table."

"I don't think you're her," Kynton argued.

"Then what's my name?" Damia asked.

"Damia."

"My *full* name," Damia said, her lips pursed together.

"Damia Lois Neimann," the words rolled off his tounge without a moment's hesitation.

Damia shook her head, another tear falling from her face, "I've told you my name. It's Damia Rosalynn Starke. Damia Lois Neimann is the Keeper Damia's name, not mine."

Kynton closed his eyes, realizing he had been calling Damia by the wrong last name all week. "I'm sorry," he said. "What can I do to make it up? I'll do anything, Damia. I promise."

Damia shook her head, now her tears were flowing steadily, but she ignored them. She looked up at Kynton and said, "There isn't anything you can do. You've already shown me the truth. You're not going to fall out of love with her. It's been eighteen years since the last time you saw her, and you're *still* madly in love with her. I'm not going to wait for you to stop loving her, because neither of us will be happy. I'm sorry, Kynton, but this isn't going to work."

"Damia, please," Kynton said, leaning closer to her. He reached across the table, hoping he could make her see how insane she was sounding. He watched as Damia stood up. As if his touch was infectious, she jumped away from him. Kynton stood as well, and grabbed Damia before she could run away.

Damia's eyes closed as she tried to ignore his emotions as they entered her mind and her body. She could feel his confusion, his anger, and his love. She tried to move, but as she tried to take a step backwards, she felt Kynton lean in and press his lips to hers. Keeping his emotions at bay was impossible now. She could feel them flooding into her, and she was now only focused on making herself see reason, making herself see that she didn't want him to leave.

After a minute, Kynton pulled away and looked down at Damia. "Please," he said. "Give me a second chance. I promise I won't confuse you with her again."

Damia slowly removed her hands from Kynton's neck, and then removed his from her back. Tears again were glistening on her cheeks as she said, "I think it'd be best if you left."

"Damia," Kynton started.

"No," Damia said, taking a step back. "I won't do it. It'll be easier for us both if we don't see each other anymore."

Kynton watched Damia as she said this, and knew that she was not going to change her mind. If there was one thing he knew, it was that Damia wouldn't say something like that unless she actually meant it. Now he had heard it twice, and he never wanted to hear it again. "Fine," he said, taking a step backwards. "Have it your way. Push away the only person you can be yourself around. How can you expect anyone else to get close to you when you have to lie to them? We were meant to be together, Damia. We were meant to spend the rest of our lives together. You just can't see that now, but you will."

"Kynton," Damia started, but he wasn't finished.

"I promise you, Damia," he said. "One day we will be together, and we will be happy."

Kynton then turned around and ran up the stairs to his room. As soon as he disappeared, Damia collapsed in the chair next to her. She stared at the empty chair in front of her, fighting a battle inside her mind. Her legs were itching to run after Kynton, to go tell him he was right and that they were meant for each other. Her throat was closing as she realized that she really had pushed away the only person who would ever be able to see who she really was. Everyone else would see her either as just a Keeper, or as a complete lie to hide the truth.

But it was her heart that did not waiver, for she knew exactly how Kynton was feeling, and what she told him had been one hundred percent true. He was still in love with Damia Neimann, and that would not change, not ever. Damia knew she had done the right thing, but that didn't mean it didn't hurt. Damia was pulled from her thoughts when she heard Kynton coming back down the stairs, a bag slung over his shoulder.

She refused to look at him, but focused on the pattern of the wooden chair in front of her. She followed the grain with her eyes over and over again as Kynton paused at the bottom of the stairs. Damia could feel him staring at her, but she didn't look. He walked over to Mahak, who was cleaning up a mess on one of the tables not too far from Damia. Damia listened as Kynton handed over the key and said his goodbyes.

It wasn't until Kynton was standing at the front door that Damia dared look up at him. His hand was on the handle, a moment away from walking out of The Dancing Bear and out of Damia's life forever. He looked over his shoulder at Damia, a pleading look on his face. Damia couldn't give in to his silent begging, she couldn't show any weakness. She narrowed her eyes and stared unblinking at Kynton.

He sighed, getting the message loud and clear.

Damia watched as his head drooped, and his hair fell in front of his eyes. She couldn't tell what he was thinking as he walked out the door, but she remembered the last thing he had said to her. *One day we will be together, and we will be happy.* Part of her wanted what he said to come true, but another part knew it would never work. Not after what had just happened, not after his love had been festering for eighteen years for someone who could never return it.

As soon as the door closed behind him, Damia could feel such a weight disappearing from her mind. She didn't have to worry about Damia Neimann and any jealousy she had ever felt toward her. She didn't have to spend nights lying awake thinking about Kynton and what she was going to do about his not so little obsession with Damia Neimann. She could go on with her life, go forward mending her relationship with her cousins.

Damia paused. She had forgotten all about her cousins. What was she going to tell them? It wasn't like she could tell them that she had sent Kynton away when she had pushed so hard for him to come along with them. How would that make her look after Aideen had stood up for her against Kendra? And what would Kendra say, other than *I told you so.*

Damia had to come up with a story, and she had to come up with one before she went upstairs to bed.

~*~

Damia was sitting at a small two person table in the corner of The Dancing Bear when her two cousins walked downstairs. It was a little past sunrise, and the two girls were groggy with sleep. They walked up to their eldest cousin, sitting in the same spot they had left her in the night before.

"Where's Kynton?" Aideen asked, sitting down in his seat.

Damia, who had been so wrapped up in her thoughts, was startled by Aideen and Kendra's sudden appearance. She quickly wiped away the tears that had formed in her eyes and smiled at her cousins.

"Did you get a lot of sleep?" she asked, choosing to ignore Aideen's question.

"Damia," Kendra said, putting a hand on her shoulder, "Have you been down here all night?"

Damia looked around, as if realizing she was sitting in the tavern rather than upstairs in bed. She shrugged, "I guess I have been."

"What happened?" Aideen asked. "Where's Kynton?"

Damia sighed, and another tear appeared in the corner of her eye. She touched it away and shook her head, unable to find the words.

"Is he upstairs?" Kendra asked.

Damia again shook her head. "He's gone," she said, her voice cracking.

"Gone? Gone where?" Kendra demanded.

"Home," was Damia's answer, though she had no idea. She had spent the night coming up with a way to explain Kynton's disappearance without telling the embarrassing story of what really happened. "He went home," she said. This time she let the tears fall, hoping they would help sell her story. She obviously had no idea where Kynton had gone. After she told him that she couldn't be a substitute, after the fight was over, he got up and left. He went upstairs, emptied out his room and returned the key. Damia refused to watch as he slowly made his way across the large room, and walked out the door.

"There was a letter for him last night," Damia continued. "It said his mother had gotten sick, really sick. He went home to see her."

"When is he coming back," Aideen asked. "He's still coming with us, right?"

Damia shook he head, "It sounded pretty serious. He said he'd try to meet up with us if he can, but how can he? How will he know where we are? We don't even know where he lives. We'll never see each other again."

"Oh, honey," Kendra said as Damia's voice cracked again and her few tears turned into sobs. Kendra however, didn't know that Damia was crying because she was the one who made Kynton leave, and that she just lied to her cousins about it. Kendra was beating herself up for judging Kynton, and giving Damia a hard time about him when he ended up being a genuinely good person. She wished she could go back and start over, this time giving Damia more time with Kynton before he left.

"I don't mean to be a snob," Aideen said, "but are you saying Kynton just took everything and left? Everything?"

Kendra caught on a second later, "Oh my god. The money. Damia, did he take the money?"

Damia looked up at Kendra, wide eyed, thinking back. Her lip began to tremble, and she sobbed, "He checked out of his room, so if he left it, Mahak already has it. He cleaned out the room as soon as Kynton left." She then paused, "It's all my fault. Peri's dead and it's all my fault. I drove Kynton away. He took the money to spite me."

"Why would you say something like that?" Aideen asked. "His mother is sick."

Damia bit her lip, "I made him leave. He wanted to stay, but I told him to go."

"Did you tell him to take the money?" Aideen asked.

"Of course not," answered Damia.

"Then it's not your fault."

"Regardless of whose fault it is," Kendra said, looking down at her two cousins, "we need to come up with eight thousand Denas by Tuesday."

"There is no way I can play that much poker," Aideen said.

"Well you're gonna have to try," Kendra snapped. "Peri's life depends on it."

Chapter Forty-Six

The Dancing Bear is the home to many poker games throughout the week. Every night there is at least one or two games started, some more serious than others. Mahak Baer finally picked up on the idea of poker as a moneymaker not only for the winners, but for The Dancing Bear as well a few years ago. Since then, he has held a monthly tournament in his bar with a fifteen Dena entrance fee.

Luckily, for the Keepers, this month's tournament happened to fall on the weekend before the ransom money for Peri was due. Even luckier for them, Aideen had already gained a reputation as the best poker player The Dancing Bear had ever seen, and many adamant tournament players were eager to try and beat her.

One of these players was Tad Dunbar, a twenty-something blacksmith apprentice with a wife and infant daughter. He had never played poker for more than fun with his friends after dark, but with the new baby came new expenses that the apprenticeship salary couldn't cover. So he signed his name under a Carr Faal and before a Clio Morris and took his place at one of the professional-looking tables set up in the center of the tavern.

He watched as the other twenty or so players took their seats, with much better poker faces than his. He could feel his stomach twist into knots, knowing that the fifteen Dena entrance fee might have been used to buy food for his wife and tiny daughter. He watched as the piano man and three waiters moved to their places behind the poker tables, the dealers for the night, and a pretty little waitress hurried between the tables getting drinks for the contestants.

The owner of the tavern and his wife hovered close by, keeping a close watch on everything and everyone. This was a big night for them, and they wanted nothing to go wrong. Tad watched as a cute little songbird walked over to the piano and began to sing to the melody she was producing on the keys. The song washed over him, calming him down, focusing him on the game, on the cash prize for the winner.

Tad studied the four people sitting at the table with him, his enemies in this competition. The only woman in the tournament, a girl younger than him actually, sat two seats away from him. Her face was locked into a look of pure concentration and determination. Tad wondered if she had anything like he did riding on this competition, maybe a dying sister in need of medical help too far out of her reach, or a baby in need of food and clothing.

He hoped not.

He wanted to be able to win this thing and not feel guilty about it. He wanted to be able to tell his wife that he had done something good for them, for the baby. He wanted to be able to make a difference in his daughter's life.

The dealer then started to explain the rules of Hold'em, and The Dancing Bear's monthly poker tournament had begun.

~*~

"I can't look. Is she winning? How many chips does she have?"

"Damia, calm down," Kendra said, watching Damia pace behind the bar. "They're not even playing with chips. And Aideen is doing fine."

"How do you know? She feels nervous. Do you think she's losing? Maybe she's having a panic attack."

"Of course she's nervous," Kendra said. "She's playing for a lot of money, and if she loses then we're not going to be able to get Peri back."

Damia paused and looked over to the table Aideen was playing at. Over half of the contestants had already stepped down, and the rest of them seemed to be pretty confident that they were going to win. To Damia, Aideen seemed like a fish out of water, so out of her element that it was making Damia sick.

"Damia, you look sick." Kendra said. "Maybe you should eat something."

Damia shook her head, "It's all my fault. All of this. Everything. All my fault. I shouldn't have been so mean to Kynton. I should have helped you save Sara Faal. I should have made Aideen stay away from that house. I should never have suggested we go for that walk."

Damia again paused in her pacing, realizing what she had just said. She looked at Kendra, whose eyebrows had knitted together, and her lips and formed a small line on her face. Damia covered her mouth, but the words had already been spoken.

"What's going on, Damia," Kendra asked. "If I remember correctly, *I* was the one who suggested the walk, not you. *I* was the one who was mean to Kynton, *and I* was the one who was responsible for Aideen."

Damia frowned, "It's this horrid Empathy power I have. I can feel everyone's emotions, and I feel them as my own. I don't even realize what's happening until I open my big mouth and get in trouble. One time I even thought I was kissing *myself* when Kynton kissed me."

Kendra tried not to vomit at the image of Kynton and Damia kissing, but it wasn't too hard. There were more important things to worry about. "That isn't good, Damia. Why didn't you mention that you were having such a bad time with this power before?"

Damia shrugged, "I was focusing on other things, like saving Peri," *and telling Kynton to leave.*

"Well, I think you should focus on controlling your power," Kendra said. "It'll take your mind off of Aideen and Peri. There isn't anything we can do now but wait for Aideen to win this tournament."

Damia nodded, "Maybe Seer Korinna can help me. I think I might go talk to her."

Chapter Forty-Seven

"Hello? Is anyone here?"

Damia walked into Seer Korinna's Magikal Shoppe, only to find the storefront abandoned. She could see a faint light coming from behind the drawn curtain separating the storefront from the back room. She approached it hesitantly, wondering why Seer Korinna had not come out to meet her. She was a Seer after all; she knew that Damia was there.

"Hello?" Damia called again, walking even closer to the back room.

"Hello," came a voice from behind her.

Damia had to hold her breath to keep from screaming. She spun around, clutching her hands to her heart. "Don't do that!" she started to say, but stopped herself when she saw who was standing in front of her.

"Kain? What are you doing here? Do you know Seer Korinna?"

"Not exactly," Kain said, taking a step forward. He frowned and looked Damia over, "What are you doing here?"

Damia blushed, "I'm having some trouble with my," she paused, "powers. I was hoping Seer Korinna could help me. Do you know if she's here?"

Kain frowned again, "I'm sorry, Keeper, but she is not. I came looking for her too, but I believe she left just moments before I got here."

"Oh," Damia paused. She was about to leave, disappointed that she wouldn't get any help when she realized that this man had known about her powers, surely he could help her control them...

"Kain, sir, could you help me?"

Kain looked surprised that Damia had asked him to help her. After only a second's hesitation, however, he said, "Of course, Keeper. What is the problem?"

"Well," Damia said, taking a seat on a stool near a large bookshelf that Aideen had spent an entire afternoon reorganizing and updating. "It's my Empathy power. I fear that none of my emotions are my own. That maybe I have been channeling everyone else's emotions without ever knowing."

"And what's wrong with that?" Kain asked, even though he knew the answer, the exact words that would come out of her mouth. The Keepers weren't the only ones with magik powers.

"I want to feel my own emotions. I want to make decisions based on what I feel, not what others feel."

"But with the proper training, you can do both. You can separate your own emotions from everyone else's. You can manipulate situations around what others are feeling. Yet you can still make decisions for yourself," Kain said, trying not to show that he was speaking from experience.

"How?" Damia asked, almost desperately. "Please help me, Kain."

Kain nodded, realizing that coming to Seer Korinna's Magikal Shoppe turned out to be a success after all. True, he couldn't kill the Seer for spilling his secrets to Keeper Peri, but he could get some information from this Keeper. From the moment she stepped inside the shop, he had been able to go through her mind, searching for any clues about what had happened so long ago.

He saw what had happened to Keeper Peri, how she had been kidnapped by the DeLucas. He saw Kynton, so in love with this Keeper, and he saw how she broke his heart. He saw Kassidy Faal talking to Trey DeLuca, and the moment that this Keeper realized that they were in love. He saw the anger Trey felt for his brother, and Kain instantly knew what was going to happen next.

Damia left not long after. As soon as she was gone, he removed the mask he had been hiding behind. He breathed easier, and with a small laugh, he knew what he had to do next, whom he had to see next. Not only had one goal just appeared on the horizon, another had just begun hurdling toward him. Ever since the Keepers had opened the door into the Trac house, into Earth, everything was going perfectly for Tárquin.

~*~

She did it. It was over. The game was over.

The pile in front of Aideen had grown so much that she knew it was impossible for her to walk away with less than enough money to get Peri back safely. Now all she had to do was fold, stop playing and let another person be the winner. Kendra doubted that was going to happen.

The glow in Aideen's red-brown eyes was sign enough that she was going all the way. There was no way she was going to stop playing this addictive game. She was going to play, and she was going to win. She had won every other game she had played in The Dancing Bear, why not this one as well?

Kendra watched as Aideen pushed over half of the pile of coins in front of her into the center of the last table left in the tournament. She watched as the only other player did as well. He was a young man, only a few years older than Aideen, and he seemed in shock that he had made it so far. Kendra knew Aideen could kick this guy in the ass if she wanted to, if she was lucky enough.

It was slow motion as he set down his cards on the table. Kendra could not see the faces of the plastic squares, but she could see the only face that mattered. Aideen studied the cards for less than a second before her face gave her own cards away, long before she ever set them down. Her mouth fell open in shock, her eyes went back to her own cards, as if she might have read them wrong, but Kendra knew she would have them memorized for life.

Kendra could feel her entire body swell with anticipation, waiting for Aideen to reveal her cards, waiting for her to reveal the conclusion of the last game of the tournament. Had they done it? Was Peri saved?

She watched as Aideen set the cards down on the table, with a little more aggression than Kendra thought was necessary for a winning hand. The only other two people at the table studied the cards in front of Aideen, and Kendra looked to Felton, the dealer. He glanced at her, and the fact that his face was not as joyous as she would have expected told Kendra what had just happened. Her realization was confirmed when Felton pushed the large pile of coins away from Aideen, and towards Tad Dunbar.

How can this happen? Kendra thought, panicking. She watched as Tad Dunbar threw his hands up in the air in celebration. The others in the bar came to his side at once to congratulate him, leaving Aideen alone on the other side of the table, and Kendra alone at the bar. Aideen slowly turned to Kendra and stood, her face molded into a look of such shock that Kendra wondered if it would ever return to normal.

She thought the same of her own.

What was left to do? They had a grand total of two thousand five hundred and thirty two Denas, and the ransom was due in less than twenty four hours. There was no way they could raise that much money working, even if they worked from that moment up until the moment it was due. They couldn't even get advanced payment, the Baers did not have that kind of money to loan out.

Kendra could feel all the hope she had felt the day before slipping from her grasp. She felt like she was drowning, and could not tell which way was up. If they could not get the money, what would happen to Peri? Would she be killed? Would the DeLucas dare harm a Keeper? Kendra knew the answer was a solid yes. They weren't afraid to harm anyone, not even if it was the very person who brought them to Hecate.

Aideen sat down in the seat next to Kendra, her shoulders slumped and her limbs limp. She stared at the floor, as if all the answers to the questions swimming around in her head could be found down there. She shook her head, muttering to herself.

She then turned and looked up at Kendra, the fire now completely gone from her eyes, and asked, "What do we do now?"

Chapter Forty-Eight

No one could sleep that night.

Not Kendra, Aideen nor Damia. Peri never slept anymore, and it had been a long time since Trey could. Ciro spent the night pacing back and forth outside of Peri's room, and Kassidy spent the night trying to figure out a way to tell her family about Trey. The only one who could sleep peacefully was Tad Dunbar, with a full stomach, a heavy wallet, and a loving wife.

The morning light gave no relief. No one was smiling that day, no one was ready for what was about to happen. Kendra, Aideen and Damia spent the morning sitting silently around a table at The Dancing Bear, trying to figure out what to do when dusk came. They were not surprised that when dusk came they still had no plan and still no money to get Peri safely back.

They were surprised, however, to see Carr and Kassidy come into The Dancing Bear just as they were about to leave. "What are you guys doing here?" Damia asked.

"We're here to help you get your cousin back," Kassidy said, and Carr nodded in agreement.

"Trust me when I say you want as much backup as possible when facing the DeLucas," he said.

"Thank you," Kendra said, though her gratitude did not show on her face.

Together, the five teenagers walked out of The Dancing Bear and down to the Willow tree, where the exchange was supposed to take place. By the time they got there, the sun had already passed behind the buildings around them, casting long shadows over the streets. They reached the Willow, and saw Ciro, Trey and Peri standing in front of it.

Damia fought the urge to run up to Peri the moment she saw her and give her a big bear hug, to apologize and to get her back to safety. Kendra looked Peri over, and was relieved to see that she looked to be unharmed, despite looking tired and strained. Aideen felt like she had just taken a kick to the stomach as she realized that they were not going to be able to get Peri back, and it was all thanks to her and her competitive edge.

Peri, are you alright? Damia thought across the open plaza.

Yeah, I'm fine, came Peri's answer. *Just ready for a nice long nap in a normal bed.*

Well you might have to wait just a little longer... Kendra said softly.

What? Peri's eyes flew open, and if the girls hadn't been hearing what she was saying, they would have thought she had been suddenly possessed by a demon. *Don't you have the money? What have you been doing all week? Playing hero to some other seven-year old girls?*

We had the money, Aideen thought quickly. *But then Kynton left, and he took most of it with him.*

What are you talking about? I thought he was coming with us?

There was an emergency back home, Damia said, looking down at the ground. *He accidently took the money with him, and we don't have any way to contact him.*

So now what? Peri asked. *I don't want to spend another night in that place. It's a nuthouse.*

Run.

The girls looked surprisingly at Kendra, who gave them each a look that said she was not going to change her mind, nor was she the least bit insane. She wanted Peri to run.

I can't just start running! Trey has a death grip on me. And besides, I'm not going to get far.. if you remember from the night I got kidnapped, I'm not much of a runner.

Well, it's either that or spend the rest of your life the DeLucas' prisoner, snapped Kendra.

Peri frowned, *Alright, fine. I'll try.*

Not realizing that the Keepers were already talking to his prisoner, Ciro took a few steps forward, leaving Trey and Peri behind him. He was less than five feet away from the Keepers and Faals when he stopped and laughed, "Well look who it is, the faggot and his whore of a sister."

Carr took a step forward, and Peri felt Trey's grip on her arm tighten. She looked down, surprised at how his hand was clasped so tightly around her. It was as if he was mad at what Ciro had said, as if he was offended by the taunting towards his enemy.

"Are you here to help these loser wannabe Saviors of Beindor?" Ciro laughed.

Carr stopped moving towards Ciro, wondering what he meant by *Saviors of Beindor*. Obviously the Saviors of Beindor were the Keepers, Keeper Peri, Keeper Aideen, Keeper Damia and Keeper Kendra. Not Thalia, Clio, Terri and Polly. Carr looked over at the three girls standing next to Kassidy, and the look on their faces told him that Ciro knew a lot more about this than he did.

Ciro saw the confusion on Carr's face and laughed again, "Oh, this is rich. Are you telling me, Faal, that the Keepers asked for your help, but didn't tell you the truth about themselves? What? Did they use fake names to trick you? How pathetic. Well I saw them, I saw Keeper Aideen's Fire. I saw Keeper Peri See the future. What did you see? Keeper Kendra bus some tables at The Dancing Bear?"

Ciro stopped laughing and turned to the Keepers, "Do you have the money or not?"

"Not," Aideen said. "But that doesn't mean you're keeping Peri. Hand her over now, and you won't see what the Keepers can do when really provoked."

Aideen, what are you doing? We have no plan! Kendra yelled. *None of us can control our powers, how are we supposed to fight them?*

We don't have to use our powers, Aideen said, her fingers curling into fists at her sides. *We just have to make them* think *we are.*

This is suicide, Kendra thought.

No, Damia said with a small smile. *This will work. Kendra, help Aideen. I'm going to help Peri.* A plan was forming in her head.

Damia, what are you thinking? Kendra asked.

Just help Aideen, Damia thought, ignoring the question.

Ciro's lips had curled into a snarl, "How dare you threaten me! I know more about you Keepers than you think. I know your powers are weak! All you had to do was get the money, and Peri would be safe. Now you've killed her!"

Suddenly Aideen charged Ciro, her fists curled so tight that her knuckles glowed white in the diminishing light. She reached him just a second before he realized what was happening, and was able to swing at him while still off guard. She punched him in the stomach, but he only laughed and swung back, catching her in the jaw. Carr was at Aideen's side in seconds, punching and kicking Ciro with such ferocity that Ciro started to back away.

As soon as Aideen took off in the direction of Ciro, Damia took off in the direction of Peri. Trey saw her running at them, and pushed Peri behind him. He put his fists up in fornt of him, waiting for an attack similar to Aideen's, and was surprised that when Damia reached them, she stopped and smiled at him. "I'm here to help you, Trey. I'm on your side."

"Damia!" Peri yelled in shock.

"It's okay, Peri," Damia said before turning back to Trey. "Let Peri go, Trey. Take me instead. I can help you, *both of you.*"

Trey was beginning to panic. Did this mean that Keeper Damia knew about him and Kassidy Faal? Had Kassidy told her? Or did Carr finally spill his guts like he knew he would.

"I can't just let her go, Ciro wouldn't understand," Trey said, wanting to know what Keeper Damia meant by how she could help them.

"Tell him that I came to get her, and she escaped, but you grabbed me before I could," Damia sad quickly.

Peri shook her head, not understanding what was going on between these two. Since when was Damia on talking terms with the DeLucas? She said, "I'm not just going to let you take my place, Damia. How could you expect me to do that?"

"Because I need to help Trey. I can't do that from over there," Damia explained, not wanting to waste time with all the details. Those could be sorted out later.

Peri again shook her head, "Fine, then take us both. I'm not leaving you behind."

"Peri, you don't have to do that. You're the one who just said you never wanted to go back to that nuthouse again. What about your nice long nap?"

"Damia, do you really think I could sleep a wink with you inside that nuthouse?"

"Fine," Damia said. "Take us both. But if you get killed, Peri, don't blame me."

Trey, still confused, said, "If you're both coming back, then we should go now, before Ciro and your cousins see us and try to stop us."

The three then snuck out of the plaza unnoticed while Aideen and Carr attacked Ciro. Kassidy and Kendra stood by, watching helplessly, knowing if they got involved, it would be more of a bloody mess than it already was. Kendra looked over to where Trey DeLuca was holding Peri, where Damia had gone to save her, and was stunned to see that the spot was empty. She frantically searched the rest of the plaza, but the only people there were Ciro, Carr, Aideen, Kassidy and herself. Trey, Peri and Damia were gone.

"Aideen!" Kendra shouted at the top of her lungs. "They're gone! All three of them! Trey DeLuca kidnapped both Peri and Damia!"

The instant Kendra started screaming, the fighting ceased and the others looked around as well, surprised to see what Kendra was saying was true. Ciro also realized that he was all by himself, and the best plan was to find his brother and their new hostages. He started running away from Carr and Aideen, and shouted, "We'd better have the money by midnight tomorrow, or else one of them dies!"

The four watched helplessly as he disappeared into the darkness, now feeling even less hopeful than ever. They were down two Keepers, and now their lives were really at stake. They knew Ciro would not hesitate to kill one of them, not while the other was there to insure the money got safely into his hands.

~*~

"Is someone going to explain to me what is going on?" Peri asked the moment they reached the room that was still apparently her prison cell and now Damia's as well.

As soon as they left the clearing, Trey had let go of Peri, and had never bothered to make sure she or Damia would stick with him. In fact, Damia seemed to be in just as much of a hurry to get to the DeLuca house as Trey was.

Trey turned to Damia and said, "I was just about to ask the same thing."

Damia smiled, and Peri wondered if she even realized that she had just been voluntarily kidnapped. She said to Trey, "I talked to Kassidy, after the two of you went to The Dancing Bear the other night. She explained to me what was happening between you, what you two have been doing for the past year or so."

"And you're going to help," Trey asked, suddenly getting excited. Maybe his dreams would come true after all. Before the Keepers showed up, he had feared he could never be with Kassidy, but now the Keepers were going to help them. He was going to be with Kassidy, forever.

Damia nodded, feeling Trey's sudden swell of joy in her chest. She smiled and said, "I have a plan, but it's going to take a lot on your part."

Trey nodded, "I'll do anything."

"You're going to have to stand up to Ciro. To your father."

Trey shook his head, "I don't care. I only want Kassidy."

Damia's smile broke into a grin, "This can work. We can get you out of this house, tonight."

"How?" Trey asked, excited but still not fully confident in this Keeper of Earth.

"When Ciro comes home, he's going to be mad, right?" Damia asked.

Trey laughed, "When isn't he?"

Peri frowned, but stayed out of their conversation. She still had no clue what was going on. And who was Kassidy?

"Well that's when you tell him that you're leaving," Damia said simply. "He won't be expecting it. He'll be thinking that you kidnapped us both, and you can corner him. We'll be here the entire time with you. Don't worry about him attacking you, it'll be three to one. He'd be crazy to do anything."

Trey nodded, taking a deep breath as he realized that in less than five minutes he would either be dead or a free man. There was no turning back now. This was it.

Chapter Forty-Nine

Slamming every door he could behind him, Ciro walked through his house. Yes, he was upset, but not because the Keepers didn't have the money, he knew they wouldn't anyway. No, it was because of Trey. He had left Ciro to defend himself against four people, two Keepers and two Faals at that.

If he didn't know any better, he would've guessed that Trey didn't want him to come out of that alive.

He headed to Peri's room, half expecting the three of them already planning his demise. He was almost there when a door to his right opened suddenly and his father stepped out. Ciro immediately stopped, and began counting how many doors he had slammed, knowing each one would earn him some sort of punch or hit. He was at five when his father interrupted him, "I noticed the exchange didn't go down exactly as planned."

Ciro shook his head, not daring to speak to this mad man.

"Did I see your brother taking *two* girls into the house?"

Ciro nodded his head, "Another Keeper."

Rico laughed, "Those girls aren't as bright as they seemed, huh?"

Ciro dared a smirk and immediately regretted it. Rico stopped laughing and his face fell into a glare. He said, "We need to stop this before it gets too out of control. Now that we have two, the Keepers might not wait to raise any more money. They might just come and get them back. I'm surprised they haven't tried to already."

"What'd ya want us to do?" Ciro asked, his eyes never going farther up than his father's chest. He was still waiting for a beating.

He watched as Rico reached behind himself and pulled a pistol from under his shirt. Ciro tensed up, fearing that his father had finally gone mental and was going to shoot him. He was surprised to watch as Rico turned the hand gun so that the butt was facing his son.

After a second, Ciro realized that his father was handing him his gun.

He took it hesitantly, not sure if he should. What did Rico want him to do with this thing?

"Kill one of them," came the answer to his unvoiced question. "It doesn't matter which one. Just kill one. That way the others know we aren't messin' around."

"Yes, sir," Ciro said. He watched as his father retreated into his room. Ciro then turned down the hall, much quieter now, but with a much more lethal purpose.

~*~

"What are we going to do?" Kendra asked, to no one in particular. She was pacing up and down in front of the piano at The Dancing Bear. Aideen, Carr and Kassidy were sitting at a table close by, watching her endless back and forth motion. She spun on her heel to face them, "We've lost two people now! Are we going to let this happen all over again?"

"Of course not," Aideen said.

"But we have until *tomorrow* to get the money we couldn't even get in a week!" Kendra yelled. "We can't just let one of our cousins die!"

"We're not," Aideen said, turning away from Kendra.

"How?" Kendra said, stopping her pacing to look at the only cousin she had left. "How are we going to save Peri and Damia?"

Aideen looked up at Kendra, "We're going to rescue them, like we should have from the beginning. No more playing by the De-Lucas' rules. We're the Keepers, damn it. We can't let some half-assed family get away with this."

Kendra bit her lip. She wanted to scream at Aideen for thinking of such an irrational, irresponsible, crazy, messed up plan that would probably get them all killed. She wanted to scream at her for not thinking it up before. "Aideen!"

Aideen cringed, ready for the normal Kendra reaction. She was surprised to see a smile break out on her face instead, "That's brilliant! They'll never expect it! We should go tonight. Sneak attack!"

"We can slip in and out. They'll never notice we were there," Kassidy said.

"And we all know you know how to do that," Carr said.

Kassidy smiled, but a small blush crept into her face, "I most certainly do."

"Then lead the way," Aideen said, standing up.

The group left The Dancing Bear and reached the DeLuca house with ease. Kendra and Aideen were surprised to see how well Kassidy seemed to know her way around the house. She went straight over to a small window hidden deep in the overgrowth on the side of the house and was not at all surprised to find it unlocked.

She pushed it open and turned to the others, "Be careful. Step only where I step. Don't make a sound. Mrs. DeLuca is a *very* light sleeper."

She then proceeded to climb down into the basement of the DeLuca house, with Carr, Aideen and Kendra close at her heels. She led them around boxes filled with old junk the DeLucas hadn't touched in years, and to the door that led to the first floor of the De-Luca home.

Once on the ground level, Kassidy quickly moved down a hall with many closed doors off of it. Only one of the doors was open, just a crack enough to let some light into the hall. It was from this room the four teens could hear voices coming. Kassidy recognized Ciro's voice immediately.

He yelled, "I'm thinking about the ten thousand Denas that we are going to collect when the Faals find a dead Keeper on their doorstep!"

Aideen then, with a sudden surge of heat in her chest, pushed the door open all the way, "That's enough!"

Chapter Fifty

Ciro had walked confidently into the guest bedroom turned prison cell, the gun resting casually in the waistband of his pants, out of sight. Peri and Damia were sitting huddled together on the mattress in the corner of the room. Trey was leaning against the far wall, hands folded over his chest, eyes closed. Peri and Damia tightened their grip on each other the moment Ciro stepped into the room, but Trey didn't move an inch.

It wasn't until Ciro started talking that Trey opened his eyes and looked at his brother. He said, "What happened back there, big brother? You left me all alone with the Keepers and the Faals."

Trey stood up, "Well, it was only half the Keepers. I was busy with the other half."

Ciro nodded, his lips pursed together, almost in a pout. He was still upset with his brother, but he had a bigger task to accomplish than beat the crap out of Trey. He then pulled the gun out of its hiding spot, similar to what Rico had done, and pointed it at the two girls sitting on the bed.

Damia, who had been giving Trey a look that said, *Now! Do something now!* yelped in surprise. She had not been expecting to see Ciro with a gun in his hand. This changed everything.

Ciro laughed, regaining the composure he had earlier in the plaza. He pointed the gun first and Peri, then at Damia, then back at Peri. "Which one of you should I kill first? I only need one of you alive to get the money."

He first pointed the gun at Peri, whose heart leapt into her throat. Would Ciro really pull the trigger on her? She had thought they had connected, had a relationship of sorts. Apparently, Ciro felt the same way, because as soon as he saw the look on Peri's face, he turned the gun on Damia. That was when Trey began to panic. If Damia was killed or hurt in any way, how could he leave all of this behind and find Kassidy. The Keeper was his ticket out; he couldn't let her die.

"You're not killing either of them," Trey said, taking a step forward.

Ciro looked at Trey, "What? Don't you want them dead too?"

"No!" Trey said, "They're the Keepers, Ciro! How could you think of killing them?"

"I'm thinking about the ten thousand Denas that we are going to collect when the Faals find a dead Keeper on their doorstep!"

"That's enough!"

The brothers turned to see Keeper Aideen standing in the doorway. Next to her stood Keeper Kendra, Kassidy and Carr Faal. Ciro immediately spun the gun on them, yelling, "You filthy scum! Get out of my house before I kill you too!"

"Ciro," Trey yelled. "Stop this! You're mad if you think you're going to hurt the Faals!"

Trey quickly moved across the room and came to stand next to Kassidy. He silently slipped his hand into hers, and she looked up at him both with shock and a look of love that made him kiss her forehead.

Ciro saw everything. There was a look on his face that Trey had never seen before. Sure, Trey had seen Ciro upset, seething even, but this was a loathing that scared him. His eyes were dilated so much that the irises were no longer visible. His breathing had slowed down so that the only way Trey could tell he was breathing was by the slow rise of his chest. Ciro faced his brother and said in a deep voice, "Move over, Trey so that I can end this fight once and for all."

"I'm not going to let you hurt them. I love Kassidy."

"Traitor," Ciro spat at Trey.

He slowly raised the gun in his hand, which was shaking slightly with anger, and pointed it at Trey. "Move," he said.

When Trey didn't, Ciro shrugged and said, "I figured as much. Only a true DeLuca would have moved."

"I'm still a DeLuca, Ciro. Just because I'm in love with Kassidy doesn't mean my family name has changed," Trey said with a sigh, wishing it could.

Ciro shook his head, "You don't understand, *brother*. You never were a DeLuca to begin with. Now I can see that you never will be."

"What are you talking about?" Trey asked, glancing at the gun still pointed at him.

"You were adopted!" Ciro shouted. "Some couple gave you to my mother. Not even your own parents wanted you, and I can't blame them. You're a worthless Faal-loving piece of shit!"

"You're lying," Trey said immediately. He shook his head, not believing a word that came out of Ciro's mouth. He would say anything to gain control again, forgetting that he was the one holding the gun. "You're just saying that to get a rise out of me. It won't work, Ciro. I'm not like you."

"I'm not lying! Father told me when we were ten years old! Why do you think you look so different from us? You look more like them than you do us," Ciro yelled, waving the gun at the Keepers.

Everyone then turned to Trey, waiting for his reaction. His face was unreadable, and Damia could feel his emotions spiking all over the place. From anger to relief to confusion and then to hate. Then he gave a small laugh and a smile broke out across his face. He looked at Ciro and said, "That's the best news I've heard all day."

Ciro obviously did not want to hear that. His lips curled into a snarl and in a sudden flash of thunder, he pulled his finger closed around the trigger of the gun. Trey had always thought the pain would be immediate. He thought that he would be able to feel the bullet rip through his chest and burrow deep in his heart. He thought he would be blinded by the pain or at least feel a pull as the speeding bullet made contact, but he felt nothing. He heard someone scream in pain and when he realized it was not him, he realized it was not him who had been shot.

Kassidy's hand slipped from his grasp and Trey had a sinking feeling he knew who Ciro had taken his anger out on. Kassidy started to fall backwards, but Aideen quickly reached out and caught her. Together, they sat on the floor and Trey was immediately at her side. "Kassidy, I'm so sorry. I never meant for you to get hurt."

Kassidy smiled at him, but Trey could tell she was in pain. Blood was seeping from where the bullet had entered her chest, where it had missed her heart by just inches. However, that wasn't enough to save her life, and Trey could see the light quickly going out in her eyes. Trey enveloped her in a hug, burying his face in her hair. Damia put a hand on him, "Trey, you have to get off of her."

Trey tightened his grip on Kassidy, too blind by love and sorrow to understand why she wanted him to let go of his lover in her final moments.

"She is going to die if you don't let Kendra heal her."

Trey looked up at Damia in surprise. *Heal?* He thought. *She was shot in the chest! No Healer can heal fatal wounds!*

He then remembered he was in the same room with the Keepers. Of course Kassidy was going to survive. As soon as he moved away from her, Kendra swooped in and placed her hand over the wound. Though she had never done it before, healing came naturally for Kendra. She placed her hands over the wounds and thought back to the moment she had healed herself, where she was floating in the water.

She watched in surprise as eater seemed to come from nowhere and wash away the wound, the hole the bullet had created and all the blood it created. Kassidy gasped in surprise, not expecting the pain to go away so instantly and so completely. She looked up at the Healing Keeper and said, "Thank you."

As much as Trey wanted to stay and watch Keeper Kendra heal Kassidy, her shooter was still in the room, still holding the gun. He turned to face Ciro, only to see a scramble of bodies on the floor where Ciro was standing moments ago. It seemed that Carr had tackled Ciro after he had shot his sister. It was hard to tell who was winning, but they were both flailing around so Trey judged it was almost evenly matched. Ciro's strength was equal to Carr's furry over Kassidy being shot.

Before Trey could help Faal beat up Ciro, he realized that the gun was no longer in Ciro's hand. Carr must have knocked it out if his hands when he attacked. Trey immediately began searching for it only to find that somebody was already holding the gun.

"Peri," he said. "Give me the gun."

Peri looked at him, still very confused. She bit her lip, "Why would I give you the gun? Are you going to shoot us too?"

"Peri, I'm not like Ciro. You heard him; I'm not even a DeLuca." He looked over to where Kassidy was being healed by Keeper Kendra. He watched as her eyes fluttered open and he smiled, "I just want to be with Kass."

Peri shook her head, "Then why would you keep me here? If you didn't want the money or to kill me?"

"I'm sorry, Peri," Trey said. "I never wanted to go along with this, honestly. I just did so that Ciro wouldn't suspect anything. I was worried he wouldn't like where I was headed," Trey paused and looked to where Ciro and Carr were still rolling around on the floor. He looked over to Kassidy and said, "And now I realize I had every reason to be cautious. He just tried to kill Kassidy."

"Are you going to kill him?" Peri asked,

"What?" Trey asked, looking back at Peri.

"Why do you want the gun if you're not going to kill Ciro?"

"I promise I won't kill him. I want the gun because I know Ciro could never make the same sort of promise."

Peri also knew that was true, but she couldn't help wishing she was wrong. It had been a week since first meeting Ciro, and despite his cruel words and violent outbursts, Peri had grown attached to him. In a twisted sort of way, she had grown to like him. She looked over to where Ciro was now punching Carr in the jaw and winced. He would never change, could never change. He was a DeLuca, a member of a family where hatred and violence is bred into you.

A tear rolled down her cheek and she blushed. "I can't believe I'm crying. They came to rescue me and I cry because I don't want to see him hurt."

"Ciro is a complicated person," Trey said with a frown. "I've seen him as the nicest one of us, and I've seen him beat up seven year old girls."

Peri nodded, remembering why she had been kidnapped in the first place. "When he would come in here with you, he was always so guarded and when he would just sit and talk, he was so open."

Trey frowned, "I've never seen Ciro open up to someone before. I really had hoped he could change."

Peri nodded and then sighed, "I suppose I should give you this then."

She raised her hand and Trey looked down. It was the gun. Trey took the piece silently, and as soon as it was out of Peri's hand, she crumbled. More tears rolled down her face and she had to turn away. In the moment the gun passed from Peri to Trey, Damia arrived at Peri's side. She had felt this particular breakdown coming, and was prepared. She brought Peri away from Trey and over to the mattress on the floor. She sat Peri down and took a seat next to her. Peri cried into Damia's shoulder and Damia quickly wiped away her own tears.

"Carr, get off my *brother*."

Everyone paused, including Carr and Ciro. Carr had been on top of Ciro, repeatedly punching him in the side of the face. Blood was dripping from Ciro's nose and from multiple cuts and bruises on his face. Carr was looking only slightly better. Carr looked over his shoulder, to where Trey was pointing Ciro's gun at them. Carr's eyes got wide and he lifted his hands off Ciro.

He slowly stood up.

He was surprised to see that Trey did not follow him with the gun. In fact, he didn't look at him at all. Trey kept eye contact with Ciro only, the gun steady in his hands.

Behind Trey, Peri looked on in disbelief. Trey had lied to her. He had said he would not kill Ciro, and here he was holding the gun to his head. She knew that Ciro deserved no better than this, and yet she was scared for him. There was no telling what Trey would do.

Trey took a few steps forward, and Ciro quickly scrambled to his feet, not wanting to give his ex-brother and ex-best friend the perfect chance to kill him. Ciro matched Trey's pace, never letting him close the gap between him and the gun. Then Trey suddenly rushed forward and grabbed Ciro, pointing the gun hard into his chest. He said in a low voice the others could barely pick up, "I never want to see you again, DeLuca, do you understand me? If I ever see your face I won't hesitate to kill you. I will crush your throat with my bare hands."

The hint of fear that was in Ciro's face hardened into hate. His jaw, bruised from Carr's fist, clenched and the veins on his neck stood out. "Threats, Trey? Is that what you've come down to? If you're going to kill me, then do it now and get it over with. Spare me the agony of watching you leave with that Faal bitch."

Trey hit Ciro so fast and so hard that it sent Ciro sprawling to the floor. Carr reached out to stop Trey from jumping on his brother, and they both realized that Ciro was not getting up. Carr bent down to check his pulse.

"What is going on in here?" bellowed Rico as he burst into the room. He stopped in the doorway, seeing Carr Faal with his hand on his unconscious son's throat. "YOU KILLED HIM! YOU WORTHLESS PIECE OF SHIT! YOU KILLED MY SON!"

Carr immediately backed away, the old man getting ready to pull out his gun, only to realize he had given it to Ciro to kill one of the Keepers with. As Carr moved behind Trey, Rico saw his adopted son for the first time. He shouted at him, "What are you waiting for? KILL THAT FAAL!"

Trey shook his head and Rico made a move to attack Carr. Trey quickly stepped in his father's way and pointed his own gun at him. Rico saw this and panicked, "Son? What are you doing? The Faal is behind you!"

"Thank you, sir, for taking me in and raising me as your own. I am very grateful for that, however, I think that it's time I see what it's like to be a Faal."

"What?" Rico yelled. "You can't just leave your family! Your father!"

Trey smiled, "Kassidy is my only family now." Trey then turned around to face Carr, Kassidy and the Keepers. He said, "Let's get out of here."

Aideen was the first to leave, she helped a shell-shocked Kassidy stand and together they and Kendra walked past Rico, out of the room and out into the street. Carr quickly followed after them, never letting either Kassidy or Rico leave his sight. Rico glared at Carr as he passed, but with Trey still holding the gun on him, Rico did nothing. Damia picked up Peri and slowly they walked out of the room.

Peri looked straight ahead, refusing to look at Rico, Trey, and especially Ciro, still passed out on the floor. Damia wrapped her arm around Peri and quickly glanced at Ciro. His eyes fluttered open just as Damia and Peri walked past him. Damia quickly ushered Peri out of the room before she could see this.

That left Trey, Ciro, and Rico alone in the side room of the DeLuca house.

Ciro quickly got up and stood next to his father. "Don't do this," Rico said. "We'll forget all of it and go back to hating the Faals. How everything was before."

Trey shook his head, "I've wanted to do this for a very long time. Good-bye, Father. Ciro."

Trey then walked out of the room and left a very flabbergasted Rico DeLuca behind.

As soon as he walked out of the house, he was met with the scent of strawberries and a flash of flaming red color. Kassidy wrapped her arms around Trey in a tight hug and said, "I'm so proud of you, Trey! Standing up to both Ciro and your father! Nothing can keep us apart now!"

"Except Father," Carr said with a huff.

Chapter Fifty-One

It was nearing two in the morning when the group reached the Faal house. The streets were all empty and the skies were clear. They walked in silence for a good part of the way. Kassidy wrapped her arm around Trey's and rest her head on his shoulder. Carr stood on the other side of her, afraid there would be an after effect of being shot and then healed by a Keeper. Plus, she was holding on to a De-Luca, and that wasn't sitting all too well with him either.

Suddenly, the door to the Faal house was ripped open and Fay Faal stood in the doorway. The group, only a few houses down from their own, hesitated. Carr and Kassidy glanced at each other, knowing the look on their mother's face. Her lips were pressed together into a small line under her nose. Her skin had been a ghostly white, but as she saw her children, her pale skin quickly began to heat and turn red.

"Get in the house this instant," she said. After a moment's hesitation from the group, she added in a slightly higher octave, "All of you!"

The seven teenagers quickly walked up to the Faal house and stepped sheepishly past Fay Faal. "Sit down," she said and they silently obeyed. It was only when her small five person table was crowded with more teenagers than usual did she realize something was up. She then saw Trey DeLuca sitting closely next to her daughter and a new girl sitting between two of the girls who had saved her daughter's life.

"Jedrek!" she yelled, and moments later, the door to the bedroom opened up and Jedrek Faal loomed in the doorway. He looked over the group sitting at the table and immediately spotted the odd one out. His face hardened and he asked, "What is a DeLuca doing sitting at *my* table?"

"At my request, Father."

Jedrek looked at his daughter, who stood, staring right back at him. She then looked at Trey and continued, "I love Trey, and he loves me. We want to be together. Trey has left his family to be with me and I am willing to do the same."

"You are, are you? Jedrek asked, his anger only increasing. When Kassidy nodded, her father said, "Well I won't allow that. No one has ever left *this* family."

Jedrek watched as his daughter did not cry nor did she beg. Instead, he watched as a look he himself had mastered a long time ago spread across her lovely features. The look of defiance that his daughter gave him only increased his anger tenfold. He studied her, and realized how much she looked like her mother. Both beautiful women with long beautiful red hair. Then he realized that his daughter was no longer the little girl he saw. She was an adult, allowed to do whatever she wants. He would be a hypocrite if he taught her to stand up for herself and then shot her down when she did.

It seemed that Jedrek's anger could not subside because his blood pressure was still spiking. However, this time he was angry at himself. He was mad that his and his father's beliefs of the DeLucas were getting in the way of his family's life. All the hot steam that seemed to be accumulating inside Jedrek suddenly evaporated and all that was left was a man who realized he had wasted his life hating someone unnecessarily.

He sighed and glanced at his wife, who was just as angry as he was, but for different reasons. He looked back at his daughter and Trey DeLuca and said, "I guess this just means we'll have to add on to the family instead."

Everyone looked at him in shock, Trey most of all. His own father could not accept him, and yet this man who hated him his entire life was able to accept him as family in less than a minute. He stood up and walked around the table to face Jedrek. Jedrek took a step back, not prepared for the sudden movement the DeLuca made.

Trey held out his hand and said, "Thank you, Sir. It is an honor to meet the man who has gotten under Rico DeLuca's skin all these years."

Jedrek smiled, "And it is an honor to meet the man who has stolen my daughter's heart."

Trey looked away in embarrassment, "About that, sir. I would like to marry your daughter, and your blessing would be an honor to have."

Kassidy gave a gasp and sat forward in her chair. This was the moment she had been waiting for. Trey had mentioned something about her father and a question he had for him. That had been days ago, and now he was finally asking... asking for her. She couldn't hold back her smile as her father looked between her and Trey DeLuca. Jedrek Faal then nodded and shook Trey's hand, "I know you will take care of her."

Kassidy stood up as Trey turned to face her. She held her breath as he walked closer to her, and a tear slid down her cheek as he knelt down on one knee. He took her hand in his and said, "Kassidy, my life was a mess before I met you. I thought that the only thing I needed to feel was hate. Hate for your brother, your parents, for you. Then I actually met you, and I fell in love. You were able to show me that there was so much more to life than that stupid feud. I was wasting my life away, but you saved me. Now I'm asking you to save me again because I know that my life would go back to that meaningless black hole if I can't have you in my life. Kassidy Faal, will you marry me?"

Kassidy did not hesitate in her answer. She knelt down before Trey and wrapped her arms around him in a hug. She pressed her lips to his and Trey knew he would never be as happy as this. Kassidy pulled away and together she and Trey stood. She said, "I have waited for you to ask me that since the day we met. Nothing would make me happier that to be Mrs. Trey DeLuca."

Jedrek was not the only one to cringe at the idea of Kassidy becoming 'Mrs. DeLuca.' Trey frowned at the sound of his own name, and asked, "Actually I was wondering if we could keep the name Faal. I never want to hear the name DeLuca again and I most certainly don't want my wife to be a DeLuca as well."

Kassidy laughed, "That's fine by me. Father?"

Kassidy and Trey looked over to Jedrek, who shrugged, "Another Faal? Why would I say no?"

Kassidy then turned to Trey and kissed him again, too excited to care that her whole family was watching. "Alright, we get the picture," Fay said, ushering Trey and Kassidy back to their seats. "I have a few questions for the lot of you. Like, who is this?"

She was pointing to Peri, who was sharing a seat with Damia. Kendra answered Fay's question, "This is our cousin Peri."

"Peri," Fay said, surprised. "I thought you were rescuing your cousin, Thalia..."

Fay then registered what name Kendra had said, and her voice trailed off. Her eyes got wide, and she exchanged glances with her husband. Then in a whisper she asked, "Does this mean...you four..are the... sitting at *my* table...? Oh, the heavens! I have been so rude! Would you like something to drink? Eat? I could cook up something real fast. Chicken? I just bought one today, not even feathered yet! I was going to plump it up for Kassidy's birthday, but we can have it now, if you would like!"

Kendra smiled, "It's okay, thank you. We're all set."

Jedrek wasn't as flustered as his wife, and was able to think more level-headed. He asked, with a frown, "How is it possible? You died twenty years ago."

"Eighteen," Aideen said. "And we were born again. Powers and everything."

Jedrek smiled, "Welcome back, Keepers."

"Thank you," Kendra said, shaking his waiting hand.

"So, what happened," Jedrek asked. "Obviously something went on at the DeLuca house, now that both Trey and Tha-Keeper Peri are with us tonight."

"We decided to stop playing their games. We went over and took Peri back," Aideen said. "It was my idea. And it worked."

Fay nodded, but it was obvious she was furious with them. Going over to the DeLucas' house in the middle of the night for a rescue mission. It was near suicidal. Unfortunately, they were the Keepers and she knew it wasn't her place to tell them what to do and what not to do. Aideen found this power rather gratifying. Before coming to Hecate, she was just another teenager and every adult felt like it was his or her place to tell her what to do. Now, no one dared object to their opinions for they were the founding mothers with all the wisdom.

Fay then asked, with slightly less authority, "Did the DeLucas see you?"

"Yes," Trey responded. "And they won't be bothering you anymore."

"Us," Jedrek corrected. "You're a Faal now, remember?"

Trey smiled, "They won't be bothering *us* anymore. Rico has too much pride to show his face anywhere around here. He'll just ignore that we exist."

"Well, that's an improvement," Jedrek said.

"What about Ciro," Damia asked. "Is he too prideful to come around looking for revenge? I know he has enough hate."

Trey frowned, "Honestly, I have no idea. He might listen to Fath-his father. Or he might steal his gun."

Chapter Fifty-Two

"Get out. Get out of my sight before I disown you too."

That's what Rico DeLuca said to his son moments after Trey humiliated him. Ciro obeyed, if only because he wanted to get out of that room as fast as he could. He knew his father's anger, and at that moment, he didn't think he could sit back and let him vent. Ciro might end up dead or an orphan if that happened. Since he wanted neither, he left without a moment's hesitation.

By the time Ciro stepped out the front door, Trey and the others were long gone. Ciro knew exactly where they went, and could probably catch up to them before they even reached the right street. But he knew that was a suicide mission, and he wasn't the type of guy to quit. Not even after his brother left him for a Faal.

Instead, he turned the other way and made his way out past the city boundaries. He didn't really know where he was headed; only that he wasn't going to turn around. The look on Rico's face made him realize he was no longer wanted. He was unwelcome in his own house, but he didn't really blame his father. His eldest son had just run away with the Faals, and his other son had let them leave.

Of course, Ciro did not intend to let them leave, but Rico DeLuca would never see it that way. He would only see the weakness Ciro possessed, and would never be able to look at him the same way again. That was okay, Ciro didn't want to look at his father again anyway. He was a pathetic old man whose only care was for his pride.

So Ciro continued to run, until the last houses of the city were far behind him, the starry skies giving minimum light to see by. He ran blindly, and with each step his anger with the Keepers, with the Faals, and with Trey increased. He thought over the events of the evening, wondering if he could have done something to change the outcome.

Would Trey have left if they had kidnapped Keeper Damia that day? Would any of this have happened if he had killed a Keeper like he was supposed to? He went back to that moment, where he was choosing between Peri and Keeper Damia. Why could he not kill Peri? She was just a girl, just a stranger who was in the wrong place at the wrong time. Why didn't he just shoot her?

There was something...something about her that made him hesitate. He couldn't put his finger on it, but there had been something. As he tried to remember, all he could think of was her eyes: large brown disks, with fear and hope blending together in them. He watched as she reached out and grasped Keeper Damia's hand. She was so scared of him, and that was when he realized he wasn't going to kill her. He didn't want to kill Peri. He didn't want to make her afraid of him. So he turned the gun on the other Keeper, and that's when everything went downhill.

Ciro shook his head, and stopped running. Even though the adrenaline was still pumping hard through his veins, and he knew he could keep running all night, his legs shut down. He stood in disbelief, thinking back at what Trey had done. He had gone against everything they had been taught. He went against his own brother. He picked a girl over his brother.

Ciro's hands immediately clenched into fists, and he wished Trey was there so he could knock him back into his place. He wished Kassidy was there too. He knew he could pull the trigger on her over and over again. She was the reason why Trey was so messed up. If it hadn't been for her, Ciro would still have a brother, a family, and not to mention ten thousand Denas. He didn't want to shoot her, he wanted to strangle her.

His hands twisted together, an unconscious act on his thoughts. He looked around, and realized he was standing on the hill on the north side of the large city. He could see a flood of lights coming from countless houses and buildings, smoke rising from chimneys as early risers got up, and night owls headed to bed. He was surprised to see how awake the city seemed from far away, when he knew the streets were deserted.

He had never seen the city from such a distance. In fact, he had never left the city boundaries before that night. He had never had a need to. His entire life was in that city, his family, his friends, his enemies. Now he had no family, no friends, only enemies.

"I can be your friend."

Ciro spun around, searching the black for the voice. He knew he was not imagining it, he could never imagine a voice so smooth, so perfect. It had come from behind him, yet there was nothing there but darkness.

"Who's there?" he yelled, panicking. He was in no condition to fight off thieves, still nursing the wounds from Carr's attack less than two hours earlier.

There was no response, and that's when Ciro realized what the mystery voice had said. He had not said a word aloud, yet it responded as if he had. He knew that it wasn't a thief he was in the company of, because any thief with the ability to read minds would not be hanging around to steal from him. He wasn't sure if that should make him feel better or worse. What kind of person could read minds?

The Keepers was his first answer, but this voice had been male. Besides, the Keepers would not offer to be his friend. They would offer to kill him instead. They would not even offer, they would just kill them with all of their freaky supernatural powers. He wouldn't even know he was dead until afterwards.

A laugh came out of the darkness, and Ciro looked around for the source. Still, there was no one on the hill but him. He was alone and apparently going crazy.

"You are not going crazy," the voice said. Ciro was beginning to freak out, still seeing not even an animal on the hillside with him.

"But you do have a very interesting mind," the voice added with a small chuckle.

"Show yourself," Ciro yelled. "Let me see your face."

Ciro then heard a disapproving cluck, and he imagined a large invisible man shaking his head at him. The voice said, "You shouldn't take such a nasty tone with those you cannot see. You never know where they could be. They could be standing with their hands around your throat, and you wouldn't even know it."

Ciro's hands flew to his throat, but the only hands he could feel there were his own. Again, the voice laughed, "You don't have to worry about me killing you. I have a job for you to do."

"Why should I help you?" Ciro asked, despite the voice's warning about that certain tone of voice. "I have no idea who you are."

"Oh," the voice said. "I think you do. And I think you will help me."

Ciro then saw a shadow forming in front of him. He paused in his search for the body that went with the voice, and watched in fear and awe. In a matter of seconds, the dark shadow became a black fog that slowly formed into a tall cylinder. As the fog condensed, forming a more solid substance, Ciro realized that this was the man who was talking to him.

Ciro only knew one man who would have the ability to do such a magikal feat. As the dark clouds disappeared, and were replaced by human flesh, Ciro knew it was really him. He recognized the pale skin, the blonde hair, and the gruesomely contrasting black eyes.

"We both want to see the Keepers pay for the things they have done," he said to Ciro, in the same silk voice that Ciro had heard before. "We both want to them to suffer. I have a plan that will destroy them, but I need your help. You are crucial to this plan working. Will you join me?"

He raised a pale hand that was almost glowing in the dark, and held it out to Ciro. He looked down at it, and upon seeing the slight glow it held, was immediately captivated by the idea of destroying the Keepers. He reached out and grasped the hand, watching its long twig like fingers wrapping around his small fleshy ones. As the hand clasped his own, the voice whispered something in that silky smooth tone.

Ciro closed his eyes, his senses suddenly overpowering him. He could feel every vein in the thin hand; he could hear every note of the voice's words vibrating in his throat. He could feel his own heart beating faster and faster in his chest, the air rushing in and out of his lungs.

Ciro opened his eyes, and found him staring back with a small smile on his face. The hand removed itself from Ciro's and he felt the brush of leather against his skin. He looked down and saw a small leather band around his wrist. He touched it, and saw there were two knots in the cord, but no way to remove it without a knife. He looked back up at him, and had a feeling not even a knife could remove the band.

"You are among friends now," the voice said.

His eyes, despite being completely engulfed by the night, were sparkling.

Chapter Fifty-Three

It had been a week since the kidnapping, and now for the first time since then, all four cousins were together again. Two weeks ago, they wouldn't want to be anywhere near each other, now they didn't want to let go. They walked together to The Dancing Bear, reeling in delight that the day had been a success; they were finally back together.

"So what was it like," Aideen asked. "Being held hostage like that?"

"Boring," Peri said. "I stayed in one room the entire time, except for the time I tried to escape, of course."

"You tried to escape?" Damia asked, "What happened? Did Ciro catch you?"

Peri shook her head, "Trey did. That's probably why I survived. Ciro was talking with his dad, if they had caught me... well they wouldn't have sent me back to my room like Trey did."

"Speaking of Trey," Peri said, turning to Damia. "How the hell did you know he had turned to the light side?"

Damia smiled, "I saw him in here with Kassidy Faal. At first I thought he was in here with you, so that's why I went over to them. When I realized it was Kassidy, I made her tell me what was going on. She explained everything to me."

"It would have been nice if you told the rest of us," Kendra said.

Damia shrugged, "It was her secret, I was just keeping it."

They reached the door of The Dancing Bear, and Aideen pushed it open. She paused, blocking the other girls from the entrance, and then suddenly screeched and ran inside the pub. The others could hear her saying, "What are you doing here? And why the hell didn't you say good-bye before you left, Kynton?"

Damia suddenly stopped walking, her heart dropping into her shoes. Kynton was in The Dancing Bear. She had thought he would be as far away from them as possible, not waiting for them in the place where he broke her heart.

Peri and Kendra pushed past her, both ready to see the man who almost cost them Peri's life. Damia lagged behind, not sure what to expect when she saw him. Would he beg for forgiveness, or yell at her for making him leave. She listened as Kendra demanded to know what his excuse was for leaving, and why he had to leave two days before Peri was returned to them. She might be sorry she was mean to him, but that didn't mean she was going to be nice to him.

Then there was silence and Damia began to panic. They were waiting for her to come in, to be reunited with the love of her life. She tried to put on a steady face, a strong act, but it didn't help her when she tried to push open the door and her arms wouldn't budge. Instead, her feet decided they wanted to do the talking. She turned around and headed away from The Dancing Bear, away from her cousins and away from Kynton.

She watched as the ground around her suddenly was lit up by the lamps from inside The Dancing Bear, as the door swung open and stayed open. She paused, as if she was a burglar getting caught robbing a bank, but the only crime she was guilty of was not wanting her heart to be torn apart again.

"Damia."

Damia turned around slowly, and saw a figure was standing in the doorway of The Dancing Bear. The shadows were too dark to make out his face, but Damia recognized him immediately as Kynton. She wanted to run into his arms, to forgive him and to make things well between them again. She wanted to scream at him and never see him again.

"Hello, Damia," he said, taking a step forward, letting the door swing closed behind him.

Damia took a step forward, but remained silent. She could feel a sudden rush of love come into her chest, into her heart. She knew it was Kynton's feelings, and she had to control them. She couldn't let them control her.

"Hello, Kynton," she said as coldly as she could.

Kynton winced, even though he was expecting some attitude, it still hurt to see the woman he loved act so mean.

She had to do what Kain said, remove herself from the situation...

She took another step forward, again letting her feet control her brain. This time, however, Kynton's feelings were controlling her feet, not her own.

She had to do what Kain said...

Kynton took another step forward, and was now less than a foot away from Damia. He quickly wrapped his arms around her, holding her tight to his chest. He never wanted her to get away from him again. He wouldn't let her. Damia could feel everything Kynton was, and it scared her. It also fascinated her.

She had to...

What did she have to do?

Damia looked up at Kynton and he smiled down at her. He touched her cheek, as if he didn't believe she was in his arms. She leaned into his touch, "I'm so sorry I pushed you away, Kynton. I was so confused. I thought you didn't love me."

"Of course I love you," Kynton said. "I love you so much. I couldn't live without you. I'm sorry I left."

Damia's eyes flew open and she studied Kynton's face. She couldn't let this happen. This man was not in love with her, she had to convince herself of that. He thought he was, but it was still the other Damia he loved. There was no way he could have changed that so quickly.

She pulled away from Kynton, knowing that his touch was not helping her think clearly. She faked a yawn and said, "I'm sorry, Kynton. I'm so tired all of a sudden. All this drama today has really wiped me out. Will I see you in the morning?"

Kynton smiled, "Yes, I have a surprise for you and your cousins."

Damia put on her best fake smile, "I can't wait."

The next morning came too quickly for Damia. For the first time in a long time, she and her cousins were able to sleep peacefully and without interruption. They slept so deeply, and so soundly that it made the hours feel like minutes, and when the sun woke them up, Damia could feel the back of her throat dry up. She wondered how the day was going to play out. Would Kynton still be with them by nightfall? Would he still be trying to make her forgive him?

Damia didn't speak much as Kynton led the four girls out of The Dancing Bear and into the city streets. She let Aideen and Peri do all the talking, asking Kynton questions about his sick mother, and whether or not he would continue on with them. Kendra was also silent, wondering how she would apologize to Kynton.

The girls were surprised to see that Kynton had led them to a part of the city they had never been to before. It wasn't as nice as the other parts they had visited, but it wasn't run down, it was just dirty. There was a lot of hay on the streets, and men pushing around carts full of manure. It wasn't long before the girls realized what their surprise was.

Kynton led them into one of the barns that lined the streets, and over to the corner where four beautiful horses were in adjoining stalls. He smiled and said, "Surprise! I thought it would be a good idea to get you some horses for your journey. You can't expect to travel across Beindor on foot."

"Holy crap, Kynton," Aideen said. "You bought us horses? That's so cool!"

Kynton laughed, "That means you like them?"

"They're wonderful!" Kendra exclaimed.

Kynton walked over to the nearest horse, "I had them each picked out for you. They are special Elvin trained horses. Very good for traveling, especially with new riders."

"Which one is mine?" Aideen asked excitedly.

"This one," Kynton said, petting the stallion's mane. "His name is Gwethar."

Gwethar was a regal looking stallion, blue black in color with the exception of a white star on his forehead and a sock on his left front foot. Aideen stepped forward and touched his nose. He gave a snort, and watched her with a steady gaze.

"Kendra, this mare is yours. Her name is Alqua."

Kendra put her hand on Alqua's light brown, almost blonde mane. Alqua was a pinto horse, chestnut overo in color. She looked back at Kendra and nudged her arm. Kendra smiled and placed her hand on Alqua's forehead.

"Peri, this is Tuilinn," Kynton said, turning to the next horse.

Tuilinn was a white mare with white mane and tail. Peri walked up to the mare and copied Aideen, not really sure what to do around horses. Tuilinn looked down at her in silence.

"Lastly, Damia, this mare is Mae'Lin. She is the mother of the other three."

Mae'Lin was noticeably older than the other three horses, but Damia noticed that she was just as strong as any of her children, if not stronger in order to protect them. Mae'Lin was dark brown in color with a patch of white on her chest. Damia approached her and held her nose in her hands, stroking it gently. Mae'Lin pawed the ground in greeting.

"They are beautiful," Damia said quietly. "Thank you."

"Would you like to ride them?" Kynton asked with a smile. The girls thought that was a wonderful idea, and soon Kynton had helped three of the four onto their horses and into the nearest riding pen. Only Damia was left in the barn.

As soon as Kynton returned to help her, she took a breath and said, "We can't do this. I can't do this."

"What do you mean?" Kynton asked. "I thought you liked Mae'Lin."

"I do," Damia said, stroking the mare's flank. "But I'm not talking about her. I'm talking about us. I still feel exactly as I did the night you left. Buying me a horse will not change that."

"To be fair, I bought the horses long before that night," Kynton said, approaching Damia. "And I would never think buying you gifts could make you forgive me."

"It's just too soon," Damia said. "I don't want you around."

"Please," Kynton said, taking Damia's hand in his. "I promise I will not slip up again. There is nothing I won't do for you, you know that. I just ask to be with you."

Damia pulled her hand away from him, "Kynton, we've known each other for two weeks. You talk as if we've been together for years."

"I feel like we have," Kynton said. "Don't you understand that?"

Damia frowned, "And that is why this cannot work. You don't love me. You never have. Maybe one day you will, but you must get over Damia Neimann for that to happen. And for you to get over her, you cannot be around me."

"Damia," Kynton started.

"Kynton," Damia interrupted. "I am done playing this game. I don't want you to come back around here anymore. I want you to leave us alone."

"I can't do that," Kynton said. "I can't be without you."

Kynton moved closer to Damia, and quickly wrapped his arms around her. He pulled her close to him, ignoring her words of protest. He hoped that if he could convince her that she loved him, then she would let him stay. He pressed his lips firmly against hers, waiting for her to melt in his arms like she had the night before.

But she didn't melt, in fact she did the opposite. She tore out of his grasp so fast, that he didn't even realize she was gone until there was a sudden sting on the side of his face. He touched the spot where she had slapped him, stunned that she would do such a thing to him. He looked down to see hate in those beautiful eyes. Her lips curled as she said, "Get away from me. I never want to see you again, Kynton. Thank you for all that you have done for us over these past two weeks, but I'm afraid you just overstayed your welcome."

Kynton took a step backwards, and almost collapsed. It didn't work. She wasn't swooning at his touch, she wasn't forgiving him or changing her mind. He had just ruined all hope of her ever falling in love with him again. It was over.

Kynton ran out of the barn so fast that he was gone before the first tear could even fall from Damia's eye.

Chapter Fifty-Four

Rico DeLuca was in pain.

He tried to stay conscious but he could feel the pull of darkness, and it was welcomed.

Anything was better than this excruciating pain, this lightening hot heat he could feel creeping up his limbs, leaving only a dull numbing sensation in its wake. He knew he was dying, he had known since the moment he saw Tárquin in the doorframe of his house.

Now, as the numbness crept into his stomach and fingertips, Rico began to see images and scenes from his life flash in front of him. He saw himself as a baby in his mother's arms, walking into a large farmhouse. He saw his childhood in Canhareth. He saw his wedding and he saw the moment Trey was given to him. He saw Ciro's birth, he saw his kids growing up. He saw the Keepers, he saw Trey turn on his family. He saw Ciro leave his home.

Rico closed his eyes to the memories.

They were too painful, much more painful than the throbbing that coursed through his body. He wondered what cruel deity would make him relive the moment that both sons left him just before he died. Whichever one it was, Rico prayed that it was not the one he would meet in the afterlife. Watching his sons leave once was enough, twice was torture. If he relived that a third time, he would die all over again.

Suddenly the memories stopped and all pain, both physical and mental, ceased. Rico took a fresh breath of air and looked around. He saw the ceiling of his own house and relief flooded in. He wasn't staring up at the black depths of hell. A shadow moved over the ceiling and Rico saw a figure was standing over him.

"Help," he managed to croak with a burnt throat.

All he could think of was a cool cup of water. Then he would find Ciro and apologize. Finding Trey would be easier, but Rico was not ready to accept a Faal-lover into the family. He knew he loved his son, but there were some things he could not forgive.

"I'm afraid no one can help you," came the smooth voice of the shadow hovering over Rico. "You took something of mine, DeLuca. There is a price to pay for that. I thank you for keeping such good care of it, but since you lost it, now I must continue my search for it."

Rico panicked. This was not the voice of someone who would save him. Tárquin was still in his house, was still bent on murdering him. Murdering him for what? Loosing something? "What are you talking about? I would never take anything from you!" Rico begged, "I'm sorry I tried to kill the Keepers. I didn't kill them, so please-" his voice cracked. "Please don't kill me!"

Tárquin laughed at the pathetic man. He was lying in a pool of his own blood, making sounds that no human could make sense of. All Tárquin could understand was the plea for mercy in the man's eyes. A plea he had seen in so many others. His step-father. His wife. The Keepers.

His mother.

Now the only thing Tárquin could feel when he saw that look was hatred. Hatred for the Keepers, his mother's murderers. Hatred for his wife, for hiding their son from him. Hatred for his step-father, a drunken mess who deserved what he got. Hatred for every single person in Beindor, on Hecate.

Rico saw Tárquin's black eyes flash red.

There was no stopping what came next.

He held out his hand, and touched it to the man's heart. He watched as the worthless man's eyes rolled up into his head and his body started convulsing. Limbs flailed around like a balloon losing its air. Tárquin didn't remove his hand until the screaming died down and the spit began to pool on the sides of his mouth.

Tárquin slowly stood and looked around at the man's greatest accomplishment. He then watched as the house spontaneously went up in flames. It would be a matter of minutes before everything the man ever earned or loved was a pile of ash in the street. Tárquin marched out of the house in a flurry of wind and fire, feeling the flames quickly spread to the house next-door.

With each new house catching on fire, Tárquin's anger burned stronger and stronger. It seemed that nothing could quench his rage, not even the destruction of a city block. He could feel the wildfire growing stronger and stronger inside him, rising higher in his chest until he wished Rico DeLuca was alive still, just so he could kill him over and over again.

How dare that man take what's mine! Tárquin thought. *They had no right. No right to take my son away from me. They've stepped out of place one too many times, and this time I will make sure they stay dead.*

Another building caught on fire, and Tárquin watched as Canharians ran into the street to see what was happing to their beloved city. Tárquin turned to a group who dared enough to stand on the same street as him. Without even raising his hand, he watched as the unsuspecting bystanders began to scream and writhe in pain. Only Tárquin could save them, but he was gone before they even knew what was happening. It was only a matter of time before they all would collapse in death.

Tárquin didn't plan on stopping with a measly group of bystanders. He wanted the entire city dead. And he knew he could make it happen. Not even the Keepers could stop him, if they dared try. There was only one thing that could make him stop. Finding his son.

Chapter Fifty-Five

"Must you be going so soon?" Kassidy asked. "We would have loved for you to be at the wedding."

Damia smiled at Kassidy, "And we would love to be here, but I'm afraid we have a very long journey ahead of us, and we have had too much delay as it is."

Kassidy nodded, "I understand.

"Don't worry," Damia said. "I promise we will see you again."

Kassidy smiled, "I do hope so, Keeper Damia."

Kassidy suddenly flung her arms around Damia in a tight embrace. "I am forever in your debt. Thank you for all that you have done for my family and me."

"We have done nothing," Damia said. "It was you and Trey who stood up to your families. We were just there to support you."

Kassidy let go of Damia and turned to Trey, who was standing next to her outside of The Dancing Bear. The Keepers were about to leave Canhareth, to start on their mission to find the four pieces of the Amîr Crystal. Their first stop was Imladun, the Caves of the West, and that was where they were finally headed. The Faals had come by the morning of their departure to say goodbye.

Sara Faal gave them each a huge hug, her thanks to them for saving her life. Fay handed them each a medium sized parcel, and with a small smile said, "There isn't a whole lot there, but it should be enough food to last a while."

Jedrek Faal shook each of their hands, trying to hide his glowing smile behind his whiskers. He still couldn't get over the fact that he had had supper and played poker with the Keepers. "It has been an honor, Keepers. Please do not be strangers, you are forever welcome in our home."

Carr also shook their hands, and with an awkward smile said, "Thank you for saving both of my sisters. I am in your debt. If you ever need anything, please know you have friends in Canhareth."

Kassidy again hugged each of the Keepers, and said, "Be safe on your journey. We will keep an eye out for you. If you are ever in Canhareth, please stop by."

"Thank you," Kendra said. "You all have been so kind to us. We will never forget that."

"It was a pleasure, Keepers," Jedrek said as the four girls mounted their beautiful new horses.

"We will miss you," Kassidy yelled after them, waving her hand as they turned down a side street and out of sight.

The Keepers rode all day, not stopping until sunset. They set up camp, the first of many, and slept peacefully under the stars. The glow of the city was faint on the horizon, but visible all night long. As the sun began to rise, the girls began to stir as well. They could see nothing but wide open plains ahead of them, and the tops of the buildings of Canhareth behind them. They could see the smoke rising from the chimneys, and could faintly hear the noises of the city.

They were about to leave their campsite, to ride until sunset once more, when they noticed a figure running towards them on the road from Canhareth. They paused for only a second to watch her, but in that second the wind carried her cries to them. She said, "Keepers! Wait! Come back!"

"Is that-" Kendra started, but Aideen finished, "It's Kassidy!"

They could now see her face and saw that it was in fact Kassidy, but she was not as they had last seen her. Her face and entire body was covered in scratches and bruises, hidden under a layer of soot. Her flaming hair was tangled and bits were burnt off. Her dress was torn and covered in dirt. She looked as if she had gone through hell and back.

They immediately turned their horses toward their new friend and reached her within minutes.

"What's wrong, Kassidy?" Kendra asked.

"What happened to you?" Damia asked.

Kassidy was bent over, out of breath. They saw that her injuries were worse than they had first thought. There was a steady flow of blood running down her face from a cut that was above her hairline, and there was also a gash on her shoulder. She grasped it in her dirty fingers as she gasped for breath.

Then, with a new, hoarse voice she said, "He's here...he's attacking..."

"Who's attacking?" Peri asked.

"Tárquin," Kassidy looking up at them. "Tárquin is destroying Canhareth."

The four Keepers looked over to the city and realized what they had mistaken for early risers where people screaming in pain and terror, and the smoke coming from people's kitchen stoves was in reality smoke coming from burning buildings.

The Keepers looked at each other, all knowing what this meant. Tárquin was back, and he was destroying the city where they had just spent the last two weeks. When he was around the last time, he was bent on killing the Keepers; and if he was back, he would want to kill them as well.

"Trey's father...he's dead." Kassidy was saying, tears running down her face, "Trey...he's gone missing...I can't find him...please...I...we need your help."

And now a preview of the sequel to STRANGE WOODS:

Infinite Realms

The Keepers, Book Two

Alexandria Noel

As this is a draft, there may be some errors. The final edition may be altered, extended, or completely rewritten.

Chapter One

At one point in time, Canhareth had been the wealthiest city in all of Beindor. It had a larger population than all the other cities in the country put together; it had old historical buildings, the established families, and a reputation of being the safest city in Beindor. Up to yesterday, that all had been true. Then one seemingly harmless night, the city was turned upside down. It wasn't a tornado or an earthquake that caused the damage, all the destroyed home, all the businesses demolished, all the lives lost. It had been a single man, a man with powers unrivaled.

Those who saw him thought he was a demon, his black cloak rippling around his body in the wind. The hood of his cloak was up; casting a shadow on his face, but the people of Canhareth recognized him immediately. They said his arms were raised, as if he was praising the gods, but it was fire that he held in his pale hands. Instead of words of worship, from his mouth came words of destruction and ruin.

All who heard these words were sent into fits of pain that no one could understand. Their screams filled the air and reached all who thought it was still safe in the city. Pandemonium spread throughout the city like wildfire, faster than Tárquin ever could will it to go. There was no stopping it, and soon the entire city was consumed by the flames.

People started packing their things, not wanting to meet Tárquin in the street. They ran out of their homes and left them to burn. Those who stayed to fight were brave, but foolish souls. They had their spears and swords, but nothing could compare to the magik that Tárquin held.

They were killed with just a thought.

"Are you happy now?" He yelled into the night, his fists clenched tightly at his sides. A group of buildings close to where he stopped exploded in a blaze of fire and smoke, shattered glass and wood. He didn't seem to notice, "You took him away from me and hid him, but I know where he is! I have found him, and you're not going to stop me from taking him back! You're plan has failed, Keepers!"

Then he was gone. With a whirl of smoke and winds more powerful than a tornado, he was gone. The streets were still glowing with the aftermath of the explosion that was Tárquin. Even though it was nearing midnight, the city was as bright as if the sun was shining down on it. There were people everywhere, screaming and dying in the streets, or running away from their ruined homes. Others were quietly picking up the mess that had recently been their lives.

One thought was on all their minds, though. *Where were the Keepers?* Wasn't it their job to protect the city from people like Tárquin, especially Tárquin. If he had survived their final battle, couldn't the Keepers have as well? Did that mean the Keepers were on their way right now? Did they have a plan to destroy Tárquin and to rebuild their beloved city?

It gave some people hope to think of the Keepers' return, but others knew it was impossible. They were dead. They had been dead for eighteen years. There was no way they could rise from the grave, even though empty caskets were buried at their funeral. If they were alive, why hadn't they come home sooner than this? If they were alive, why would they let their city get destroyed?

No one could believe the truth.

~*~

"He's here...he's attacking..."

"Who's attacking?" Peri asked.

"Tárquin," Kassidy looking up at them. "Tárquin is destroying Canhareth."

The four girls were sitting astride the horses they had gotten as gifts from their first friend in Canhareth. The horses were the most beautiful creatures they had ever seen, raised and trained by the Elvin of Taurëfor, the forests north of Canhareth. They were fidgeting under their new riders, aware of the danger in the city they had left the previous day. They also seemed to know that their riders were about to point them in the direction of the danger, instead of away from it like every other person in Canhareth.

But these four girls weren't like every other person in Canhareth. They were the reason why Canhareth was built, and they were the reason why it had been destroyed. They were the Keepers; at least, they were in their past life. The Keepers really did die eighteen years ago, but before they died, they made sure that they would live again. Less than twenty-four hours after they passed away, they were born again. Now, eighteen years later, they were back in Beindor.

"Trey's father...he's dead." Kassidy was saying, tears running down her face, "Trey...he's gone missing...I can't find him...please...I...we need your help."

The four cousins looked at each other, knowing what they had to do. There was no way they could refuse their new friend's plea. Kendra, even though she was the youngest of the four cousins, had quickly emerged as the leader in the past few weeks. She looked down at the beaten and bleeding Kassidy, "Of course we'll help you."

Kassidy, too weak to smile, sighed in relief. Her eyes started to roll up into her head, and Kendra quickly jumped off her mare, Alqua, to catch her. She pressed her palm to the cut on Kassidy's head, and watched as the blood disappeared. The wound on her shoulder also shrank and disappeared as Kendra's Healing Water washed it away.

Kassidy opened her eyes in surprise, not expecting to be Healed so quickly and so suddenly. She smiled at Kendra, and whispered, "Thank you."

Kendra smiled back and turned to Damia, "Can she ride with you? You'll be the first to know if anything goes wrong."

Damia agreed, knowing that her Empathy power would tell her immediately if Kassidy's health worsened. She helped Kendra lift Kassidy onto the back of her mare Mae'Lina, and then Kendra mounted Alqua again before they rode back to Canhareth. They galloped as fast as they could toward the city. With each mile they grew closer, the worse the damage looked.

When they were on the border of the city, they slowed down to a trot. The buildings closest to them were almost unrecognizable, except for piles of rubble on the path into the city. The few people who were around these buildings looked up at the four large horses in amazement. Their gazes then drifted to the riders, who must be of some importance, maybe Elvin come to the rescue of the city to the south.

The rumors started immediately. Those who were alive eighteen years ago had some suspicion as to who these strange women were, but they were only guesses. It was those who had been born on Earth and traveled to Beindor with them who recognized the teenagers before them. They were the ones who spread the word throughout the city, the ones who fell to their knees as the group of girls walked their horses through the city.

By the time the five girls reached Kassidy Faal's home, there was a large assembly of curious onlookers behind them. Ignoring the crowd in the street, Kassidy brought the four girls into her home, where her family was waiting for them. As soon as the door was closed behind them, Fay Faal flung herself at Peri, wrapping her arms tight around her and sobbing into her neck.

"It was terrible," she was saying. "I thought we were all going to die! We woke up, and the roof was on fire!"

She broke away to point at the ceiling, where the girls could see a large hole smoldering over the front room of the Faal's house. "Luckily, Jedrek, Carr and Trey were able to put it out before it spread to the bedroom or to the rest of the house. The neighbors weren't so lucky."

"Their whole house was on fire," Jedrek said, stepping up. His face was covered in ash, and the clothes he wore had holes burned through them. "So of course we went over there to help them. Both Joshua and his son Aaron were able to get out, but Joshua's wife Evangeline and their daughter Grace were still inside. Trey was the first inside."

Kassidy interrupted her father with a small sob. She covered her mouth and buried her head in her mother's shoulder, who had moved away from the cousins to comfort her daughter. Jedrek continued, "Evangeline came running out moments later with little Grace in her arms. She said that Trey was right behind her, but he didn't come out. I was about to go in and get him when the roof collapsed."

Kassidy's sobs grew louder, and Fay tried to calm her daughter, but Kassidy couldn't listen. She turned to the girls, tears rolling down her face, "We put out the fire and searched the debris for Trey, but he wasn't there. Nothing. No body, alive or dead."

"We don't know what happened to him," Jedrek said, but the look on his face told the Keepers that he didn't think Trey had made it out alive. Kassidy had a more positive outlook. Despite the tears, she looked rather confident as she spoke, "I know he's alive. He escaped, and now he's somewhere in Canhareth. You have to help us look for him."

"Don't worry, Kassidy," Aideen said. "We'll help you look."

Kendra glared at Aideen for a second, she obviously was not willing to help the Faals look for someone who was more than likely a pile of ash. Aideen quickly shrugged and turned back to the Faals, "Do you have any idea where he would have gone?"

"Maybe to his house, to see if his father really is dead," Kassidy said. "The word is that Tárquin killed him himself, before he destroyed the city."

"Okay," Kendra said. "Have you gone over there yet?"

Kassidy shook her head, "I could barely get out of the city, let alone farther in. It was chaos everywhere."

"Well then I guess that's where we're going to start," Aideen said. She and her three cousins started for the door, Kassidy and Carr following close behind. Fay hugged her youngest daughter, Sara close to her and Jedrek put his hand on his wife's shoulder. He smiled sadly at the Keepers, "I think it's best if we stay here. Good luck."

"Thank you," Aideen said before the group left.

They were immediately swarmed by the huge mob of people that had crowded around the Faal house. People were coming at them from all sides, shouting questions and demanding answers from these Keeper-look-a-likes. The six teenagers were being crushed by the mass of people. Then, rather suddenly, the door behind them swung open and they rushed back inside the house. Jedrek looked at them in alarm, "I guess Canhareth has heard of your return."

Kendra groaned, "How are we supposed to do anything now? We can't even get outside the door, let alone go all around Beindor peacefully!"

Peri frowned, "You don't happen to have a back door, do you?"

Fay shook her head, "But we do have a window in the bedroom,"

Aideen shrugged, "That's good enough for me." They followed Fay into the second of the two-room house, and quietly climbed out the small window and into the alley behind the house. Placing their hoods over their heads, the six teenagers snuck down the alleyway and onto a not-so-crowded street. Kassidy led the way to the DeLuca home, a silent parade down the devastated streets of Canhareth.

When they reached the DeLuca house, all were shocked to see what lay before them. There was no longer the large four-bedroom building in front of them. Instead, there was a huge pile of smoldering wood, brick, and ash. There was no distinction between caved-in walls and collapsed ceilings.

Kassidy's resolve quickly dissolved. The wells of her eyes filled with tears almost instantly, and she had to grip her brother's shoulder for fear of her knees buckling beneath her. Carr watched her; worried she would pass out, or worse, try to find Trey in the rubble. He placed a hand over hers and she turned her watery gaze on him. He saw her lip tremble before she buried her head in his shoulder, shaking with despair.

Carr turned to the Keepers, "I think we'd better head back."

Kendra nodded and headed the procession back toward the Faal house. They almost made it there when suddenly they were on a street they had never seen before. They paused at the end, caught off guard by the large number of people gathering in the square that the street opened up into.

It was a large square, where a few thousand people could pack in. It was surrounded by buildings on all sides but south, where only the one street ran into the square. A large platform was built into the buildings on the north side of the square, and it was to this platform that all the people of the square were faced. On top of the platform were four large portraits, leaning against the building behind it. Surrounding the portraits, and covering every other inch of the platform, were flowers, candles and other gifts. A plaque hung on the wall behind the portraits read:

In Memoriam,
The Keepers of Beindor: Earth Keeper Damia,

Air Keeper Peri, Fire Keeper Aideen, and Water Keeper Kendra. You governed us as just Queens, you pro-
tected us as brave Soldiers, you watched over us as
loving Mothers. You were taken away from us before
your time, and will be dearly missed.
  –Written by Rohak Moorel

"Whoa," Peri said, taking a step forward. "Is that *us*?"

"In a few years, but yeah... I think so," Aideen said, coming to
stand beside Peri.

"What are we doing up there?" Peri asked, but then she
gasped, "Is this where we're buried?"

"No," Carr said. "The bodies were never found. This memorial
was built a year after they –you died."

"Okay, not that I'm not honored to have a memorial built after me," Kendra said, "but we really need to get away from all these
people. We don't want to start another riot."

Peri, Aideen and Carr quickly turned around and followed
Kendra's lead out of the square. Damia started to go with them, but
paused and looked again at the backs of the multitude of bodies. A
strange feeling was passing through her, something she had never
felt before. It was a calm feeling, but with such a strong vibe of panic,
that Damia's heart went out to these people. They were looking for
guidance, and they had turned to the only people they knew could
ever give it to them, their Keepers.

"Damia," Kendra whispered. "Let's go!"

Damia shook her head, "They need us, Kendra. They've asked
us to come help them, and look: here we are. We have to do something. We have to give them some confidence in themselves, in their
city."

Kendra's stomach dropped to her toes. This couldn't be happening *again.* "We can't, Damia. Remember last time you did this?

You got Peri kidnapped and we wasted an extra week in Canhareth."

"But you also saved my sister," Kassidy said, tear stains running down her cheeks. "Maybe this time you can save the city. And Trey."

Kendra gave a little groan, "What do you expect us to do?"

Aideen answered, "Let everyone know we're back."

Kendra's eyes grew wide and she shook her head. "No way. You saw what happened when they were just curious if we were the Keepers. If they found out it really was us, we'd never leave!"

"What's more important, Kendra?" Damia asked. "Our personal mission or rebuilding the city for people who suffered because of us?"

Kendra knew she had lost. Aideen had already stuck up for Damia and her crazy ideals, and Peri was giving her a look that made her realize she was the only one on the losing side. She pursed her lips and gave a curt nod, "Okay. We'll completely ruin our plans and tell the city we're back. How do you suppose we do this?"

Aideen then turned and pointed to the memorial behind them, "Up there."

She then started walking through the crowd of people. At first, it was almost impossible, with her shouting to get people's attention and shoving to get her way around. Then, about half way through the throngs of people, they started to part for her and the others. They turned to face them, watching with large eyes as they moved closer and closer to the pictures of themselves on the dais. Whispers spread like tremors through the crowds, and then as soon as the noise started, it stopped.

The four girls walked up the stairs and picked their way over the flowers left by mourners. They came to the center of the platform and stared at the many faces looking expectantly up at them. Peri leaned over to Kendra and whispered, "Good luck."

Kendra laughed, "Oh, I'm not saying anything. You're the

ones who wanted to do this, you're going to be the ones telling them."

Peri looked over at Damia and Aideen, suddenly her throat closed up and she couldn't breathe. Damia's face was bright red, and it looked like she had stopped breathing as well. Aideen locked eyes with Peri, and upon seeing the panic there, sighed and said, "Okay, fine. *I'll* do it."

Peri smiled at her and Damia glanced at her, her face only going even redder. She looked even more worried, as if she knew Aideen was going to trip over every word and make a fool out of herself and her cousins. Kendra frowned at her, but didn't stop her. It was too late to do anything; they were already on stage.

"People of Canhareth," Aideen started. "You've been through much these past few days. You're looking for something to believe in, someone to guide you. You've turned to the Keepers, the four women who guided you through many tough times while they were alive. But they died almost twenty years ago, how could they possibly help you now? Well, my cousins and I are here to tell you that though the Keepers died, their souls live on. They live on in us, the Keepers Reincarnate. We look just like your Keepers, we have their powers and their morals. We are the Keepers. We are here to help you through these tough times, we're here to do what we can for you. We just hope that in the years to come that you will learn to trust us as you have our predecessors, that you come to love us as we love you. So please, spread the word. The Keepers are back, and we are here to protect you."

As the final words left Aideen's mouth, the crowd reacted as a single body. The hush that had come over them when the Keepers climbed the platform suddenly was swallowed up by the large applause. Everyone was shouting in joy, hugging their neighbors and praising the four girls standing in front of them. There was an abrupt explosion of optimism in the square, where before it was filled with misery and dispair.

The Keepers were back.

Aideen glanced at her cousins, each with a different expression on her face. Peri was smiling at the crowd, not as nervous to be standing in front of them. Damia was watching Aideen with large eyes as the people were. She was in shock over what Aideen had said, but a smile began to creep over her features. Kendra, although she was trying to hide it, was glowering at Aideen. She just promised that they would be there for the people of Canhareth and Beindor for an indefinite amount of time. How would they ever get home now?

4590028

Made in the USA
Charleston, SC
15 February 2010